The Last Troubadour

SONG OF MONTSÉGUR

BOOK I

The Last Troubadour

A NOVEL

Derek Armstrong

LARGO, USA

THE LAST TROUBADOUR

For information, contact Kunati Inc., Book Publishers in both USA and Canada.
In USA: 6901 Bryan Dairy Road, Suite 150, Largo, FL 33777 USA
In Canada: 75 First Street, Suite 128, Orangeville, ON L9W 5B6 CANADA,
or e-mail to info@kunati.com.

FIRST EDITION

Designed by Kam Wai Yu
Persona Corp. | www.personaprinciple.com

ISBN-13: 978-1-60164-010-9 ISBN-10: 1-60164-010-2
EAN 9781601640109 FIC000000 FICTION/General

Published by Kunati Inc. (USA) and Kunati Inc. (Canada). Provocative. Bold. Controversial.™

http://www.kunati.com

Library of Congress Cataloging-in-Publication Data

Armstrong, Derek Lee.
The last troubadour : a novel / Derek Armstrong. -- 1st ed.
p. cm. -- (Song of Montsegur ; bk. 1)
Summary: "Historical thriller focused on the 13th century Cathar crusade, the development of tarot cards, Pope Innocent IV, Saint Louis of France, the Holy Grail, based on true history"--Provided by publisher.
ISBN 978-1-60164-010-9
1. France--History--13th century--Fiction. 2. Carcassonne (France)--History--Fiction. 3. Troubadours--Fiction. 4. Albigenses--Fiction. 5. Inquisition--France, Southern--Fiction. 6. Tarot cards--Fiction. I. Title.
PS3601.R575L37 2007
813'.6--dc22

2007028101

DEDICATION

Always for Kam,

A true troubadour.

The City of Carcassonne around the time of Ramon Troubadour.

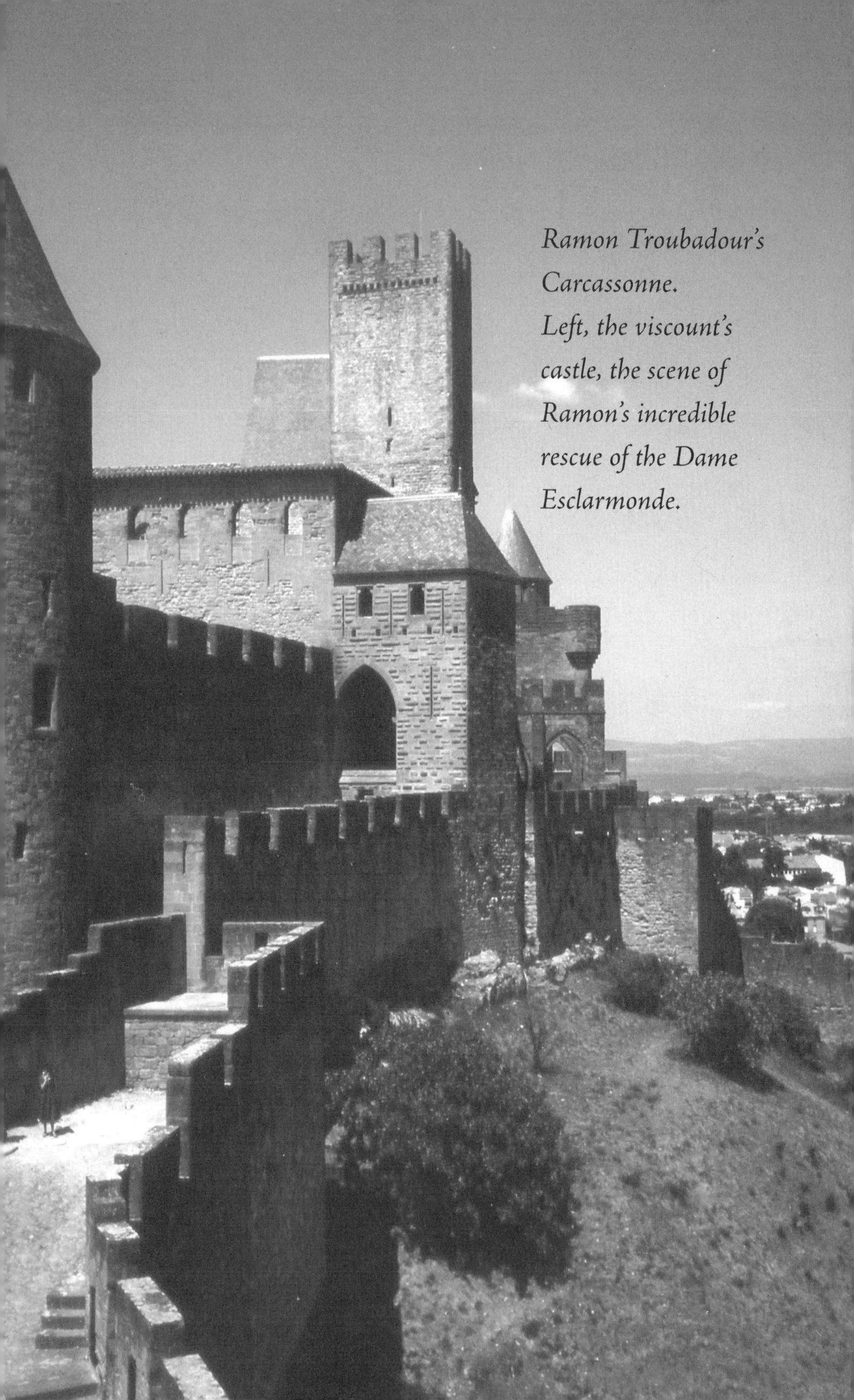

Ramon Troubadour's Carcassonne. Left, the viscount's castle, the scene of Ramon's incredible rescue of the Dame Esclarmonde.

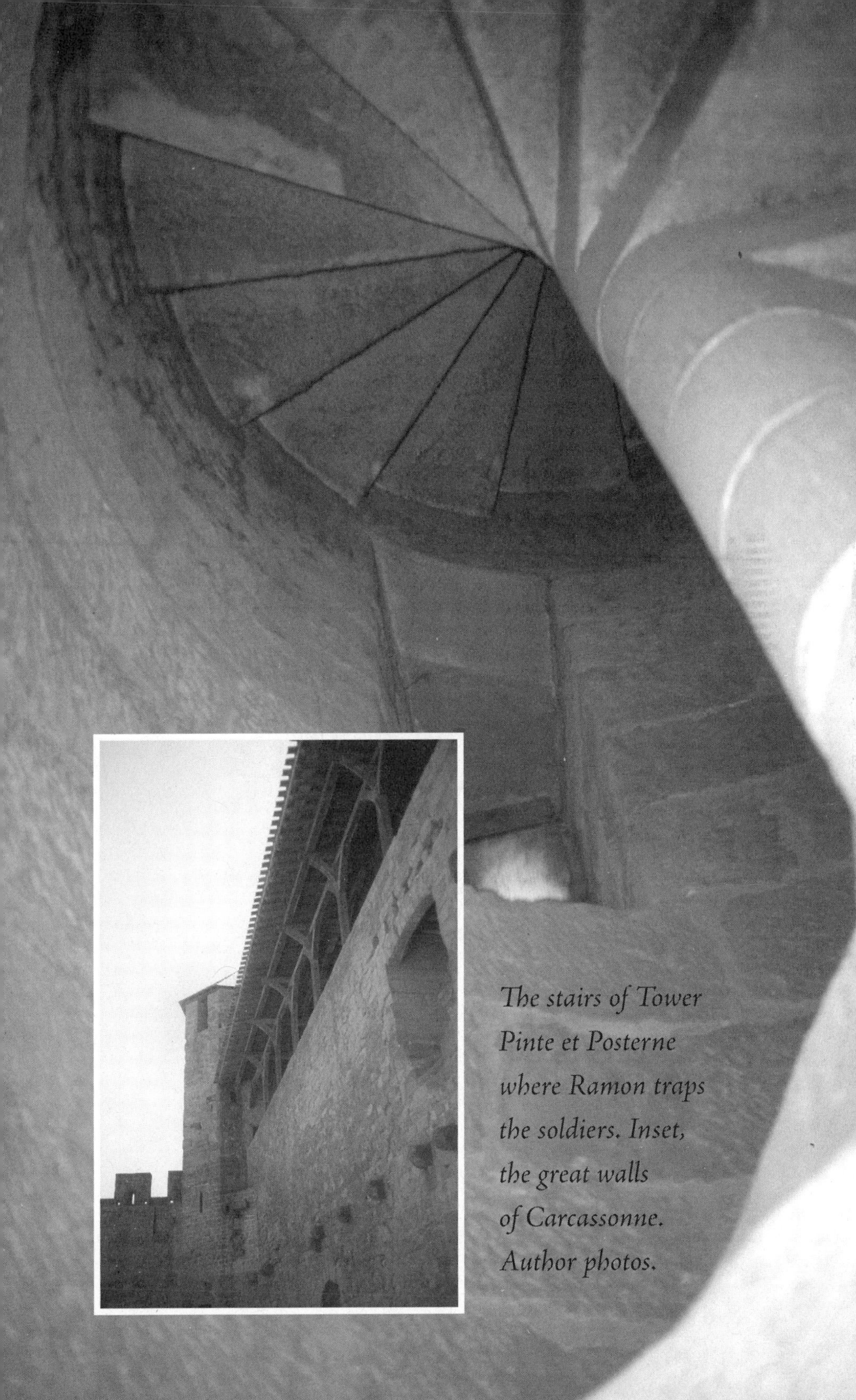

The stairs of Tower Pinte et Posterne where Ramon traps the soldiers. Inset, the great walls of Carcassonne. Author photos.

A Cast of "Tarot" Characters and Events

Song of Montségur recalls the rise of the brutal monastic Inquisition in the South of France, an epic story of heroes and villains of the 13th century. Rather than spin a dark tale of glory and death, I fancifully retell these momentous events with your reading pleasure as my goal: two cups adventure, a pound of real history, a large dollop of humor, a dash of tragedy and hopefully enough mystical juice to create a buzz, roasted over a fire of heretics and witches. Enjoy!

From The Silver Dame of Montségur to the terrible witch-hunter Diableteur, all of my larger-than-life characters are drawn from history. Many legends (and half-baked histories) associate the development of the Tarot cards with the Cathar heresies and this period in history. In *The Last Troubadour*, you will meet my "inventor" of the first tarot deck, Nevara of the Baug Balar "circus" and the characters from history that inspired her deck. Although we know the full decks appeared around this time—the four-suited Turuq came earlier—associating Nevara with major trumps of the Tarot is pure imagination. All major characters and events are historical, fancifully dressed up here with Tarot attributions.

Character Cards

The Fool	Ramon, last of the Occitan's famous heretical troubadours
The Magus	Nevara, the albino pagan sorceress of the *Baug Balar* "circus"
The Priestess	Dame Esclarmonde de Foix, the High Lady of the Cathar Christians
The Empress	Magba, the ever-pregnant mother of the *Baug Balar* entertainers
The Emperor	Hugh d'Arcis, conquering Viscount of Carcassonne
The Hierophant (Pope)	Cardinal Sinibaldo Fiesco, the future Pope Innocent IV
The Lovers	The Grand Duo, the famous rebels Doré the bastard and Osric the hammer
The Chariot	Arnot, the disenfranchised Templar

Justice (Adjustment)	Perce de Mendes, too-loyal squire of the famous Cyclops Seigneur
The Hermit	Guilhem d'Alions, the ancient Perfectus of the Cathars
Fortune	Adelais, the rebellious daughter of the conquering Viscount of Carcassonne
Strength (Lust)	Seigneur, the "Cyclops" one-eyed crusader
The Hanged Man	The suicidal Dominican monk, Brother Jaie
Death	The Diableteur, feared witch-hunter
The Devil	Archbishop Peter Amiel of Narbonne, worldly leader of the crusaders

Song of the Fool

Carcassonne, 1241

1

THE APPROACHING MAYDAY festival drew larger than normal crowds to the unholy city of Carcassonne. A driving rain and threats from the Inquisition did nothing to dampen the spirit of the pagan festival.

From the top of a centuries-old olive tree, downslope from the twin towers of the south gate, Ramon Troubadour watched the steady stream of minstrels, mummers, acrobats, bear-wrestlers, costumed visitors, and traveling merchants with their carts of wares. Mayday was the day when the church lost her grip on ancient pagan traditions. Springfest brought the city alive with memories of an enlightened age of tolerance, of the time before the crusading land-hungry knights occupied the Occitan. There could be no better time for a heretic, a pagan and an atheist to get past the scowling Inquisitor at the gate.

Torrential rain and two days of lightning could not keep away the spring celebrants. After a long winter huddled around never-quite-warm-enough fires, the entire county was ready to play. The sweetness of cherry and olive blossoms invigorated young and old, conquered and conqueror, serf and lord in a floral festival of new life as intense as a celibate monk's first orgasm.

"Colorful birdy hanging in a tree," called his friend Nevara, her voice thickly accented.

Ramon Troubadour smiled down at his friends. Ramon's bright troubadour garb would be conspicuous in the gray-green foliage of the ancient tree.

"A gangly cock rooster," shouted his grumpy friend Arnot. Ramon's little dog Mauri barked up at him, circling the great tree with tail wagging.

A cock rooster in the hoary olive tree he must seem, a splash of color surrounded by fragrant white olive blossoms and busy hummingbirds, with his high green-feathered cap, knee-high blue boots and the bright scarlet of the sash at his waist. His too-long legs splayed on either side of crook of the old tree. Flowing golden hair, as fine as a woman's, trailed to his waist, pulled back in a long mane behind a feathered cap. An unbuttoned, over-sized surcoat, a green tunic embroidered with intricate vines and grape motifs, completed the persona of the fool. Everything about Ramon spoke of spring, from his smile to his festive green clothes.

"Much use I'll be in your daring venture," shouted Arnot. "My armor is soaked through and rusting. I'll be sneezing soon!"

"Blame Nevara," Ramon called back. "She claims she conjured this storm."

"We asked for fog!"

Only Nevara didn't laugh. Her magic was at the best of times erratic. "I calling up some lightning to zapping your armor," she said, sounding sulky.

"We could have been dry inside the city by now," complained Arnot.

Ramon smiled but didn't answer. He was soaked through as well, chilled yet oddly comfortable in the sprawling tree, nestled in the shelter of his own nostalgia. This had been the very tree he had escaped to as a child when his father's belt came out. Even as a toddler Ramon had been a rebel, running from Papa's stinging strap, most often seeking refuge in this olive grove. His mother told him the sacred olives had been planted by the city's namesake Dame Carcas in honor of her victory over the Franks in 760, nearly five centuries ago.

It comforted Ramon, those old trees, reminding him that once the Occitan had fought back and won against the northern invaders. Most of the trees had been cut down by the besiegers thirty-two years ago, and the years of neglect since then meant the old trees bore less and less fruit, yet they remained a symbol of Ramon's conquered people. Survivors, even if they weren't bountiful.

Ramon raised his hand to shield his eyes from the rain and studied the scowling monk at the gate, who crossed himself over and over as he questioned the line of visitors. Ramon couldn't hear the monk's words, but no doubt he mumbled about "witches and devilry" as the guards waved through tellers of fortunes, wishboat vendors, pagans, heretics, witches, Muslims and Jews. Even in the Lord's year 1241, Springfest and Mayday meant everyone was permitted to wander the glorious walled city of Carcassonne except enemies and rebels. Even so, Ramon had seen the Inquisitor arrest dozens.

There could be no better time for Ramon's wild plan, and for their return to his home city. Any other week, they would come under scrutiny. Today, God willing, a joke, a bluff and a bribe would get them into the city. Only the Devil's own luck would get them back out. Fifty-six towers, two great walls, curfews, rebels, thousands of soldiers and the new Dominican Inquisition made Carcassonne the most dangerous city between Castille and Constantinople.

Not every visitor bribed the gate guards. The steady stream of Dominican monks and Christian knights with their retinues bypassed the line of merchant carts and celebrants and entered without a toll.

Ramon knew these throngs only presaged the spectacle-seeking audiences who would arrive over the next few days. Though the guards questioned each muddy visitor, watchful for rebels and searching every wagon, they detained only a few dozen out of hundreds, and Ramon could see that the sentry's purses grew heavy.

As Ramon expected, at sunset the scowling Dominican Inquisitor left the gate for his vigils. It was time.

The swollen sun broke through the storm clouds, sending God's own holy light beaming through demon cloud. The shafts of gold illuminated the twin western mountains the pagans called Epona, the Earth Mother's Tits, a spectacular backdrop to the towers of Carcassonne.

The last of the rain stopped almost miraculously as the Dominican disappeared into the shadows under the gateway. Ramon took it as a good omen.

Cold fingers of rain penetrated his floral tunic, making him shiver. Either Nevara's mists would come or not. Her "magic" was as predictable as her temper.

Ramon delighted in startling big old Arnot. He swung down out of the tree in an elaborate acrobatic tumble and landed in front of the scowling knight. Startled, the grizzly warrior's hand snatched at the haft of his old Templar mace.

"Christ's bloody tears, you fool!" Arnot growled. He plucked at his mail shirt. "Are we going to loiter here all day? My armor is seizing."

Ramon's tiny white dog Mauri barked and jumped up into his arms. "We go, fog or not. Where's Nevara?"

Arnot shrugged. "Conjuring fog, I guess. Her magic's as powerful as your sense of humor."

"I hearing that!" said Nevara, her Novgorodian accent thick, and she stepped around a tree, her face as stormy as the sky. "Coming now, it is."

Ramon smiled, set down his dog and picked up his lute and spear. "Then we go."

"I hope the Jewel is worth our lives," said Arnot, still scowling.

"It is worth the lives of every man, woman and child in the South. It is our hope." Ramon rubbed numb fingers. It would have been simpler to steal into the city with the *Baug Balar* performers, his adopted family. The famous troop of entertainers had made their festive entrance hours ago, led by tumbling acrobats and their famous dancing ponies. Thirty-eight men and women, dozens of children, forty-two horses, a leashed bear, sundry knife-throwers, acrobats and performers had filed through the narrow gates with eighteen colorful wagons.

Ramon didn't regret his plan to make a separate "grand" entrance, even if it was risky. If things went terribly wrong—as they often did with Ramon's complicated plans—his adopted family would remain safe from prosecution.

Nothing was more important than rescuing the Jewel of the South, not even the *Baug*, his family. Thousands would die if Ramon and his friends failed. Loup de Foix, the leader of the Caspins would march on the city to rescue the Jewel, and he and his soldiers would certainly die. The landless, oppressed and conquered would rise up against the invaders once more—and perish. The king of Castille would send his armies. From Armagnac to Provence, rivers of blood would run again.

Ramon Troubadour stared up at the old stone walls of Carcassonne, now touched with the blood of the dying sun. Mist or not, they must be inside the walls before curfew. A hundred wall guards, the Inquisition, not even the Devil himself would stop Ramon from returning to Carcassonne after twelve years away. All that was precious to him had died here. He might die as well.

But he was home.

THE MUDDY WASH of storm runoff slowed to a brown trickle that sluiced across the green grass. The lineups at the city gate became a dribble of latecomers. With the growing night chill came eerie coils of mist snaking along the hilltop road like a biblical curse, willowing across the stagnant moat water.

"There'll be no space in the wayrooms." Jaspre the gate guard said. He drank deep from their flask of apple bitters, grateful the watch was over.

"Still more, Jaspre." Henri, his fellow sentry, pointed with his spear.

"A fool to come at curfew." *A fool in appearance, too,* Jaspre thought. The prancing man with the green-feathered cap crossed the drawbridge, followed by some kind of dwarf horse. The colorful specter danced through the growing fog. Already the miasma, reeking like marsh gas and tinged hell-red by the sunset, churned and swallowed the high walls of Carcassonne.

"What is this creature?" Jaspre said, shivering as fingers of vapors explored his already damp cloak. He sneezed into his sleeve.

"Another jester?"

"But is it a boy or girl?"

"An unmentionable?"

Jaspre was thankful the Inquisitor had left them for prayers. The church frowned on the unmentionables, the men who kept company with men, one of a long list of heresies. The visitor was "pretty" and effeminate, not in the way of Jaspre's wife, a solid beast of burden, but in the useless manner of a lady in waiting at court. Jaspre's laugh huffed out like a limp flag. Something about the intense green eyes of the straggler, luminous in the spooky haze, made Jaspre shiver.

Crickets chirruped and a fox yipped but the only other sound was the clop of the visitor's booted feet and the hooves of his dwarfish horse.

"Is that a dog or a pony?" Jaspre asked.

"It's like them circus ponies we saw before," Henri answered.

Henri was right. The dancing horses of the spectacular Baug Balar had been just like this little pony. "Maybe he's one of them?" Jaspre said.

The pony followed without a lead rope, like an obedient dog. It carried itself with a strange, fluid gait. As it resolved from the haze, Jaspre realized it was not one color but two. He had seen spotted horses before, but this one, with its big patches of black and white, reminded Jaspre more of a cow than a horse. The horse nudged up close to the fool and some sort of rat or dog ran alongside, weaving in and out of the hooves, a tiny white creature with a wagging tail.

"Should we call back Brother Scowling Face?" Henri asked.

Jaspre shook his head and stared at the stranger. A Southerner almost certainly, judging by his fine hair and eyes. A boy of good birth or affluence, Jaspre guessed, because this womanish man had a full set of chompers. Jaspre himself had only three precious teeth left.

He walked with a staff, but he didn't lean on it, instead twirling it like a baton. Then Jaspre realized it was not a staff at all, but a lance, tipped with a two-edged blade. He recognized it from the crusades, an obscure *hasta,* a Roman weapon, popular with the Occitan nobles of the South. Not as dainty a weapon as it looked, it could be wielded sword-like, or thrust like a Greek spear to penetrate armor. Jaspre weighed him. Unmentionable, girlish-boy or jester, but not harmless. This gangly insect had a sting.

"Qui va là?" Jaspre challenged, finally remembering his duty. "Who goes?"

"Who asks?" the boy said in a strong, melodic voice.

Jaspre glanced at Henri. His friend seemed equally startled. In all their years as sentries, no one had challenged them in such arrogant fashion. Even knights and lords deferred to gate guards.

"A simple enough question, fellow," said the fool, grinning. "I asked your name."

Flustered, Jaspre snapped. "I am the guard of the gate. Give me your name and business!"

"How do I know you are the sentry?" challenged the boyish-girl, still smiling. "I see by your fat purses you grow rich on the toll. Are you truly the guard?"

Jaspre, angry now, lowered his long spear. "Answer now, or go to the pit for questioning."

"Then let us play a guessing game." The girlish man nodded at Henri, Jaspre's companion. "You, sir, your name, would it be Henri? Henri of Clairveaux?" The fool smiled a brilliant smile. "You have a chubby wife who bore you three sons and one daughter. Your friend here is Jaspre, who has both a wife and—"

"But this is sorcery!" snapped Jaspre, cutting off the fool before he could mention the—secret things. He felt abruptly certain this devil-boy knew of the two women who warmed his straw matt in the barracks on alternating nights. Jaspre felt a suffocating sense of terror and certainty. He suddenly wished that Brother Scowling Face was with them at the gate. Jaspre crossed himself then spat for good measure to ward off what could only be Satan's own imp.

The fool laughed, a cheerful sound, and all the more brilliant for having all his teeth. "I am that good, am I not?"

Good enough to draw the wall guards on the outer wall. Many of the sentries on the southern curtain crowded the allures, peering down through the fog with toothless grins.

Jaspre ignored them. This boy would have to be arrested, not for arrogance, but for suspicion of devilry. The Inquisition would want this boy in their pit.

The fool snatched a strap that lay across his chest.

Jaspre came to attention, spear lowered, expecting a weapon or some witchery. Instead, in a deft movement, the boy-man spun a musical instrument into view. A lute. Few minstrels carried lutes anymore, not since the persecution of the Southern troubadours. It was well known that troubadours were heretics and mockers of the church, perhaps even sorcerers and devil worshipers. Hundreds had been rounded up and now languished in Inquisitors' pits. In the South, troubadours were almost always of noble birth, irreverent and heretic, and sang of pagan gods and the glory of women. A few troubadours had been burned as heretics, but most had renounced and given up their mystical trade to become simple minstrels or *trouvères,* forgoing the forbidden lute in favor of harps and flutes.

What bull's balls this boy had! Demonstrating sorcery and a forbidden instrument in the very heart of the archbishop's city! The boy strummed a few quick, magical notes.

"Minstrel, jester, *trouvère,* Ramon at your service, good Jaspre." Ramon bowed. "What's the difference between a black-haired archbishop and a red-headed lord?"

What by all the imps in hell did that mean? Jaspre wondered.

"One has black-haired children," answered Ramon with another girlish smile.

For a moment, Jaspre heard only the snort of horses. Then a nervous cascade of laughter. The small crowd of guards on the wall leaned over the stone curtain. Their laughter drew the attention of more soldiers. Jaspre almost joined in. If their black-haired archbishop heard of this joke, he would have all the guards castrated. Their lord the viscount, with his flaming red hair, would probably laugh.

"A jokester!" Henri laughed.

The jester Ramon stared at Jaspre. "Good Jaspre, I must have your smile."

"I be on duty," Jaspre grumbled.

"Duty is no reason not to have fun." Ramon bowed.

"What's your business here, jester?"

"You won't believe this, but Saint Mary appeared to me in a vision and told me I must seek out the hospitality of the archbishop."

Several soldiers on the wall laughed.

"He'd like you, girlish boy," said a faceless voice in the fog. "He likes anything young and pretty."

"Didn't you know?" asked the jester Ramon. "A cleric each day keeps the black plague at bay?"

The laughter rolled out of the thickening fog.

"The Inquisition will hear of this, fool," Jaspre warned. In spite of himself, he liked this boy. If he would just be quiet, or stop insulting the archbishop, perhaps the boy would survive the night.

But the fool pirouetted in a deft acrobatic move, nearly falling off the edge of the drawbridge. "How do you think I got so tall?

"How?" Someone shouted from the wall.

"I was once a burly man like you good soldiers. Then the Inquisition put me on the rack! Stretched me thin!"

This time even Jaspre laughed. He had rarely met a boy with such courage. That alone begged mercy. "On your way. But get to a wayroom, fool. The curfew is imminent!"

"Come see me perform for the viscount!" the boy said merrily, as he and his dog-like horse and rat-like dog passed by.

"I, for one, will seek out his performances," Henri said.

Jaspre realized he was still laughing "A cleric a day! The viscount's court has need of this merry boy." But his laugh faded as a new shape resolved out of the early night mist. The flow of Mayday visitors was not complete.

Jaspre's hand tightened on the ash haft of his spear. This was not some foolish boy, but a hulking shadow on a massive horse.

"A Templar knight, by the Almighty," said Henri.

"Or a vagabond. His surplice is in shreds, and no beard." Jaspre watched, wary. Where the boy-fool had surprised and delighted Jaspre, making him forget the chill, this new visitor put him back on high alert. Perspiration prickled through Jaspre's crust of days-old sweat. Templars always brought trouble. This knight was something of a squat giant, not towering, but massive in nearly every other dimension. He reeked of death, the stench of moldy gore on his armor. His mail was dented and rust colored, except Jaspre felt certain the discoloration was blood, not corrosion. Similar stains decorated the fierce man's over-tunic, discoloring the torn cloth browner than the red of the small Templar cross on his upper left shoulder.

He did not wear the traditional *chapeau de fer* but everything else about the monkish warrior was traditional Templar: the Turkish mace on his belt, the two-handed thrusting sword slung on his back, mailed boots and spurs jangling as he rode. The string of four horses was the only suggestion of affluence, each horse skirted in mail and slung with shields and lances. Jaspre distrusted Templar destriers, big snorting creatures that trampled foot soldiers—infantrymen like Jaspre—on the battlefield. The Templar was scraggy, his face marred by badly healed old wounds, his head shaven like a monks and his cleft chin equally naked.

"My Lord," Jaspre managed to finally challenge the Templar. What had he done to deserve such evil portents? "May I have your name, messire?"

Hard eyes fixed on Jaspre, a killer's gaze. Templars were not used to being challenged. Even the Inquisition had no authority over the mysterious knights of the Temple of Jerusalem, who answered only to His Holiness. Jaspre's own blessed King Louis had once bowed to the master of the Templars. They always meant trouble, with their strange blend of savage chivalry and monkishness. Like any humble Christian, Jaspre remained in awe and fear of them. Death was their constant companion.

"Brother Arnot de Ridefort, companion knight to Master Marshall." The knight's voice sounded gravelly, as if he rarely spoke, but his words were enough. Jaspre bowed, and as he bent he spat to ward off evil. After the Master of the Temple, the Marshall was the most powerful man in the Templars, the leader of the army, the largest standing permanent army in Christendom, and feared from Jerusalem to Rome. No good could come of such a visitor.

It occurred to Jaspre that this was all some fabrication at his expense. The knight was far too grubby to be companion of the second most powerful man in the Temple, and where was his traditional beard? And knights of the Temple never traveled without their brother sergeants. But Jaspre could hardly chance it. Confrontations were best left to the archbishop, the viscount himself, or the Diableteur, who feared nothing on earth. Jaspre kept his eyes down.

"You are welcome, Lord," he said. He had no choice but to let the

Templar enter the city. He kept his head down as the scowling knight passed him, leading his four great horses.

"Another, Jaspre! This day must never end." Henri gawked at a third stranger, an ethereal white specter in the growing fog.

Jaspre stared at the woman's mountainous love-pillows, bulging out from a clinging white garment. If the Templar shocked Jaspre, this woman both terrified and aroused him.

"Look at the udders on that," Henri said.

"Your wife will pluck out your eyes, Henri." Jaspre scowled. This woman would almost certainly bring the Dominican monks, the Inquisitors, sniffing and whining like frustrated dogs. Which meant—a long night for Jaspre.

Sentries up on the open allures of the outer city wall whistled and called out to the brazen lady who approached the gates, leering at her as they hung over the wall between the stone merlons, their faces suspended in the fog like specters. Brazen was the only word that seemed to fit this "lady" with her thrusting breasts and low cut gown of pure white cloth, all mysterious and frightening in the fog.

But it was not her mouth-watering milk-makers that kept his attention. Jaspre's mouth felt dry as he stared into her colorless eyes. Soulless eyes, it seemed, as if some manic portrait artist had not taken the time to color her pupils. And her hair was pure white, like her gown. An albino temptress, almost certainly the Devil's own mistress. Her delicious love-bags spoke of youth, a strange contrast to the hag's hair. The locks were shining and wavy, like the foamy white of a mountain waterfall, cascading around a magnificent face with high cheeks and no lines. And no color at all. Take away the elder-hair and the ghostly eyes, and she was quite the temptress. Even her horse was white, a short-legged pony with a flowing mane and a tail that trailed on the drawbridge planks. Another late Baug Balar troop member? A torque hung about her delicate throat, riding high on those magnificent mountains, thick braids of gold and silver, twisted in the manner of the ancients and set with a glittering red stone. It reeked of pagan rites by moonlight, a symbol he had seen often enough in the tolerant South, but not since the crusade ended.

He had heard of such ladies, legends of the Southern sorceresses. It was such as these that had enraged frowning bishops, stirring them to preach their crusade against the heretics of Albi, sending soldiers south from their thatch homes in France in quest of loot. This brazen temptress, with her pagan symbol—did she not know the Inquisition would have her in irons by daybreak? Since the Cathar crusade ended, and the Inquisition replaced it, Jaspre could not remember seeing such a lady parading on the streets, although he'd seen a few thrown to the fires to the cheering of the crusaders and the tears of the decimated Southerners.

"She's bewitched me, Henri," Jaspre whispered. "I'm as stiff as a spear shaft down there."

Henri crossed himself.

The part of Jaspre that unwillingly belonged to his piggy wife was less disapproving of the delightful witch. She would be in the Inquisitor's cellar before dawn with her long foamy white hair and her wide, ridable hips that even now thrust side to side like a deadly battleaxe. Jaspre found himself momentarily plunging into a mad fantasy. He'd arrest the witch, take her aside for "questioning" and search her down to the warm harbors of her womanhood. Would she be white down there as well?

She had a satanic stink about her and Jaspre shivered, partially for fear of the witch, but mostly because it meant Inquisitors would soon interrogate Jaspre and his troop.

Over forty soldiers, nearly the entire south wall garrison, had left their watch posts and crowded over the gate looking down, pointing and leering. Such theatre was rare.

"And your name—Lady?" Henri asked, his sarcasm not disguised.

Before she could answer, Jaspre felt a blast of wind, a flurry of motion, and as if by magic a ghost of a creature appeared on the woman's shoulder. It was large, perhaps as long as Jaspre's arm, and white, with little black demon eyes that glittered even in the mist. An owl! But such an owl. It was pure white, with a long hooked beak that rested near the woman's ear, and it extended its ghostly plumage to help it balance on her shoulder.

Devilry! A witch bird!

It made an unearthly barking sound, like a huffing.

Jaspre willed himself to breathe. A sorcerer's bird! A white owl! He crossed himself again. He had seen owls, but never snowy white owls such as this. This witch stroked its hooked beak, and now the great bird seemed to pant like a dog, and it sidled up close to her hair, preening her in return. Jaspre shivered. A Devil's familiar.

"I am being called Nevara," said the white-haired witch, her accent thick. She sounded like Jaspre's friend Smolensk, a crusader from Novgorod.

"Nevar? To snow?" Jaspre shivered. An appropriate name for this creature, whether nickname or real.

"Snowing storm," she said, her pink eyes frosty. They froze his soul and he looked away, not willing to be cursed. He would rather face a dozen enemy spears than a witch's gaze. He crossed himself and spat for good measure.

Henri grabbed his arm, steadying him. He leaned close. "Should we fetch Brother Scowling Face?" he whispered, but Jaspre felt panic and superstitious terror in the painful grip.

This witch looked fully capable of curses and devilry, with her unholy owl. The owl's head swiveled, black, black eyes taking in everything. He wanted no part of it. "Let her be," Jaspre said. Then louder, he snapped, "Go on your way." And one more time, just for safety, he crossed himself.

After shift, he would rush to the basilica and splash his face with blessed water. But he would not detain her. To do so would be to risk her curses. She might curse him to lose his few remaining teeth and all his hair. Or make his skin rot like a leper. Or worse, curse him to impotence.

After she passed through the suicide-way between the two gates, he looked at Henri and said, "Henri. Go inform the Diableteur."

"Not I," Henri said. "I won't go near that—my lord Diableteur."

Jaspre shivered. If Henri would not report, it was left to him. But Jaspre was more afraid of the Diableteur, that foul witch-hunter, than the Devilish trio who had just entered the ancient city of Carcassonne.

2

RAMON TROUBADOUR WATCHED as the Snow Storm resolved from the mist, appearing as if by magic. His little dog Mauri barked at Nevara, front legs squatting down and tail wagging.

"The guard not knowing to arresting me or to ravishing me," she said, smiling, and slid from her little horse. Ramon felt the wind of Bubo, a stirring of white in the mist, and, almost magically, Nevara's great snowy owl appeared on her shoulder. This time his little dog Mauri growled. Bubo often swooped down, hoping to make a meal of Mauri.

"You have that effect on most men," Ramon said, laughing lightly.

She lifted her breasts teasingly. "And you?"

"You're my little sister," Ramon said, trying not to blush. Nevara had always attracted him. Since he turned fifteen, he had been breathless at the sight of her, but it was difficult to think of her as anyone but a sister, even though he was just another of the many adoptees of the traveling Baug Balar, misfits and outcasts from every country. For more than a decade, she had taught him everything he knew of horses, healing and happiness, but his love for her was still like unbaked clay, still forming and fragile, as likely to crumble as to transform to beauty.

"I think they were more terrified of Bubo than of your pink eyes," Ramon said.

Nevara tickled Bubo under his beak. She had found him as an abandoned hatchling, fallen from the nest and nurtured him with mice and snake bits, and now she was the only person he would tolerate. Bubo had learned many tricks from Nevara, the Baug's sorceress and animal-talker, but he remained a wild creature. He had once taken a chunk out of Ramon's index finger.

"I think Ramon's performance was better," said a gruff voice from the mists. "Though the vision from Saint Mary was a little over much."

"You used to love my jokes," Ramon said, as a burly silhouette on a massive horse emerged from the fog. "My humor confused the sentries."

"Craven guards, too afraid to stop a prancing fool and a sluttish witch," the Templar grumbled.

"Even brave men fear magic," Ramon said, smiling wide. "And everyone fears a grouchy Templar with blood-stained armor." Of course the "blood" was nothing more than one of Nevara's red dyes.

"You're a fop and a cretin," said the Templar as he swung down from his big warhorse with a grunt, his armor clanging. "But I love you anyway, little brother." He slapped Ramon hard across his shoulders, sending him sprawling forward.

Ramon allowed the momentum to carry him, spun into a handspring, then tumbled back around with acrobatic ease. As he swung back in a sudden move, he managed to pull down his old friend with a slice of his long legs. The Templar fell with a grunt to the cobbles. Now the laughter spilled out of Ramon again, unstoppable. Arnot sat on the cobbles, scowling.

"I should chop down those long legs," Arnot said, refusing to smile as Ramon helped his friend stand.

"Then he'd being your height," Nevara said.

They laughed quietly in the fog, their voices echoing hauntingly off invisible stone walls. Nevara and Arnot hated each other, but they were both bonded to Ramon by love and history. They separately owed Ramon their lives, and Ramon owed them as much in return. Any adventure bringing together Nevara—the snowy pagan—with Arnot—the fiery Templar atheist—was akin to a winter storm sweeping south on a hot summer's day. Separately, they were magnificent, Nevara chill and stunning, Arnot blazing and terrible, but together they became the chaotic tempest.

"The stench in this vile cesspit of a city is unbearable," growled Arnot. "You grew up here?"

Ramon nodded, his smile fading. "Before they executed my parents. Just there by that tower. Back then, Carcassonne was the envy of the

South, the roads lined with cherry trees in blossom at this time of year." He could see a tree stump used as a corner post for one of the hovels that crowded the lane. The invaders had ruined his green city, turning it into a soldiers' privy. "An enlightened city of freedom."

"Dirty French," said Arnot.

Ramon chuckled. "You're French."

Arnot scratched his rear end in an exaggerated movement, then sniffed his finger. "Like I said, dirty French. Our towns and cities are filthy sties compared to the South, oui? That's why I became a Templar. To get away from the reek."

"Leave the jokes to me, friend Arnot."

Nevara scowled. "We must be off the streets before the curfew guards picking us up, no?" The white-haired temptress had more to lose than either of them. Women and pagans were no longer welcome in Carcassonne. Her albinism marked her as the Devil's child, and her Occitan name Nevara, Snow Storm, branded her a pagan magician or witch. Her real name was unpronounceable. Worse, her thick accent made her unwelcome in Christian cities, reminding the superstitious that she was one of the unwelcome wanderers of Novgorod.

"They'd never dare arrest our atheist Templar, would they Arn?" Ramon scooped up Mauri, his little dog, and gave him a kiss on the snout. Nevara's ghost owl made a guttural, *"krufff-guh-guh-guk"* sound, a threat not lost on Mauri who growled in return.

He loved these two, but he was risking their lives. Better two lives than the entire Baug Balar. If he was to stop a war, he must rescue the Jewel, and to do that would require more than just two accomplices. "We must find the *Auberge de Terre* in your infernal mist."

"Now you complainings." She glared at him, her pink eyes sharp in the fog. "Are you sure these two rebels, they being there?"

"Guilhem promises so," Ramon said.

Nevara spat. "That for your old hermit."

"When is he ever wrong?"

"Always being wrong that old fart."

Ramon kissed the haft of old Guilhem's spear. The *Spear of Zaleucus* was very old, a Roman weapon given him by the old hermit mystic Guilhem d'Alions. Guilhem, a craggy old Cathar, was a frequent visitor to the Baug, for all his hermitic reputation, and had become Ramon's on-again, off-again teacher over the years. He had trained him in Roman spear work: the *Aquila*, the deadly Eagle Strike, a flying leap and plunging stab; the *Tonitrus*, the Thunder Strike, a dizzying acrobatic spin and slice; and a dozen other killing moves Ramon had never once used in real battle. "This spear, it has magic," his old master Guilhem had told him, "Never throw this spear, Ramon. It is for defense and stabbing, but never throwing, aggression or killing. Sleep with it. Let no one else touch it. It is *Zaleucus*, the lawgiver. Whoever carries it, if he fights for law, is protected from harm."

Ramon said, "Guilhem is a great Perfect."

Nevara laughed. "You be so full of pigshits, I can smell it tumbling out both your holes." She continued to smile. "So, telling me now, how did you do that? With the guards?"

"Magic."

"Pigshit."

"I asked the people in the village by the river if they knew of the sentries."

"Trickeries!"

"And you don't use tricks?" Ramon squinted at Nevara. Sometimes, in these misty moments, he felt her "magic" was real enough, that the fog was evidence and not coincidence, but she often used tricks to fool the gullible. Only last week he had seen her terrify a village Inquisitor with a toss of her famous black powder in a fire pit. The explosion had sent the entire village, monk and guard included, running for their thatched huts. Her "trickery" had given them time to rescue the twelve-year-old girl, already roasting on the Inquisition's spit. The girl was fortunately only lightly basted.

"We all be using ploys," Nevara said, her voice angry. "Real magic, it being hard work. It draining on me. Why waste it on the superstitious?" She vaulted on to the back of her beloved white tarpan horse Wizigard.

Nevara's true magic was her way with her animals, and not just Bubo the owl and the Baug's wrestling bear. The Baug Balar said she spoke to animals. She needed no reins or spurs with her beloved tarpans. A herd of her horses traveled with the Baug Balar, their famous dancing horses, the main draw for the crowds and their coins. Though Ramon had lived many years with his adopted family, those dancing horses always amazed him. Twenty horses, all in sequence, rearing back on hind legs, front legs spinning in the air, jumping over each other, riders and all, hopping from foot to foot while rearing back, and a hundred other steps. It was always the horses that drew the acclaim wherever the Baug Balar performed. They were the best horses Ramon had ever ridden, although they tolerated no saddle. Nevara said they were descended from the small Hun mounts, smooth and fluid in gait, responsive to legs rather than reins. Ramon could even sleep on the wide, flat back of his little horse, just by wrapping his fingers in his long mane.

Izzy, Ramon's own tarpan, was a rare gift. Year after year, Nevara had seen how Izzy doted on Ramon. After a few months of his asking, she had finally parted with the little black and white spotted horse. "If Izzy telling me you mistreated him," she had said, "I be turning you into toad." Izzy hated toads, his one peculiar trait. One night, years ago, Ramon had found Izzy rearing and stomping on toads. Izzy was one of Ramon's best friends, along with his little dog Mauri. The horse insisted on sleeping in Ramon's tent, following Ramon inside and lying down on the floor like a guard dog.

"No magic will help you if you don't find this Auberge de Terre before your friends at the gate set loose the Inquisition on you," said Arnot.

"Nevara would curse them with ten thousand farts if they tried," Ramon said.

"I am to save that for you, fool," Nevara said, stroking the head of Bubo.

"I should stay with you until you're safe," Arnot said.

"We not be needing you," Nevara snapped.

"Be silent, witch! Your magic is no protection from my crushing mace."

"I not fearing you." She held her fingers splayed in a warding pose.

Ramon sighed. His two closest friends fought constantly.

"You are condemned by the church," Arnot said, his voice a low growl.

"And you are spurned by the church!" She spat. "You believe in nothings."

"I believe you'll bleed red enough if I crush your old hag's head!" His gauntleted hands were balled into fists. "Your curses mean nothing to me."

"Because you believe in nothings."

Arnot grinned. "You are right, witch. You have no power to scare me. I have no soul to curse."

Ramon stepped between them, afraid of both of them. He believed Arnot was on the verge of murder again, and—like most sensible men—he believed in magic and Nevara's curses. "Save the anger for the damn French."

"I be French!" Arnot shouted and turned on Ramon.

"For the damn papists, then. Arnot, you are yelling. The soldiers will come." He watched Arnot's once-handsome, now scarred face. The man believed in nothing but his mace and sword, had lost God in his life, and it was only their tenuous friendship that he had faith in. Slowly the fury left Arnot's glaring eyes. In high Norman French, the language of the nobles—a language Nevara had never mastered—Ramon said, "Let's not fight amongst ourselves. There'll be plenty of killing." Arnot smiled at that. "Come, let's get off the main road, before the curfew patrols find us."

Silent now, the three turned onto a smaller road, not much more than a winding path between dilapidated hovels that resolved out of the fog in dripping collages of monotone chaos. He had not returned to his home city in a dozen years—not since the dark day his mother burned—and he could see that the occupation by the French had ruined Carcassonne, the pride of the South. The mud road was piled with refuse, dumped from the shuttered windows of rotting houses, and even now the pigs ran the streets, cleaning the slop but leaving behind the stink of pig shit.

They sought the after-curfew refuge of the Auberge de Terre, a forbidden *grendincroix*, a rogues' crossing, hidden amongst the slums of the outer city. In Ramon's youth, the *Lices Hautes*, the long stretch between the outer and inner wall, were left clear for defense, a killing field into which arrows and hot oils would pour. Before the conquest, his people lived in the stone and daub houses inside the main wall, ruled by the just hand of Count Trenceval. After the invasion, the crusaders allowed the native Carcassonnians to build new villages between the two defensive walls—little more than a prison. The slum grew into a dangerous hut city, full of poverty, rebels and heresies. Every space was filled with hovels, wayrooms and straw-and-daub shops, connected by barely passable tracks that meandered in patterns that baffled the French conquerors. The Crusaders stayed out of these disease-ridden quarters at night, curfew or not. Even by daylight they could be dangerous.

"Here we must part, good Arn," Ramon said, still speaking in high Norman French.

"Are you certain, Ray? Perhaps in the morn?" The Templar halted his string of horses.

"Certainty is for Popes, Arn." He smiled when he saw the worried frown on Arnot's face. Arnot feared nothing. He could courageously face a dozen knights in a tourney, stand up to the Inquisition, and his temper scared even Ramon, but his overblown sense of parental protectiveness for Ramon was nearly as irritating as his temper.

"'Tis dangerous." Arnot growled.

Ramon swung his weight to one leg, striking a martial stance, his other leg drawn up like a viper, his spear poised. "I'm dangerous. *Serpentus*, the Serpent Strikes. Ha!" His front leg slid forward, his long legs stretching until he felt the cobbles on his thigh, then stabbed upwards in a strike so fast, the Templar's shield missed. He stopped a knuckle's-breadth from Arnot's crotch.

"You be a fool, naught more." Arn knocked the spear aside with his shield, grumpy he had missed the strike again. "These juggler-acrobat skills, they're just pretty. One good sword stroke, and you have no head!"

Ramon spun, dipping the spear under his arm in a move so quick the tip came within an inch of Arnot's neck. "*Transmuto*."

"Must you name every move?" Arnot's voice became a low snarl.

"My teacher instructed me so."

"That's because that old Guilhem was a crazy hermit. He speaks to birds and spears." Arnot laughed. "Your acrobatic skills with a twig of a spear and midget horse be no match for the rogues at this grendincroix. Or the patrolling soldiers. Or a furious ex-Templar knight in armor."

"You're just jealous. You have to spend the night with the archbishop. Just don't share his bed. I hear he's quite the lech. Sleeps with anything. Even scowling old Templars."

"Ray, your tricks and jokes are not going to keep you alive in a rebel wayroom." Arnot growled the words, but his concern was genuine.

"This is my city. My people." He grinned. "And I have Nevara's magic."

Nevara made an obscene gesture at the Templar, who spat in return. "Go sucking the archbishop."

The Templar stepped close to Nevara, barely keeping his famous rage in check.

Ramon touched the big man's shoulder. He felt the tension. Arnot's temper was the one thing that most worried Ramon. Would he be able to maintain his role of aloof Templar? Arnot's fury had resulted in his expulsion from the hallowed order of Templars after he murdered a brother in rage. "Our plan depends on your new—ah, friendship—with the archbishop, Arn." He gripped the mailed shoulder, pressing between the armored shoulder plates so his friend could feel his fingers.

"I won't sleep with the sleazy old devil."

Ramon fell suddenly to his knees, his hands held up in prayer. "Then woo him with your gentle manners, I pray you." Both Ramon and Nevara laughed.

"You just take care, Ray," Arnot said, finally, offering a grudging smile.

"I will. I do my best work when I'm performing for a crowd." He swung back onto his heels and sprang up with the grace of youth and practice. "And don't slit the archbishop's throat. You kill him, the whole city will be on us."

"You tell me this too many times. I know the risks." Arnot hesitated, then smiled. "Tell me one joke before I go."

Ramon smiled. How he loved this crusty old Templar. Like most of Ramon's friends, Arnot was an outcast, a wanderer and an outlaw. In these dark times, being condemned marked a good man, a man to be trusted and a man to be feared. Was it only three years ago that he met Arnot, on the run from the Templars for killing a brother knight? Nevara called Ramon's friends and allies "Ramon's misfits" and perhaps they were, dark souls that found a spark of humanity in troubadour songs.

Ramon bowed to his friend. "A quick jest, then. A Templar knight returned to Jerusalem after months in the field and reported on his exploits to the King of Jerusalem. 'Your majesty,' he said, 'I have killed dozens of your enemies to the east.' Shocked, the king replied, 'Sir knight, I have no enemies to the east!' The knight blushed red, bowed, and said, 'Then, you do now, sire.'"

Arnot laughed hard, gathered his reins and led his horses into the mist. His laughter could be heard even after he disappeared into the night.

Ramon wondered if he would ever see the cantankerous Templar again.

"I be thanking Freyja he is going," Nevara said. "He's such a brute." But her voice sounded sad.

3

RAMON TROUBADOUR HEARD the clink of armor and weapons in Nevara's magic fog. Soldiers. There could be no doubt.

Nevara's fog obscured them, but voices called out, spectral sounds that chilled. Without a word, Ramon slid onto Izzy's back. He had committed them to a path of utter idiocy, three against the entire French army, but for a prize like no other. To stop a war. To save the Jewel. But, now, in the fog, in the growing dark, in his dying city, it seemed a fool's quest and doomed to failure. They would be facing the torturer's inquiries by morning.

Nevara was already mounted on Wizigard, her little white horse. The clever mountain horses' hooves were quiet, even in squishy mud, but they still went slowly.

The sounds of the soldiers faded and they rode on, ducking under leaning shanties that jutted into the muddy alley. There were no cobbles on the inner alleyways. Here, in the heart of the lower city, rebels, peasants and rogues mingled, slopping in the muddy alleys barely wide enough for a single horse and ankle deep in muck. The alleyways spider-webbed in every direction, without plan or reason, and soon Ramon, a native Carcassonnian, was lost.

Now their biggest fear would be starving brigands, out after curfew to hunt the foolish. Mauri, Ramon's dog, whined, and jumped up on his lap. The little dog always felt safer on Izzy's back.

Ramon fought fatigue. For now, all he hoped for was a bowl of broth and a patch of space on a common-room floor.

Tired, Ramon saw his mother's smiling face in every alley. As unfamiliar as these newer slums were, his heart felt he was home. Home for the first time since her death. The French might have ruined his city, but it remained his home, a haunted place, but home. The mist and dark played on his tired mind. As they rode, he saw Mama bickering with a vegetable vendor, laughing at a juggler and pulling down child-Ramon's leggings to give him a good hard smack for running off with the other children before his chores were finished. Then she brushed off her apron and smiled as she handed him apple bread, and papa laughed with his friends on the old stump in front of their house—all bittersweet memories. He remembered the smells too: honeyed oat bread and pickled olives and dried apples.

He heard the horn blow at the gates and a crash as the portcullis slammed down, chains rattling.

Formal curfew.

Somewhere above, in the dusky sky, invisible in the fog, he heard the flutter of wings as Bubo, the ghost owl, circled overhead. They were not safe yet.

He looked around for a wayroom, a hostel, or a common-room. For now, they did not need to find the Auberge de Terre. Any refuge from the curfew patrols would be fine. He saw only a single darkened brew auberge. The wind-worn sign, faded paint difficult to read in the dark, swung on rusty chains. He slid off Izzy's back, tried the door and, finding it locked, pounded with Zaleucus, his spear, but there was only silence.

Mauri whined and both of their stomachs rumbled in chorus.

He didn't re-mount. Izzy and Mauri squished along beside him in deep mud. Nevara followed in silence. Ahead he saw two soldiers making rounds and they dodged into an even darker alley. He waited, allowing his eyes to adjust to the deeper gloom. This alley was so narrow that Nevara was forced to slide off her horse. The leaning daub and wattle houses that rose around them appeared to have been hastily built and crowded every inch of space, jutting out into the roadway at odd angles. Mauri whined, his tail between his legs.

"I know, Mauri. It'll be all right." He bent and rubbed the dog's fur.

He heard a muddy slosh behind them. Mauri heard it too and growled with a sudden ferocity that belied his size. Ramon tensed, crouched beside his dog and feeling vulnerable. He squeezed past Nevara to face the threat.

Three faceless men, silhouettes defined by the dim light of moonlit fog, blocked the alley behind him. Ramon had lived long enough to know their intent. Years of occupation by the crusaders had transformed Carcassonne from enlightened city to a slum of starving beggars. No need for words, or pleading. They wanted whatever he had and they'd kill him for a crust of bread and his boots.

"We're armed," Ramon said.

One man laughed, his breath so foul Ramon covered his nose. The bitter vinegar stench made it clear the man hadn't eaten in days.

"I have bread." It was the last of their bread, but he would gladly give it.

"We want your meat, boy," the brigand said, his voice a mad cackle.

They saw a girlish boy and his mongrel, and a white-haired woman. Two horses with good meat. They wouldn't let Ramon and Nevara go.

Ramon didn't hesitate. He tumbled, acrobat-style—a flying move taught him by old Guilhem. He levered off his spear-staff and landed back on his feet—behind the nearest man. The alley was too narrow for three to fight, so it would be one on one. His spear sliced down, scraping the daub wall as it arced, its wind a loud whistle. He used the butt end. He saw no reason to kill a starving brigand. "Never kill with Zaleucus," his teacher had told him, "unless the cause is just." There would be time enough for killing. These brigands were hungry, not evil.

His swing missed as the man ducked aside but Ramon swung around and up, catching the man on his chin with the haft of Zaleucus. The second brigand ran over his companion as he charged at Ramon. The troubadour bent his knees and slid low, sweeping his free arm and spear in a full arc. The black wood bent as it wrapped around the man's chest, then snapped back. The brigand fell back with a shout. "Broke my rib! Broke my rib!" Ramon rapped him on the head for good measure. The third came at him. He swung quickly, Zaleucus a blur. Ramon pirouetted, hitting the close wall, slid to the ground and swept out the man's legs with his spear. He heard a sharp crack of bone, then a cry.

Without waiting, he vaulted past Nevara, and ran on up the alley. "Quickly, Nevara!" He glanced back only once and saw Nevara following but nothing of the attackers.

The fog was too thick. He heard angry cries. "I be all right. Get the bastard!"

"He's down here!"

Ahead, he heard more voices. They were surrounded.

The voices rose louder. He remained still. They were deep in the maze of lower city alleys, in a place where soldiers probably never came. The alley was so tight the walls pressed Izzy's sides.

The voices ahead were different, though, laughter mingled with drunken singing. It must be a wayroom or an auberge, a refuge, perhaps even the one they sought. Only a grendincroix, a rebels' crossing, would be open after curfew. He rounded a leaning shack, puffing and out of breath, and saw the light pouring out of a badly shuttered window. He studied it. A wayroom opened after curfew in a dark alley could be a haven for drunks, thieves and renegades.

"It's being safer than out here, fool," Nevara said.

"What of the horses?"

"Taking them inside, or they be meat."

What would the innkeeper and patrons think of two bizarre strangers and their horses charging right into their common-room? He couldn't wait to find out. The door opened into a large, sagging area filled with people and smoky with fire pits. He stepped in, and without hesitation Izzy walked in after him.

"No horses," a voice called out in the langue d'oc, the Southern tongue. The roar of voices fell to silence as Ramon's green-feathered cap swept the low thatched roof. He stared at their scowling, shocked faces. Nevara rode in behind him, leaning forward and hugging her short horse's neck. She slid off, and all eyes were on her, most of the men greedily staring at her breasts.

The reaction varied slightly, from town to town, but not much. Always the stunned silence, the gaping mouths, followed by nervous glances, spitting to ward off hexes, and sometimes nervous laughs.

But this auberge was different. The only sound was the crack of the several fires in low stone-ringed pits. It was a surprisingly big common-room, big enough for forty to sleep, but low raftered and intersected with dozens of crudely squared pillars. It reeked of spilled brew, urine, rats, and unwashed patrons. Smoke coiled below the thatch, whisking along in rivers to the smoke holes, and so thick that Ramon coughed. Most of the patrons were on the reeds on the floor, sitting at low tables where the air was sour with urine, but free of smoke. Izzy and Nevara's horse Wizigard made the room feel crowded.

He heard a gruff voice, "Non! Not them!"

Ramon's shoulders relaxed. They spoke the language of the South, his own people. A grendincroix, then, perhaps even the one they sought, the Auberge de Terre. His eyes adjusted to the dim light of the fire and he grew accustomed to the oppressive stink and smoke. He scanned the scowling faces of the wayroom's patrons. A lot had changed since he was a boy. At least they were Southerners. His people. Ramon and Nevara pushed along the wall, trying not to step on out-stretched legs. Izzy and Wizi stepped lightly, necks arched and big eyes alert.

"Look at that, Domer!"

"Are them horses or dogs?"

By the time Ramon and Nevara found a table, the occasional chuckle grew to a rumble of laughter. The cheer brought the chubby waykeeper from his kitchen. Laughter was so rare in Carcassonne in these days of French occupation.

As the kitchen curtain flew back, the smell of savory broth made Ramon's stomach rumble. The waykeeper approached them with a scowl. "Non, non, we don't allow horses here!" Even as he said it, Wizi's flowing tail cocked up and healthy, steaming dung piles fell out of her. By then, the waykeep's eyes were fixed on Nevara's spell-binding bosom. Ramon kicked rushes on top of the fresh manure.

"Good master, we can't leave our pets outside," Ramon said, and he tossed the waykeeper a sou. He leaned his spear-staff on the wall, sloughed off his lute, and sat.

The waykeep's beady eyes glared out of the pouches of cheeks as round and red as beets—as friendly a greeting as they'd had yet in Carcassonne.

"A brew and some turnip broth, if you have it, Sir Waykeep," Ramon said, keeping his voice cheerful. "No meat, if you please."

The fat keeper snorted. "If you please!" He laughed. "You'll get no meat here, less'n I put your little rat-dog in ma' cookpot. Does we look like nobles?" He glared at the horses. "And you'll clean up the dung, young master." With one final glance at Izzy and Wizi, who were now munching on the floor straw and reeds, the waykeep padded into the kitchen.

Ramon heard a loud screech and then the waykeeper's voice, "Nough, woman, just stir th' cauldron!" and her even louder voice, "You lazy ox, stir it yersel'!" and then a clatter of wooden bowls.

Ramon closed his eyes for a moment, allowing his breathing and pounding heart to return to normal, suddenly overwhelmed with a hot flush of memories. This was home. The place where he was born. Where his mother died. Where he swore revenge. A ruined place.

Could twelve years really make this much difference? The music and light of Carcassonne were gone, replaced with starving brigands and a suspicious citizenry. The reek of desperation clung to the rafters, wrapped in greasy smoke.

He wiped sweat from his face with his tunic sleeve. The odor of his fresh perspiration mingled with dry sweat and reminded him that he hadn't bathed in nearly a month. He sighed. A grendincroix was not likely to offer the hospitality of a wash barrel or even a privy.

Nevara and Ramon sat with their backs to the wall. The rushes were fresh enough, and there was a nearby fire pit. Izzy and Wizi nudged up close, dropping their heads to nuzzle Ramon and Nevara with warm muzzles. The people and the small space did not terrify the tarpan horses, but they did frighten poor Mauri, who jumped onto Ramon's lap.

Ramon studied the room. He guessed that most of the patrons were rebels or freeholders caught after curfew. They eyed him with open hostility, gathered in tight circles around firepits, drinking bitters and ale from bowls.

The plain barmaid ran back and forth with bowls of brew. She thumped two down in front of them, spilling it on the splintered tabletop. She gave Nevara a disapproving glare. Ramon wrinkled his nose at the odor, but he drank the slop with the relish of a tired traveler. It tasted, as it smelled, as if brewed from moat-water sewage.

The heat in the room was oppressive. They sat at a table for the first time in three weeks and they had, against all hope, survived the gate guards and the hungry brigands. He began to relax. It became increasingly difficult to keep his eyes open. An occasional burst of drunken laughter caused his eyes to flutter open and he glared around and gripped his dagger before drifting off again. Mauri lay in his lap, already asleep.

"Talk to me, Nevara," he said in her language. "I fall into sleep."

Nevara, who never seemed to tire, leaned closer, her shoulder touching his. "We be lucky so far, beloved."

He nodded. "I thought you did not believe in luck. Fate and magic, but luck?"

"Always you joke."

How did she manage to smell so fresh and feminine? She had spent as many miles on the road as he had, without a bath, yet her face was as clean and white as her hair, even her white garments bright and clean. Of course, she'd tell him it was her magic that shielded her from the grime of the road, and he'd mostly believe her.

He glanced around. The rumble of voices gave them a degree of privacy. They could speak freely, especially in her Novgorod language, which was easier for him because when she spoke langue d'oc it was crude and accented. "Did you really create the mist with your magic?"

"Do you mock me, Ramon Troubadour?" Her voice took on a richer, more ominous tone in Novgorod.

"Do I ever mock you?"

"Always mocking, mocking, mocking."

Ramon waited for her answer. He knew it would come, eventually. He was very conscious of the curious eyes, the hostile stares, the gossip all around them. Of course, how often did a green-eyed fool and an albino witch—with two dog-like horses and a rat-like dog—visit this rogues' crossing, speaking an alien language?

"You saw me call the weather." She sounded indignant.

"You must know there is fog at night when the weather changes."

"Not on the hilltops. Not after a thunder storm." She smiled. "Always you are the doubter."

"I believe in magic. Everyone does. That's why the church fears sorcery. Magic is everywhere."

"But not in me?" Her voice simmered, dangerous and hot.

He smiled back. "Why don't you call up the mist right now. Here in this room." He challenged her this way all the time. She never gave in.

"I am tired."

"Always the magician's evasiveness."

"Do you believe in anything, Ramon Troubadour?"

"I believe in many things, Nevara. I believe in magic. I've seen enough of yours to believe you are a real sorceress. At least sometimes. And I have seen the power of the Silver Dame."

Nevara snapped forward, leaning on the table, eyes as intense as a stallion scenting a mare in season. "You've met the Dam?"

"The Dame. Yes. It was the Dame who brought me to the Baug

Balar." His fingers drummed the table. He didn't want to be drawn into that dark memory. Not yet. Not until he must.

"Tell me."

"Later."

"Is she as powerful as they say, yes?" Her voice was breathless and fast.

"More so. Although she would say not. She's not pagan, Nevara."

Nevara spat, a big gob that landed by his bowl. "Dear Ramon, you are such a fool. There is room in my world for all gods and goddesses, even your sacrificed carpenter God."

"The Dame's a Perfect, not a sorceress."

"But she's not an ass-licking papist, thank the Goddess." She spat again.

Ramon stared at the unladylike gob of spit.

"You do not believe in me?"

He wanted to say, *Don't sulk,* but instead he settled for, "I believe in you, dearest Nevara."

"But not my magic?"

"I know you have powers."

"Elemental magic requires the right elements. I cannot conjure water out of fire. Over these many years, have you not seen my skill?"

He nodded, happy he had distracted her away from the Silver Dame. "We'll need such powers to succeed." He closed his eyes, but he could feel her staring at him.

He almost gave her platitudes: *it will not come to that; your magic will protect us; I have this all planned.* Then, he realized how tired he was. A man risked castration if he gave Nevara a trite response.

"Do you think they'll come?" Nevara asked.

A sudden cool draft interrupted his answer. The door to the wayroom banged open. Ramon was grateful for the diversion. Two strange men stood in front of the low doorway and studied the room with alert eyes.

"Here they are, I think," said Ramon.

Nevara's mist swathed them for a moment, wrapping the men in an obscuring cloak. Ramon thought they might be mercenaries; they were similar to soldiers-for-hire he had met in Venice. These peculiar men, every bit as extraordinary as Nevara and Ramon, threw their heavy travel cloaks on the unswept floor, revealing weapons.

The larger of the two men appeared to be a tradesman of poor birth, big enough in the shoulders and leg to pull an oxcart. The giant's plain wool tunic could not conceal hardened muscles and his shaven head touched the rafters. Swinging at his right side was an immense mason's sledgehammer, gray metal but dappled with darker splotches. The goliath had an easy smile on his dark face as he made his way to a table by one of the fires where he greeted many of the patrons with a wave or a slap on the back. He had the look of the Hun. Ramon, who had traveled as far as the Empire of Bulgaria, had seen Mongol-like swarthiness in the offspring of Hungarians, and occasionally in the children of Italy and Occitania. Two of the Baug Balar were pure Hun.

"Your kin," said Nevara, cocking her head in the direction of the second, smaller man. Ramon smiled. He did have the look of a traveling *goliard*, or a fellow troubadour. Blue eyes flitted back and forth with nervous energy, Ramon would have taken him for a Venetian trader for he wore a broad hat with a battered feather and a gay tapestry of embroidered surcoat and tunic. Not nearly as large as his companion, he swaggered with the confidence of a hardened fighter and as his hips swung, twin short swords slapped leather breeches.

Old Guilhem had promised Ramon he could find the Grand Duo here. The Dandy and the Hammer. There could be no doubt that these two were the famous rebels.

The dandy halted in the middle of the wide wayroom and whistled. The red-faced barmaid emerged from the kitchen doorway with a laden tray.

"Doré!" she cried, all but dropping the heavy tray. She rushed into his arms. He gave her a long, happy kiss and then thrust her aside.

"Mon Dieu!" He laughed, a girlish laugh. "T'would think I'd been gone for years!"

"Too long! Where have you been, you rogue? I never thought to see you again!" The barmaid clung to his arm.

"Oh, you knowest me, ma chère," he said, his voice jovial and oddly disarming.

She looked around then cried, "And there's Osric." She ran across the room with a squeal of delight and fell giggling into the arms of the colossal man. "Osric! Osric!" She kissed him repeatedly. "You bastard! You didn't even bid me adieu when you left!"

Osric squeezed her. "We 'ad to leave in a hurry, Brigitte. You know 'ow the local militia loves us so." He winked at her.

"Oh, you bastards! You beautiful, hateful bastards!"

Doré sat on the table and took Brigitte's hand. "We missed you, chéri."

"You lie, filthy worm! How many hearts have you broken since mine?"

"I really couldn't say." He looked to his big companion for help. "Do you recall, Osric?"

Osric continued to smile and shook his head. Brigitte glared at him, and Ramon thought she was about to slap him, but instead she burst out laughing. "You must be hungry!"

"Oui, and thirsty, mademoiselle!" Doré gave her a slap on her generous bottom that sent her flying to the kitchen. She came back a moment later with beer and watched as they drank a bowl each in one long, hard chug.

Ramon and Nevara stared. Ramon stroked Izzy's muzzle, smiling, watching the two strangers. "These are the two we came for," Ramon said to Nevara in her tongue. His information had been good. They were unmistakable. The Dandy and the Hammer. The Grand Duo. He had never met them, but he knew their reputation. According to the speakers of langue d'oil, the French, the Grand Duo were murderers, monsters, butchers, thieves, and even—as the years passed and they remained uncaught—rapists, fiends, killers of priests and monks. But to the Southerners, the Grand Duo remained heroes, rescuers, saviors of mothers and children—and Ramon's favorite: "tax collectors of the French." They robbed wealthy church coffers, caravans and nobles and "redistributed the wealth."

The Dandy wore expensive felt and suede leather, embroidered with gold thread, and under his deeply scalloped tunic, Ramon saw the glint of a fine mail coat—nothing more than a light fencing hauberk. Draped over his shoulders was a cape of fine green cloth, trimmed in fur, clasped with a large jewel. Obviously the man came from a family of consequence—perhaps a dispossessed Occitanian noble, judging by his extravagant clothes—for though his face was tanned and weathered, his fine features had the cultured look of a Southern lord. A fine gold chain hung around his neck with a peculiar pendant on the end—the symbol of the sacred star. The star of the South. Any who openly wore it would be dangerous rebels, sworn to die fighting the French invaders.

Yes, these were the men he needed. But they would be infinitely more dangerous than the brigands in the fog, or the curfew patrols. And they would not be superstitious fools like the guard gates.

Doré stared at Ramon now, hard blue eyes that never seemed to blink, killer's eyes, yet soft and enticing at the same time.

"Your food, garçon!" The barmaid slammed a crock of putrid pottage in front of Ramon, thick with overcooked turnips and cabbage and a hard slab of stale horse bread. Mauri stood on his lap and peered over the edge of the table, panting.

Nevara wrinkled her nose. "We cannot eat that."

"It's better than your pottage," Ramon said, trying to sound light. Nevara never cooked.

Ramon held out a chunk of the horsebread to Izzy. Izzy nickered lightly, sniffed, then ate the coarse-grained bread. Ramon dipped another chunk of bread in the foul pottage and gave it to Mauri. Then, holding his breath against the stench of turnips, he lifted the bowl to his lips and drank broth.

His eyes met Doré's and for a moment, they locked gazes. Then the dandy tugged on the brim of his green felt hat and nodded. Ramon waved back.

Home. After twelve years he was home. His own people now lived in shacks outside the inner wall in a chaotic slum, while the French invaders plundered the inner city; but still, Carcassonne was home. His parents had died here: his mother Musette Midwife burned as a heretic; his father Burc Tailor hung as a rebel. Most of his neighbors would either be dead, rotting in chains, or starving in this very slum.

The barmaid cleared their table without a word. Ramon took another bowl of brew. He slouched on the bench and listened to snatches of the whispered conversations around him: he heard whisperings of old Count Raymond, flogged on the steps of the Cathedral in Toulouse as penance for supporting heresy in the South; various burnings in the market square; hints of rebellion and secret meetings.

"They distrust us," Nevara said.

Ramon nodded. Every eye in the grendincroix was fixed on them, glaring, unfriendly eyes. "They think us French."

"I'm of no country." She spat again. "That's what I think of all kingdoms."

Ramon smiled. Nevara's mother was of the wanderers, the displaced Novgorodians who wandered through Europe, reviled and feared by all. She never understood Ramon's patriotism for the Occitan. "They will not let us out of here alive."

"I'll turning them all into rats," Nevara said, reverting to her crude langue d'oc. "So they can spreading the plague on the piggy French."

"A good plan. But let's try mine first."

"Your planning is reeking of danger. All your tricky plannings are too dangerous."

He shrugged. "More fun that way, dearest."

She spat, to ward evil, as the two killers, Doré the Dandy and Osric the Hammer, crossed the common room and moved towards them.

Song of the Magician

4

PETER AMIEL SHIVERED by the fire. He opened the front of his woolen robe, enjoyed the heat on his skin and held out meaty hands, rubbing them together.

He glanced out the narrow slit in the stone wall. Not yet sunset. His felt slippers whispered on cold stone as he paced. Gray stone and dark rooms. Drafty halls and low ceilings. He sighed. He missed his villa in Narbonne with its extravagant glass windows, tapestries from Firenze—his favorite, an image of Saint Sebastian pierced by eleven bloody arrows—and the small luxuries he took for granted, especially the soft Venetian carpets.

He heard the scullery maids clattering in the bailey kitchen as they brought the common pots to the boil. How sound traveled in the palace. He heard the kitchen boys cursing as they heaved barrels of brew from the undercroft. He smelled the sweetness of stuffed pig roasting on the spits. His stomach rumbled. An afternoon of sport always made him hungry.

He turned and contemplated the girl in his bed. She was asleep and only half covered by the bed furs, tiny bosom exposed. Young, perky breasts. Her mouth parted in a snore and one of her arms moved, delicate fingers closing around the blanket. Her smell was on him now, salty and syrupy, mingling with his moldy-oats odor.

Sweet child, he thought, and together with that, the guilt. They always came together: the yearning, then the remorse.

Longing—he thought about having her again—but shame made him sit instead on a stool by the fire.

He threw another log on the embers, scattering red sparks. He liked fire. It was a living thing. It hungered, ate, grew. The flames licked the fresh food and he heard a hiss as the flames wrapped their prey.

Bark cracked and fell into the coals and the naked wood darkened. He leaned closer and closer to the flames and watched as a yellow-striped spider, clinging to the apple wood, glowed red and evaporated in tangy smoke. Pleasant memories enveloped him like the heat.

Fire. It purified. It cleansed. With fire, he had remade Occitania.

A hand touched his shoulder. A child's hand. "Your Grace."

He did not turn. "You should go."

She caressed his shoulder under the wool cloak and stroked his skin. He felt the familiar rise, the thudding in his temples, the stirring in his loins. He fixed his eyes on the glowing ember of the spider.

"Go."

He did not watch her dress and leave even when he heard her soft crying. His eyes remained fixed on the hungry flames.

A mouse chattered at his foot.

"Leave me alone," he said to the mouse.

Tiny eyes stared at him. He kicked at the mouse and the mouse scampered away, turned, and sat back on its hind legs, looking at him with an expression that said *I'm faster than you, fat man, try to catch me.*

The mice and rats were so bold in Carcassonne. In the common-room, even crowded with feasters, the mice scampered everywhere. And in the pit, where the heretics waited for trial, the rats were nearly as big as cats, fat and well fed.

He threw one of his slippers at the mouse, but it didn't run away. "Go mouse." He shivered.

He hated mice, ever since he had heard the story of Hatto, Archbishop of Mainz, devoured by a swarm of mice in the tower now nicknamed the Mauseturm, the Mouse Tower. Punishment for wrongdoing, so the legend went.

Amiel trembled, remembering the old witch twelve years ago, burning to her death, her flesh melting as she screamed out her curses. *"A mouse shall destroy you. A mouse shall be your bane!"* Everyone knew a dying curse was powerful. Ever since then, he saw mice everywhere, in eating halls and cathedrals and sleeping chambers; he dreamed of mice and in his dreams they devoured him like Archbishop Hatto. He feared nothing in the world—except mice. A rat was no problem. A mouse ... He shivered.

At first, he ignored the soft knock at his door but on the second rap the mouse scampered away and disappeared into a crack in the wall. His breathing returned to normal and he answered on the third attempt. The door opened and his archdeacon peered in. The scarecrow of a man averted his eyes when he realized his archbishop was dressed only in a sleeping robe.

"Your Excellency. My apologies."

Archbishop Amiel waved him in with an impatient "Come." The deacon entered with his head dropped. "Well, Verdun?"

"Your Excellency. We have a visitor. A most important visitor."

"Is that so?" He wondered if the priest had seen the cobbler's daughter leaving—*perhaps I should give the cobbler a chicken or two,* he thought—then, he shrugged to himself. It didn't matter. "Who is this important person?" Less than the pope himself was unlikely to interest Amiel.

"Your Excellency, a Templar."

Amiel drew his robe closer. Templars. How he despised those self-righteous pricks. They thought themselves exempt from the power of the Church—just because of the charter of His Holiness Honorius II, at the urging of that fool Bernard of Clairvaux. For more than a century, the Templars had plagued the Church with their power and demands, and pope after pope gave in, exempting them from the authority of kings and archbishops. Amiel shivered. What did a Templar want of him? A damnable nuisance.

"Well, Verdun, who is this knight?"

Verdun looked away, clearly terrified. "Brother Arnot de Ridefort, companion knight to Master Marshall Bertrande."

The Master Marshall's lieutenant, here? What could this mean? "Well, fool, why do you stand there? Make yourself useful. Help me dress."

Amiel frowned as his archdeacon picked up the thrown slipper and held it out, his eyes fixed on a flickering candle. "Am I so monstrous?"

"Your Excellency?" The priest seemed unable to swallow.

"Look at me. You can't dress me blind. My best ceremonial robes.

And my crozier!"

Verdun helped Amiel dress in his ceremonial robes with fumbling hands. The archbishop wore his tallest mitre and his most colorful vestments. In need of reinforcements, he lifted the ceremonial crozier, the firelight glittering on its golden crook. He would need all his symbols of power. An archbishop was nothing next to the lieutenant of the Marshall of the Templars. The Marshall commanded the greatest standing army in all of the lands, greater than the German Empire, while the archbishop's men-at-arms counted only seventy. Only the Mongol Khanate commanded more horsemen than the Templars.

"My sword."

"Your Excellency?" Verdun seemed shocked. The archbishop normally only wore his sword on the battlefield, never on the Church's business.

Amiel held out his arms as Verdun belted on his sacred sword, a gift from the pope himself. "You must take the sword of Saint Michael on your crusade," His Holiness had said, and he presented his legate with the sword, beautifully inlaid with gold filigree depicting the Archangel Michael, the very sword hand of God. That sword had killed many enemies of God.

"I will meet this Templar in the great hall," Amiel said, caressing the crossed hilt of the holy blade.

"Yes, Your Excellency."

"Oh—and Verdun—"

"Yes, Your Excellency."

"Give the cobbler two chickens."

Verdun stared stupidly at his feet and made no move.

"Did you hear me?"

"Yes, Your Excellency." Archdeacon Verdun ran from the room, a hopeless man who disapproved of the archbishop's little vices. Thank God he wasn't his confessor. The archdeacon's only virtue was that he was totally pious and easy to control. He did a reasonable job as the liaison with the local Inquisition, and he truly believed in the good work of cleansing heresies, though he was not ambitious enough to be of any real value as an archdeacon.

The Templar was nothing like Amiel expected. More killer than monk, with eyes that demanded respect even by the low light of rush torches—they seemed to say 'look at me, fool, or suffer my sword'—but what surprised Amiel was the man's shoddy clothing and the stink of death on him. He had killed recently, Amiel felt certain. Both his chin and head were shaven, breaking tradition with his brother knights' penchant for beards. There was no respect in that hard face, no glimmer of fear of Amiel's lofty office. He had led a string of four horses, two destriers and two light riding horses, into the great hall, between the low feasting tables, and even now the horses munched on the floor straw. Amiel saw his steward hovering nearby, trying to grab the reins of the beasts to take them to the stable.

Amiel felt his own heat, certain he was blushing, but he tried to control his rage. Horses in his great hall! He wouldn't allow such disrespect from the viscount himself.

Neither the archbishop nor the Templar moved, and they stared at each other stiffly. Even Amiel was unclear of the protocol. The Templar did not bow. Neither did Amiel. There could be no doubt as to this knight's mission. He had come for the prize, on the scent like some scruffy, starving wolf.

Verdun cleared his throat. "His Excellency, Lord Archbishop Amiel of Narbonne, Legate of His Holiness our Blessed Pope Gregory the ninth, I present Brother Sir Arnot de Ridefort, companion knight to Master Marshall Bertrande of the Knights of the Temple of Jerusalem."

Still no bow. But the knight stepped closer to a rush torch. The shadows played across scars, making him appear to be the Devil's own messenger. "Your Grace," the growling voice said finally. "God's peace on you."

Amiel nodded. "Brother Arnot, may Our Lord watch over you and guide your sword in His service." He offered his holy ring but Sir Arnot made no move to kiss. Stiffly, feeling the heat again, he dropped his hand. "Pray, tell me what brings you to my court?"

"I have come for *The Jewel*." He offered a hint of a smile, a twitch of his mouth, and his hand rested lightly on the haft of his Turkish axe.

"I have many jewels. Which jewel?" But Amiel knew. This bastard Templar knew about *The Jewel*!

"*The* Jewel. The only Jewel a Templar would care to possess."

Amiel thought about denying it, calling it a rumor, but he sensed such protestations would be futile. The Jewel was not a secret that could be kept for long. Monks were breezy gossips and by now half the land knew of The Jewel. Which meant, in all likelihood, His Holiness would know as well. "What business is this of the Temple?"

"All the treasures of the Holy Land are the business of the Temple, Your Grace, you know this."

"The Jewel is not of the Holy Land, brother." Amiel barely controlled his rage. They had only captured The Jewel six weeks past. How could the Temple know so quickly? He had kept it secret from all for fear of the Temple. Monks were terrible gossips, so even the Abbott of Carcassonne did not know.

The damnable Templar spat. Right there, at Amiel's feet, in his own hall! Amiel could barely stop himself from calling the captain of the guard.

"The Jewel leads to the holiest relic of all," the Templar said.

Amiel struggled to disguise his shock and dismay. The Templars commanded the greatest standing army in Europe and the Holy Land. They could not be dismissed. Even their sainted King Louis would never stand against the Temple.

Amiel studied the ruffian. There could be no doubt he was a Templar in high office. Only the Temple knew the legend of the Holies. But where was his retinue? His brother sergeant? Would more Templars arrive? Were they outside? Amiel silently weighed the risks of having Brother Arnot dispatched, perhaps thrown head-first into the privy cesspit.

No. He must play the Templar. Discover what they knew. "Brother, The Jewel is not in my possession. But I offer you the hospitality of my palace."

"Who possesses The Jewel?" The voice was harsh, no expression of gratitude for hospitality, just demands. It had always been so. Templars were the bankers of Europe, always taking, taking, demanding,

demanding. Even Holy Mother Church, especially after the pope fled to Lyons, owed the Templars vast sums of money, borrowed to fund the defense of papal palaces from the rogue emperor, various crusades and the growing demands of the new Monastic Inquisition. He vowed that when he became pope, he would obliterate the Temple forever.

The Templar stepped closer, his face set in a sneer, the Turkish axe half drawn from his belt.

Amiel stepped back. His captain of the guard, until now hidden, stepped out from the archway behind the archbishop, with five of his men. "Brother, I ask you to respect the office." Amiel rapped the floor with his crozier, then tilted it forward as if it were a weapon of war.

The Templar laughed, a deep, rolling sound that prickled like thorns. "I accept your hospitality," he said, still sounding amused.

Amiel considered again. Kill the Templar now? But curiosity had him. If he killed this knight, he might never know. And if he tried torture, the Master Marshall of the Temple might send his great army against Carcassonne.

Gently, he said, "You are most welcome." *You sheep-fornicating son of a heretic.* "Would you join the feast in the viscount's hall? I bless the feast each night."

"I would be grateful, Your Grace. Allow me to tend my horses and freshen my clothes."

"No groom? No brother sergeant?" He asked it genially, smiling.

"I rode ahead of the main contingent."

Amiel felt his shoulders sag, all pretence gone. If the Templars had sent a troop, and sent this lieutenant on ahead, they meant to have The Jewel with all urgency. But the prize, The Jewel, had been Amiel's life mission, and not even the Marshall himself would take it from him. The Jewel would ensure Amiel earned election as the next pope against his chief rival, Cardinal Sinibaldo Fiesco, all the more important now that his spies told him that His Holiness Gregory was dying.

"My servants will see to you." He clapped his hands. Three nervous men ran from the shadows of the hall.

As he watched the fierce man gather his string of horses, he knew this Templar must die.

5

CARDINAL VICE-CHANCELLOR SINIBALDO FIESCO kissed the ring of His Holiness, holding the skeletal fingers of the dying pope. He felt the brittle vellum-thin skin. It sloughed off the wasting flesh and he felt a pang of grief as he realized his old friend would soon be gone.

Pope Gregory sat crumpled in the plush throne, a shriveled shell of the man he had once been, asleep but not at peace, his arms twitching and his grayish lips trembling. By the light of the cheerful braziers on either side of the marble dais, Holy Father appeared gaunt and ancient. He had slept since that afternoon, first drifting off as the archbishop of Agen reported on the heresies in his archdiocese. Fiesco had hustled all the petitioners from the grand audience room, even those who had waited months, then sat at the gilt chancellor's desk, placed between the pillars to catch the afternoon sun through Saint Michael's window. He used the time to quill another exhortation to the king of France to march on the unholy emperor of Germany. He would stamp it with the papal seal, of course.

Then Fiesco leaned back in his chair and watched his dear friend sleep in the papal throne. Holy Father twitched and spoke in his sleep, often calling out the name of the damned emperor, his sworn enemy. The pope's ashen face took on the colors of the stained glass in the afternoon sun, then later the torchlight. Patiently, all day, Cardinal Fiesco waited, even after the pages brought him the urgent request for audience.

There could be no doubt Holy Father Gregory must die this very year. When Fiesco had campaigned to have Cardinal Bishop Ugolino Conti de Segni elected Pope, he had expected his old friend and mentor to live a year or two at best. Ugolino, now Pope Gregory IX, had already reached eighty years of age and lived on and on, due in part to Fiesco's ability to shoulder many of the papal burdens. Regardless of infirmity, the stress of war with the excommunicated emperor, which had forced the pope to flee Rome to Lyons more than once, and his advanced age, Holy Father had presided over one of the most important papacies in recent history: Canonizing Saint Francis of Assisi and Saint Dominic de Guzman, creating the Blessed Monastic Inquisition after preaching the crusade against the Occitan and the Albigensians. The Inquisition alone had already changed Europe, driving pagans into hiding, rooting out heresies, bringing Christianity into full blossom. Fiesco could only hope he would be as well remembered when he was elected Pope Innocent IV. He already knew that would be his papal name. He would see to it. Fiesco's support in the college of cardinals was overwhelming, and the Holy Father was soon to die.

"Holy Father," Fiesco said, and he kissed the ring once more.

The pope started awake, his eyes revealing momentary confusion. "Sinibaldo, dear ..." He lurched forward on the throne in a fit of coughing. Fiesco snatched a silver chalice of wine, and held it to the dying pope's grayish lips.

"Drink, Papa," he said, addressing his old friend informally only because they were alone in the audience chamber.

Holy Father drank then continued to cough.

Fiesco sat on the stool at the pope's feet and prayed silently for his friend. As much as he hoped his own time as pope was near, Ugolino had been as a father to him, a mentor, a teacher. Fiesco had risen from bishop to archbishop to cardinal, all because of his dear Ugolino. But Pope Gregory's time was finished, and Fiesco prayed for a painless, dignified death.

"I would walk in the gardens ..." Again Holy Father's voice trailed off into a fit of coughs. "To smell the ..." More hacking coughs.

"In the morning, Papa," Fiesco said. "We have an important visitor."

"Yes, Sinibaldo?" He coughed again, spraying pink spittle on his white glove.

Fiesco dabbed the pope's bloody lips. If they hadn't been alone, he would never have presumed. He felt the pope's forehead with the back of his hand. Papa's skin was too hot, but he was shivering. Fiesco stood and pulled the pope's fur-trimmed cloak forward across the papal vestments. "Papa, Diableteur comes with important news."

He felt the pope stiffen. Diableteur rarely visited Rome, and then only with big news. His last visit had been at the end of 1239, just before the pope delivered an important advent mass, and Diableteur came with the announcement of his triumphant burning of 183 heretics at Montwimer.

Fiesco both admired and despised Diableteur, an experiment in fear gone possibly too far, a persona deliberately created by Fiesco himself to reinforce the fledgling Inquisition. Diableteur was all about the appearance of terror.

The less educated screamed when they saw him riding his white horse, the biblical death rider of the apocalypse, cowled face hidden, black gauntlets clenching his terrible weapon. Parish priests closed their eyes and prayed when he rode into their villages. But even men such as Cardinal Fiesco and Pope Gregory might feel a moment of superstitious dread whenever Diableteur appeared. Only last year, Diableteur had denounced and arrested the bishop of Tulle as a heretic. If the Diableteur, the great heretic hunter, freed from all restraint by the pope's own authority, would dare to arrest bishops, who was safe from his accusations?

As long as Diableteur had the support of the college of cardinals, even Holy Father could not curb his powers. Diableteur was a past abbot of a fringe sect of the Dominicans, a grand-nephew of Saint Dominic himself, and once a highly revered cleric. When he had taken on his new duties, he said, "I must be allowed to do this my way. Only terror can win this war on heresy." His weapon of choice had always been fear.

Every part of his facade was crafted to elicit dread, from his cowled black robes and his scythe to his haughty white horse. In the beginning, he had not bothered with arrest and trial by the Inquisitors, favoring instead summary judgment, executed by his small troop of forty-four fealty-sworn martial monks who wore his black robes, rode white horses, and carried his standard of the white rose on black. It was all very dramatic and improper. Fiesco had complained, campaigning to have Diableteur work more closely with the monastic Inquisition, but the Diableteur's authority came directly from the pope, much like the damnable Templars, and he always rode the gray area between crusader and Inquisitor. He frightened the pagans into conversion, and the heretics into hiding, so even Fiesco grudgingly approved of his work.

"Does he still carry his scythe?" Papa asked.

Fiesco's laugh was nervous. "It seems to work in the villages well enough."

"The reaper." Papa's laugh became a long, gasping cough, and Fiesco could smell the sourness on his breath, the bitter precursor to death. The irony wasn't lost on Fiesco. Perhaps Diableteur's dramatics would be enough to terrify the pope to death. He doubted it, since the pope had known the former abbot as a friend, before he fell into dark madness. His Holiness had tolerated Diableteur's fringe beliefs, even encouraged the radical militant order. Fiesco had argued to have the order disbanded. "How can monks be soldiers?" he had argued. But the pope called them his "soldiers of God" and financed their training in arms and their ongoing needs. Even rumors of Diableteur's own heresies and wild stories of dark sorcery had not been enough to sway Papa from encouraging the group. Now, it seemed to Fiesco, Diableteur and his deathstalkers had gone too far, bowing to no authority, arresting even churchmen, executing suspects without trial—all in violation of Church law. Even His Holiness feared this rabid dog he had raised from a pup.

At last His Holiness said, "Let him enter."

Fiesco stood to the right of his pope and rapped the dais with his staff. The great double doors of Saint Michael swung open, pushed by the papal pages. Diableteur swept into the grand hall, his face invisible behind the long black cowl. He appeared, at first, to be a towering monk, lank and black, but the cowl and the long sleeves were cut longer and deeper, designed to hide his features. He walked with his staff-high scythe clutched in a black gauntlet, its metal-tipped haft clacking on the marble as he walked. No facial features were visible. Fiesco realized, abruptly, this could be anyone—a spy or an assassin from the Emperor Frederick or an Occitanian noble seeking revenge.

"The hood," Fiesco said, rapping his staff again. Four guards appeared at the door, alarmed by his stern voice. "You will remove the hood."

The Diableteur, grown arrogant in his power, hesitated a moment, drew taller and more menacing. The four guards with their pikes hung back, their faces revealing unusual apprehension. Death incarnate had come to the grand hall.

Then the head bowed. The Diableteur properly fell to his left knee, still tall in this pose, and set his scythe on the marble floor. Slowly his black gauntleted hands reached up and he pulled back the long cowl.

Fiesco drew in a long breath. The last time the Diableteur had revealed his face in Rome, three of the cardinals in the grand chamber whimpered. His face was the Devil's own, the melted flesh of one cheek flowing into a fold of flesh where his ear should have been. There was no flesh on the bridge of his nose, just two gaping nostril holes where the scarred flesh bonded to shining bone, and half of his lip was gone as well, so that half of his mouth hung open to reveal grinning teeth.

The abbot had once been dear to both Fiesco and Papa, one of their most devout Inquisitors, a compassionate Dominican—at one time. The fire in the chapel had changed him. He had nearly died that night. What was left of the Abbot Dimitri became even more devout, and he formed his splinter order of militant monks. He became a twisted man, a man convinced that his suffering in fire had been God's own will, that the flames had purified him just as pyre flames cleansed heretics in the moment of their deaths. Fiesco realized the ordeal had simply driven him mad, but Papa seemed to believe Diableteur was God's own hand, molded by the holy flames of the chapel fire. If Fiesco had been a more spiritual man, he might have believed, as Papa did, that it was all part of God's plan, that the accident in the church had been God's way of creating this Diableteur, a creature needed in the world. Diableteur was a weapon designed to bring God to superstitious folk who still celebrated pagan rituals alongside mass, or who misunderstood God and practiced dangerous heresies.

Diableteur was close enough that Fiesco could smell the ripeness of mortified flesh—clearly, the abbot still practiced self-mortification with his whips. The abbot had always been one for austerity, often fasting for days, flagellating his own body, even cutting the flesh. He believed that purity came from suffering, that their Lord Jesus had suffered to redeem mankind, and a monk's duty was to do the same. Years of personal abuse and mortified flesh had created this thing that stood before them. There was no compassion or Godliness about the ex-abbot. If Fiesco feared this mad creature, what must the superstitious of Southern Occitania think of him?

Fiesco could not repress a sudden expulsion of breath, a loud sigh, and he realized he had been holding his breath. This was no spy, no assassin, but their own Diableteur, or what was left of him. Except for the glittering black eyes, fiercely alive and clearly mad, Diableteur seemed to be Death incarnate. He stepped forward and kissed the papal ring of St. Peter. As the scarred flesh of his lips touched the fisherman's ring, Fiesco saw Papa stiffen. Fiesco didn't hold out his ring. Diableteur was exempt from all but papal authority, much like the damnable Templars, and he had long ago shown his reluctance to dignify Fiesco's important office as Vice-chancellor of the Church of Rome. But he did nod once, the respect of equals, or perhaps in recognition of his old friend. Diableteur was not a man of politics, but he certainly knew Fiesco would be the next pope.

"God be with you, Holiness," said Diableteur. His voice was the last and most frightening aspect of the demonic persona. His voice had changed that night of the fire, his throat damaged as much as his ear and cheek, and he never spoke unless he must, for it clearly pained him. His words sounded like a moaning hiss. "And with you, Eminence."

"Welcome Father Abbot," Pope Gregory said, using Diableteur's proper title.

"God be praised on your safe return, Dimitri," Fiesco said. He knew it was pointless to dabble in social niceties with the heretic-hunter. The Diableteur would stay only long enough to deliver his message, then leave as mysteriously as he came, surrounded by his forty-four deathriders on white horses. "What news have your brought us?"

Diableteur's glittering black eyes studied Fiesco for a moment, perhaps deciding if the news was for him or just for the pope's ears.

"You can speak in front of His Eminence," Papa said, but he bent forward in another fit of coughing, and both Diableteur and Fiesco waited.

"Close the doors, Holiness." It was not much more than a hissing whisper.

Fiesco rapped his staff again, and magically it seemed, for there were no men visible, the doors glided closed. The pope and the future pope were alone with death and his scythe.

Typical of Diableteur, he wasted no time. "The Jewel of Montségur is found."

Neither Papa nor Fiesco spoke. Diableteur remained on his left knee, his horrid face glaring at the pope. Fiesco fell into a numb shock. *The Jewel!*

"Where is The Jewel?" Papa demanded suddenly, his voice alarmingly loud. He seemed abruptly agitated, angry even. "Why did you not bring it?"

"Carcassonne. I was prevented, Holiness." The whispery hiss carried an angry thrum. Fiesco couldn't imagine any force on earth that could resist Diableteur's authority. What fear couldn't compel, his forty-four sworn knights would. Fiesco wondered again if he would strip Diableteur of his authority when he became pope. There were advantages to having this monster at large, as long as he never became so arrogant that he ignored the pope's authority.

"You understand its importance?" Fiesco demanded, suddenly.

The Diableteur nodded, his black glittery eyes glaring.

"Then who would dare stop you?" But even as he asked it, he knew the answer. The Jewel led to a prize so great that many powerful men would try to stop him.

Diableteur stood, and though he was two steps down from the dais, his tortured face was level with Fiesco's. "The archbishop and the viscount prevented me."

Papa's face tightened with anger, a fury that made him suddenly appear younger. Fiesco was convinced it was rage that kept the old pope from dying. Rage about his own failed plans, about heresies out of control in Europe and an emperor, Frederick, who ignored the papacy, kept him from going to God's glory.

"Did you speak with Archbishop Amiel?" Fiesco said, hoping to calm his pope.

Again the arrogant nod. "He blames the viscount."

"And the viscount?"

"He blames the archbishop." The hissing voice dropped lower, dripping with hate. Diableteur despised Archbishop Amiel, that was clear.

As did Fiesco. Though only an archbishop, he was Pope Gregory's Legate in the South and well-supported in the college, and Fiesco felt sure the archbishop planned to use The Jewel to make a move for the papacy. He had even built his own small army. An archbishop with The Jewel, which led to the Holiest of Holies, might very well win election, even if he was just a Papal Legate. Fiesco felt a rage he hadn't felt since the last time the emperor chased the pope and the cardinals from Rome. There could be no doubt of Amiel's intentions. Diableteur would have threatened the archbishop with either excommunication or accusation of heresy, and obviously Amiel had not caved in.

The viscount had also already proven immune to Diableteur's threats. As seneschal for the glorious King Louis, the viscount of Carcassonne was fearless and unshakable. "King Louis will be a saint," Pope Gregory had once told Fiesco. "You'll make sure of it, won't you?" And Fiesco had agreed, for King Louis was the greatest hero of Christianity in Europe: he aided the mendicant orders and the Inquisition, propagated synodal decrees of the church, sheltered the pope when he fled the wrath of the emperor Frederick, built leper hospitals, collected holy relics—and would lead the great crusade to free Jerusalem. All of which made the viscount, the king's own seneschal, untouchable.

"Cardinal Fiesco, you must return with Diableteur," Papa said, abruptly.

Fiesco glanced at his friend. The Pope seemed younger, straighter and angrier than he had seen in years. Diableteur had just given Pope Gregory a new purpose in life. What could be more important than the Holy of Holies? Fiesco felt it dangerous to leave his friend's side at a time like this. The pope was vulnerable and weak, infirm with age. The college of cardinals might campaign against Fiesco's impending election. Attempts could be made on the weakened pope.

As if understanding Fiesco's concerns, Papa said, "The viscount and archbishop must listen to you." For the first time he did not cough. "At any cost, bring The Jewel."

"But Holiness..."

The white glove, stained pink with blood, snapped up, interrupting Fiesco's argument. "I know all you would argue, Eminence. Understand that nothing is more important to Mother Church than The Jewel."

Fiesco attempted only one argument. "The Vice-chancellor of the Church can succeed where the Diableteur cannot?"

"You have my authority to excommunicate, to arrest, to do whatever is required. The Jewel must be brought to Rome!" Fiesco had not heard such fierceness in his friend's voice for many years. The pope sat straight on his throne, eyes alive and excited.

Fiesco kissed the fisherman's ring. "I will not fail you, Holiness."

"The ultimate prize is within our grasp!" Pope Gregory said. "See that you do not."

6

THE GRAND DUO approached Ramon and Nevara, hands on their weapons. Ramon knew their reputation. By legend, they had killed hundreds of French invaders, which probably meant dozens. Either way, they looked darkly dangerous. He had been a fool to assume he could easily charm them into helping him. But the French feared the Grand Duo, and everyone in the South loved them. The two rebels had succeeded in fighting the French in a way no one else had, not since the first crusade launched against the South decades ago.

Osric, the massive, dark-skinned mason, scowled down at them, his Hun-like features scrunched into a frown of intense disapproval.

But it was the kindlier Doré who spoke, in the langue d'oc, "What brings strangers to our cité?" His voice was unnaturally high pitched and musical, almost as if he were a troubadour himself.

Ramon sighed. He had hoped for more rest. He swung his long legs under him and sprang up, like a siege engine releasing, landing on top of the table and sending their empty bowls flying. Osric and Doré, the Grand Duo, stepped back, startled.

"Good sirs, we come for rest and ale," Ramon said, putting on his best jester façade. He blew Doré a kiss. "And what is a dandy boy and his big ox boyfriend doing in a dungeon like this?"

"You speak our language." Doré ignored the insult.

"No. 'tis you speak my language." Ramon maintained the smile, a crafted expression he had perfected across years of journeying and entertaining.

"We test you, boy," Doré said, but now he was smiling.

Ramon winked, his eyes watery from the dense smoke in the wayroom. "And what are you, good sir? Do you threaten my trade? Are you in training as a troubadour?"

A hush fell on the room. Ramon had deliberately admitted his own heresy, in a time of hungry flames. A test of his own.

"You are a troubadour?" Doré stepped closer. "You must be, by the sight of you. Or a madman to admit such an offence publicly."

"Or a jester!" the Hun-like giant Osric snapped. "A long-legged fool!" He spat.

Ramon danced a quick jig, then flipped onto the table into a handstand. He stood on one hand, upside down, staring up at frowning Osric. "Don't let my long legs fool you, big man. The inquisition stretched me on their rack. I was once as squat as you." He had used this joke with the gate guard, but he was too fatigued to think of something new.

The patrons in the Auberge de Terre laughed. Only Osric retained his frown.

Ramon switched hands and waved. "Come, friend, I jest with you."

"I be no friend of you or yours," growled the mason, his melon-sized fists wrapping the haft of his rock-smashing hammer.

"Then you stare at me because you think me fetching?" Ramon

batted his teary eyes, still balancing on the one hand. "Shall we off to your hovel or mine?" Ramon half closed his eyes, hoping the hammer wouldn't sweep out of the belt to crush his head. "Many mistake me for a girl." Snickers of laughter rippled through the room. "But I bend over for no man." Stunned silence, followed by a loud guffaw, then the entire room rumbled with laughter.

He tumbled back to his feet and blew Osric a kiss. "'tis not the size of the wand that matters, but the magic within."

Osric cracked a smile. Who dared to joke about heresies, magic and sexually-forbidden topics but a jester?

"Come, now, good Osric. Didn't your mother teach you—a laugh a day keeps the clerics away?"

The smile widened.

"Fine. Have me your way." Ramon spun on the ball of one foot, flipped up his tunic, and bent over. He pulled down his breeches, revealing his bare arse. "I'm ready for your hammer, Osric." The laughter churned through the room like a gale. Ramon peered between his legs and saw that Osric laughed. His job done, he yanked up his breeches and turned with a flourish.

"Ramon Troubadour, at your service. And sometime jester." Only Nevara didn't laugh, and he knew it was because she was too used to his antics.

Doré couldn't reply for several moments. He and his big friend Osric laughed so hard they had to lean on each other. "Ramon Troubadour, I care not if you are the archbishop's own," he said, finally. "I needed that laugh."

"I hear the archbishop favors much younger than I," Ramon said, smiling.

Light laughter, but now Ramon knew he had them in his power. He jumped from the table and bowed once again.

"Do not bow to me," Doré said, and he slapped Ramon hard between the shoulder blades. "But tell me of your friend, good Ramon."

Nevara rose with typical drama, sweeping up her trailing sleeves. "Nevara, the storm!" Her voice was loud in the crowded hall, as abrupt as a thunderstorm in the mountains.

"You certainly are," Doré said, smiling, thinking she was joking as well.

"That being my name," Nevara said, her accent so thick most in the room appeared puzzled.

"Snow blizzard?"

"I warn you, friends," Ramon said. "Her storm is terrible. No sense of humor. She spits curses. And she's a sorceress of great power. Earlier this night, she threatened to turn me into a toad."

"An improvement," Nevara said, her albino-pink eyes spearing him.

"She admits to sorcery?" Doré pointed at her pagan gold and silver torque. Or, perhaps at her breasts. "Or is she an entertainer as well?"

"I not being a jokester!" She drew herself up to her fullest grandeur. She was at least as theatrical as Ramon in her performances, knowing just how to flourish and gesture. She stood, one arm raised to point at the sky, so long it touched the low rafters, and her sleeve slid down her arm to reveal the wrist-to-shoulder tattoos. Her other arm pointed down, and her face was thunder, eyes flashing. Ramon felt, in that moment, her magic.

They had lived together in the Baug Balar for twelve years, but even as a child she had been mysterious. To the Baug, her white hair marked her as belonging to the Goddess, and even her venerable teacher seemed in awe of her. "She is special," the kindly old magician had told Ramon once, when he asked why the adults of the Baug deferred to a girl no older than Ramon. He was sixteen then, and she was only fifteen, but the old magician told Ramon that Nevara's white hair and pink eyes marked her as ageless. "She's also gifted." The old man had laughed. "She's already learned all I have to teach. She's a greater magus than I ever can be."

These common folk in the wayroom would see her as something terrible and wonderful, the female magus. The fires in the pits seemed to flicker, and the wind rose in that dramatic moment, howling in the high smoke holes.

Then the moment passed. She smiled. "I have taking away the fog," she proclaimed.

The wayroom patrons stared at her. The one nearest the low door opened it and stared out.

"The fog is gone!" he shouted.

"Gone with the wind," the rebel Doré the Dandy said. He stood closest to Nevara, and his eyes did not blink, even with the smoke in the room. "Well. A heretic troubadour and an admitted magician. In a city that burns both for sport. How bold you two are."

"There being a time," Nevara answered, her voice hard, almost imperious, "when people of south welcomed both troubadours and the wise."

"I'm not sure how wise she is, though," Ramon said. "Although she did conjure this night's mist to help us slip through the gates at curfew."

No laughs. The patrons glanced at the open door. The man standing there slammed it shut. Several of the more superstitious spat or made a warding sign, but no crosses.

Nevara sat down, regal in her fury.

"Then what of a song, troubadour?" Doré said with a smile. "If you be a troubadour, let's hear you then."

Ramon and Nevara had forged a small link with his people, but they were rebels in a city occupied by the Church and King Louis of France. Many of their friends had died in the crusade. After the war, their neighbors had been tried as heretics and their midwives as witches. A song would quickly build their new relationship with the underground of Occitania.

"Well, boy?" the giant Osric bellowed. "You'd best know a tune!"

Nevara sighed, *a must we go through this again?* sound. She handed him his lute.

Ramon sat on the edge of the low table, in a sticky puddle of spilled brew, settled his lute on his lap and tuned the strings.

Doré and Osric sat in front of him and watched with wary smiles. Ramon looked at his feet, focusing. He plucked the strings with his practiced fingers. Even the rat near his feet paused and looked up at him. Then he sang, in the forbidden language of the troubadour.

He lifted his head and looked into the startled faces of his audience.

Even the fat waykeeper came stumbling out of his kitchen and stood gaping at the curtained door. Always, everywhere he went, it was the same. The shock. A fast blinking of eyelids, then the smiles. Even sour old kings sang along with Ramon's sweet, almost girlish voice. He sang of the fall of Minerve to Simon de Montfort, a song of the invading French he knew would be popular with Southerners. He sang of the day when tens of thousands of their fellow Occitanians fell to French swords. Even little Izzy and Wizi swayed with his music, their heads lifting and ears arching forward.

Though the song told of tragic events, the Southerners pounded the table and roared approval. On the second verse many stood and sang along in coarse, drunken voices.

Doré stood up and slapped his back, and Ramon nearly lost his grip on his precious lute. "Merde! You sing with magic, boy!"

Ramon's face heated. Even the fat keeper had wet eyes and joined the peasants in pounding the tabletop.

Big Osric sat on the table beside Ramon, tilting the top. He put his arm around Ramon.

"I joked about being ready for your hammer," Ramon said, shrugging off the arm.

The patrons laughed amid the tears.

Ramon cradled the lute, pleased with the praise. "I am Ramon Troubadour, son of Burc Tailor and Musette Midwife."

"I 'member the son of Burc an' Musette!" A man stood at the back of the room. "You were but ten or twelve, last I saw you."

"Oc, I remember, too!" A bearded tradesman stepped closer. "This little boy swore to kill the Diable—"

"Non!" Nevara pointed at the bearded man, and he fell silent. "Not saying that name here!" Her voice silenced the room, and in that moment an abrupt draft swept under the door, feeding the low fire pits. Flames snapped dramatically higher.

Everyone stared at Nevara, and Ramon knew these simple folk were convinced of her magic.

Ramon stared at the flames as they wrapped around stinking dung faggots. He knew Nevara's sense of dramatic timing had filled the room with superstitious dread, as she intended. But as he stared at the hungry flames, he journeyed to a different place, a terrible place. Memories crushed him with a sudden weight of nightmare intensity. He had put that day out of his mind for many years, burying himself in the craft, the song, and later in his passion for rescuing his people. He rarely faced that memory. He had locked it away in a dark room in the cellar of his memories. One time, when he had rescued the old midwife in Rabastens, a silver-haired woman so like his mother, the door to the locked memory room had rattled and the lock strained.

But now, for the first time in years, the door stood open. There was something about being in Carcassonne, with his people. Some of them had been there, twelve years ago. He had only told the story once, to his uncle the troubadour, one time that brought wretched tears and terrible dreams. But now, he needed to tell them. He needed to speak of his mother, to see she was remembered by her own people. He needed to build trust in these people, Carcassonnians who could help them. He especially needed the help of the two rebels, the Grand Duo. And he needed to release for himself. He had never entirely let go of his grief.

He barely realized he was speaking. "I was twelve." They stared at him now, but he focused only on the flames. The hungry fire. He leaned closer, hands outstretched, feeling the heat. And then he told them the story, fighting the tears.

Song of the Priestess

7

"AFTER MORNING PRAYERS they would burn my mother as a witch. I was only twelve, but this day burns on in my nightmares, the day I became a man, the day I learned to hate the French and the Church, the day I swore a man's revenge.

"I remember every detail, every smell, every word spoken. The dawn glow of the summer sun painted the streets of Carcassonne in warmth and the still air behind the stone ramparts sweltered with the heat of the gathered crowd. I remember that heat most of all. My clothes clung to me like garlic peels.

"The clamor of the crowd echoed off the ramparts, raised voices mingling with the shouts of children running in gangs through the streets and hawkers calling their wares.

"I recognized almost every sweaty face in the tide of people that packed the market square outside the castle—people who came to see my—my mother die.

"They crowded between the carts of the tanners, candlestick makers, armorers, brewers, potters and cutlers, and they fell silent, staring at me, probably seeing an angry boy, his unwashed face streaked with the rivers of old tears. Or maybe they saw a boy aged beyond his years, stooped, no longer crying, but with eyes so red they would know he had shed tears for days, his long golden hair tangled, his clothes torn and muddy. That's what I imagine, anyway.

"The burly bootmaker, a family friend, grabbed my shoulder and spun me around. 'Ramon, 'tis not safe!' But I remember pulling free, afraid he'd drag me off to his shack by the river and lock me away. I needed to see. More than anything, I needed to see.

"I hid under a baker's cart. The aroma of syrupy bannocks reminded me of my Mama's baking. But still I didn't cry. I had cried for weeks. I was all dried up. All I had left was precious rage.

"From under the cart, I stared up at the old castle that dominated the city. The walls seemed festive with the blood-red banners of the viscount. Sentries stood vigilant because of the growing throng, even though the drawbridge remained up. The aroma of roasting mutton drifted down from the hilltop kitchens of the seneschal's castle.

"A drum silenced the mob. The drawbridge dropped in lurches, chains rattling in stone slots.

"I could still escape. I could run across the market square and down the steep hill to the peasant's gate, cross the wide river on the foot bridge and into the sacred olive groves.

"But then the bridge landed with a heavy bounce, and it was too late for me to run like a child. I would stand, a man.

"The market stilled—as quiet as a cathedral during confession. That stillness stays with me, even now. I feel it in the quiet moments, a hole in me so empty it felt like death. Why was no one helping? Why had no one spoken for my mother? What kind of God would allow his priests and monks to roast old women whose only crime was to heal a neighbor?

"From under the baker's cart I simmered, watching the procession march out of the gate, led by the sheriff on his towering black horse. I was a child, verging on a gangly man-child, but against an entire troop of soldiers I was totally helpless. I couldn't even lift a sword in those days.

"The sheriff wrapped a gloved hand around the hilt of his sword, hard crow eyes scanning each face. The bailiff followed on a tan palfrey, leading the soldiers who surrounded the monks of the Inquisitional Court, and their prisoner—my mother.

"A towering man in black robes rode at the head of the procession of Dominicans, astride a great white horse with nervous eyes and flaring nostrils. Though his face remained hidden under a long hood, I knew him. The Devil's own creature, nothing less, riding the white horse and carrying that scythe of death. I caught a flash of his scarred and melted face.

"'The Diableteur,' said the baker, and he spat then shuffled around behind the cart to hide. 'Mother of God save us!'

"A frightened murmur rippled through the crowd and city folk turned away.

"But I had given up that boyish fear the night he took my mother. I could never forget the night the Diableteur had come to our rickety house by the south tower. It had haunted my dreams in the months since.

"I glared at him. I pressed my lips together until it hurt, struggling against the urge to shout obscenities at this monster. I pulled my own hood to shade my face.

"At the end of the procession, my mother came into view. She stumbled under the weight of her chains and the Master Executioner pulled her like a leashed dog, jerking her to her feet. She fell again.

"For a moment rage consumed me. Then I burst from under the baker's cart and dove forward between the guards. I was small but tall for my age, like now. My Papa Burc used to call me *Mouse* because he said I could slip through wall cracks. The soldiers couldn't get a hold of me. All I knew—all I cared about—was reaching her, to help her stand, to tell her she was not alone, to let her die with my words in her ears—but at least to help her stand.

"Hands finally grasped me and threw me to the cobbles. I scrambled up, but soldiers grabbed my arms.

"The hate burned hotter than the summer heat now, hot like a pot of my mother's bubbling cassoulet.

"My Mama shuffled to the stake, dragged by the Master Executioner, surrounded by a ring of soldiers. I stood, ringed on all sides, unable to move, only able to cry. But no tears came.

"Musette Midwife. Mama. A harmless mother whose only crime was to heal a neighbor of the palsy. Her piercing yellow eyes marked her—and me—as different.

"Two soldiers dragged her the last few steps and hauled her onto the high pile of wood. They jerked her bruised wrists above her head and tied her to the stake with rough hemp.

"I could not stop the trembling now. Still no tears came, but it felt as if the entire city was shaking, as if God Himself was smiting the city with his mighty hand.

"The soldiers faced outwards with lowered spears. By the pyre stood the monk Duranti—the man who condemned my mother—and the Master Executioner. The Diableteur on his great white horse, gripping that long black scythe, approached the base of the pyre and turned to face the crowd. The white horse pawed the cobbles and snorted.

"The Inquisitor Duranti raised his arms and looked westward and up. I followed his gaze and saw the audience on top of the central tower. The Viscount Hugh d'Arcis stood leaning on the wall, splendid in his scarlet tunic, flanked by his wife and the Archbishop Peter Amiel, who made the sign of the cross and nodded.

"Duranti's sharp voice bellowed, like a father scolding a child: "Musette Midwife! You have been found guilty of heresy and witchcraft. Given an opportunity to repent, you have clung to your errors and—"

"The city erupted in a fury of fists and cries.

"'She's our healer!'

"'Our midwife!'

"The Diableteur's horse reared, egged on by glittering spurs and a hard yank on the reins. An uneasy funereal hush settled on the courtyard.

"I could not see the face beneath the long cowl. I wanted to see it and remember it. Someday, I would kill this creature. Though I was brought up a Cathar Christian and didn't believe in hell, I wanted to send this creature to hellfire. The Diableteur on his fidgeting horse towered over Duranti. This creature had inhabited my nightmares, a specter in the darkness, a blacker shape in the night, his long staff with its curved blade sweeping down to stab at me. I would always wake before Death could touch me, but I would always remember the red eyes, glowing in the shadows of the cowl. Now, as I looked up at the creature, I saw those eyes. Perhaps it was a child's imagination, but I saw red, demon eyes.

"Duranti shouted now, over the crowd. 'And separated from the body of Mother Church you have been handed over to the secular authorities who have sentenced you to perish in flames. It is not too late to repent and be welcomed back into God's family. What say you?'

"I felt a stir of hope, an empty, burning feeling in the pit of my stomach. My mother would beg mercy of the Church and Duranti would stop this. The monk would raise his arms and smile and welcome her to the Roman Church.

"Her head lifted. I tensed as her eyes sought me out.

"How could this be my mother?

"Her cheeks were pale and hollow, sunken to the bone, her skin yellowish and waxy. She had lost some of her hair and the bald patch was scabbed. She made a tired effort to smile, then stiffened and heaved in a fit of coughs.

"Not my Mama. This could not be my Mama.

"I shouted, 'Christ's mercy! She is a Christian!'

"And she was. She was the most devout Christian in Carcassonne, preaching in her little makeshift church in the stables, just like one of the Perfecti, speaking on the compassion and love of Christ. She was not Catholic but a more devout Christian than any jeweled pope—she believed, as true believers do, that hell is on this earth and that Christ our savior taught us to escape hell not through rituals but through right actions—and for this she would die. As they had dragged her out of our hut by the south tower, she had screamed at me, 'Don't cry baby, I leave this hell for God!' But I had screamed and cried, anyway. And the Inquisitors had ignored my puny fists as they carted her away.

"Now, all around her, the crowd took up the cry. 'Christ's mercy!'

"Duranti's unblinking eyes found me then. He smiled. 'See, Musette Midwife. Your son calls out to you to recant.' He waved his arms, and the soldiers stepped back from me.

"I stepped closer, then right to the foot of the pile of faggots, right under the snorting white devil horse of Diableteur. The horse pawed the ground, and I couldn't resist looking up. If this world is hell, that creature is the very Devil. I saw that face, the melted flesh, the lifeless eyes. And I screamed. As I tried to turn away, that great scythe swept down, wrapping around me. And I screamed again, the back of the black blade trapping me.

"My mother's voice called out, her voice suddenly strong, 'Get away, my baby!'

"I sobbed and fell to my knees. 'Mama! I love you Mama!' I looked up into her face, ignoring the Diableteur now.

" 'Ramon! No crying!' She pulled herself up by bleeding wrists, her head lifting, her voice rising. 'I join my dear heart Burc. And I go to God.'

"I met her eyes. Even now, so strong. She smiled at me, revealing toothless gums, her strong, white teeth gone. 'My sweet baby. There will be no pain. The Dame is with me.'

" 'Silence, witch!' The Diableteur's voice was inhuman, a windy sound, hoarse and quiet, but ominous enough that the crowd stilled. The scythe lifted and the horse wheeled suddenly, great hooves knocking my face against the cobbles. As I rolled over, the black thing bent from the saddle and snatched the torch from the Master Executioner.

" 'Repent!' The flaming torch hissed as he waved it from his tall horse. My eyes followed the torch as he waved it.

"Then, lip bleeding from my fall, I stood up, too terrified to think, a boy again, not a man. A shivering, sobbing, terrified, helpless child. I feel the shame of my cowardice even now.

"Mama spat at the Diableteur. She turned her head and aimed at Duranti. Spittle splattered the monk's cheek and he stepped back, his arms flailing.

"I found I could not breathe. '*No!*'

"I clambered onto the logs and kindling. Soldiers grabbed my arms and dragged me back. I stomped on their boots.

"A soldier threw me back into the crowd. I felt the impact and cried out. My rage overcame fear and pain, and I ran back at the soldiers. But they weren't paying attention to me. Like the crowd they stared at the spectacle above them, forming a ring of spears to prevent a child, and the crowd, from attempting a rescue.

"Diableteur waved the torch. 'To God I commend you. *In nomine Patris, et Filii, et Spiritus Sancti, Amen.*' He sounded like a monk, in spite of the windy, damaged voice, for he had chanted the words, and for a moment I thought he would relent.

"Then he threw the torch into the kindling. 'May the flames purify you of your heresy.'

"The monks began a mournful chant: '*Credo in unum Deum, Patrem omnipotentem, factorem coeli et terrae...*'

"The Master Executioner took another torch and walked around the pile, the torch trailing slowly across the firewood.

"The Dominican monks bowed their heads and continued a mournful chant:

'Bone Jesu, libera nos a peccatis nostris...' And most astonishing of all, I realized the raspy voice of Diableteur chanted with them.

" 'No! Christ's mercy, no!' I flung myself against another soldier, a man as unyielding as an elm tree.

"I already felt the heat of the fire, saw the hungry flames consuming the dry wood and faggots.

"I fell to my knees and crawled between the soldiers' legs, scrambling in the dirt, struggling as I felt hands seize me. 'Where are you going, little mouse,' said a soldier, and the others laughed. 'You want to join your Mama?'

" 'God's mercy!' I struggled in the arms of the soldier. The man leaned close, his breath rank with apple ale. He whispered in my ear, 'You'll be next, little yellow eyes!'

"The hungry blaze devoured the wood.

"I finally tore myself free and weaved between the clutching arms of guards and monks, using my mouse slimness and speed to evade them. I rolled to one side. Three soldiers tried to tackle me. They crashed together with a clang of weapons and shouts.

"I ran between the cracks, dodging and spinning and changing direction like a mouse cornered by a cat. I slipped past two more. Finally, I was at the base of the high pile of wood, but I could do nothing, for the heat pushed me back. I could do nothing but join my mother. It was too late to rescue her. I could only join her and go with her to paradise. But I couldn't. And my cowardice brought wails of self-contempt that made me feel more guilty. I was not crying for my mother, but for my own weakness.

" 'I beg God's mercy!' I shouted. I reached out my arms to Duranti. I had heard the monk preach love and peace in the basilica. Surely this monk could see it was not God's way to burn mothers. Duranti stared at me, his lip pressed into a hard line. To him, indeed, I was a mouse, nothing more.

"The sheriff shouted at me, and I turned in time to see him point at me. More soldiers closed around me. I dodged aside and tumbled to the ground again, tasting straw and sand.

"The Diableteur's horse pranced forward, cutting me off from escape. I saw only the great legs towering over me. And then I was the mouse again, scrambling between the legs of the creature as it reared. I flew out between its hind legs, under its long tail, and sprinted into the crowd of shocked onlookers.

"Then my mother screamed, a long agonized shriek. I stopped, turned. No one around me moved. The soldiers forgot me—for a moment.

"I stared, terrified, unable to move. *Oh God. Dear God.*

"The flames caressed her bare feet.

" 'Run!' my Mama called out. 'Run my little Ramon!' Then she screamed again.

"But I didn't run. I looked up at her, my vision blurred with tears.

"'Go!' she shouted.

"I hesitated another moment. Then, the mouse coward, I ran. God help me, I ran. I pushed into the crowd, shielded by my neighbors, and they closed around me, protecting me, hiding me. They interlocked arms, a barrier the soldiers could only penetrate with thrusting spears. The soldiers hesitated. The crowd teetered on the verge of riot. Even the mouse-boy knew it.

" 'Back to your posts,' shouted the bailiff. The soldiers reformed their line around the pyre.

"I peered between the city folk, crying like the boy I really was. My fists clenched and unclenched, and I think I stopped breathing. Shivering, I watched as the flames spread, twigs melting into red embers. The smoke wafted over the crowd, choking me so I could not breathe.

"I jumped as a man put his arm around my shivering shoulders. 'You're a man now, Ramon. There's always revenge.'

"I looked up into the eyes of Merle the bootmaker, a family friend, and I wanted to scream at him, *I'm a mouse. I'm a coward.* But I just looked away, and stared at my mother. I would, at least, remember her agony.

"The soldiers, the sheriff, Diableteur, the archbishop and the lords and ladies on the chateau tower—all had forgotten me. They stared at

Mama as she thrashed in her bonds.

"Then Mama found a screech of new intensity.

"The monks stopped their chanting.

"Mama sagged in the ropes, her robe in flames.

"She shouted, her voice growing louder with each word, 'I curse you, Diableteur! I curse Duranti. I curse you Archbishop Amiel and Viscount d'Arcis! You will all suffer—you will die in sickness and shame and violence. You will be impotent! None shall love you! You will burn. A mouse shall destroy you. A mouse shall be your bane.'

"Duranti winced with each word. His face paled and he bit his own lip, drawing blood. He backed away and made the sign of the cross and mumbled the Paternoster. Even I knew the curses of the dying had special power. I prayed it would be so, willed with black hate. Die Duranti. Die Diableteur. Squirm Amiel and d'Arcis. And let me be the hand of the curse. The Mouse!

"The flames enveloped Mama's hair now, hungry, tasting her—a burst of orange.

"'In Christ's name,' whispered Merle Bootmaker. I felt him shaking, probably because my trembling had stopped. I felt only fury and hate, now.

"And Mama stopped struggling, her face suddenly calm.

"Staring.

"Black smoke drifted down into the crowd. No one spoke.

"I pressed hard against Merle Bootmaker and listened to the growl of the inferno. A shower of sparks flew skywards and embers spat out into the crowd. My mouth opened and closed as if I was trying to speak, but no sounds came.

"Nearby, I heard a voice: '*The Dame. The Dame—*'

"All around me they chanted it. '*...The Dame, the Dame...*'

"I stumbled forward, pulling free from the bootmaker's grip. I could not take my eyes from my mother's peeling skin. Why didn't she scream? Why didn't she cry out to God? The last of her clothes burned away as glowing fragments lifted on the wave of heat. I could see Mama's wilting breasts. The heat magically erased her features—the kind face that had smiled at me in play and frowned at me in mischief—it dripped like a beeswax candle.

" '*The Dame. The Dame...*' The crowd chanted, a windy sound.

"My mother's eyes, so calm. Somehow still conscious. How could that be? So tranquil. As if she had found peace.

"Not looking towards heaven. Not looking at Ramon.

" '*The Dame. The Dame...*' Rising in intensity.

"I followed my mother's gaze.

"And I saw her—the Lady in Gray. There, yet almost not there. Brilliant, shimmering. White, yet dark. Between light and shadow. Silver or gray. The smoke from the fire seemed to have gathered around her in a gray cloud, obscuring her. Her arms lifted. Her lips moved, but no sound came.

"The Silver Lady seemed to glow. I couldn't bring her into to focus, as if she were part of a waking dream.

"Kind eyes. Silver hair. Smiling. The Lady's eyes stared at Mama.

"I shivered. What did it mean? Who was this woman? I turned away, staring again at my Mama.

"I must see her last moments. She no longer seemed to be Mama—just reeking, melting flesh. Where her skin burst open, fat bubbled out and fell into the flames, splattering outwards in little explosions. Oh God, I remember that. Dearest sweet Jesus, I remember every detail.

"She still moved, yet she no longer danced her agony. She seemed at peace. One eye burst, leaving an empty socket. But the other eye stared at me now. I felt she was still there, watching me. How could that be? There was nothing left of her, but that one eye. How could she stand the pain?

"I fell to my knees as she sagged in the ropes.

"But I kept my eyes fixed on her charred remains fused with the pole.

" '*Be at peace, Ramon,*' said a voice as soft as a summer breeze. The voice came from above me. I felt it, rather than heard it. Was it Jesus speaking to me? I looked up.

"A smiling face hovered over me like an angel, sky blue eyes a sharp contrast to her parchment pale face and cascading silver hair. The Silver Lady knelt and touched my head.

"I flinched but I didn't move. I could only stare at her. Nothing else existed in that moment.

"And—this is hard to explain—I felt my own pain draining away. I felt warmth and comfort. A fragrance like peach blossoms swept away the reek of burning meat.

"I closed my eyes, thought of my mother. Of her plump, smiling face. I smelled her—not the roasting reek—but her living, musky sweetness. The hand on my head seemed to belong to my mother, not to some strange woman in gray.

"After a moment I opened my eyes. I lay on the ground, clutching a handful of dirt, surrounded by staring neighbors.

"The Silver Dame was—gone.

"Neighbors crowded around me, shielding me.

"A woman sobbed. 'Your Mama's gone.'

"Another said, 'She was not alone.'

"A third clutched her two children to ample bosoms. 'What is to become of us?'

"I felt numb. My mother. Gone. The Silver Dame. Gone. My father, years ago, gone. I was twelve. And I was alone.

"The stench descended on me again, sweeping away peach blossoms and sweetness. I had hallucinated in my grief, but now the darkness returned. And the rage.

"The Diableteur's fire had taken away my blessed Mama and burned a hole in my soul. I felt it like a real thing.

"The bile rose. It bubbled out of my mouth and ran down my chin. 'Mama.'

"I pressed my face into the hard cobbles until my blood mixed with the vomit.

"There was only one thing left for me. A man's path.

"I clenched my teeth until it hurt.

"I looked up at the citadel tower at the Viscount d'Arcis. Then, at the somber Archbishop Amiel.

"I stood, my knees wobbly, and raised my small fist. The words erupted from me: 'Death to you all! Death to Diableteur! Death to the archbishop! Death to the viscount!'

"They all stared at me. I had crossed over from grief to heresy and treason.

"'Run! Ramon, run!' The bootmaker pulled at my arm.

"I saw the soldiers, pushing through the crowd, lances lowered, faces set in scowls.

"'Death to all the damn French!' I shouted.

"Then I ran for my life."

8

THEY WERE ALL staring at him, crowding around his table, and there was not a dry eye in the wayroom. They had left their tables and firepits and now fifty Occitanians crowded him, crying along with him. Ramon was back in the *Auberge de Terre*.

Nevara slipped her arm around him. "I understanding now."

Ramon had told them the story in more detail than he intended. His memories of that terrible day had spilled out in a torrent, like a mountain river after the snow melt.

"I never told that story," Ramon said. "Not like that." He hadn't been here, in the wayroom, he had been back there, in the market square, watching his mother die as if for the first time. The hate had not faded over the years. And for the first time, he realized his real reason for returning to Carcassonne. Not for The Jewel. Not to see home. Not to help his fellow Occitanians. For revenge.

"A revenge curse," Nevara said. "We are being here in completion."

Ramon stared at her white skin, her pink eyes glistening with tears.

"A revenge curse can no being stopped, ever." She bent and kissed his cheek. "Mouse. I liking that name. I calling you Mouse."

"Do not." Ramon closed his eyes and held his breath.

"Yes. A Mouse shall destroy you. A Mouse shall be your bane!"

Nevara kissed his cheek. "That's you, little Mouse. The archbishop's bane!"

"I am no longer the Mouse."

"But you still being the fool." She shook her head. "A blood curse cannot be avoided, but you are foolish to take on the entire French piggie army."

"I have your magic, Nevara."

She nodded. "You are wiser than you thinking." She kissed his cheek.

Osric, the burly Mason, slapped Ramon's shoulder again. "Another song," Osric said. "A 'appier song this time, friend Troubadour."

Ramon put down Mauri. The songs always took away the sadness.

They sat around him in a ring of expectant faces as he sang.

Fatigue and grief slipped away as Ramon performed song after song, lighter now, comic romps, and slowly the tempest of past furies lifted. Music and humor had always been his defenses. The audience of peasants hummed along and drank brew and cried real tears and banged the tables in approval. Ramon knew that he had them in his power. No one tended the fire as it burned down and the barmaid Brigitte was reluctant to fetch brew, unwilling to miss any of the songs. When Ramon paused to drink, they hollered at him for more.

Finally, he stopped. His throat hurt. The silence continued for a while and they stared at him, waiting for the next song. The squeak of a hungry rat was the only sound.

Osric the Hammer smiled at him. "You be a true son of Carcassonne, Ramon."

Ramon lowered his lute, his shoulders sagging as exhaustion overwhelmed him. "I am tired. We have journeyed from Toulouse and—"

A crash interrupted him as the door burst open and a voice bellowed: "In the name of the seneschal!"

Ramon set down his lute.

Osric and Doré lurched to their feet.

"Silence!" the soldier shouted. "In the name of the seneschal, be silent!"

Doré the Bastard and Osric the Hammer—the Grand Duo—stood alone in front of the soldiers. Ten soldiers crowded into the common-room in their too-familiar surcoats, yellow tunics emblazoned with the red griffin of the seneschal of Carcassonne, the Viscount Hugh D'Arcis. The colors of mother-killing barbarians, the monsters of his dreams.

The other patrons backed away. The seneschal's soldiers drew their swords.

Ramon scooped up Mauri. He leaned close to Nevara. "You must not be here," he said.

"I knowing" But she remained beside him. "Are you sure, Mouse?"

"I am sure. Get these people out of here. I will hold the soldiers. Go to the Baug Balar."

Osric and Doré remained calm. Doré gripped the hilts of his twin short swords, though he did not draw. Osric gripped the handle of his sledgehammer.

Ramon stared at the soldiers, controlling his anger. He had planned to meet the Grand Duo, to befriend them and seek their help. Guilhem d'Alions, his master, had told him they were the leader of the Phantom Rebels, the displaced Southerners who haunted the Phantom Wood that surrounded the city of Carcassonne. Instead, it seemed, he had condemned them with his singing. Did he stand with the rebels now, or escape with Nevara and make a new plan? The Jewel was more important than the Grand Duo. Yet if he stood with the Grand Duo, the rebels would accept him and trust him more readily.

"Who is in charge here?" demanded the captain.

The waykeeper shambled forward. "I am, capitaine!" He held out a bowl of brew in shaking hands. "Brew for your men, lord"

The captain smiled, showing rotting stumps of teeth. "You are guilty of operating a gredincroix after curfew."

"Non, non, capitaine! This is only a humble wayroom. Dieu! These are my guests, here for th' night!"

The soldiers laughed and the captain stepped forward.

Nevara leaned close to Ramon, kissed him lightly, then slowly moved to the back of the room, toward the kitchens, while the soldiers were distracted. She tugged on the sleeves of the wayroom guests, nodding towards the kitchen. Some followed her, others remained frozen like stunned rabbits.

The captain swept a row of half full bowls from the table with his sword. "I see no bedding. I see only tables and drinking bowls!"

"My lord, we are communing before—"

"Plotting, more likely! I heard your rebel songs!" The captain shoved the waykeeper backwards into Brigitte and they both fell against the soldiers. The captain glared at Osric and Doré. Then he smiled. "Well, a few guests for the lord shérif, I think." He looked at Brigitte and then at Nevara, staring at her bosom. His smile broadened. "And for the barracks." His sword came up, and he caressed Brigitte's hair with it. Then he stepped forward and his hand squeezed her breast. She screeched and backed into another soldier. The soldiers pushed her forward and she fell into the captain's arms. Without a word, his tongue flicked out and tasted her lips as he squeezed her nipple harder.

"*Diable maudit*!" Osric stepped forward with his big mason's hammer unslung. Doré stepped beside him, his twin short swords drawn. Ramon slipped over the table with athletic grace and snatched up the Spear of Zaleucus.

Then Nevara cast her magic powder. She threw the black powder into a firepit. The pit erupted in flame, blinding the soldiers, and she stood in front of the pit, shrouded in billowing smoke, her arms raised. The smoke filled the room, and everyone began coughing as the soldiers shouted, the horses shrieked, and little Mauri growled.

Osric took advantage of the confusion and grabbed the captain by the hair, yanking him backwards and pressing the handle of his sledgehammer across the captain's exposed throat. "Get back, or I break your capitaine's neck!"

Osric had moved so fast that the soldiers hesitated and it was obvious to Ramon that they had not expected resistance. Dense smoke hung in the air like a fog, choking them with the stench of sulphur. Ramon saw that Nevara was herding the Carcassonnians out the kitchen door.

Doré snatched Brigitte and pulled her behind him. He pushed her across the room at Ramon, who caught her.

"You dare lay hands on the king's men?" the captain shouted, his voice high-pitched and fearful.

Osric yanked back harder on the captain's hair, and spat into his eye. "I dare whatever I please."

"You will hang for this!"

Osric spat again, into his other eye. "Not before I make you suffer, French pig!"

Brigitte pushed Ramon's hands off her arm and ran to Osric. "Osric, no! They'll kill you!"

Osric smiled at her. "Brigitte, I'm not afraid of these piggie soldiers. They are not my match!" The soldiers edged forward, grumbling. "Back, you piggies! Or I kill him!"

"So kill him!" said his lieutenant.

The captain stared up into the face of Osric and, for a moment, Ramon felt pity for the man, northerner or not.

"No, don't—" said the captain.

Osric smiled, contemplating.

"No, Osric, not in my—" The waykeeper waved his arms.

The soldiers edged closer. They lifted swords and glared at Osric.

Osric shrugged and seized the captain's throat in one of his big hands. With hardly any effort, he tore open the man's windpipe and threw him dying to the floor.

The soldiers yelled and rushed forward, swords swinging.

"Now!" Ramon shouted at Nevara.

He saw her hand flash upward. Her voice rang out, and the soldier's hesitated. Her words were strange, even to Ramon's ears, eerie and unsettling. Then, her hands flicked again.

Ramon shielded his eyes.

The fire pit exploded in white-hot flame, blinding in intensity. Smoke billowed up and out.

"Devilry!" shouted the lieutenant.

Ramon knew he could have left in that moment. He could have escaped with Nevara and the horses. She was already leading the horses through the kitchen, most of the city folk ahead of her. But he had the goodwill of Osric and Doré. He would not leave them now.

As the smoke cleared, the soldiers and the guests of the auberge still didn't move.

"Where did the white wench go?"

"Witchcraft!"

Ramon felt his own smile, in spite of the situation. Nevara and the horses had vanished in the smoke. An old ruse, but it never failed to amaze him.

The soldiers crossed themselves.

The waykeeper stared at the pool of blood creeping across his floor. The captain was writhing as ugly spurts of blood shot out of his gaping throat and painted the floor reeds in red. "Non! Non!" The waykeeper wailed now. "Mon Dieu! Do not fight in here!"

Mauri wriggled in Ramon's arms. He smelled blood. The rats were already swarming over the captain's body. Ramon looked away, sickened.

Doré moved fastest. Catlike, dodging the blade of one soldier, he jumped over a fallen bench and parried a second soldier, then ducked into a third. His two short swords seemed no match for the soldier's broad swords, but he danced between them and pushed their bigger blades aside with glancing blows. The soldiers milled around Doré and managed to dodge his rapid swipes. Then Osric's first hammer blow fell. The great sledgehammer cleft one soldier's skull, spilling his brains. Osric glanced sideways and knocked another soldier's shoulder from its socket. Another man howled as Doré's blade plunged into his stomach and twisted.

Ramon's mouth parted and his eyes blinked several times. He must help his friends but not get arrested for it.

He watched as Osric's hammer swung and fell in a red blur. The big mason knocked the soldiers aside like puppets. The soldiers closed rank and fell back, stabbed with long swords, then fell back again as the two renegades danced around the clumsy weapons and plunged in with their own. Osric's hammer, now a dripping mess, fell with thuds and his voice called out "*Courroux de Dieu*!" with each skull crushed.

Ramon set Mauri down and danced around behind the troops who paid no attention to the fool. Osric roared his hoarse cry, and Doré laughed a strange, chirping hoot. And then Ramon struck for the first time, using the back of his staff, in the *Plaga Ignava,* the lazy blow intended not to kill but to immobilize. He struck the soldier in the temple, above his helmut's cheek guard. The man's eyes widened, but he was unconscious before he could cry out. Then he sliced to the right, in the *Sectum Inferum,* tangling the feet of two soldiers. He danced along the wall, wreathed in Nevara's lingering smoke, unseen but a nuisance. The Mouse attacks.

"Stand and fight, cowards!" one soldier bellowed as he tried to stab at Doré, unable to slice or swing his broadsword because of the low rafters. Doré's twin patula swords parried and counter-thrust every stroke. He danced with agility and whirled around the stunned soldiers.

Doré and Osric dispatched five soldiers, some dead, some squirming as they lay in the gore on the dirt floor. Ramon whacked two others, still wrapped in the shadows and smoke of the wayroom corners. He took down another soldier by rolling under the tables and tangling his boots.

The soldiers inflicted no crippling blows as Osric's hammer smashed bones and Doré's short swords sliced flesh. Ramon inflicted no mortal blows, only striking with the capped bottom of Zaleucus. His hatred of the French was as vivid as any Southerner's, born of his father's hanging and his mother's burning. He wanted to drive his long spear into the chest of a French soldier—any soldier. He saw a soldier maneuvering in his direction, attempting to outflank Doré. Zaleucus flashed out and down, and the soldier fell at Doré's feet.

Ramon had no love of soldiers, hated them as much as any, wanted to crack their heads and stab them. They had taken away his mother, father, friends, uncles and aunts, cousins, nephews and nieces. None were left. Street festivals and laughter were dreams of another time. But he must be the Mouse.

He watched now as a soldier backed towards him and shuffled behind Doré; the Bastard of Costonot was too involved in his fencing to notice. The soldier slid along the wall, his back to Ramon and his sword lowered and ready.

Again, he felt the urge to call out a warning to Doré.

No. Ramon must not yet reveal himself, for all his hate of the Français.

A shout made both Ramon and the soldier look up as a dozen more soldiers poured into the room. It was hopeless. Osric continued to laugh and hammer on heads as if he was splitting building stones.

The soldier was about to ambush Doré. Ramon's spear thrust forward, slicing down, a movement so swift it was invisible in the shroud of smoke, and it nicked the man's sword wrist. The sword dropped, the man cried out, and Ramon was revealed as a rebel.

"I've done it now, Mauri," Ramon whispered. He looked around, wondering who had seen his crime, wondering what it must feel like to hang. Only one soldier had noticed his attack and now approached Ramon.

Ramon swept his staff in a fast arc, and brought it to a defensive *Paratum*, the ready stance. The soldier tried to brush it aside with his sword, sneering at the colorful fool he faced.

"You die now, fool," said the soldier. The soldier was nearly as tall as Ramon, and twice as broad, with muscles that pressed hard against a leather tunic.

The man plunged in, stabbing with his broadsword. Ramon stepped aside, swinging around, and brought his staff up and into the man's crotch. The soldier howled, stumbling back. His face a mask of fury, the soldier lunged forward again, sweeping widely with his sword. Ramon stepped back, pressing against the mantel. Zaleucus sliced up, blade tip out this time, cutting fine and hard through the leather tunic.

The man howled, sure he had been sliced open, but his tunic fell open, revealing a naked chest. Ramon had only scratched the skin.

Ramon smiled. "I undress you, sir!"

The soldier swung around and brought his elbow into Ramon's arm. Ramon fell into a table, scattering drinking bowls and bread loaves, but he was already tumbling into a full somersault. He flew back up and to his feet, landed on top of a table, spun with one knee bent and one leg out, and snapped frontward with a sharp kick to the man's chin.

Mauri dove in, tearing into the soldier's ankle. The man yelled more from surprise than pain and kicked. As Mauri flew into the daub wall, Ramon drove in with Zaleucus, nicking the man's thigh, then his arm. He danced around nicking and cutting until the man was bleeding from a dozen cuts, none more than flesh wounds.

The soldier howled, stumbled back, flailing with his sword. Ramon spun and drove the back of the spear into the soldier's unprotected neck. The man clawed at his throat, his eyes full of rage, but already he was sinking to his knees, like a tree toppling slowly. The man grunted in surprise, staring at the foolish boy who had beaten him, then fell to his knees, his mouth working, trying to speak perhaps a curse or a cry for help. Instead, eyes still open, the elegant falling tree landed inches from Ramon's feet, his fingers still moving, clenching, trying to grab Ramon's boots.

For a long moment, the sounds of battle, of clanging swords and shouting soldiers, seemed to fade away as Ramon stared at the man. Had he killed him?

Around him, the fight carried on, everyone seemingly oblivious of Ramon's crime. Doré and Osric seemed tireless, stabbing and hammering. The sweet smell of blood and the sour odor of sweat were heavy in the air.

Ramon backed into the hearth in a cold sweat. Mauri ran to his feet, barking, his teeth bloody.

He gritted his teeth. He would hang now, like his father, even though he had yet to kill. These were the seneschal's soldiers. With both doorways blocked, he had no choice but to fight with the Grand Duo.

But before he could intervene again, it was over. Osric and Doré struggled in the grip of four soldiers, their dripping weapons on the red floor. Doré winked at Ramon and nodded his head in thanks. They knew.

The soldiers grabbed Ramon and tied his hands behind his back. One soldier seized Mauri, who growled and snapped, but the burly man just held the dog's snout and carried him by the scruff.

Ramon's throat was dry. He knew he was doomed to the torturer's art.

Ahead, he heard Mauri's whimpering and he wanted to call out reassurances, but when he realized there was no hope, the comforting words went unspoken.

9

VISCOUNT HUGH D'ARCIS—seneschal for King Louis for all the lands south of the Loire—sat on a raised dais. He watched the juggler's clumsy antics with only half-focused eyes as he held out his hands for the laverer. The poor boy trembled as he massaged Hugh's hands with a damp cloth steeped in sage and rosemary.

Hugh dried his hands then sipped a sweet Pisan wine with great enthusiasm. Flies buzzed around the leavings on the table, swarming the uneaten mortrews and capon bones. The fragrance of the feast, so sumptuous when they had entered the great hall, was now a vile perfume of carcasses and sopping bread trenchers. Not even the sweetness of milk-honey pudding could bring back Hugh's appetite. But it had been a wondrous night.

The archbishop had swept into the hall with melodramatic flair, and introduced their important visitor, a Templar, and not just any Templar. Hugh had fought alongside Arnot in Jerusalem a dozen years ago. Arnot was the Marshall's own lieutenant, and one of the fiercest combatants Hugh had the pleasure to know. They had exchanged a few pleasantries and Hugh insisted Brother Sir Arnot sit on his right in the place of honor. They had exchanged war stories and tales of comrades who had perished in the great crusade, while the damnable archbishop sat in his normal place to the left of Hugh.

In all, a fair and happy night, if only he could get rid of the nagging archbishop.

Conversation rumbled through the great room, mixed with peels of laughter and the raised voices of drunken knights boasting of past counts, and no one could hear the wailing song of the court's dreadful minstrel. Some of the seigneurs and chevaliers were already snoring on the rush-covered floor, passed out from wines and feasting, while others continued to devour roast wild boar and good German brew. Three jugglers performed acrobatics in the center of the floor.

Nothing, not the buzzing flies nor the dreadful entertainment, could spoil Hugh's rare good spirits. Today had been a day of triumph. They had the Jewel, the treasure of the South, a kingmaker. And the unexpected arrival of Arnot, obviously a clumsy attempt by the Templars to take possession of the Jewel, had only increased Hugh's good spirits. Thank God his wretched wife had taken her leave after the announcement of their daughter's betrothal. The guests had cheered and his wife had made a rambling speech, but even his wife's whining couldn't spoil Hugh's mood. Hugh's daughter would marry into the royal family, albeit a distant cousin. His mood improved vastly with the early departure of his harpy wife to the bedchamber. Adelais, his precious daughter, still caroused around the room, flirting with drunken chevaliers—in spite of her formal engagement—and he watched her game with wary goodwill. Hugh's chevaliers knew better than to dally with his precious daughter.

Now she sat on a table and told one of her scandalous jokes to his knights. They roared with laughter. Hugh smiled. Today was a good day—a day no one could spoil for him, not even the archbishop.

Hugh felt half fogged by the vast quantities of wine. "Before God, Arnot, I am glad you are here." He leaned forward and rapped the table with his knife. "But you don't go touring around Occitania without reason. What brings you, good friend?"

"Your old comrade came seeking the prize," Archbishop Amiel said, his voice mocking.

Hugh straightened. He had suspected as much, but he would have to make a show of sternness, old friend or not. "Not the prize. *My* prize. It would do well for both of you to remember it!"

"Too important a prize for the Temple not to be concerned." Arnot's voice was hoarse from yelling over the crowd in the room, but he offered a smile.

Hugh shook his head. "Be as concerned as you like, damn you to my wife's bedchamber, but the prize will remain mine."

Arnot no longer smiled. "You would deny the guardians of the sacred treasures of God their very most Holy of Holies?"

Hugh's fist slammed hard into the table, and the heavy oak planks jumped, drinks spilt and capon bones went flying. "It is my Holy of Holies."

"If you find it," said the archbishop calmly. "The Jewel is only the guardian."

"I will find it!" Hugh felt the coursing of his own blood, the pounding of it in his ears, a feeling he normally only enjoyed during the heat of battle.

"It belongs to the Church," Amiel snapped back.

"It belongs to my king!" Hugh said.

"You are both wrong," barked Arnot, his voice rising loud. "The Temple is the guardian of the Holies. Not the church—" and the fierce monk stared at Amiel, "And not any one king."

His eyes met Hugh's now, extraordinary eyes in their anger. Hugh remembered Arnot in Jappa, fighting Saracens, his eyes filled with that very same rage. Arnot would be dangerous in this moment. Arnot was a terrible killer. When the passion of Christ was on him in the battlefield, no one stood against him. There was a madness about Arnot, a pureness of rage that protected him like a holy shield. On one campaign, Hugh had fallen from his horse, surrounded by Saracens, hewing about him with his favorite crusade weapon, his great two-handed broadsword. Most of his men had fallen. It had been Arnot, and fourteen Templars, who had charged in, his fury impossible to withstand, saving Hugh from certain capture, or worse. Hugh had seen dozens fall before Arnot's bloody sword, had seen the utter insanity in those eyes. Arrows never seemed to touch him, swords never came close, and Arnot's bloodlust was never fulfilled until every Saracen lay dead in pieces around him. Arnot had saved his life that day, perhaps oblivious of it, for he and his men continued their charge past Hugh, ignoring him, continuing to hack the fleeing enemy. Hugh knew better than to anger the mad Templar.

"It belongs to the finder," Hugh said, trying to sound reasonable.

"Then that would be me!" shouted a new voice. The Seigneur de Castleneau—known to all simply as The Seigneur—stood at his table.

The Seigneur's one remaining eye glared at Hugh. Hugh stared back, with familiar unease. Seigneur recognized no liege lord and served at his own pleasure, a formidable and deadly opponent. As much as Hugh might never wish to see Arnot angry, he had never seen Seigneur angry at all. The implacable lord wore no emotions, and was the one man in all the world Hugh knew he could never best in honest battle.

Seigneur was the most striking lord in the South, almost certainly, the "beautiful monster," Hugh's wife called him. He had clearly been a strikingly handsome man at one time, with his golden hair cascading in curly waves past his shoulders, almost womanlike, but those shoulders were anything but feminine, as wide as a horse's withers and just as muscular. His face, too, combined both beauty and bestiality. On the left, an almost delicate manly beauty, yet on the right there was little of the original flesh remaining. On the left, a bright blue eye that rarely blinked, as if to compensate for the missing right eye in its ugly empty socket. Half angel, half devil, Hugh's daughter called him.

He wore white, too, though the colors of Castlenau were blood red. Hugh had known Seigneur back in the days he wore red, before the knight was captured in the Holy Land. Back then, he had been the perfect legendary knight, beautiful yet manly, unbeaten in the joust, the most eligible young knight in the crusades, desired by every woman in France. He returned from that crusade a broken creature, appearing in the desert, dying of thirst, scarred beyond recognition. He would not speak of his ordeal. When he recovered he took white as his color, with no insignia. No stag of Castlenau decorated his white shield. No color of any kind. Riding his black horse, friend and foe feared the Seigneur, the white lord with his cyclops eye. Some called him Cyclops. Some Seigneur. No one spoke his name, for he would not allow it, though Hugh remembered it well enough. And everyone feared Seigneur, even Hugh himself.

"Well met, Seigneur," said Arnot the Templar, also standing. All four of the great men stood now—Hugh, Amiel, Seigneur and Arnot the Templar—and every person in the room fell to silence. They had seen Hugh and Amiel argue on occasion, but never a spectacle such as this.

"You are well, Brother Arnot?" Seigneur's gruff voice replied.

"Well enough, Seigneur. I see you are as ugly as ever." A smatter of laughter cascaded around the great hall of knights.

Hugh didn't bother asking how they knew each other. He assumed they had met on crusade since Seigneur de Castlenau, the nameless lord, had served with distinction in the Holy Land. Nor did he want to engage in a competition of combat for the prize.

"The prize is in my possession—but I will consider all of your claims," Hugh said diplomatically. It would give him time.

Seigneur nodded and sat, but his one eye continued to stare at Hugh. He was ugly/beautiful and deadly, this Seigneur, with his uncovered scarred eye socket and the hand's-length scar down his right cheek. He was Satan's own Seigneur, yet all in white: white cloak, white mail, white gauntlets, and a single glittering eye. Seigneur had, indeed, captured the Jewel in one of his raids, but many of Hugh's knights rode with him, for Seigneur had only a small retinue, only eight surviving knights who wore his white without insignia, and one squire. But even with only eight knights—perhaps as good as eighty ordinary knights—Seigneur was not a man to have as an enemy.

Arnot had remained standing, as had the archbishop. They glared at each other.

Hugh laughed. "Enough! We shall settle this properly, and not here." He shook his head. "Those damnable Dominicans. They're worse than women for gossip!" News of the Jewel had traveled the land like the black plague, carried on the flapping lips of the traveling Dominican monks. All of Europe knew of the capture by now. Soon other claimants would be arriving in Carcassonne. Emperor Frederick, King Louis of France, King Jon of Aragon—soon their representatives would be buzzing around Carcassonne like flies on a corpse.

"They make great spies in wartime," said Arnot, smiling at last.

"That they do, friend Templar, that they—" Hugh paused as the great doors opened and his own squire entered, erect and all-business. "Oui, Gileet?"

His squire knelt on one knee, head tucked. "One of your patrols wishes an audience, my liege."

Hugh sighed, folded his arms and leaned back in his big chair. "Let it be so." He knew Gileet wouldn't interrupt the feast for unimportant business.

A dozen soldiers prodded three men laden with thick ankle and wrist irons into the great room. Hugh studied them with some amusement. He noticed Arnot sat abruptly straighter, showing interest, and for a moment it seemed the Templar recognized them. Then the scruffy knight sank back in his chair.

Hugh examined the prisoners. Strange creatures—like most Southerners: all Southerners loved their colorful clothing, women who revealed cleavage, wines, and their odd festivities—a truly alien culture. Yet even so, these three astonished and delighted Hugh. The oddest one, an over-tall man-boy with girlish features and hair wore unusual clownish colors and, in spite of his chains, clung to a stringed instrument. A second man was dressed in expensive green suede and felt, with a long traveling cape and an immense jewel, appearing vaguely like an Italian noble.

Strange, no one confiscated the jewel, Hugh thought.

The third man was a giant freeman who towered over the soldiers and could probably more than match Hugh, Arnot and the Seigneur together, in a wrestling match.

"What is this all about, lieutenant?"

"These men were arrested for murder, rebel plotting, and breaking curfew, my liege!"

Hugh glared at his lieutenant. "Then why have they not been taken to my shérif?"

"My liege, these two have killed your capitaine and twelve of your best men!"

"Twelve!" Hugh eyed the prisoners with new interest. Most of his men were hardened from several campaigns—three years fighting the Moors, five years killing the Saracens, and several years battling in Occitania. "Well. That is very distressing, no? Still, I don't understand why you have disturbed our feasting, lieutenant." He shook his head like a disappointed father. "And I am not pleased with your performance! Twelve men!"

The lieutenant's eyes remained steady. "My liege, these two are identified as Doré de Costonot and Osric d'Albi!"

Merde! The Dandy and the Hammer. The Grand Duo! The great room fell as still as the morning after a storm. A jongleur's voice trailed off in mid-story, "El Cid's great black stallion pawed the sand ..." The minstrel stopped his dreadful harping. Even the one-eyed Seigneur de Castlenau stared at the prisoners, silent and attentive.

The Lady Adelais, Hugh's daughter, stood up on a bench, leaning on a squire's shoulders, eyes bright with curiosity.

Hugh studied the prisoners unable to believe his good fortune: his daughter's engagement, the capture of the Jewel, and now two of the most notorious renegades—all in one week! His soldiers had been hunting these two for years. He could hardly enjoy better luck.

The silence continued a moment and he forgot the twelve killed men and the unannounced interruption. "Ah, très bien, lieutenant! Très bien! You are to be commended, no?" His eyes sparkled, and he vaulted off his dais with sudden energy.

He halted in front of Doré, studying the Bastard's clothing with amusement. He smiled and his fingers drummed on the hilt of his great broad sword. "Well, well. Doré. The son of the Lord of Costonot, no? I knew your father." He smiled. "I helped take his castle from him." Doré spat, narrowly missing him. "I don't know your mother? She was the town whore I believe?"

Doré spat again. "Garra!"

Hugh stepped in front of Osric and looked up at him. "I had heard you were big, but—" he gestured widely with his gloved hands, "I never imagined. Mon Dieu! You must have trouble with doorways, no?" He laughed to himself. "I believe you used to build castles. A master builder? And a mongrel by the look of you. Hun?" Osric did not answer and his eyes refused to look up from the floor. "We'll need a higher gallows for you, I think. I am delighted to have you both in my chateau."

"This is the castle of Viscount Trenceval!" shouted Doré, the Bastard.

"So it was. Matters naught. Just as the chateau de Costonot used to be your father's, no?" He held out his gloved hand and closed it slowly into a fist. "Now, both Carcassonne and Costonot are mine." He laughed. "What? No spit left?"

"The ownership of castles is never permanent, d'Arcis. Trenceval had a son!"

"Yes. Yes. His son did try, I suppose, to take back his father's lands. Just last year. 'Twas likely you were part of all that? Not much of an effort, really. Scampered away like a dog with his tail 'tween his legs." A cascade of laughter rolled through the great room.

"Garra!" Doré spat again and a great gob of bubbling spittle soiled Hugh's spurred boot.

The lieutenant's gloved hand shot out and clipped Doré's head. "Lord Seneschal to you, son of a whore!" The soldier was caught off-guard as Doré lunged into him, pulling big Osric with him by the chains. He knocked the soldier to his knees. The lieutenant drew his dagger and struck Doré with the hilt, drawing blood.

Hugh's lieutenant raised his dagger again but Hugh snapped, "Enough, lieutenant! I need these two men in one piece for the Inquisitor." He smiled, thinking of the tortures of the secular arm of the lay Inquisitors. He was disappointed that Doré showed no fear at the mention of the Inquisition. "You are a brave bastard, no? You might even have been a chevalier if your mother had not been the village whore. But then how can you be sure Fabrion was your father anyway? I heard she lay even with some of my men! In fact, I lay with her myself!" Hugh's men laughed and he smiled with them. "Mayhap I am your father then? What think you?"

"I'd rather be the son of a Saracen!"

Hugh's hand shot out and grabbed Doré's chin. "Such a pretty face. Perhaps I should have the Master Torturer leave you alive after they skin you. Do you think the women would like your face with no skin?" He pushed Doré away. "Matters naught." His eyes settled on the gangly boy beside Osric, who still clung to his lute in spite of the chains. A fool by his smile. "And who is this grinning idiot, lieutenant?"

The soldier shrugged. "He will not speak my liege."

"Truly? A brave boy, no?" He studied the bright blue boots and the feathered cap. "Well boy? Who are you?"

"He does not know us, d'Arcis!" Doré snapped.

The lieutenant snarled, "Viscount to you, dog!" and struck Doré again. Doré stood up, rubbing his jaw, but did not speak the title.

Hugh glared at the boy. "Then who is this smiling misfit? Lieutenant, why have you brought him?"

"We picked him up at the Auberge de Terre with these renegades, my liege."

"And what has he done?"

"We think he killed Louis!"

Then Hugh laughed. He imagined this scrawny creature taking on bull-shouldered Louis, a veteran of three campaigns. "Did any see it?"

The lieutenant sneered at Ramon. "We were busy, Lord Viscount."

Hugh looked at the boy's tall blue boots and green leggings. A fool indeed. "You assumed this skinny thing was a companion of these proud renegades?"

"My liege, he had this!" The lieutenant held out a short spear.

"You are a fool, lieutenant! This is a toy spear. My daughter has one like it."

"Oui, my liege!"

Once again, Hugh stared at the womanish idiot's face. "Well, boy. Who are you? Be quick. If you do not answer you have not long to live!"

"A jester, my lord, come to serve. And a passable minstrel."

"You look the part. Humor me." When the boy looked confused, he snapped, "Quickly, or you go with these renegades!"

The jester's smile widened. "A woman brought her son to a cemetery to visit his grandfather. As they walked among the great stones, the mother read the inscriptions out loud for her son. And the son asked, 'Mama, why do they bury two people together in the same grave?'" The jester delivered the joke with a perfect little boy's voice. "The Mama said, 'Why would you ask me this?' And the son replied, 'You told me the stone back there read, 'Here is buried a priest and an honest man.'"

Hugh laughed, for though it stank of heresy, the jester delivered it with mimicked voices, the mother's voice just perfect, and the little boy sounding just like a five-year-old whelp.

"Blasphemous!" snapped the archbishop, jumping to his feet and glaring at the boy. "And what is this—a lute? A forbidden instrument of the troubadours."

"A troubadour!" Hugh's daughter jumped off the table and ran to her father's side. Hugh smiled at her enthusiasm. She had been six when they left Paris for Occitania. He remembered warm nights on the banks of the Seine with Blanche de Castille on his arm, strolling as they listened to the famous troubadours of Paris. And even after the South was conquered by French armies, the troubadours were in every city, wonderful and smiling. Men such as Amiel had seen them as heretics, with their songs of magic and heroism and monsters and dark sorcery. Even their love songs were deemed devilish, especially if sung in the langue d'oc.

The fool bowed. "Ramon Trouvère, part-time jester, at your service, my liege. I came to serve."

Hugh laughed. "To serve me, fool?"

"Only you, my liege. Sadly, I came after curfew, found myself in the company of these fellows here."

"They are rebels," snapped Hugh.

"The big one, he offered to poke me with his hammer," the fool Ramon said.

"Yes, you are a pretty boy," Hugh said, playing along.

Ramon puckered his lips. "I kiss noble ass with the best of them."

The boy's delivery was impeccable. Hugh roared laughter.

"My Lord Viscount, why do Vikings never use lanterns?"

Hugh winked. "Why, good jester?"

"Why light a mere lantern when you can torch the church on the hilltop?"

Hugh laughed again, and the entire room joined him. "Enough, Ramon." Hugh gaped for breath. "You'll choke me with your good humor!" Hugh nodded. "So you seek employment from me, no? Who is your patron?"

"I have no patron, my liege. I am a student of the great Ansel d'Avignon."

Again the Viscount laughed. Ansel was probably the best-known trouvère in France. His patron was King Louis himself. Hugh had never been so lucky in a single day: two infamous rebels, Ansel's student, the Jewel of the South, all in his keeping.

"Oh, papa! Let's keep him!" Adelais seized her father's hand.

"'Tis not a horse, my Adelais."

"Papa! But he's a troubadour. A real one! Not one of these mournful minstrels that sound like tortured cats. Keep him!"

"Troubadours are heretics!" snapped the archbishop.

She frowned at Amiel. "I meant trouvère! Please, Papa!"

She kissed him on his bearded cheek and he relented. "Anything for you, my Adelais. A gift for your wedding."

"Oh, my own troubadour!"

Again laughter rippled through the room as Hugh returned to his seat between the templar and the Archbishop. The jester was making faces at the archbishop, mimicking his scowl and crossing himself.

"Quite the catch, today, my Lord," said Archbishop Amiel, who had not seen the insult.

"You were always lucky," said Arnot, the Templar.

Hugh smiled, but his attention remained fixed on the prisoners. He rubbed his whiskered chin. "So, these are the famous renegades Doré the Bastard and Osric the Hammer!" He sipped his wine. "You do not seem so formidable."

The archbishop's voice was loud in the hall. "They killed twelve of your men. And one of your capitaines!"

Hugh sneered, his mood too good to be spoiled. "So what shall I do with such famous enemies?"

"They are heretics, my liege. They must be burned—sent to hellfire!"

"Roasted renegade, no?" He glanced at the massive ribs of the boar on the table. Smiling now, he played with his long tail of hair, wrapping it around his neck in a coil. "Not yet, Lord Archbishop. They know all the rebel leaders and heretics, no? They will talk—first. Take the prisoners for questioning."

Song of the Empress

10

NEVARA FOUND THE Baug Balar camped in the market square near the southern outer wall of the city. It was the poorest neighborhood, a reeking ghetto to which the new French overlords had banished the Jewish folk.

She used a spell of concealing to make her way past the guards posted around the square. Three of the men from the wayroom, frightened of her magic but thankful for her help with the soldiers, had guided her through the lower city and past patrols. They led her through a maze of meandering shoulder-width alleys between the wretched huts that crowded every inch of space. She found herself breathing through her mouth, covering her nose to the stench of sewage dumped straight out on the alleys. The walked through shit, pushing aside the foraging pigs that ran freely. Bubo flew in circles over them, swooping down occasionally in a great display of white to scatter screaming piglets.

Her new friends had led her to an obscure rutted path between the shabbiest daub and wattle huts, not much more than windowless shanties. As they approached the Jewish market, she found only one guard before she saw the glowing pavilion of the Baug. Her people were camped in the center of the market square, swimming in mud and surrounded by smaller tents of hide. She whispered, "I thanking you," and promised her guides blessings and friendship in exchange. "Bringing your families to the Baug on Mayday," she said. "Bringing everyone and I show you magic like you never see!" They promised her then scuttled off into the shadows to hide from the curfew patrols.

The lone guard on the pathway was asleep, propped up against a house beside the barely visible gap between the buildings. The opening was barely large enough for Izzy and Wizi and the only light was the glow of the Baug tents, a riot of color in the muddy market square of Carcassonne's poorest neighborhood. She whispered a chant of concealing, and slipped past the sleeping sentry.

The herd of tarpans sensed her, nickering as she melted into their midst, unseen. Izzy and Wizi joined the herd of tiny horses, nuzzling each one in turn. Nevara smiled then made her way to the largest tent in the square. The pavilion, made of leather hides painted with stick figures that appeared both primitive and festive at the same time, was taller than the surrounding thatch houses. On one side of the pavilion was a crude pictogram of home, showing the Volga and Oka rivers. Home. She closed her eyes, just for a moment, and her spirit journeyed home to Nizhny, to the beautiful towers and stone houses on the rivers. She had never seen such beauty among the Germanic and Frankish barbarians and she missed home, though she knew they would never return in her lifetime.

The laughter of her people brought her back to dirty Carcassonne with its roaming pigs and muddy streets. She knew her people had paid well for a week's tenancy in the market, and would pay again as taxes to the viscount from their performances. They would be exempt from the curfew for as long as they remained in the market square.

The Baug always found something to laugh at. There was singing, too, and hearty, drunken voices. And the smells of home, the sumptuous stinging spices of Novgorod, lingering sweetly on the air, the incense of civilization, pulling her in from the barbaric stench of Carcassonne.

As she neared the wide flap to the pavilion, Orus moaned at her, and Bubo swooped down to tease the big bear, brown and shaggy, with one missing canine, but a savage array of remaining teeth. His claws were unclipped, unlike other performing bears. He ate a man's weight in precious food every week, throwing up a cloud of noxious gas after a gorging that always reeked through their camp, but he was one of the Baug's star attractions. Peasants threw coins when he wrestled their "strong man," especially if the bear won. Now, sadly, he was in chains, necessary in towns and villages, but when they rode the wilds, the Baug always unchained the great bear.

"There you are Orus." She knelt beside the bear, scratching his chin. Jealous, Bubo swept past the bear's head in a flurry of ghostly feathers and long talons. Orus's long claws came out, striking upwards. "Go away,

Bubo!" Bubo pivoted elegantly, wings extending, flapped twice, and flew to the top of the pavilion, twin black eyes glaring down on the bear. Nevara leaned and stroked the bear's shaggy chest and he scratched his round belly in response to her caresses. He always itched, poor Orus. "Did they feed you?"

She heard the twins laughing inside and she gave Orus a parting scratch before entering the pavilion. Her people fell silent as she entered, and the singing stopped, although the instruments continued to play. The entire Baug sat around a fire in the center of the tent: the knife-throwing twins, the "strongest man alive," their lithe escape artist, all the acrobats, singers, horse handlers, stilt and rope walkers, wrestlers and dancers, and the unwelcome old Guilhem d'Alions, the mystic. Earlier, they probably danced around the fire, but now they were in a circle around Magba, their Baug's great mother. Magba meant 'mother,' and was her only name. All except Magba and the old mystic Guilhem crowded around Nevara, their laughter and kisses a warm welcome.

Magba waited for her by the fire, sitting beside old gray Guilhem. Her hair remained golden, swept with only one streak of grey, and she wore a loose white gown decorated with flowers, the robe she always wore when she was pregnant. Magba was Nevara's own teacher, and also the mother of twelve of the men and women in the Baug, but she seemed younger than Nevara because of her wavy golden hair. She was probably twice Nevara's age, but ever smiling, always serene and nearly always pregnant. Her husband, the Baug's strong man, was a lusty man who, during the Mayday festivity, would load a wagon with ten Carcassonnians and lift them clean off the ground. In Paris he had managed eight men and the wagon! "These Southerners are smaller," he had said to Nevara, laughing at her concerns when she told him she worried for his bones.

Nevara knelt in front of the Magba, then stood and leaned forward until their foreheads touched in the traditional greeting.

"Blessings, Nevara," Magba said in Novgorodian, her voice lyrical. "The abundance of the Goddess upon you."

"Long life, Mother," Nevara responded, bowing her head. She was not actually Magba's own daughter, but all of them in the Baug were

Magba's adopted children, even Ramon.

She nodded at the old graybeard Guilhem, and spoke polite words. "The Goddess smile on you, Graybeard." The old man's hood was up, hiding most of his wrinkles and those mocking eyes, but the braided gray beard revealed him as a Perfect.

"Christ's blessings on you, child," said Guilhem in halting Novgorodian.

"I need no carpenter God's blessings!" She warded his curse with her fingers.

Magba sighed, used to their rivalry, but not approving. "Ramon, he was captured?"

"I'm sure of it," Nevara said, sitting on a log by the fire.

"Then it is as he wanted, child," Magba said.

"But not as we planned." Nevara had planned to stay with Ramon, helping him until he presented himself at the viscount's court as a "traveling minstrel." She glared at the old mystic now. "This is your doing, old man!"

Guilhem's ancient gray eyes regarded her. He nodded. "I admit it, my child."

"I am no child of yours!" She spat to ward his magic. She hated Christians above all others in the world. Their carpenter God had brought more death and suffering to Europe than the great Hun horde. In the name of this sacrificed God, crusades had been fought, Druids slaughtered, pagans oppressed, and now they had unleashed their Inquisition. It did not matter that Guilhem was not a Papist. He was still a Christian, and worse, he had a hold on Ramon. Ramon remained a follower of this sacrificed God, and old Guilhem had become his master, teacher, guide, even though he visited the Baug only on rare occasions. Was it only jealousy that made Nevara hate old Graybeard?

Guilhem bowed his ancient head.

"You come to us two weeks ago, and suddenly we must come here, to this filthy city!"

Guilhem nodded.

"Ramon is in great danger!" she shouted, and everyone in the Baug stared at her. The music stopped.

"We've taught him well, daughter," said Magba. "No one gets the better of Ramon."

"But Ramon might be tortured."

"Then he will suffer gladly. Do not worry, my daughter. I have seen a dark future for Ramon, but not in this place."

That made Nevara feel better, for Magba was once the greatest seer in Novgorod. More than sixteen years ago, they were chased out of their home city by a ruthless bishop jealous of Magba's fame as a wise woman and teller of fortunes. Back then, the Baug had been seven, all Magba's sons and daughters plus her husband, the strong man, and her adopted daughter, Nevara. As they traveled Novgorod, other outcasts joined them, including Atta and Hatta, the knife-throwing twins, and Eline, the archer. They lived as nomadic entertainers and it was a good life, breeding their tarpan horses and building their covered wagons. Even lands at war would let the Baug pass, for smiles and songs were a precious thing. Along their nomadic travels they picked up Ramon and this old Graybeard, Bubo the owl, Orus the bear, and a few other misfits.

Nevara had no secrets from the Baug, her family, or even from the old Graybeard, and so she told them everything that had happened, including what Ramon told her of the Jewel.

She ate, sang some songs, then made her way to her personal covered wagon, a space so low and small she had to bend to enter. Bubo stayed outside. He rarely came inside, preferring the top of her hide-covered home as a perch. Unlike most owls, Bubo was diurnal and hunted during the day, occasionally at night, sinking his talons into lemmings, voles, mice, hares, muskrats, marmots, squirrels, and the occasional fish snatched from the surface of lakes. Bubo preferred to catch his own and did not like closed spaces, but he was never far from her. When Ramon had found the nestling, twisted and dying on the ground, he had brought it to Nevara. She fed it chunks of meat and nurtured it, hoping to turn it free in time and return it to the wild. Bubo never left her. There was no way to drive off the ghost glider. Often, Nevara felt his emotions. She didn't train Bubo in any formal way, unlike her horses, but Bubo always seemed to know her mind.

Nevara lit the lanterns in her wagon. She had no family yet so her home was barely big enough for two people, small and round, of course, as all things magical must be, and painted with her symbols of protection, a dangerous thing in this time of Inquisition, even for "entertainers." It was no more dangerous than her fortune telling at festivals. The fearful Catholics tolerated them only because she put on her grand facade as the artiste whenever they came sniffing around. She could stand only in the middle of the wagon, where the hides domed to an apex. She saw the shadow of Bubo on his perch.

Everything in her small space was of magical significance, but disguised. Only her hand-painted cards—the superstitious Inquisitors would call them Satan's own work—might give her away, but even they were tolerated, for during Maydays and other quasi-pagan-Christian festivals, peasants and nobles alike came to hear of their futures, paying her with whatever they could afford: the nobles might give a gold florin for a good fortune, the bonded serfs a precious loaf of flatbread, and the destitute nothing at all. Village priests and monks tolerated her sorcery because, secretly, they came to her to have their own futures told. Once, the bishop of Prague had come to her to find out if he would be the next archbishop.

Now she chanted as she cast her circle of power. She laid out a circle of rune-marked stones and fanned the area with smoldering dried herbs, then placed burning wick in an oil bowl at the four directions. She sprinkled precious salt and blessed water and gave her chants. On his perch, Bubo spread his wings and flapped then flew off. He would not stay when she made magic, but he would return when she was done. She called on her guardians.

Almost immediately, she felt them. In her mind's eye she saw them. One was fierce and fiery, another cool and unsmiling, the third wispy and laughing, and the last a small gnome-like creature. She welcomed them each equally. Her master had always taught her "The guardians are your servants, not your friends," but Nevara loved them. They had been her childhood friends. She spoke to them, befriended them. They were always with her. Ramon never saw them, even when he tried, and thought her crazy because of it.

She sat down with her precious painted cards. Magba called them

Turuq—"four ways" in Arabic. She had spent years painting them, embellishing on what Magba had given her, imprinting them with her own vision, painting her own version of the fifty-six elemental designs taught her by Magba—cards Mother said were given her by a Moorish Holy man. Over their years of nomadic wandering, she had added her own cards based on those things in her life that were important: people she knew and loved, respected, feared or hated, forces in her life, the blessed Goddess and all the forces of the universe.

In Toledo, when Ramon joined the Baug, she added her first card, although it was a child's painting, for she was just fourteen at the time. By the time the Baug reached Paris, where they performed for King Louis, she had added two more. Down to Milan, Verona, magnificent Venice—where they picked up Arnot, the drunken Templar—then to Rome. There they performed for the Pope and had their first confrontation with the Diableteur—only the Pope's intervention had saved them. "Leave them be, brother Abott," the Pope had said, wheezing. "They are but entertainers!" Diableteur terrified a young Nevara, and she added a new card. Their two-year journey to Constantinople gave her time to paint a dozen more. The cards were her most precious possession, and no one but she could touch them, not even Magba. She would kill any who tried. The cards spoke to her.

Nevara chanted in the smoky interior of her tent, calling on the Goddess. Her hand quivered over the cards. Did she really want to see? What if she could do nothing against the darker power of the Diableteur? Ramon was already arrested, and anything the cards might show would almost certainly be terrible.

Ramon was a fool, pure and simple; in fact, she had painted one of her new cards, one of the twenty-two grand cards, to reflect his unique personality and special nature. She called the card *Arpayk*, The Fool, and painted it with Ramon's green-feathered hat, and his little dog Mauri, showing him stepping off a cliff into oblivion. She painted him that way because he was always fearless, always rushing off to some new adventure. Everywhere the Baug traveled, they found a heretic to be rescued, a petty thief to be saved from hanging or an Inquisitor to torment. Ramon, for all his smiles and antics, always targeted Inquisitors.

Now she knew why. She resented Ramon in that moment, although the feeling surprised her. He had never told her the story of his mother for all their years in the Baug, not in detail. Now Nevara understood why Ramon had been all tears in that first year in Castille. She had thought it was because he was among strangers, but now she understood he had been mourning his mother. He had been full of hate in those days and fought the other children, but no one lived with the Baug in misery for long. Within a year, he had become the laughing fool, and Magba had sewn his over-sized embroidered tunic. "He'll grow into it," Magba had said. "See how he sprouts already?"

He lived with the Baug and he was dear to them but why had he never told them this story? Perhaps Magba knew Ramon's story. But now, for the first time, Nevara felt she truly understood Ramon, even though she might never see him again. Why would he tell this story to a room full of strangers, yet not to the people who had loved him these last twelve years like family?

She was not surprised when the first card she turned was *Arpayk*, the Fool. Ramon. She used the old language to label her great cards. She stared at the card, so like the outer Ramon. She thought about gathering her brushes and painting a new card, reflecting what she now knew about her friend, reflecting his actively vengeful inner nature, perhaps adding a mouse to the card. She kissed the card, and set it down. No. The card was still right. Ramon didn't actively seek revenge. There was something else driving him, something nobler.

The next two draws she didn't understand. One was *Yapar*, the lusty card of Strength, one of her first, painted many years before. A fierce Sampson-like man with golden hair and white robes wrestled a lion, prying its mouth open. The third card was equally mysterious. It was a card Nevara had created, modeled on Magba herself, although she titled it Empress to hide the pagan associations from the sniffing hound dogs of the Church, the Inquisitors. But what did it mean here?

For clarity she drew another card—the one she feared more than any other. She knew it would come. *Xmertyl*. Death. She had painted it when she first encountered the plague in a village of the dying. Later, after Rome, she embellished the card with the creature she so hated and feared—the Diableteur.

She stared at the Death card, cursed it, spat in her small fire. She felt a sudden chill.

Confused and unsure of what she was seeing, she drew a trinity of cards, placing one above, one below, one crossing, but they too puzzled her. The card above was *Negralim*. The Priestess. But who could that be, in this Goddessless land of men who feared women? The card below was *Ilana*, the Priest, representing a carnal Holy Man, a card she had painted after Rome when they performed for the Pope. The card that crossed them was the *Exparn*, the Questing Hero and his chariot. All three were very powerful cards. She closed her eyes, allowing her intuition to take her to the meaning of the cards.

In the darkness of her mind, the cards came alive. A Holy Man who was not holy was coming into Ramon's life. A woman, someone Nevara had not herself met, was a high priestess of great power. The carnal Holy Man crossed the Priestess. They were opposites and enemies. The third could only be Arnot, the Questing Hero, a man in search of God, with the empty soul. She had painted that card for Arnot, two years ago when he joined the Baug, hoping it would sympathetically influence him, help him find compassion and the spirit again, and she depicted him in a great chariot drawn by a white and a black lion because he had once been the companion to the Marshall of the Temple, also known as the Templar Charioteer.

What did it all mean? A priestess, a woman of true spirit and belief must oppose a fraudulent holy man and crossing them was Arnot, a man with no soul.

Nevara picked up the Priestess card and held it by the edges between her two outer fingers, chanting the words of power, staring at the dignified face, serene and pale like a full moon in a clear sky. The image shimmered as she concentrated, the face glowed, and suddenly Nevara found it impossible to keep the image in focus. She went with the vision, not trying to bring clarity, intensifying her chant. And for a moment, just for an instant, the face dissolved, revealing a jewel. A glowing, wonderful jewel.

Nevara gasped. The Jewel! The very object of their quest, perhaps the very thing that would destroy Ramon.

Calming herself, she re-dealt the cards in a final trinity for an outcome. As she turned the first card, her small fire snapped to new life, fed by a sudden breeze through the flap of her tent. She shivered.

Ramon's card, the Fool.

Then Death. Diableteur.

Xmertyl on top of *Arpayk*. The tears came then. She stared at the Death card, cursed it, wiped her tears, then picked up the Fool card and kissed his face. Ramon could never stand against the Diableteur. The last card was the *Kakoban*, the Burning Castle, the ruined Tower. She shivered. She held her breath. Disaster! She had painted this card in memory of a city of good folk in Bulgaria that fell to the Hun, depicting it as it burned.

As the card that crossed Ramon and the Diableteur, it almost certainly meant disaster.

She sat for a long time, staring at the fire, conscious of the elementals whispering outside her circle. The shock of those three cards gave way to anger.

She opened her eyes and saw, just for a moment, a shadow in the shadows, a shifting malevolent spirit. It was outside the ring of firelight, but it was there, dark and hungry. She warded with her fingers, spoke words of power, felt it recoil from her.

Hand shaking, she took the *Yapar* card of strength. She had no idea who it represented, but her inner spirit told her he was an enemy. She had painted *Yapar* from a dream of a golden-haired Sampson in flowing white robes, wrestling a great lion. She crossed the mysterious *Yapar* on top of the Fool card and chanted a bonding. She wrapped the cards in cloth, tied it with a binding rope, then blessed the bundle with smoke, ash and dirt, bringing her enchantment to life with the elements. She even shed some life force, some blood, and smeared it on the bonding rope. She performed a knotting charm with the rope, then closed her eyes. She heard the murmuring in the dark, the sound of her spirits responding.

She continued chanting, staring into the shadows. A vision formed there, hazy at first, then startlingly real. She saw Ramon laughing and dancing, oblivious of his danger, his pretty face full of joy. He was alone in a forest, surrounded by towering pine trees, and Nevara smelled the sweetness. The night was full of crickets. A wolf howled. Then the night became still. Nevara felt it first. The evil had come to the fool. The Diableteur emerged from the shadows, his black cloak a shape in the night, eyes glowing red. She chanted faster. A wind rose, an elemental wind, and the Diableteur's hood flew back. Nevara screamed. Beneath the hood was a skull, grinning, empty except for glowing red jewels for eyes. Nevara chanted faster, moaning, swaying, sweating.

The scythe made a hissing sound as fleshless fingers swung the great weapon. Nevara gestured with her fingers, her voice rising. Black flames filled her mind and smoke erupted around the dancing fool and the grinning Diableteur. A man with golden hair stepped out of the smoke and flame, a sword in hand. He swung. The blade clanged against the scythe, stopping it. Black flames and white hot flames erupted from the collision of blades. The fool turned, surprised by the sudden battle, black on white. She smelled blood, but already the vision began to fade. She chanted faster, calling on her elementals, but something stopped her. She lost the vision.

She opened her eyes, tears falling down her cheeks. She had done all she could.

This knight, this strong man, would become Ramon's ally. And together, they must defeat the Diableteur.

She gave her thanks to the elementals, banished the spirits, and fell into an exhausted sleep, the cards still clenched in her white hands. And she dreamed of terrors beyond her comprehension.

11

RAMON TROUBADOUR RUBBED his raw hands, and studied the viscount's hall. It was a crude, vile place, filled with dunged straw, the stench of pork and urine and vomit from drunken knights.

He stood in the center of the great hall, surrounded by four immense tables. The knights and ladies sat along the outer perimeter of the table, their backs to the glowing hearths and facing the center of the hall where the minstrels, goliards and jugglers performed. A glowering minstrel with a primitive harp spat at Ramon, and a juggler sat despondent by a fire, but most of the rest of the crowd were watching him with drunken anticipation.

Now what? So far his plan had spun off in a wild direction, as if a drunken puppet master played with his strings. He had contacted the infamous rebels as planned, only to get them all captured. He tried not to think of what they faced in the viscount's pit. His best friend, his dog Mauri, might soon be in a soldier's cooking pot. His songs had always saved him from the pit, the fire or the whip. Few lords would squander precious talent, and Ramon had always enjoyed some impunity from prosecution for his coarse jokes and insults, even for crimes, as long as he wasn't overtly heretical. At least Arnot had been successful. He sat between the archbishop and the viscount, an honored guest.

"Let's hear another joke, jester!" the viscount said.

Ramon bowed. "My lords and ladies. An Inquisitor on his rounds visited a remote village in the Pyrenees. When he arrived, tired from his journey and expecting food, the villagers immediately dragged out a haggard woman, an elder with a wrinkled face and dressed in rags. 'This lady is a witch! Burn her. Burn her.' The villagers took up the chant, 'burn her, burn her.' The Inquisitor, who had looked forward only to rest and food, sighed wearily."

Ramon paused to see if he had the audience. This wasn't one of his funniest jokes. The trick was in his acting of the roles and his clever and dramatic voices. He could sound just like an old hag, a tired monk, a pleading child, a terrified woman or an angry man. Already, it seemed he had captured everyone in the viscount's great hall, even the archbishop. Adelais, the viscount's daughter, smiled expectantly. Arnot wore an expression that said, *Couldn't you find a less controversial joke?* The viscount was neutral. So Ramon carried on.

"The villagers chanted, 'Burn her! Burn her to a crisp!'

"But the Inquisitor was tired and not so easily fooled. 'How do you know this to be a witch?'

"'She is ugly!" shouted one villager.

"'She looks like a witch!'

"The Inquisitor sighed, put down his traveling bag and looked at the villagers each in turn. 'Why does she look like a witch?'

"'See her wart!'

"'I have a wart,' said the Inquisitor.

"'Burn her! Burn the witch!'

"'Tell the truth,' the Inquisitor said.

"'Her farts are so foul the entire village chokes,' the village priest said. 'It must be the devil inside her!' Then, the Inquisitor heard the woman fart, a long and disgusting sound, followed by a stench that brought tears.

"'See, she is a witch!' the magistrate of the village pointed at her.

"'Monks fart too,' said the Inquisitor, holding his nose. 'My abbot smells just like this. My farts smell worse.'

"'She chants and mumbles in her sleep,' shouted one villager.

"'I chant and mumble in my sleep,' said the Inquisitor, in no mood for a burning.

"Now the crowd became truly angry and crowded around the monk.

"'Grab the witch,' shouted the village priest.

"And the villagers grabbed the Inquisitor by both arms and chanted, 'Burn the witch! Burn the witch.'

The silence hung for a moment in the great hall. Then an old grey-haired knight guffawed. Then another. And soon the whole room filled with laughter. The old grey-haired knight chanted, "Burn the witch! Burn the witch!"

"This is not funny!" shouted a new voice. The room stilled, instantly.

Ramon turned and stared at the monk near the back of the room. His scowl marked him as an Inquisitor. He hadn't realized any were in the room, not that it would have stilled his tongue.

"This is dangerous talk!" shouted the monk.

"Nonsense, Brother Duranti," said the viscount. "Jesters must have free licence to mock anyone from peasant to king to pope." Ramon noticed that the viscount was a man of good humor, his smile large and attractive.

"I will not have it," said the monk.

"This is my hall, brother," said the viscount. "You may go if you wish."

Ramon could just hear the archbishop's rebuke. "You err to criticize the Master Inquisitor, my Lord."

"Have a caution," snapped the viscount. "I like this boy. This is my hall. I don't joust in the cathedral, do I?"

Ramon hid a smile. He hated the viscount, would never forgive him for his part in the suffering of his people and the death of both his parents, but at least the man had a sense of humor.

Ramon rubbed his raw wrists again, re-inspected his precious lute for damage, then forced another smile. He studied the hall of his new "patron." He danced lightly across the open floor towards the viscount's table. Adelais, the viscount's daughter, kissed her father's cheek. "Papa! Make him sing for me."

"You are not to call me that in court," the viscount said, frowning. When her flashing smile remained, he relented: "Oui, my Adelais."

"A romantic song, my lord!" She sat on the arm of her father's chair and put her tiny hand over his.

The viscount glared at Ramon. "Well, boy?"

"My lord?" Ramon stared at him, forcing a smile. The viscount hadn't changed much in twelve years. There was perhaps a hint of silver now in the red beard, but the man was as imposing and powerful as he had been to a young boy's eyes, standing on his tower, laughing over the roasting of Ramon's blessed mother.

"I said, sing for us, boy!" The viscount's voice was loud, but he seemed amused. "Are you dim?"

"My liege, I—"

There was no patience in the hard lines of the viscount's face. "You are a troubadour—pardon, Lord Archbishop, a trouvère—I do hope, for your sake. It's not too late to join your rebel friends in the pit!"

"Oui, my liege, but my dog, my liege. Mauri. He is my friend."

"A dog?"

"Your soldiers said something about him being a fine addition to their stewing pot."

The room filled with laughter.

"Already you entertain us," the viscount said. "Now sing!"

Ramon pointed at the doors with his lute stem. "He's hardly a morsel, lord."

Again the laughter swelled, echoing off the vaulted ceiling. "Impress us, then, boy. Then mayhap we'll find your mongrel."

Ramon pointedly slid his instrument on to his back, a signal he would not sing.

"You play a dangerous game, boy." The viscount's voice sounded angry, and he looked furious when his daughter whispered again in his ear.

Ramon had to stand firm or Mauri would not live. He shook his head. "My dog, lord." The minstrel snorted, glowering at Ramon, probably hoping the viscount would change his mind and send him to the pit.

He thought the viscount would fly into one of his famous furies, but instead the lord waved his hand and shouted: "Sergeant! Fetch the dog before the cook gets hold of him!"

The silence hung.

"A joke, then, while we wait." The viscount's glare was terrifying.

Ramon bowed. A religious joke always made knights laugh. "Once, there was an abbot." He paused as the archbishop sat forward and glowered at him warningly. "This abbot was very vain and dressed splendidly with a ruby cross about his neck." No one laughed at first, then the viscount chuckled and everyone joined him. Most stared at their own archbishop, who wore a ruby cross. "Father Abbot was also quite fat, for he indulged in only the best foods." More laughter, but a piercing glare from the archbishop. "One day Father Abbot traveled the country on a mission to investigate heresies in Toulouse. There, he stayed in an inn, for the monastery was not yet rebuilt after the war. The abbot ordered a grand feast for himself, but plain pottage for his monks who accompanied him. When the serving wench returned with the food, she served the monks first. The abbot was enraged. 'How dare you serve monks before me?' And the serving girl dropped the bowls, bowed low and said, 'Forgive me, Father, I was blinded in crusade. But I should have known you were the holiest one in the room by your blessed farts.'"

The archbishop stood up in a fury. Arnot and the viscount smiled. The room howled with laughter. Ramon waited to see if the archbishop would arrest him.

Fortunately, the sergeant appeared with Mauri and the archbishop, red faced, sat down. Mauri yapped, squirmed so hard in the soldier's arms that the man dropped him. He ran across the floor, barking and jumped into Ramon's outstretched arms. Ramon let Mauri lick his face and he kissed his snout.

"Well, boy," said the viscount. "You have your rat friend. A song and be quick!"

Ramon put his dog down though Mauri rubbed up against his legs and barked. The viscount's greyhounds growled.

"My lord, your soldiers stole my possessions."

The sergeant sneered. "He had nothing, my lord. Just a toy spear."

"That is my toy. It was my uncle's." Ramon continued to grin, but he made no other move.

"Sing, damn you, or I'll condemn you to the pit!" The viscount's good humor was fading, but Ramon couldn't give up the precious Spear of Zaleucus. He didn't move. He might be a fool, but he was a freeman, not a bonded servant, and he would not move until Zaleucus was returned.

The viscount's daughter whispered in her father's ear again. He shook his head. She pouted and even pounded her father's shoulder. "Boy, you had better be the best damned-to-hell trouvère in all of Christendom. Bring him his toy!"

The sergeant gave Ramon a look that was part admiration, part hatred. Probably he had never seen anyone stand up to his lord before. Moments later Zaleucus was returned, but carried by the lieutenant this time. He held it out. When Ramon reached for it, the lieutenant snatched it back. The crowd laughed. When the lieutenant held it out a second time, Ramon danced forward, snatched it, yanked it to one side, spun it around and brought the point up under the soldier's chin. The room erupted in cheers, although the lieutenant had murder in his eyes. He had been bested by a fool in front of his lord, and Ramon knew he had an enemy for life.

Ramon stepped back, settled the spear in the crook of his arm, then, with a flourish, he spun the lute off the strap and into his hands and struck a chord across the strings. He must sing his best or he would join his new friends in the pit. Expectations and anger ran high. He was careful to sing nothing heretical, nothing the archbishop might use to prove he was one of the mystical troubadours, rather than a humble trouvère. He sang of Tristan and Iseult, a long and tragic ballad that never failed to bring tears. He sang his popular Christianized version, the one he sang in Paris at the king's court, not the Celtic myth taught him by his uncle. In his version, it became a tale of a noble knight and beautiful princess trapped by magic, a story of noble virtue but also betrayal that knights and their ladies so loved to hear.

He spun his own form of magic, pouring all his spirit into his song, his voice rising to the heavens. He escaped into the song, losing himself in the spirit of the muse, feeling the ecstasy of music. Almost instantly, he had the crowd in his power, even the archbishop, equally the viscount, and especially the viscount's daughter. He saw them all come alive as his soprano notes echoed from the rafters, and he forgot everything then, the viscount and the archbishop, sworn enemies, Nevara and the Baug, even Mauri, and sank into the music and his special world. When he sang, he escaped the miseries of the physical world. It was a trick taught him by Uncle Ansel, the troubadour. "To make a song truly come alive, live it," Ansel had said, over and over. He used his imagination—his spirit, Nevara would have said—and journeyed to Ireland as Tristan. He saw the physical beauty of Iseult, and the green hills of her country. He was there in his mind, no longer in the reeking hall of the viscount. He felt Iseult's touch, he made love to her as Tristan. It was all very real to him.

Back in the viscount's hall, another Ramon, dimly aware, moved about, plucking the strings, meeting the astonished gaze of each and every knight, lady and squire in the room. Even the stuporous knights, near oblivion from the strong ales, came alive to his song. Most of Ramon's spirit was in Ireland with Tristan, in love with Iseult, tortured with guilt over his betrayal of his king. Being there made his voice come alive. He visualized every detail. He smelled the heather on the Irish hills, and the sea. He felt Iseult's lips on his.

The "physical" Ramon paused at the end of one table and sang for the minstrel and juggler as well, and their hurt and angry expressions transformed to wonder.

Ramon was enough in both worlds, imaginary and real, to see that one knight in the room didn't respond to his voice. A scarred knight, all in white, simply glared at him through a single eye. He had obviously lost an eye to battle, but he did not deign to cover the ugly flesh with a patch. He wore no emblems, no griffins or dragons or eagles or symbols of any kind. Just a hauberk of silver polished mail against a white tunic, white breeches and white boots. The terrible face was carefully neutral.

Ramon nearly lost the cadence of his song as his imaginary world shimmered and faded. He hesitated under the gaze of that one, angry eye and nearly lost Tristan and Iseult.

Ramon moved along the table and finally back to the head table where he sang the tragic conclusion for the viscount and his daughter. He pretended not to notice Arnot's secretive smile.

He waited through the stunned silence, then bowed as the room erupted in roars of approval. Knights pounded the table. Women stood and reached out their arms, tears in their eyes. Even the viscount shouted acclaim.

Ramon had spun his magic.

12

SQUIRE PERCE LEANED forward, chewing on the rib of boar and enjoying the sweetness of the meat. After nearly a moon on the trail—dried venison munched from horseback during the day and a stew of salt meat over a campfire at night—the viscount's feast was a delight of sensations: Piers' famous hotch-potch, forfar birdies and trenchers of hearty colconnan. Bless old Piers.

He had expected to return to a quiet time at court: a couple days of drinking with the other young squires until he passed out; a few more days of making Adelais swoon over his tales of valor; as his confidence grew, the same stories, by now pregnant with adventure, told to rivals; and the mundane tasks of cleaning Seigneur's white tack and armor, and sharpening the swords. He hadn't expected so much excitement on his first night home.

He threw the bone at a rat. The Grand Duo! Dieu! The capture of Doré the Dandy and Osric the Hammer threatened to overshadow even Seigneur's great triumph.

And this cocky young troubadour! What a stunning voice. Pure magic, especially for one so young. Although Perce was probably the same age as the troubadour, this Ramon had perfected his art, whilst Perce de Mendes remained a humble squire, struggling to earn his spurs of knighthood.

The fatigue of their mission fell away, and Perce was caught in the spell of this heretic troubadour.

His foot tapped along. He watched Adelais sway to the music. The viscount smiled and seemed oblivious of the mead that ran down his chin.

Only Perce's master, the one-eyed Seigneur, seemed impervious and sat with folded arms, his single eye half closed.

Perce stared at the boy and his dog. The sweet voice of an angel, the look of a fool. During his travels with his Seigneur, Perce had heard the best troubadours: in Spain, the stringing of the famous Dominic de Capio; during the crusade to Egypt, he listened to the captured infidel Saliman sing with a honeyed tongue; in Constantinople he had heard the haunting melodies of Glandeville de Borne. This fool was easily their master.

Only the court minstrels, jugglers and goliards frowned, no doubt thinking their employment was suddenly in jeopardy. No one conversed or laughed or snored as Ramon sang his beautiful songs and strummed on his lute. In between ballads, the room erupted in thumping, cheers and applause. Adelais' voice was the loudest of all—most unladylike—not that Adelais was famous for genteel behavior.

She stood up, lifted her arms and hooted like a man. Perce saw her father's disapproving frown, but she was clearly a fanatic for this trouvère. Perce stared at his sparkling nymph. All the men in the room wanted her, in whispers they talked of having her, though none would dare. More than one careless chevalier had been humiliated, sent off to some degrading duty, or spurned from the court, by her protective father. One knight, a likeable man who distinguished himself in the defense of the city last year when the rebel lord attacked, vanished from the court the day after his too-obvious courting of Lady Adelais.

Her eyes remained fixed on the troubadour—it was clear to Perce this was a troubadour, protests notwithstanding—as he sang a courtly love song. The melody was melancholy and Perce was a little scandalized when he realized he was singing it in the poetic *langue d'oc*.

When the boy stopped singing, the room erupted in loud praise: fists thumped tabletops, hands clapped loudly, voices cheered and hooted and called for more.

Adelais' infectious cheering kept them applauding.

Sir Albaric, to Perce's left, shook the table, and hollered for more. "Sing another!"

Ramon bowed to the dais. "Perhaps I could rest, my liege. I need a drink to soothe my voice."

The viscount nodded and Adelais, not waiting for the servants, seized two bowls of mead from the head table and ran with them to the troubadour. Ramon drank one in a long chug and smiled at Adelais as she held out another. "Merci, ma Dame."

"You do credit to your teacher, Ramon," the viscount said.

The chevaliers pounded the tables in agreement. "More!" yelled Albaric, joined by other drunken knights, but Ramon chugged back mead and swung his lute on its strap to his back.

Sir Albaric winked at Perce. "Have you ever heard such a voice, carrot head?"

I'm sure you haven't, cockroach, thought Perce. How he hated this knight. Sir Albaraic was Seigneur's main rival. The golden knight was simply called The Lion in court, because the emblem of his family and fief in Laon was a golden lion, and he was perhaps the only knight in all of Europe who rivaled Seigneur for fame and ferocity. One day, the two rivals would almost certainly fight, for Albaric, the Lion, suffered no rivals.

Perce ignored the reference to his hair—after all, the great Seneschal Viscount Hugh D'Arcis was red-haired. He forced himself to answer politely: "No, Messire. A wondrous voice he has!"

Albaric smiled. "Oui!" He took a fresh bowl, obviously quite drunk and drained it in a single draw. "What do you think, Seigneur de Castlenau?"

Perce was surprised when his one-eyed Seigneur replied, "I was entertained."

Clearly startled, Albaric stared at the colorless Seigneur. "I have never known you to enjoy entertainments, Seigneur."

The Seigneur did not look at his rival but continued to stare at the troubadour sitting in the center of the hall. His only answer was a curt nod of his head.

"I have not yet congratulated you, Seigneur," Albaric said.

Seigneur glared at him.

"The Jewel of Montségur is a great credit to you. I am most envious of your triumph."

When his white Seigneur refused to answer, Perce said, "You have many achievements to your credit."

Albaric slammed the flat of his hand into the table. "I did not speak to you, carrot head!"

Seigneur's unsmiling face turned to his foe. "My squire is honoring you, Messire."

They glared at each other, two eyes into one, one eye into two, neither speaking nor turning away, and Perce squirmed between the two great warriors, sweating. Finally, Albaric broke the confrontation: "I am told this Jewel, this Dame, is sworn never to know a man!" He chuckled. "Tell me the truth, Seigneur. Did you take her flower?"

Seigneur's face did not reveal the answer. Perce tried to prevent his own blush. All those weeks on the trail, with Seigneur visiting the Dame Esclarmonde in her caravan nearly every night. The low murmurs of their voices. The rumors amongst Seigneur's troops. The silences. Seigneur often didn't emerge until the morning.

Perce tried to change the subject, sensing a drunken feud was imminent. "I wonder why they call the Dame 'The Jewel.' "

"She is precious," said his master softly. "Precious to the Southerners."

"Precious?" Albaric snorted. "She is an old wench with a dusty patch of womanhood between her legs."

"Have a care," said Seigneur.

Albaric the Lion gulped more brew. "Did you not wish to be the one who could say he ruined the virgin Lady?" Sir Albaric no longer laughed and Perce knew, without doubt, that the knight of Laon would have deflowered the Jewel for sport had he captured her. A picture of it invaded his mind and it sickened him: Albaric tearing at her silver gown, squeezing her breasts—and all the while the placid Dame would have smiled at him and said, 'I forgive you, my son.' And Albaric, angry, would strike her and ...

Perce scowled and drank more brew. The very real memory of his Seigneur visiting the Dame each night—his lord with a heretic Dame!—and the nightmare vision of Sir Albaric raping her—vile thoughts both.

Albaric smiled at him. "What about you, squire? I hear you are still a virgin. Did you not want to take your carrot and plunge it into the holy bush?"

Perce refused to be provoked, although he was sure his face burned as red as his hair. "I do not know what you mean, Messire."

"Did you not want to take your tiny manhood and put it in her womanhood. Do you not know what I mean?"

Now Perce felt the heat in his face. "No, Messire, I do not."

"You did not wish to ravish the Dame of the Cathars? To take the Jewel and make her shine. The perfect revenge for your father's death at the hands of these rebels!"

Perce looked down at the leavings on the table, now a pile of gnawed bones and spilled brew. The chevalier Albaric the Lion never tired of mentioning his father's defeat at the hands of the Cathar rebels. Angry, Perce focused on the ring on his second finger, with his father's crest, a hunting bird, talons extended for the kill, and he had the unmanly urge to shed tears—followed by the manly urge to drive Albaric's drunken face into the table until brains spilled out to join the putrid leftovers. Of course, Albaric would have cleaved him in two. The knight of Laon was possibly the only man in the room who could equal Perce's one-eyed lord, more than a match for a squire's anger.

"Messire Albaric, she is probably fifty summers of age," Perce said, but the anger rose in him like a pot coming to the boil, hotter and hotter. Perce turned away and scanned the room, looking for anything that might divert him. He focused on Ramon, the magnificent new voice of the court. The court's ladies swarmed the performer, surrounding the trouvère like fanatics, touching him inappropriately. One grabbed Ramon's backside. Ramon tried to smile as they demanded to know where he was from, who was his teacher, whether he was married, did he have a sponsor.

Perce scanned the rest of the room, refusing to look at Albaric. Arnot the Templar, a knight known to Seigneur, sat silent, staring at the troubadour. The court minstrel glared at his new rival, the troubadour, and resumed his dreadful harping. The jugglers were suddenly clumsy. One dropped a flaming torch and stomped the dry reeds as they caught fire. Beside Perce, Albaric laughed as he told his squires about his latest conquest in the whorehouse, the Fleur de Joie.

The diversions didn't help. His anger simmered. Seigneur's hand squeezed his leg under the table, as if to say, 'Let it go.' Perce felt his fury draining, comforted by his placid master, and he took a fresh bowl of brew.

The great hall rumbled with activity. The *pâtissier* fell down in a clatter of trays, tripped by the drunken provost. He gathered up his pastries and sweet cakes and served them anyway, now sprinkled with the chaff of straw from the floor. The kitchen clerk saw the commotion and shook his head as he made a note in the ledger. Two sweepers moved in quickly on the remaining cakes, batting away rats with their brooms. Threading his way through the pandemonium, the cupbearer topped up bowls of mead and brew.

The room was lit by torches and two great stone hearths with fires that roared to the height of a man, one behind the dais of the Lord of Carcassonne and the other on the opposite wall. A scullion threw logs on the lord's fire. Near the fire, a wet nurse fed a knight's baby.

Seigneur Shérif argued with the viscount's lieutenant, probably over possession of the rebels Doré and Osric, this bizarre twosome. The shérif's glowering eyes and his wide-legged stance seemed to indicate he lost the verbal sparring.

Sir Albaric slammed another empty bowl to the table and stood up. He untied his breeches, hitched up his leather tunic, and urinated into the reeds beside the table. Perce frowned at him, annoyed at the disrespect. It was generally unacceptable to expel at the table and he held his breath against the beer-vinegar stench.

Albaric exaggerated the arc of his stream, lifting his manhood. "Is this more to your liking than the Dame?" he asked, loud enough for several knights to hear.

They all stared at Perce. The fury could not be contained. Albaric was a knight who could far out match Perce in any contest, but an insult could not go unaddressed. Perce started to stand, his hand on the hilt of his sword.

The Seigneur's hand whipped out, grabbed his arm and pulled him back onto the bench.

Albaric chuckled, retying his breeches. "Oh, I forgot. Seigneur is more your taste."

"I think you've had too much mead, Sir Albaric," Seigneur said, his voice a harsh whisper.

"I've had not nearly enough, Seigneur." Albaric drank more, the brew running down his chin, across a three-inch scar on his throat, a failed attempt by a Moor to execute the knight.

"If you provoke my squire, you provoke me." Seigneur sounded bored.

Sir Albaric and Seigneur stared at each other for a long time and the conversation in the great hall faded. Even Viscount d'Arcis and the archbishop watched the confrontation with interest, a conflict long overdue.

"I was just offering your squire my hospitality," said Albaric.

Adelais stepped between the two rivals, staring squarely at Albaric's breeches. "Not much entertaining there." Half his height, tiny fists on her hips, she was imposing enough to make Albaric blush. Then she tittered with laughter and most of the knights joined in.

The viscount frowned at his daughter's interference. "I see the Cyclops and the Lion are arguing," he said, with a tone that really said: 'You two behave. I have more important matters than two feuding knights.' Instead, he said, "I think perhaps they've had too many spirits!" General polite laughter filled the hall, echoing off the high stone arches of the roof. The viscount glared at Albaric who stood for a moment, defiant. "Do me a kindness, Messire Albaric."

"Oui, my liege." The golden knight bowed.

"I wish you to bring the Dame Esclarmonde de Foix to my hall!"

The only sound was the scurrying of mice. Perce watched as one of them scampered across the archbishop's foot. The archpriest yanked back his foot, looking afraid. Scared of a mouse! Perce nearly laughed. This man, who had the ear of the pope and influenced the king, was terrified of mice!

Albaric glanced one more time at Seigneur, then drew his golden cloak over his shoulders, bowed, and left the hall without a word.

Abruptly, the room erupted in shouts and excited voices.

"The Silver Dame is here!"

"I hear she can heal with a touch."

"She's a witch!"

"Be careful she does not look at you, she may curse you to impotence."

Perce felt the tension around him. A few superstitious knights left the room.

"Is she a witch, Seigneur?" Perce asked.

Seigneur shook his head.

"Of course not!" Adelais giggled. He had forgotten she was there, still sitting on the edge of the table. She looked like a mischievous elf herself, at the same time magical and dangerous. Her nickname in court, before her breasts developed, had been Tiny, and in those days most, including Perce, had treated her as a boy. Then one day, almost over night, she had breasts—perky, bouncy things that pressed against her boyish clothes. Neither the viscount nor his wife could convince Adelais to dress as a lady, apparently not even on the night of her betrothal announcement.

"Then why do they call her a witch?" Perce demanded.

"Because she's an enemy, of course," Adelais said. "Really, Perce, I love you more than the Devil, but you can be such a clod at times!" She grabbed his arm and pulled him to the bench. Her leg pressed his. "I'm sorry, my squire. I was teasing only."

Perce glowered at her. The child in him found it easy to love her in her playful moments. But the squire, the emerging man with a driving desire to obtain the coveted knighthood, to be Sir Perce de Mendes and serve king and country—that man despised her antics. Yes, they enjoyed their moments in the stables, at risk of life and Perce's career. She was not only delightful, fun, enticing, and provocative, she was a danger. Now that she was betrothed to the royal family, any intimacy could destroy Perce's advancement. Perce needed his spurs, his knighthood, to take back Mendes. He would take his revenge as a knight.

"Come, Perce. This is a day for rejoicing. My Father—my apologies, Seigneur—your Seigneur has captured the Silver Dame! The leader of these Cathars! And now my father has two of her most famous rebels. And that delightful troubadour!" She pointed at Ramon.

"And you, dear Tiny, are engaged," Perce snapped back.

"Bah!" She spat at a scurrying rat.

"Not bad—for a boy."

She punched his arm. "Ow! You damn *milites* and your mail!"

"Your own fault."

"Bah!"

"So is it true? You're to marry?"

She put her hand on his thigh, squeezing. "Are you sad, dearest Perce? Don't worry. Marriage is just a convenience. He's royal or some nonsense." She winked, leaned close and whispered, "I'll still meet you in the stables!"

He pulled away, looking around quickly. He laughed to cover his fear. "Bah yourself!"

She pinched him. Hard. "Have a little fun, Perce. You are always so dour!"

"I like being dour."

"Oh, have it your way." She kissed him on the cheek, and danced across the room.

He watched her for a moment, then turned to face his Seigneur.

Perce remembered vividly every moment of the long journey to Carcassonne. The Dame was as serene and fearless as the Seigneur. She laughed often with her captors and talked to them as equals. Even when a soldier was rough with her, or threatened her virginity, she smiled. She smiled and she smiled. She was almost certainly not human. Who could smile in the face of her own ruin?

The Dame's capture should be a career builder. Perce's role in her capture moved him one step closer to his spurs, his title. He was of the age of knighthood, already eighteen summers since his birth in Mendes. If not for Sir Albaric's interference, he might already have achieved the dubbing ceremony. It would take only a good word from Seigneur, a man even the viscount feared and respected, and Seigneur had promised that word. Before the moon was out, Perce could be fasting for the dubbing ritual! He felt a surge of excitement. To be Sir Perceval de Mendes. He would continue to follow his Seigneur de Castlenau, his liege lord, wreaking havoc and revenge on the Southerners who took his family lands. But he would be a knight of the realm! The viscount could hardly refuse him a knighthood after their heroic capture of the Dame of the heretics.

"Seigneur?" Perce said. The single, cold eye turned on him. "Did you feel her power?"

Seigneur seemed to hesitate. "Adelais? She seems to have some power over you."

"No, Seigneur, I meant the Dame."

Seigneur nodded, once.

"Is that magic? Witchcraft?"

"Don't be stupid, Perce."

The great doors of the hall thudded open, and the herald's voice boomed: "The Dame Esclarmonde de Foix!" Albaric strode into the room, dragging the Dame. Perce felt anger as the Lion dragged her by her chains, and she barely kept her feet. He treated her as a dog on a leash rather than a Dame of noble birth, the sister of the Count of Foix. She was the most important living Perfect, the last remaining influential heretic in the South, and her people would die for her. She was precious.

Albaric pulled her roughly to a stop and she almost fell, but with light-footed grace managed to remain standing. Her plain silver dress covered all her flesh, except her face, which was plain but handsome. Perce knew she was at least as old as Seigneur, yet she possessed a calm beauty, and she smiled even now, her blue eyes full of defiance and life. Her hair was a cascade of shining silver.

How can such a woman be a witch?

When Dame Esclarmonde de Foix saw Seigneur, she immediately lifted her hand. Seigneur waved back.

The viscount stood. "I am the Viscount Hugh d'Arcis, Seneschal of Carcassonne for his royal majesty King Louis!"

Perce was surprised when the Silver Dame curtsied. "I am honored, lord."

The viscount scowled at Albaric. "Remove the Dame's chains. She is my guest."

The Dame curtsied again. "I am grateful, Lord Seneschal."

The Dame stood alone in front of the dais as a scowling Albaric withdrew.

Perce had never seen the viscount's hard-drinking, hard-fighting knights so furtive. They glanced at the Dame, then looked away—as if she might curse them.

Perce was astonished at who broke the uneasy silence. The troubadour Ramon crossed to the Dame Esclarmonde with a bench. He bowed low and said, "My Jewel." He stayed down on one knee, head dropped.

"Do not bow to me," said the Dame.

"I must. You are the Jewel."

Perce, like everyone else in the room, waited, silent, for an outburst from the archbishop or the viscount.

The Dame touched Ramon's golden hair. "I remember you, dear child. Please. Stand." She turned to face the viscount, who was as astonished as the rest. "I am grateful for the comfort of the viscount's hospitality."

Ramon placed the bench behind her. She sat and smiled at Ramon. "Thank you, my son."

Ramon bowed and stepped back. "My Jewel."

"I wish you to be comfortable, ma Dame," The viscount's voice sounded angry. "You are to be my guest for a short time." He tugged on his mustache. "And then the guest of the archbishop of Narbonne."

The Dame nodded at the archbishop. "I know your reputation, Your Grace."

The archbishop looked pale. "And I know yours," he said, his voice stiff. He glared back and forth between the hated witch and the viscount. Probably trying to decide who he hated more.

"Are you hungry, ma Dame?" The viscount stood up and clapped his hands and the servitor ran forward. "Food for the Dame, and wine!"

The Dame Esclarmonde shook her head. "My liege, do not trouble yourself. I was well treated and fed by your noble Seigneur de Castlenau. And I am sworn never to eat meat or drink of spirits." Her voice was almost hypnotic and Perce found himself looking at the plate of leftovers in front of him with sudden revulsion. A shard of gristle clung to a rib bone and an untouched trencher of mortrew was host to a cloud of buzzing flies.

"A loaf and goat's milk then?"

Again, a big, flashing smile. "The bread with gratitude, my liege. Perhaps some well water?"

"So be it!" the Viscount bellowed and his steward ran to the bailey to summon the pantler. "Ramon, sing another of your sweet ballads!"

Ramon stepped forward again into the brighter torch light around the dais and appeared flushed. He sat on the floor on a pile of clean rushes, between the Dame of the Mountain and the Lord of the County and tuned his lute. His dog settled at his feet.

Ramon sang of the old world, stories of the fall of Troy and other Homeric tales. And he sang of the Morte d'Arthur and of Perce's namesake, Sir Perceval and the Quest for the Holy Grail. Again, everyone in the room stopped their talking, unusual in this hall, and listened to the wondrous voice.

When the troubadour stopped singing, the Dame Esclarmonde stared at him for a long time. "Your voice is from God, my son. God bless you!"

The archbishop popped up like a crossbow bolt, his face as red as the embers of the fire. "Blasphemer!" He pointed at her. "You enchanter. Devilress! How dare you defile the name of God in my presence? Do you not know who I am?"

"I know who you are, Your Grace. I know well." Her voice was soft, like a mountain breeze.

"You'd do well to remember it, defiler of God's name."

She smiled, fearless. "Do I defile God's name, Your Grace?"

"Your guilt is clear."

"Then I am sorry for you, Your Grace."

"Despicable." He shouted and circled the table, his crozier tapping as he approached her.

"I am sorry I've distressed you, Your Grace." She bowed her head.

"Do you see the error of your ways?" He stood over her now, face purple with fury.

"Your Grace?" She looked up, her calm eyes like placid pools confronted with a summer thunderstorm. Even Perce, a terrified Catholic, wondered how she could be so dangerous.

"Admit your heresy!"

She smiled. "I'll pray for you, Your Grace, that you find the peace of Jesus."

"Defiler! Abjure! Renounce your evil ways!" The archbishop's voice was thunder, but his howling wind did not disturb her calm waters. Several knights crossed themselves and looked away in fear. "I warn you to keep silent, witch! You have already condemned yourself with your own words."

She stood up and held out her hands. "You have nothing to fear from me, Your Grace. I honor God."

"Then on your knees to the Almighty!" He yanked his ruby studded cross from his neck and swung it at her. In spite of his anger, some knights chuckled, perhaps remembering Ramon's earlier joke about the abbott with the ruby cross.

She did not flinch. "I honor your beliefs, Lord Archbishop. Can you not respect ours?"

"Fear God!"

"I do not have to fear God. God is love."

"You will burn in hellfire! Your words have condemned you."

"We are in hell already, Your Grace. It is heaven we must strive for." She sat down.

The archbishop glared at her, started to say something then stopped. Suddenly, without a word, he strode from the great hall, the silent crowd parting for him like the red sea.

The knights, squires and ladies watched the archbishop go and no one spoke. They listened to the clink of his staff receding until they could no longer hear it, then the room erupted in excitement.

Perce felt some satisfaction. The Dame had shown her heresy, and her demise would be a sure step to his knighthood. After the recounting, when the viscount would listen to the full report on the capture of the Dame, Perce's dubbing was assured. In capturing the Dame, Perce had killed six rebels with his own sword, more than any of the others. It made losing his gray stallion, a good friend, almost worthwhile.

Perce turned to his Seigneur to ask him to demand the recounting. Seigneur's eye was openly staring at the stool where the Dame sat, and it seemed that his face was full of admiration. In an evening full of surprises, Perce thought this show of emotion from the Seigneur was the most shocking of all.

Song of the Emperor

13

RAMON HAD FELT SOMEONE following him almost the instant he left the castle. He saw nothing in the shadows under the portcullis. He and Mauri walked lightly across the stone bridge that connected the viscount's castle with the vast hill top marketplace, his spear Zaleucus tapping on the stones. They merged quickly with the morning crowds. He turned and watched the small man in the brown robes dash out of the gates. He knew it was one of the archbishop's dogs, a Dominican monk and probably an Inquisitor.

Ramon glanced over his shoulder at the young Dominican, then, lute slung on his back and spear Zaleucus in hand, he plunged into the crowd, followed closely by Mauri with tail in full swing.

His stomach rumbled, enticed by the delightful scents of savory hotch-potch and roasted blackmanger on the carts. He bought some spiced carrot pies and sat in the spring sun on the castle's sloped counterscarp to eat.

The monk pretended to browse a cart of gundies and savory treats. Ramon smiled. The Inquisitor was not much more than a boy. The turmoil of the market filled the Place du Chateau with morning life: hollering merchants tried to outdo each other, women chattered with neighbors as they squeezed vegetables, starving beggars cried for alms and held out calloused hands for any scrap. All classes of people—from serf to lord on foot and horse—stirred up a great cloud of dust.

Ramon watched a one-legged minstrel play a small rebec and sing huskily for food. He tried to listen to the wailing song, forced a smile, and tossed the haggard man a coin. The "minstrel" stopped his ballad long enough to glare at Ramon before he went back to his clumsy strumming.

Ramon made sure the monk followed him. Mauri trotted at his

booted feet. He passed stalls of herbs and mustard from Dijon, and toolmakers, and an old, balding bootmaker who looked vaguely familiar.

Though he could have lost the monk easily, he decided this day must start with some fun to overcome the utter despondency he felt in this haunted place of death. He refused to descend into morbidity and fixed a smile on his face. He would have fun with the monk.

He circled around, followed by Mauri, until he was behind the Dominican. He saw the man's tonsured head whipping back and forth, looking for him.

Ramon jumped out from behind the bootmaker's cart with a shout, "Here I be!"

The monk jumped, stifling a shriek then put on his most intense disapproving frown, quite unconvincing on his youthful features. He couldn't be much more than a novice.

"Come, brother, if we are to play seek-and-find, I must have your name." Ramon said. "I'm sure you know of me." He bowed. "Ramon Trouvère at your service, brother." He picked up a bannock tart off the baker's cart, tossed the startled merchant a sou and held it out for the monk. The monk stared at him. Ramon shrugged, bit into the tart, and smiled. "Sworn a vow of silence, brother?"

Ramon guessed the monk to be too young to be a scowling Inquisitor. "Let me tell you a joke, brother."

The monk walked on but Ramon stopped him with the haft of Zaleucus. "Come, one joke." Mauri circled around the monk's feet, barking.

The handsome young man's eyes blinked quickly, darted left and right for an escape. He tried to duck into the crowd, but Ramon circled around and jumped in front of him with a cry, "Magic!"

Passersby gawked at Ramon, this fool dancing around an Inquisitor and shouting forbidden words. The nearby people, a moment before surging and flowing like the spring runoff of a mountain river, abruptly stilled. Children pointed and laughed. Parents stared, horrified. No one confronted or made fun of Dominicans! Ramon noticed several nobles in the square, watching him, including a red-headed lord from the viscount's festivities the night before. The viscount's daughter Adelais was on his arm.

An audience had gathered to watch the colorful clown and the Inquisitor, so Ramon raised his voice, "There once was a novice in a monastery vowed to silence." Ramon winked at the silent monk, who blushed bright red and tried to escape again. Ramon easily cut off his escape, and this time he threw his arm around the monk, squeezing his shoulder and holding him. "Now this monk had to spend his first ten years in total silence. He could speak only three words every year."

Ramon noticed the Lady Adelais and her consort had pressed through the smiling crowd and stood only two strides away. Adelais appeared even more boy-like in daylight, with her plain, smiling face, short hair and men's leggings and tunic. Ramon continued his joke: "At the end of his first year, the Abbot allowed the novice to say his three words. 'Terrible food, father,' was all the novice said. Another year passed, and the Abbot asked him again to say his three words. The monk said, 'My head itches' and he scratched his tonsured head. The next year he said, 'Too much silence.' Finally, a year later, the monk said, 'I'm leaving, father.' And the Abbot, grateful, said, 'Thank God, my son. You do nothing but complain.'"

He felt the monk's shoulders quiver. Ramon glanced sideways and saw the lip tremble in a half-smile. It was the Lady Adelais and the red-headed lord who broke the silence with their laughter. Then the crowd let go, cheering.

The young monk pulled away from Ramon, turned, and stared at him with a look of incredulity. Ramon saw that he wanted to smile, maybe even laugh, but the monk's training took over. He scratched his tonsured head. Ramon winked in reply. "Your head itches?"

At last, the monk smiled.

"Forgive me, brother. I am Ramon the jester. Ramon the minstrel. I cannot help myself."

Intense brown eyes fixed on Ramon now. "The heretic troubadour."

"Come, brother, you say heretic, I say entertainer. Did you not enjoy my songs in the viscount's hall last night?"

"I was not in the hall."

"Ah. So you follow me now for a tune?" Without waiting for an answer, Ramon spun his lute to the end of its twine and settled it in the crook of his arm.

"No. No Devil's songs!" The young man held up his hands as if to physically push away the music.

"Monks can sing like birds, can't they brother?"

"Holy chants!" He crossed himself.

"You're a Southerner aren't you? From Carcassonne?" To Ramon, it seemed impossible that any Southerner would join the religious orders, but the man's accent betrayed him. "What's your name, brother?"

"I am the clerk of the Inquisition!" the young man snapped, and he tried to glare but failed miserably. "You must fear me."

Ramon could only smile. "Then I feel for you. How must it feel to record those miseries?" The handsome young monk glared—it appeared more of a pout. "Give me your name, brother."

"Have a care, Troubadour!" The sleeves of the monk's cassock fell back to reveal gnarly forearms, almost certainly the working muscles of a farmer's son.

"What good farmer raised you, brother? I might know the family."

The monk crossed himself.

"Come, your name. Your name, or I'll tell another Dominican joke!"

The crowd, forgotten by the monk, seemed to press closer, perhaps anxious for another joke, or just wanting to hear what the Inquisitor would say.

"I am Brother Jaie. And I know who you are."

"Yes. I told you." Ramon winked.

"No. You are Ramon, son of Musette the witch! I have the records! Brother Duranti has recognized you."

Ramon strummed the lute to steady himself. The twelve-year-old boy had been recognized! Brother Duranti was the Chief Inquisitor, the man who had complained about his monk joke, the joke that saved him from torture and the pit. But how could the man recognize Ramon as the twelve-year-old boy who had screamed curses all those years ago? Of course, Ramon recognized Duranti as the very man who had condemned his mother.

Ramon bowed. "Ramon the troubadour, son of Musette and Burc the Tailor, at your service, good Brother Jaie." He forced a smile, but the monk's revelation had obliterated any clownish feelings. It was as if the monk had punched Ramon with his big callused hands, the crusty fists of a farm-raised Southerner.

The monk's scowl was intense, but there was something in the brown eyes, a message of warning, a fellow Occitanian pleading for Ramon to leave. Leave now, or suffer, they seemed to say. "I will be the brother at the clerk's tables, recording your confessions for the Inquisition."

"Then I'll be famous," Ramon said, and he bowed.

The monk sighed, shook his head, then abruptly pushed through the crowd and disappeared. The crowd roared with laughter once more. Lady Adelais and her red-headed consort laughed the hardest. Lady Adelais laughed so hard the tears were flowing. "You are a precious one, to be true, Ramon."

Her consort waved his arm and shouted, "Move on, friends. No more jokes today!" The crowd reluctantly went back to their shopping.

The young noble was dressed as a lord in fine silk and velvet, scarlet and gold. His surcoat was emblazoned with a gold falcon, against a crimson field. Even his curly hair was the color of strawberries. His sword's hilt glittered with jewels. Could he be Adelais' brother? He had the same red hair as the viscount.

"Thank you, lord." Ramon bowed slightly.

"He's not your lord, Ramon Troubadour," said Adelais.

Ramon bowed to Adelais. "Fairest maiden, I have sung in the highest court, fought mighty battles, braved the unspeakable, slain my enemies, all but for a moment to bask in your angelic presence."

She giggled.

"She's no lady," said the red-headed noble. "Look at her, Ramon. Dressed like a man. Scandalous!"

Ramon looked at her. She managed to appear nymph-like and clever, and her smile was utterly charming, but somehow, she was alluringly feminine in spite of her clothes.

The young man laughed. "I am Squire Perce de Mendes, in the

service of Seigneur. You just call me Perce."

Ramon glanced at the young redhead. If this Seigneur had a squire so richly dressed, the lord must be a powerful master. "I'm sorry. Who is the Seigneur? The viscount?"

"Not *the* Seigneur. Seigneur! Everyone's heard of him!"

"Seigneur who?"

"Seigneur de Castlenau. He has no name so far as I know. Some call him Cyclops. The one-eyed lord."

"No name? If you are his squire how can you not know his name?"

Perce's handsome young features were spoiled with a scowl. "No name and no colors. He wears only white." He stared hard at the troubadour. "For a singer you ask a lot of questions."

"Good questions!" Adelais snapped, then wrapped her arm around Ramon's shoulders. "Come, Ramon, I think we shall be friends."

Squire Perce nodded. "Anyone brave enough to insult an Inquisitor like that, he is a friend of mine."

She giggled. "It's all right, Ramon Troubadour. We'll protect you from the Dominicans. We are admirers, dear Troubadour."

"Trouvère," said Ramon with a quick smile.

"Tosh, good Troubadour." She astonished him by kissing his cheek. "The Inquisitors can find other fuel for their fires. You're under my protection now. And you are my troubadour, not one of those horrid trouvères. I want mystical songs. I want songs of Heracles and his labors, not saintly hymns. I want to hear of knightly love, not quests for some idiotic holy cup."

Ramon stared at her in astonishment. She had very nearly blasphemed. Her boy's clothes were emblematic of her courage, too, it seemed, or her father's absolute power in Occitania. "I am your humble servant."

Mauri barked, scratching at Ramon's boots.

"And who is this little creature?" Adelais held out her arms. Mauri jumped into her outstretched hands and she held him to her chest. He licked her cheek. "Oh, he is delightful."

Ramon was now hopelessly in love with Adelais. He had been determined to hate her, this daughter of the viscount whom he had sworn to kill. But this fearless, laughing girl—how could he not adore her?

"So, here's this leering fool, insulting Inquisitors and archbishops and viscounts," said Perce with a smile. "He looks an idiot, and speaks with a loose tongue. But he's no jester. He carries a sting, doesn't he?"

Ramon twirled his spear like an acrobat.

"See, very pretty! But can you use it?" Perce was a blur of scarlet, as fast as a diving hawk. Ramon barely registered the movement, his eyes locking on the glitter of metal as the sword thrust at him.

Ramon's daily training triggered a block. There was no calculating it, only the instinct of defense. But Zaleucus spun down and out and Ramon stepped back into a lunging bear stance, one leg dropping back, knee bent. Zaleucus knocked the sword aside easily.

"Oh, very well done! Did I not tell you, Adelais? Not a harmless jester at all!" Perce took two short half-steps, his sword stabbing, then quickly sweeping sunwise in a clever slicing motion. Ramon grinned, aware of the laughing children and the disapproving parents who stood in a circle around the two men. He enjoyed a workout and this squire was damnably good. This time Ramon counter-attacked, going low for the feet, a diversion, then levering hard around, spinning his entire body and bringing the haft of the spear to within a finger's width of Perce's nose.

"Fantastic!" shouted Perce, staring at the hovering haft. "You bested me."

Ramon bowed. "I think you held back, squire Perce."

Perce winked. "I would not waste your voice. Yet you were admirably good. Yes, admirably." He sheathed his sword and held out his arm. "Come, we will be friends, good Ramon."

Ramon gripped the man's outstretched arm in the northern fashion, clenching him around the forearm. "Friends."

They strolled the market. Adelais held Mauri, who sat comfortably in the crook of her arm. Perce remained ever smiling, often stopping to speak with the young ladies who shopped the carts of combs and jewels. He seemed very popular with the ladies and they clung to his arm and giggled when he whispered in their ears.

Ramon liked them both and he needed new friends in this city of enemies, especially with his new allies, the Grand Duo, Doré and Osric, in the pit, and his precious Jewel trapped in the viscount's tower. Yet now he felt the urgent need to get to the Baug, to let them know what had happened. It occurred to him that this magnificently attired squire might be his enemy, a spy.

"I smell nutmeg tarts!" Adelais put down Mauri and bought four tarts. Mauri whined and held up his little paw and she chuckled as she fed him an entire tart. They washed them down with cuckoo-foot ale, thick with the flavor of ginger, basil and anise. The aroma was as delightful as the taste.

"I hear the Baug is in the city," Perce said, wiping away crumbs from his chin.

"I saw them once in Paris!" Adelais said. "Their horses can almost talk! They're so funny. They walk on hind legs!"

"No!" Perce winked at Ramon, his eyebrows lifting as if to say, *Humor her.*

"Yes, on their hind legs! And they can tell your fortune."

"The horses?"

She punched his mailed shoulder. "Damned armor! Not the horses, idiot. The Baug have tellers of fortunes."

Ramon frowned. "Won't the Inquisition be after them, then?"

"No! They're entertainers, Ramon! Really! You're not a clod, you know better." She grinned. "You would love them, Ramon Troubadour. They dance. They throw knives! They sing! Their horses can dance, too! And they have a wrestling bear, and acrobats, and—"

Perce laughed. "If they are so splendid, why would they come to Carcassonne?"

"They sent my father a letter, telling us they performed in Toulouse. I told my father it was to be my engagement present!" She grinned like a boy.

Ramon smiled. The letter to the viscount had been his idea. Since he was sure Adelais would eventually discover that he knew the people of the Baug—after all, he was an entertainer himself—Ramon decided there was no harm in disclosure, especially as she was an admirer of the Baug, and no supporter of the Inquisition. He needed allies, especially powerful ones. "I am friends of the Baug Balar."

"Non!" She stared at him, those childlike eyes growing wide. "Why didn't you tell me? Ramon!" She spat like a boy. "We must go right now! Right now, do you hear me?"

"I think the whole marketplace heard you," Perce said.

She tugged Ramon's arm, leading him towards the central hill road. "Come, you can tell us as we walk how you know them."

Adelais held his arm, totally inappropriate behavior considering his profession and her noble status, but he could hardly stop her.

"I am a trouvère, dear Adelais."

"A troubadour!" She snapped it, but she laughed instantly.

"I have played with the Baug in several cities," Ramon admitted.

"But you were not in Paris. I didn't see you there. I would have remembered."

"I was singing for the king," Ramon said, remembering that season, five summers ago, when he had played for Blanche de Castille and her son Louis, the king of France. He had used Blanche de Castille then, as he planned on using Adelais now.

"The king!" Now it was Perce's turn to be impressed. "You played for our king?"

Ramon smiled. "One night only. The queen mother wanted me to stay, but I was due to play for the doge in Venice."

"The doge!" Adelais' grip tightened. "He's my distant cousin. My father promised to take me there, then this damnable crusade got in the way."

Adelais stopped to inspect a cart of jewelry near the gate to the lower market, browsing the necklaces of garnet and silver and the broaches of bronze. She picked up a Roman gold torque.

The jeweler ambushed them at once. "Very valuable, ma Dame, very valuable—"

"Nonsense. I can tell by the weight it's not gold!" She tossed it carelessly on the cart.

But Ramon wasn't paying attention to her spoiled antics. He stared at the broach and stopped breathing.

"Ah, master has good taste!" The merchant picked up the nine-pointed star pendant and handed it to him. Trembling, Ramon turned it over in his hand. It was the size of a child's fist, silver and gold and studded with coral and turquoise. And heavy.

"How much?"

"Forty *deniers*, master, only forty."

It might as well have been a gold bezant—two years' pay. Still, Ramon couldn't put it down. Doré's pendant. He was sure of it.

"Very unique, master! Nine-pointed star, see? You'll never see another!"

"Where did you get it?" Ramon stared at the fine star jewel, completely in its spell.

The merchant snatched it out of his hand. "Good master mustn't ask such things."

"Can you hold it for me?"

The merchant laughed. "Am holding it now, aren't I?" He held out his hairy hand with the massive pendant.

"You like it?" Adelais giggled and Ramon turned, startled. "Shopping for a lady already, Ramon?"

Ramon managed to meet her searching gaze. "Nay, Lady. Tis a memory only."

She smiled. "I'm certain of that." She glared at the merchant. "Give this boy that pendant and the viscount will be grateful."

"But lady—" The man closed his hand over the jewel, hiding it.

"Stop whining, you grasping old frog. How much jewelry have I bought from you?" Her booted foot tapped.

"Lady, this is very valuable, very unique, see the jewels—"

"Nonsense! Common stones and poor silverwork!"

"Lady, tis my best piece—"

"Only because you stole it!"

The small man dropped his face. "I bought it lady! From one of your father's lieutenants—"

"Then he stole it!" She laughed, a chirping giggle that made the passersby pause and stare at her. "You have your cart here at my father's sufferance. I'll not argue with you. Just think of this as a tax."

Ramon frowned. "Lady Adelais—"

"A gift, dear Troubadour. Never had our chateau felt such joy before you came with your songs of romance and adventure. Take it as a gift of your patron."

He shook his head. "I sing for you because it pleases me—"

"Nonsense!" She snatched the pendant from the trembling merchant. "You sing to save your skin from the Master Torturer." She held out Doré's jewel. "Take it. As a down payment on your salary if you like."

Still, he didn't move.

"Take it, Ramon, or I'll pout."

Perce nudged Ramon. "Don't let her pout, Ramon. It'll last days!"

She held it out, smiling. When he didn't move, she untangled the chain and hung it around his neck.

"See, Ramon. I won't claw you. I'm a gentle cat." She tilted her head back to enjoy the sun. "A fine day for the tourney!"

"I suppose."

She stared at him. "But surely you're going. Perce is fighting this afternoon!"

"I don't like the *bohort*."

"Everyone likes the tourney!" Perce snapped.

"Bloody and violent," Ramon said.

"They fight with blunted weapons. Don't be silly," Adelais said.

"People are still hurt."

"You're squeamish!" She howled. "Ramon's squeamish!"

Ramon nodded. "I am, Lady. I see more than enough bloodshed without seeking it out for sport."

"Come. I'll not take no for an answer. You're coming to the *plaisance*! You'll take us to the Baug this morn. I'll take you to the tourney this afternoon! We'll embarrass poor Perce by cheering for his opponent!"

"Adelais, I—"

"I seem to repeat myself a little too often with you, Ramon!" Her voice was stern. She pointed at the nine-pointed star pendant. "Well, they don't really match, do they, such a fine jewel with your jester's garb? We'll have to do something about your ridiculous clothing."

"This tunic was my master's." He turned the pendant so that one of the rays of the star pointed up, as he had seen Doré wear it.

"You do fuss! Fine. But those leggings and that hat must go!"

"I'm an entertainer!"

"Don't pout! Fine, we'll keep the hat. The leggings are ridiculous." She put her hand on his skinny thighs. "I like the boots though. Very fine craftsmanship."

Ramon felt the heat of his own blush. "Lady, it is beneath you to escort such as I."

"Such as I!" Her laughter made eyes turn, and he felt the heat rise in his face. "Oh, Ramon, you are so dull! I do as I please! I cannot abide these dull lords and ladies. Who will dare stop me?"

"But Lady!"

"Call me that again, and I'll have you hanging in that pit yet." Then with a smile, she took his hand. "Come. Let's go to your friends in the Baug!"

He pulled his hand away. He couldn't predict what would happen if he appeared suddenly at the Baug, especially when the children saw him. "I want to visit my old home. To see if my birth-house still stands."

She stroked his arm. "There. See, we can do both. Where did you live?"

He sighed. "Near the Tour du Casteras."

Perce said, "It's on the way to the Baug Balar."

Ramon knew it was pointless to argue and it seemed that everyone was staring at them. They passed through the gates of the lower city and stepped into the deep shadow of the narrow suicide way, the channel between the two gates where an enemy could be trapped and slain by arrows from the slits above. From there they stepped into brilliant sunlight in the ghetto of crusting mud and hovels. It stank from the pigs running loose among the refuge tossed in the streets. When he was a boy, the lower city had been as fair as the upper, and he had lived with his mother and father by the south wall in a small daub and wattle hut. There would always be long lines of people at their door, people waiting to see Musette the healer, Musette the midwife.

Ramon fought the despair of the sudden memory as they arrived in the small square, jammed with temporary hovels.

"Not happy memories, I'm guessing," Adelais said

Ramon didn't answer. He resented her presence, and she must have sensed it because she grabbed Perce's arm and pulled him to the opposite side of the square.

The west marketplace was smaller and less noisy than he remembered it. In his youth, the merchants had rolled in their carts of produce before cock's crow, fighting over the vacant corners. The loud arguing of hawkers and craftsmen woke Ramon each morning of his childhood, and he ran out the door, ignoring the calls of his mother to be careful.

He remembered the crowded market with its endless rows of wine-sellers, ale-makers and sellers of livestock. Now the bustling marketplace of his memories was a ghetto.

"I am home, Mama," he whispered.

He stopped in front of his birth house and the tears came.

The house was abandoned. The daub fell out between the timbers in large dried chunks, and the shakes had fallen off the steeply pitched roof, lying scattered on the ground.

Ramon squatted and hugged Mauri. "There are ghosts here." Their names were Burc and Musette. A father and mother, one hanged, one burned to death by the father of Adelais.

He could see them, the ghosts of his beloved parents. They stood at the door, smiled at him, but didn't speak. Ramon's hand instinctively reached for the little leather pouch hanging around his neck, where he had a lock of her hair.

"Mama," he said, his voice catching with emotion. "I miss you, Mama." And he saw her there, unaged and perfect. The ghost waved at him, smiled, and Musette cried as well. Then, suddenly, she was gone.

He brushed away his tears. He had seen enough. The past was gone. He had returned home to rescue the future, to save the Dame from his mother's fate—and to abolish his past.

But he had found that his ghosts remained.

14

FLICKERING SHADOWS lashed across Brother Jaie's face in the torch light. He squinted as his quill scratched observations. He stopped writing when no one spoke. At his feet a rat squeaked but he kicked it away and reread his notes:

Brother Duranti: Confess, my son. Confession is the first step to salvation! The Church wishes to welcome you back to her sanctity.

The accused: no answer

Brother Duranti: Proceed Francis

Master Torturer: Oui, mon Père.

Jaie sighed, his quill poised as he peered in the candlelight, noting every detail. The light sputtered in a macabre dance across the pale white features of Master Torturer Francis. Jaie hated this necessary violence. And he hated this room in the undercroft of the bishop's palace, reeking with the stale urine of terrified subjects, rat droppings and the vomit of both victims and witnesses. True, the torturer would not shed blood. The Church may not shed blood in pursuit of confession or redemption and Francis was most skilled and diligent, the viscount's best interrogator. He would break bones, stretch limbs and even burn flesh, but not one drop of blood would be shed.

Jaie heard a loud crack. The dandy rebel Doré didn't scream. He wrote: *The accused heretic's thumb cracked.* He glanced at the journal and added: *The accused did not scream.*

He sighed again and glanced behind his table at the archbishop who sat with crossed legs in the bishop's chair. The archbishop rarely missed an Inquiry, eyes always sparkling with interest, no matter how long the questions went on. He was not an Inquisitor, but he was their most avid sponsor in Occitania, and legate for the pope. Thank God His Holiness thought to send so diligent an advocate. The archbishop smiled now, clearly delighted at this opportunity to save another heretic.

Jaie thanked God for Amiel at every mass.

Brother Duranti stood in front of the clerk's table and stared at the prisoner. The Dominican leaned on the writing table, his dark skin drawn as taut as dry leather on a soldier's shield. A holy brother of privation, Brother Duranti was a man of his vows. Jaie had never seen him smile.

The heretic clenched his teeth. Jaie made a note that his honor, the master torturer, was applying a thumbscrew. The prisoner spat blood and yelled: "*To hellfire with you!*"

Brother Duranti's voice was kind. "Now, my son, we do not wish you to suffer. But we know that through suffering your soul will be cleansed. But confess, and you will—God willing—find your way finally to grace."

The prisoner refused to scream, a sure sign he was under the power of some demon, even as the screws crushed his finger with a loud crack that echoed in the vaulted room. The dandy passed out.

"Revive the wretch." Impatient, Brother Duranti strode to his table and sat on a chair. Beside him was Brother Ferrier and Jaie's own confessor, Frère Balfour, the diocesan deputy. Balfour signaled Jaie to cease recording, and his quill hovered, waiting.

"This dandy is certainly a sorcerer!" Brother Duranti snapped. "He resists with inhuman calm! He is entrenched in the Devil's ways!" They all crossed themselves.

"Without a confession we cannot even excommunicate him," Balfour said.

"I do not seek his excommunication! I seek his renunciation."

They all nodded. Brother Jaie looked at the dandy. This rebel was almost certainly the most infamous prisoner they had ever investigated, known throughout the lands for attacks on the king's men, a personal friend of the ousted count of Carcassonne. Besides the Dame herself—a prisoner the viscount put under his protection—the Inquisition had never had so great an opportunity to compile a list of heretics and rebels. Handled well, this one prisoner's knowledge could bring an end to years of conflict. If only he would admit his faults.

Jaie stared at the too-pretty face. How could something so attractive be evil? Sandy hair, long and wavy, framed an angel's features. How could such loveliness be touched by the Devil's hand? Jaie grew angry at himself for lustful thoughts. He looked away, feeling his own heat. Where did these feelings come from? Lately, he found himself more and more drawn to the physical, away from the spirit, and it infuriated him. He punished himself every evening with bloody mortification and other privations, but always the urges returned. He had felt the same, earlier today, when confronted with the peculiar jester-troubadour. Almost certainly, Ramon Troubadour would be arrested in the next few days. Soon it would be Ramon on the table, his foolish grin disappearing as he saw the first of the master torturer's tools. Again, those lustful thoughts. Jaie felt the rise of something terrible and uncomfortable under his robe, and his forehead prickled with sweat. But Ramon was so beautiful! He could only be a servant of Satan himself.

Jaie smiled, remembering his confrontation with Ramon yesterday. Always the bright smile and the jokes. And the voice! Jaie felt a flush of heat, realized Duranti was staring at him. He concentrated on his breathing, half closing his eyes.

"We will try the iron," said the master torturer.

The dandy groaned as torturer Francis untied the tunic. They would lay the hot iron on the dandy's bare white flesh, not piercing the flesh, mortifying it for God's great purpose, but not drawing blood.

Jaie hated the smell of burnt flesh and acrid smoke and the screams that haunted his nights. But he admired the skill of the torturer. The master Frances never crippled or killed a prisoner, a reputation of which he was justly proud. He always obtained the necessary confession—eventually. The master torturer saved many souls.

When a heretic finally understood the error of his ways it was a beautiful thing. *More beautiful than the cooing of turtle doves or the sweet song of a chaffinch,* he thought. Yes. *Far better, far more beautiful, to see the godless find God than to revel in the perfection of God's universe.* A confessing heretic begged for God's Church and renounced his evil ways. What work of the Church could be more rewarding than the conversion of a heretic? Even when the secular court sent the unrepentant to the flames—the heretics who were excommunicated from the body of the Church for refusing to recant—there was still a feeling of satisfaction. Jaie believed that flame purified and saved the soul of the condemned. He had seen it many times: the heretics' anger was transformed to terror and made them realize their error as the flames blackened their skin and their corrupt flesh melted. And perhaps their fear of God was enough to send them to purgatory instead of straight to hell. They almost always cried out for forgiveness, asked to be freed from the flames.

This dandy was different. He resisted torture with magical calm. Jaie had no doubt he would face the flames with equal serenity. And that was always unique. Only twelve in his memory had been so calm in the face of torture and the flames. All twelve had been Perfecti, the leaders of the Devil's church.

Frère Balfour called a short recess as the torturer Frances heated the irons. The heat from the furnace was oppressive. Thankful for the moment to relax, Brother Jaie stood and stretched. His hand was cramping from endless scribing. The interrogation was far longer than normal for an inquiry of this sort.

He bowed to the archbishop. "Your Grace, may I be excused a brief moment?"

The archbishop nodded and extended his ring. Brother Jaie kissed the gloved hand and left the chamber. He needed a little fresh air. He tasted the tang of urine and the smoke of seared flesh. He climbed the narrow stairs and emerged in the courtyard of the bishop's palace. He hadn't realized it was almost sunset. They had been seeking a confession since morning matins, breaking only for prayers and a modest lunch with the Cistercians.

The blossoming lilacs cast long shadows in the courtyard, their perfume enveloping him. Soon the honeysuckle would burst into glory. All of God's beauty! Why couldn't the heretics see this divine beauty? It was all so ridiculous: the Cathar heretics believed this lovely garden was an illusion, an illusion created by their own cravings, and not a divine creation. So misguided. If only he could teach them.

Jaie paused by an arch of linden trees and looked out over the city.

From the bishop's gardens he could see over the two city walls to the valley below, a verdant green that clothed the twin mountains, the *Earth's Bosoms* as the pagans called them. Couldn't they see this was god's awesome art, not the breasts of some pagan earth goddess? He scanned the city, busy and dusty now that the mud had begun to dry. In the lower city he could just see the Jewish market, where the Baug Balar had their camp, a brilliant splash of color in the midst of grey stone. Soon, he knew, the archbishop would move against them. The Baug Balar were famous for spreading vile heresies. Archbishop Amiel would become famous as the man who stopped them.

Jaie sighed. He understood the great work. He understood that they saved so many. But he couldn't reconcile his feelings of horror and revulsion whenever he descended to the reeking vault below his feet. Every night, in his tiny cell, he whipped himself with the seven tails, trying to beat out the feelings of compassion he felt. He knew the work was good, but why did it feel so wrong? He saw the agony on countless faces—children, women, men—and it agonized him. He barely slept at night.

Jaie looked up from his dark thoughts as he heard the guards challenge someone at the gate.

Two big men, one in yellow, the other in white, approached on horseback. Jaie held his breath. The viscount himself and the one-eyed Seigneur! Should he run and warn the archbishop and Duranti? Both of these men terrified him for different reasons: the viscount because he was the lord of all the land and the archbishop's main rival for power; Seigneur because—well, every sane man in Europe feared Seigneur. Only Diableteur inspired more awe than the scarred, one-eyed crusader with his empty eye socket and disfigured flesh. The wavy golden hair, bright white mail and cloak, and the left side of his face, all so pure and beautiful; then the appalling transformation, the right side of his face creased into deep scars, the missing eartip, the bald patch—and that horrible blank eye. Jaie could see that he had been a beautiful man, once. He still was, in his way, with his broad shoulders, the muscles that pressed hard against his mail, and the golden hair. What horrors this creature had known. A lord with no name, no colors and no emblem, who never smiled, rarely spoke and inspired fear from all in the city.

Jaie shivered and bowed low until the horses stopped.

"My Lord Viscount. Seigneur de Castlenau!"

"Get up, Jaie." The viscount's voice was mocking.

The white knight, Seigneur de Castlenau, said nothing as he dismounted. He held the reins of the viscount's horse as the great lord swung down.

"Jaie," Seigneur acknowledged, coldly.

"My lords, we did not expect you." Jaie could not keep the tremble from his voice.

"We are here to witness the interrogation," said Seigneur, his voice a low rumble, as if he was unused to speech.

"My lord, the inquiries into heresy are closed to the secular."

"Nothing is closed to me," said the viscount.

The viscount and Seigneur swept past Jaie, their long capes lifting.

Jaie stared for a moment in shock, terrified, certain some sort of power struggle was about to ensue. Finally, he ran after the two lords, bounding down the stone steps in time to see that the assembly was equally surprised by the abrupt entrance. The archbishop rose from his chair.

"My Lord Viscount? Seigneur de Castlenau. What brings you to this holy court?"

Jaie slipped past the two lords and took his seat, noticing that only the viscount kissed the holy ring. Seigneur merely nodded as if to an equal. "We wish to witness the proceedings," said the viscount.

"Witnesses must be invited. This is a closed proceeding."

"Invite me, Your Grace."

"Of course, my lord." The archbishop clapped his hands. "Chairs! Quickly!" His clerk, the bumbling Verdun, ran from the cellar and returned a few moments later with another priest, both carrying chairs. They were placed at Jaie's table, and suddenly Jaie found himself surrounded by the great lords of Occitania. He found he couldn't breathe.

Brother Duranti looked down his long nose at both of the lords and seemed to sneer as he rapped the table. "Call to order. We will continue to inquiry. Revive the heretic in God's name."

What could bring the noble viscount and horrible Seigneur to a church court? Did they not trust the viscount's own torturer to extract the needed information? Jaie glanced often to his left, fascinated by the scarred face and single eye of the Seigneur. Although the viscount was the lord of all, the Seigneur was the more fascinating of the two.

Doré's eyes fluttered open, piercing green and alive with hate, fixed now on the new arrivals.

"Come for some entertainment?" said the voice, suddenly strong and defiant. The dandy spat blood, splattering Jaie's parchment.

"I came for information," said the viscount, rising to his full height, his head brushing the low cellar rafters.

"This is irregular," said Duranti.

The viscount spared the Inquisitor a single glance, and the monk instantly sat. The lord circled the table and looked down on the dandy's pale face. "The great Doré de Costonot. You do not seem so terrible now."

Jaie couldn't see Doré's face with the viscount standing in front of the table, but the voice was defiant and full of sudden energy. "I feel your pain. The king's leash chokes you, does it not?"

Jaie held his breath, expecting the viscount's fury. Instead, in a calm voice, he said, "I require the names of all of your rebels."

"Just step outside. Every person on the streets hates you. The entire city is ready to rise up against you."

"The names of your intimates."

"I love them all."

"The names of your lieutenants."

"They're all my lieutenants."

"Tell me, or we'll have your big friend Osric castrated."

Jaie waited in the long silence, with the others, his pen hovering, waiting. Neither men had spoken in anger. Both spoke without emotion, with controlled voices.

"The archbishop threatened that yesterday," Doré said, finally.

"I'll set loose the Diableteur on your friend."

"You will, regardless."

The viscount returned to his seat. "I shall enjoy this." He nodded at the master torturer. "Proceed."

The Master Torturer lifted a rod from the brazier. It glowed red. "Ready to continue, Brother."

"Do so," Duranti said.

Torturer Frances folded back the untied tunic of the dandy.

"Dear God in heaven," Frances said.

Duranti spun around. "What is it Frances?"

Frances stepped back.

Jaie gasped, horrified.

The white Seigneur snorted laughter. The viscount said nothing, but simply stared.

The archbishop stood up.

And everyone stared at the dainty pink nipples of a young woman.

15

THE LOCAL JEWISH children ran with Baug offspring, laughing and playing in the mud. Nevara could not help smiling. Magba's eleventh son saw Nevara, ran to her, and reached up his arms to be picked up. She swept him up out of the mud and swung him around as he screamed "Wheeeeee!"

Now six other Baug children tugged on her long trailing sleeves. She picked them up one by one, spun them, then set them down with a spank and an "on your way to lessons!" As they ran off, she yelled after them in Novgorodian, "Do not leave the camp!"

The camp was buzzing with Mayday preparations. Even pregnant Magba, the matriarch of the Baug, forked hay from a wagon to the horses while two of her older children shoveled dung. Everyone worked in the Baug and nearly all of their income from their traveling shows went to the upkeep of their precious horses and the children. It was not a rich life, but a good one.

The horses grew excited as Nevara approached, crowding around her and leaving their hay. Izzy and Wizi pushed against her, their soft muzzles rolling back to smell her. She kissed them all, one by one, fussing especially over the pregnant mares.

"Ostara is getting close," Magba said, wiping the sweat from her brown forehead. Her muddy hands left a streak of dirt on her handsome lined face. Magba bent to look at Ostara's milk bag.

Nevara ducked under from the other side and saw that Ostara's teat seeped. "A couple days." It worried her a little. The Baug was used to fleeing with young children, but if Ramon accomplished his rescue then half of Carcassonne's garrison would be pursuing them.

Ostara went back to her haystack and Nevara pointed at Magba's belly. "You as well, mother." Magba might end up giving birth in the back of a bouncing covered wagon as they fled the soldiers. It wouldn't be the first time. But they might also have a newborn foal trying to keep up, with great, thundering war horses galloping in pursuit.

She kissed Magba's cheeks. The Mother smelled of earth and mud, a wholesome musk, and faintly of horse dung.

"Bah. I am weeks off yet." Magba straightened her loose gown. She barely showed and she would work right up until delivery and the very day after.

Nevara adored Magba, the very walking incarnation of the Earth Mother, always full of bright energy, never tiring, ever at work or in labor. Her word was the law, but she was rarely harsh, always just. She wore plain loose gowns, grew more beautiful as each year passed, with her always flushed sun-kissed complexion and plump cheeks. She was wise in all worldly things, and her moods went with the seasons: in spring she had boundless energy, in summer she blossomed, in fall she was breathtaking, and in winter her mood shifted to cool and pensive.

"A boy," Nevara said.

"I know," Magba said. "I hope Ramon comes today."

"He's already on his way," Nevara said. She knew it with certainty. "And with company." She reached out her arm and Bubo fluttered down from a nearby rooftop, sidling up to her shoulder.

Magba nodded. "I think the Inquisitors will come today as well."

She spoke the word Inquisitors in the barbaric northern tongue, for in Novgorod there was no word for such creatures.

"I have hidden my tools."

"That is well." She smiled as a gang of Novgorod children ran through the mud, three of them her own. "Back to your lessons!" she shouted, her voice a bellow. The children halted immediately, then ran off to the great pavilion. They didn't fear her, no one in the Baug feared Magba, but the people never wanted to disappoint the mother.

"We will have to flee two days after Mayday," Nevara said.

"So soon?" Mother took a long breath. She looked unusually fatigued.

"I have seen it."

"Then we will pack the day before." Magba's calm facade dropped and revealed naked fear. It was one thing for the Baug to be involved in one of Ramon's rescues of a nobody, some condemned heretic in a small village. But here in Carcassonne, if they managed an escape at all, the archbishop, the county Inquisitor, the viscount and an entire army would be in pursuit.

"Is the prize worth so much risk?" Nevara hadn't meant to ask it. She never questioned Magba. But the children, the people, the horses—everything was at risk.

"Life is risk, child." Magba's calm masquerade returned.

"Ramon lied to me about the Jewel."

Wizi nudged her from behind and nipped her calf for attention, but Nevara ignored her baby.

"Not a lie, Nevara." Magba's voice sounded like a sigh. "He just did not tell you everything."

"The Jewel is a person."

"The Dame Esclarmonde. A great lady."

"But just a lady! And a Christian! We risk so much."

"One life is worth every risk, child." She smiled, pure sunshine. "The Silver Dame is the hope of these Southerners."

"Not our people!"

"Ramon's people. He is our people. What has always made our people great is our willingness to sacrifice to help others."

"But why is she special?"

"For the same reason we are special." Magba reached out a big calloused working hand and rested it on Nevara's shoulder. "Nevara. We stood against tyranny in our own city and went into exile because of it, taking those of our people who would not suffer misrule. Here, we have a chance to make a difference for these people. The Jewel is their holy woman. She has saved countless lives. She takes away their suffering."

"She is their mother? Their Magba?"

Magba smiled with the full warmth of spring sunshine. "More precious than that. She is their priestess. Their inspiration."

Nevara leaned forward until their foreheads touched. "As you are mine."

"Bah!" Magba pushed her away.

Nevara laughed. "I will conjure a storm for the night of our escape."

Magba sighed. "More mud. Please, not so much rain the wagons get stuck!" Magba smiled. "And here is Ramon. As you said, not alone."

Nevara turned and saw Ramon and two strangers enter the mud-bogged square. The children swarmed Ramon, not just Magba's own children but all the little ones of the Baug. Ramon picked them up and kissed them one by one, but Nevara focused on the two people with him. One appeared to be a splendid French noble, all scarlet and jeweled, with a sweeping cloak that trailed in the deep mud. Beside him was a slender boy. Then Nevara realized it was a girl with short hair and boy's clothes. This boyish girl dropped to her knees in the filth and hugged the children.

Why had Ramon brought northerners to the camp?

The strange entourage approached Magba and Nevara followed by a long line of giggling children.

Ramon kissed Magba's cheeks. He smiled yet seemed wary, and his luminous green eyes warned them to govern their words. He greeted Nevara with a kiss.

"Magba is the mother of the Baug," Ramon said to the strangers. "And Nevara is the teller of fortunes."

Nevara gave Ramon a sharp look. In this time of Inquisitors, it seemed provocative to volunteer so much information.

"May I present the lady Adelais d'Arcis, daughter of the viscount, and her escort, squire Perce de Mendes."

Nevara stared. He had brought the very daughter of their enemy into the camp! But this boyish-girl was grinning, like a child herself, and she held the hands of two of the Baug children.

Magba held out her hand. Nevara was surprised as the viscount's daughter kissed the hand and bowed in respect. Magba smiled and greeted them in Novgorodian, "Come, please, we are all friends here, dear."

Ramon translated. "Magba doesn't speak the langue d'oïl. She asked you not to be so formal. We are all friends."

The squire nodded his head stiffly. "Greetings," was all he said. He seemed less comfortable and he didn't offer to kiss Magba's hand. Nevara found him quite attractive, muscular and young with pouting lips and bright eyes that rarely blinked. Unlike the viscount's daughter, this boy wore his emotions naked on his young face and right now he sizzled with tension. A conflicted man.

"Being welcome to the Baug," Nevara said, in her crude French.

"Merci!" Adelais' voice was full of enthusiasm and her smile was genuine. How could this be the daughter of the monster who slaughtered so many of Ramon's people?

"Adelais insisted that we come," Ramon said. "I told her there was nothing to see yet!"

The horses had begun to crowd them now, as always friendly and curious, and the two strangers were jostled by Baug children and horses both.

"We must offer our guests hospitality," said Magba, smiling. Ramon translated then led them to the great pavilion. Others of the Baug crowded in too, until most of the adults and children surrounded them. Ramon's friends patted his back or kissed his cheek, and they waved or bowed to the strangers. Inside the big tent, big enough for all of the Baug, the hospitality fires always glowed and they settled in large rings around the simple hearth. To the Baug, the hospitality fire was the heart of the people. Even when they moved on, the "fire keeper" would keep coals from the last fire alive in an ever-hot iron pot in Magba's own wagon.

The Baug brought food, meager morsels by French standards but the best they could offer. They served flatbreads slathered in olive oil and rosemary. A child sat on Adelais' lap, Magba's daughter of three summers, plucking at the girl's hair and laughing. One of the older Baug boys, nearly a man, knelt in front of squire Perce, speaking in broken French. The squire seemed to relax, enjoying the attention, and soon he was telling stories of his exploits.

Ramon left his new friends and led Nevara and Magba to the back of the pavilion. The knife-throwing Mongol twins, Hatta and Atta, Ramon's closest friends in the Baug, followed them. Ramon hugged them both.

"Missing your songs, we do," Hatta said in his unusual accented voice.

"Missing your jokes, too," Atta said.

No one could tell the twins apart, even their closest friends. They were very short, their wiry bodies wound into tight knots of muscles. They dressed identically in worn leather breaches and boots. They rarely wore clothing on their bare chests, showing off the scars of a dozen knife accidents. Braces of throwing knives on belts crossed their dark hairless chests. The Baug loved to joke that they slept with their knives. They were orphan boys, left for dead at six summers of age by the Hun on the attack of a village south of Novgorod. Magba had adopted them, as she did all vagabonds, but they proved to be her fiercest challenge as Baug Mother. Even at six they were unruly and beat the other Baug children bloody, always angry and fierce. But they were the best riders in the Baug and, even as children, masters of the knives. Their small deep-set eyes were ever full of a fierce energy. They could juggle swords, spears, and they could shave a whisker off a man's face at thirty paces with their throwing knives.

Ramon grinned, resting a hand on each of the twin's shoulders. Nevara was jealous of their affection. Ramon had been gone only one night, but the twins acted as if he had returned from a long journey. Ramon said, "The two rebels, the Grand Duo, are captured by the

Inquisition."

"What of the Jewel?" Magba didn't reveal anything on her always-smiling face.

"She is kept in the north tower under guard."

"So, you are alone, dearest," Nevara said.

"I am never alone," Ramon said. He brushed her hand with his. "You forget Arnot."

"I forget nothing. But you planned to use the Grand Duo and their network of rebels!"

"I still do." Ramon frowned. "I must rescue them all."

Nevara sighed. "You expect too much of yourself, dearest. Rescuing the Dame is nearly impossible. Now, you must rescue these rebels?"

Ramon nodded. "The Baug's grand performance will distract the French. Nevara's magic and the twins' knives will keep the city enthralled. I brought Adelais and Perce here, so that you can show off. They will tell all the French of the Baug's wonders. We will put on a grand show. Worry not, Snow Queen, I have a plan."

Nevara put on her fiercest scowl. Ramon's plans meant great danger. And as she listened, she realized just how hopeless his mission was.

"I have bonded you to a new ally," she said. Each night she chanted over the two magic cards, Ramon's Fool Card, and the Strength card, the lion wrestled by the golden haired man in white.

"Be watchful. A man in white, a powerful man, a man who seems to be an enemy, will help you. Listen to him."

Ramon winked at her. "Of course, my love."

"Menace," Nevara said.

"It is a dangerous plan," Ramon agreed.

"No, no. Something dangerous arrives in our camp." She pointed at the door to the pavilion. She shivered, certain they were in jeopardy. She smelled blood. "Hurry!"

Ramon and the twins, Atta and Hatta, ran for the door without questioning her perception. They flung back the flap and stepped out into the blinding sunlight.

Nevara heard loud voices. She followed Ramon and the twins outside, followed by the two French strangers. They emerged from the pavilion to a frightening spectacle. The camp was full of French soldiers, who were turning over baskets and searching wagons. Ramon and the twins were surrounded by soldiers with spears lowered. Two monks stood in front of Ramon, one smiling, one scowling.

"It is known that the Baug practices devilry and witchcraft," said the younger, smiling monk.

Ramon waved his spear in an arc and it settled under the young man's nose. "Tricks and entertainment, Brother Jaie." Obviously Ramon knew this young monk.

"We shall determine that," said the older monk, a man with one eyebrow and a deeply furrowed forehead.

"And who are you, brother?" Ramon swung his spear left until the point was an inch from the older Inquisitor's nose.

"No jokes, please, Ramon," said the younger monk, but Nevara saw a ghost of a smile on the Dominican's face. "Meet Brother Duranti, the senior Inquisitor in Carcassonne."

Ramon didn't drop the spear, and continued to smile, "Are you saying Brother Duranti has no sense of humor?" The younger monk winced. Nevara knew Ramon was about to lay on the offensive religious jokes. She stepped forward quickly. "We are all just being entertainers here," she said in her rough French.

"You must be the famous witch Nevara," said the older monk, Inquisitor Duranti.

"I being a player of tricks and games," Nevara said.

"I shall determine your devilry," Duranti snapped. He waved his arm, and three soldiers stepped forward.

"Come, friends, the Baug is for celebrating, music, fun, jokes, and tricks!" Ramon stepped between Nevara and the soldiers. He winked at the younger monk. "So let me tell you a joke. Yes? In a monastery in northern Italy—"

"Enough!" Duranti interrupted. "No more sacrilegious jokes."

"Tis what we jesters do. Anyway, one day a new monk was copying manuscripts in the scriptorium. He asked the precentor, 'How do we know we're not copying someone else's mistakes?' The precentor said, 'You are right to ask, my son,' and he took one of the copies down into the vault to verify against the original."

Ramon paused, and Nevara noticed that this younger Brother Jaie was grinning now, and the scowling monk Duranti did not interrupt.

"When the precentor didn't return, the worried monks went down to find him. Through the door they heard him sobbing, and they found him crying over a new copy of an ancient book.

"'What is wrong, Reverend Father?' asked one of the monks.

"The precentor did not look up as he said, 'My dear, sweet Jesus. We have copied this a dozen times! The word should be "comitas" not "comissatio!"'

"And the young monk, who understood little Latin said, 'Will anyone notice?'

"And the precentor wailed, 'It should say Jesus' *kindness* not Jesus' *orgy*!'"

Jaie snorted then covered his mouth. Duranti refused to smile, but his lip trembled. The soldiers hesitated then several of them turned away, hiding grins.

"Perverted nonsense!" snapped Duranti. "Arrest him!"

The soldiers, some fighting back laughter, hesitated.

Suddenly, as if by magic, a pair of knives protruded from the two soldiers' boots. The two men stared at their feet white-faced.

The twins held knives in both hands. Ramon's spear was cocked and ready.

"Lieutenant, you shall arrest Ramon and all these people," Duranti said.

The lieutenant was the very same man who had arrested Ramon the last time. He stepped closer, his eyes wide and unblinking. Nevara could see he was afraid of Ramon. At any other time she would have laughed. One more step and Ramon's short spear swung around in a whistling rush, heard rather than seen, and cracked hard against the lieutenant's chin. The man lifted physically in the air, arched his back, and cried out as he landed on his back.

The soldiers roared with laughter. Nevara smiled. To be bested by a girly jester! It was all too funny.

"I want them arrested now!" Duranti bellowed.

The soldiers ran forward, spear tips thrusting at Ramon's unarmored chest.

Ramon's long legs slid apart, his front heel splashing in the mud, until his crotch was flat in the muck. The spear tips flew over his head. He thrust upwards and tapped first left then right, and both of the soldiers' spears went flying through the air. Ramon's legs slid in reverse, and he rose, a sudden erection from the mud. His spear spun around and up until the tip was under Duranti's chin.

The senior Inquisitor's hand came up. "Hold!"

The soldiers, terrified, froze in mid-attack.

Nevara looked behind her and saw that the twins had two knives ready in each hand.

"You dare to attack a papal legate?"

"I dare whatever I please." Ramon grinned but dropped his spear. "Do you have grounds for an arrest?"

"I have grounds for an investigation." The monk's face was cherry red with rage. He threw back his cowl, and the bald pate of his head was afire.

"Then investigate. Without the spears."

Again the soldiers lunged. This time the twins threw their knives, two in each hand, released all together. One soldier howled and fell back, a knife in his spear arm. A second took a blade in the shoulder.

"You dare? You dare!" The monk was purple. Nevara wanted to laugh, though she knew that this monk and these soldiers could unravel all of Ramon's plans and land them in chains.

Ramon's spear was nothing but a blur as he parried and thrust, careful not to hurt. On one thrust, sparks flew. Two more soldiers fell face down in the muck.

"Enough!" The voice was that of Adelais.

Ramon and the soldiers fought on for another moment. The haft of Ramon's spear caught the tip of an enemy blade and they slid toward each other, their chests slamming together.

Little boyish Adelais stepped between them, pushing their spears apart. "Ramon is under my protection. The entire Baug is under my guarantee of safe passage!"

The only sound was the squish of boots in the mud and the snort of horses. Finally, Duranti broke the spell. "Lady Adelais, this is Inquisition business."

"I don't give a damn if the Holy Mother Mary sent you. My protection and my bond." Adelais stood in front of the monk, one foot shorter but tall in her ferocity, her fists on her small hips, her eyes blazing. For the first time, Nevara found she liked the little scamp.

"You watch your tongue, lady," said the senior Inquisitor.

"You watch you don't end up on my father's rack. You are here by his permission!"

Everyone stared at her now. The soldiers grinned, and that told Nevara that she was always fiery and unpredictable, but it seemed outrageous to all of the Baug performers, certainly to Nevara, that this little sprite could intimidate a legate of His Holiness, the blood-thirsty pope.

Her companion, the handsome young squire, stood at her side, his sword drawn and shining in the sun. Nevara found him even more attractive.

"Now, now," said Ramon. "We're all just playing, aren't we?"

"There's nothing funny in this," snapped Adelais. "You will withdraw, Brother Duranti!"

The monk bowed his head, but Nevara caught a flash of fury in his glassy eyes. "Yes, lady."

"And you will not bother the Baug Balar or my favorite jester." Her voice remained fierce.

"Yes, Lady." But as he turned, he said, "But I will be visiting your father, young lady. You can count on this. And a letter will go to His Holiness in Rome."

Then, he squished through the mud, holding up his long robe, followed by the soldiers. In mid-squish, Nevara heard a loud fart.

The Baug Balar laughed with one voice. Several of the children held their noses.

The Inquisitor reached the small street that led up the hill towards the inner city. He turned, raised his arms, and said, "By the way, lady. My lord Diableteur and his forty-four have returned."

Nevara found she had stopped breathing. The Diableteur. Their situation had just become as dangerous as a winter blizzard in the Alps. She felt a chill.

Song of the Pope

16

LORD VISCOUNT HUGH D'ARCIS bowed to Cardinal Vice-chancellor Fiesco. Hugh bowed to no man except his king, but Fiesco was a man to whom even kings must bow, widely expected to be the next pope. Hugh bent, his movement quick and disrespectful, and his lips did not touch the cardinal's ring. Flushed and angered by the demeaning gesture, he snapped back, ignoring the smug face of Archbishop Amiel, his main rival for power in the South. Amiel delighted in lecturing Hugh on the seven deadly sins and how the viscount was the perfect expression of all seven. Hugh couldn't disagree, but of all the deadly sins, he cherished pride the most, which, according to Amiel, would condemn Hugh to suffering the worst hell of all.

"You'll be broken on the wheel by foul demons, your body smashed over and over for your pride," Archbishop Amiel had told him every Sunday. "Then, you'll be thrown into freezing water until you scream—for your envy. Later, you'll be dismembered alive for your anger, cut slowly with dull knives by gibbering fiends. Then, when your arms grow back you'll be thrown into a pit of snakes for your sloth. The next day you'll be put in cauldrons of boiling oil to help you remember your greed. For your gluttony you'll eat rats, toads and snakes. Your lust will earn you fire and brimstone." And Hugh always laughed and said, "I've suffered all of that on the crusades, even the eating of toads and snakes. And I imagine I'll be seeing you in the seven hells."

Hugh feared no one, not even his own king. He was lord of all—land, people, priests and church included—in the lands south of the Lorre. It galled him to bow to Fiesco, but one did not ignore protocol with the man rumored to be the favorite to replace the pope.

The rivals for power met in Hugh's private apartments in the west tower: Diableteur in his dark splendor; the one-eyed nameless Seigneur, equally threatening even in his shining white robes, fearless and his own man; the future pope, Cardinal Fiesco; the fat and pompous Archbishop Peter Amiel; the Templar Arnot; Sir Albaric, the new city champion; and Hugh. The tension ran high. The two lords, one in white, one in black, Seigneur and Diableteur, glared at each other, their hatred polluting the sanctity of Hugh's private chamber. Both were feared. Diableteur answered only to the pope; Seigneur answered to no one. Diableteur had his forty-four black-robed hunters, feared from Constantinople to London. Seigneur rode with his eight hardened white-robed crusaders, men who had butchered Saracens, heretics and enemies of King Louis, from Jerusalem to France. Seigneur's eight were worth eighty ordinary knights and followed him without question, a fierce loyalty that was rare and precious.

The archbishop was no more than a nuisance, but a dangerous one for all that, a bloated rival for Hugh's power in the South who held Hugh in check with threats of the newly powerful Inquisition and threats of excommunication.

Diableteur against Seigneur; Hugh against Archbishop Amiel. But the delicate balance was upset by the unexpected arrival of the future pope, by all accounts the current pope's closest friend and advisor. And Hugh knew Arnot well enough to know the Templar was a man to have beside you in a fight, a taciturn and dedicated man; the same could be said of Sir Albaric, the new champion.

The faint stench of death hung in the air, a cloying sweetness that seemed to cling to Diableteur. Hugh knew his burned flesh was the source of the sweet reek. He shivered. For all his courage, Hugh could never overcome the unholy feeling of anxiety that the black-cloaked beast of Pope Gregory aroused in him. Who else but a devil could live with those terrible disfigurements? Who but a demon could tolerate such pain?

Archbishop Amiel had once told Hugh that Diableteur endured constant physical agony from his wounds, every day a trial. "It is what made him our perfect hunter," Amiel had said, with a nervous laugh. Hugh had seen Diableteur fully uncowled two years ago, and for all the terrors he had seen in his many years of crusading—and the countless heretic burnings he had witnessed—there was something unspeakably perverse about a man living with such pain and ugliness.

Diableteur had transformed himself into the very image of a fiend risen from the flames. His monstrous appearance made even Seigneur appear beautiful by comparison, with his empty eye socket and scarred cheek. Only hate or hope could keep such a thing alive. Every sane person feared Diableteur, including Hugh.

To survive such constant pain, Hugh believed Diableteur had aligned with dark powers, perhaps the devil himself. Hugh believed Satan existed. The world was evidence enough of the dark lord's work. Fortunately, he had the archbishop to mete out penance for each of his sins, which was the only reason he didn't personally slice the archbishop's throat. Without his weekly penance, Hugh would be doomed to hell. Amiel's price was always the same: "You will seek out and arrest or kill each and every pagan, heretic and witch in your lands." Which meant allowing Diableteur almost unlimited power.

Hugh focused on Cardinal Fiesco, an aging man, with deep worry lines sharply etched around each eye and permanent frown creases around his unsmiling lips. "I have sent for the Dame, Eminence, as you requested. May I offer wine?"

"Mulled," Fiesco said, without acknowledging Hugh's title.

"Eminence, I hope you can attend the Mayday Tourney?"

Fiesco shrugged. He stared intently at Arnot the Templar. "How is it, Brother Arnot, that I have not heard of you?"

"I am companion knight to Master Marshall Bernard de Ridefort," said the Templar.

"So you say. If you are his companion, how is it you are here alone?"

Arnot did not flinch under the glare of the second most powerful man in the Church. "Brother Bernard trusts me with his most sacred mission."

"That being?"

Arnot smiled. "I assume much similar to yours? What brings so lofty a cardinal to Carcassonne?"

Hugh knew Arnot as a fearless Templar from past battles, but even he was astonished at the arrogance.

"My business is my own."

"As is mine," Arnot said.

"Impertinent," snapped the cardinal.

"I answer only to the Marshall," said Arnot.

"The Templars might be exempt from my direct authority, but your disrespect is noted," said Cardinal Fiesco, his rage barely controlled. Hugh assumed he really meant, *I am to be the next pope, you fool, at which time you will be under my authority.*

Hugh smiled. The grizzly old Templar was shrewder than he remembered, although no one could doubt that Arnot was utterly fearless in battle. Few would dare to stand against the second most powerful man in the Church.

"Your disrespect is equally noted," said Arnot, folding his arms.

The Diableteur stepped between them, facing Arnot the Templar and towering over the big knight of God. Hugh watched with renewed interest as Arnot stared hard into the shadow under the hood. "Call off your dog," Arnot said, blandly. "He doesn't frighten me, Eminence."

Diableteur didn't move. Cardinal Fiesco seemed equally fascinated. The Diableteur, when he spoke, whispered, a harsh croaking hiss, his vocals unused to speech. "*You will fear me.*"

"I might fear your foul breath. My God, man, do you never wash?" Arnot grinned, staring at the scarred face.

Amused, Hugh clapped his hands. "Do you think it appropriate for Diableteur be in the room? Perhaps both the Templar and your hunter should withdraw?"

"And why is that?" Cardinal Fiesco said.

"I find people rarely speak in the presence of Lord Diableteur."

"Your friend the Templar seems not to hesitate," said the cardinal. "And I doubt the Dame, this much revered Jewel of the South, will fear Diableteur." He sat in Hugh's throne-like chair by the fire. Diableteur stepped back and stood behind him, face hidden, eyes glittering.

A good insight, Hugh thought. The Dame had shown no fear in any of his meetings with her. Her utter lack of emotion unnerved him, as did her power, even as a prisoner. Ever courteous, always smiling, it was easy to understand why men such as Fiesco and creatures such as Diableteur might regard her as dangerous. There was something unearthly about her.

The door opened and Hugh turned to greet the Dame, his honored guest and condemned prisoner. But it was not the Dame. Senior Inquisitor Duranti and his clerk Jaie entered, red-faced and out of breath. They sank to their knees in front of the cardinal, kissed his ring, then bowed low to the Diableteur and Amiel.

"I am grateful for your safe arrival, Eminence," Duranti said. "I come with a complaint."

Fiesco sighed. "Surely this is a matter for the archbishop?"

"I came to see the viscount," Duranti said, although he made no eye contact with Hugh, and spoke as if he wasn't in the room.

"You were not invited." Hugh kept his voice curt.

"A matter of urgency," said Duranti, giving only the slightest nod of his head in respect of the office.

"Speak and go. We have business." Hugh folded his arms and glared at the one-eyebrowed monk. He hated monks. Self-righteous, imperious and sacrilegious, all of them. The revelation that Doré the Dandy was a woman had thrown the Dominicans into a frenzy. It explained a lot, now that Hugh thought about it. The rumors that the Grand Duo, the dandy and his big escort Osric the Hammer, were in fact lovers, made for a fascinating legend. He had always assumed they were "unmentionables," men loving men, something he had seen many times on long crusades where men camped in absence of the fairer sex. But Doré—the viscount's greatest enemy—a woman! Now it made sense. The diminutive size of the rebel, the high-pitched voice. It was a wonder no one had guessed before. Hugh had interrupted the proceedings, and ordered Doré and Osric returned to the north tower of the castle. Torture, it seemed, would no longer be necessary. He would extract the information by threatening Doré—in front of his apparent lover Osric. He assumed that Duranti was here, again, to complain about the transfer of Doré and Osric, woman and man, to the castle. He was wrong.

"Your daughter interfered with the business of the Inquisition again," snapped Duranti.

"My daughter is Her Ladyship to you, Brother Duranti," said Hugh, controlling his rage. He hated that he had to defend her all the time, but she was precious to him, he had no sons, and no one would disrespect her in public. "You might also remember she is betrothed to the royal family." Sir Lantar might be a distant nephew of King Louis, but he was royal nonetheless, and if he survived Adelais' antics, he would be a valuable asset to Hugh.

"*Her Ladyship* put a bond of protection on the Baug Balar and your new jester!"

Hugh played with the hilt of his sword. "And? She is the lady of Carcassonne. She is of my blood. She has the right." He was proud of her fearlessness and annoyed at the same time, but he was not about to reveal his disappointment in front of his rivals for power. "Besides, if we terrify all the entertainers, what a boring world we'll be left with!"

"They are heretics. All of them!"

"You have proof of this?" asked the cardinal.

"Eminence, I ..." The senior Inquisitor bowed and said no more.

"He means no," Hugh said. "Get out, Brother Duranti. We are conducting the business of your betters!"

Duranti glared at Hugh, looked once more at the cardinal, who shook his head, then to his archbishop, who shrugged. "I will investigate further."

"You will not go against the wishes of Lady Adelais!" Hugh snapped.

Duranti met Hugh's glare for a moment, an expression of loathing, then bowed to his cardinal, Lord Diableteur and archbishop. With no bow to Hugh, he strode from the room.

"Duranti!" Hugh shouted.

Duranti re-appeared. "My lord?"

"You forget yourself."

Duranti flushed. He bowed.

"You may leave," Hugh said.

The fury on Duranti's face was a beautiful thing.

Fiesco sighed, sipped on his warmed wine and said, "You are in command here it seems."

"I am."

"The iron fist of D'Arcis, no?"

"Yes." Hugh nodded to the cardinal, so as not to appear arrogant.

"We would do well to remember that Brother Duranti has saved the South from these vile heresies, almost single-handedly," snapped Archbishop Peter Amiel.

Hugh stepped closer to Amiel. How he despised this fat, child-molesting priest. "You give yourself too little credit, Your Grace. But if by 'saved the South' you mean reduced my tax-paying tenants by half, then you are quite right."

He never understood the Inquisition. Fear was necessary, yes, if there was to be order, but the Inquisition seemed more like an out-of-control and petulant child, a sadistic toddler out to prove it was better than its parent. Hugh had fought Duranti's arrival in the South, and only an edict from Pope Gregory and a letter from King Louis had changed his mind. The king, and especially his powerful mother, were beyond devout. The Inquisition did serve a purpose, but they applied their powers too enthusiastically. Their work emptied farmsteads and not enough northerners made their way south to replace the lost souls and the taxes. The remaining Southerners lived in constant terror, a sure path to rebellion. Fighting revolutionaries cost money.

"You exaggerate, my lord," said Amiel.

The cardinal held up his gloved hands. "I did not come here to settle disputes." His voice was soft but firm. "The Church is our mother. Our children must be saved at any cost. Sometimes firmness is required." He stared at Hugh.

"Eminence, I agree," Hugh said, nodding his head. And he did agree. Did a parent hold back a beating from a child who misbehaved? "But I do need revenues from the land. Half the vineyards were ruined in the crusade."

"Your mundane interests," said Fiesco, waving his hand as if to brush away a buzzing insect. "You led one of the butchering armies yourself."

"Yes, Eminence."

"Is it not better to send a few hundred heretics to the flames than to put thousands to the sword?" Cardinal Fiesco smiled. "There, my Lord, let us not bicker. I came to honor your great triumph."

"The Dame?"

Fiesco's bright blue eyes were alive with energy. "Certainly that interests me. But it is the knowledge she possesses that the Church must have."

"Legend. Myth." Hugh forgot titles. This 'Holy of Holies' nonsense was a tiring debate the archbishop brought to every dinner feast. "How could a hive of heretics in the mountains come to possess so powerful a relic when the Templars have searched for it for more than our lifetimes?"

"Diabolical powers," Amiel snapped.

"Wicked imagination more likely!" Hugh forced a smile. "I have seen the powers of this Dame. Simple serenity and resignation to her fate. I doubt she'll scream on your pyre. But if she is this fearsome witch, why does she not turn herself into a crow and fly away back to her mountain refuge."

"You are in her spell." Amiel's voice rose, perhaps embarrassed that Hugh would confront him with their old argument in front of his betters.

"They say four of our precious Holy Relics are in high Montségur," said Cardinal Fiesco, his voice quiet, but commanding attention.

"That is what they say," Hugh said.

"But you do not believe it?"

"No, Eminence."

Amiel's voice was a little too strident. "Eminence, I have asked the viscount many times to lay siege to the refuge of these devil-worshipers to rescue our holy relics."

"The castle is impregnable," said Hugh, tired of the old argument. "I would have to throw my entire army against the keep for possibly years. Chateau Montségur sits atop a mountain. They have provisions for a full year siege."

"But Montségur would eventually fall!" Amiel seemed to have forgotten the cardinal, his chubby cheeks red with rage as he warmed to his old argument.

"Yes. And who would feed my army and pay them for a full year? For what? A lump of rock."

"The relics!"

"Rumored relics. And sixty or seventy Perfects for your fire."

"Who spread heresies throughout your corrupt lands!"

Fiesco's quiet voice interrupted them. "That is quite enough, gentlemen." He smiled. "If I deem it appropriate, the Church will pay for such a siege. Let us talk first with the Dame. Perhaps her ransom will be sufficient to bring us these precious relics."

Hugh saw something then, in the cardinal's eyes. A hunger. He believed in the relics. He wanted them. Hugh could imagine why. Any one of those relics would make its possessor a pope. Installing the relics in Rome would bring pilgrims with money from all over Europe.

"We would ransom the Dame?" Amieil asked, a tremor in his voice. "But it is the Dame who keeps these heresies alive in our lands."

Fiesco set down his wine goblet, eyes abruptly hard. "You forget yourself, Amiel."

Amiel bowed his head.

A knock at the door interrupted what might have been a splendid confrontation. The Silver Dame entered, and all the men fell silent.

The Dame intrigued Hugh D'Arcis. She was not beautiful in the classic, youthful sense, but her serenity was astonishingly appealing. She was slightly older than Hugh but seemed ageless, her face unlined and plain, and if not for her silver hair, he'd have guessed her to be thirty summers of age. Shimmering silver-gray robes couldn't hide a true woman. She was rumored to be a virgin, but she was ageless femininity personified. Even now, she smiled as she bowed to each of them in turn, starting, appropriately, with the cardinal. She even bowed to Diableteur, who nodded his head.

"Cardinal Fiesco, may I present the Dame Esclarmonde de Foix," Hugh said, and he took her hand and kissed it. He saw Amiel smirk at that.

"Eminence," the Dame said, bowing again. She surprised Hugh by kissing the proffered ring.

"Ma Dame," the cardinal said, with an odd smile.

Hugh clapped his hands. "A chair for the Dame!"

The Silver Dame shook her head. "I am fine standing, thank you, Hugh."

Hugh felt a little heat at the familiarity. Had they become so intimate in their daily conversations that they were now on a first-name basis? "We have called you here to decide your fate, Dame Esclarmonde," he said, formally.

"This tired body is yours to dispose of, my lord," Dame said softly, her voice neither sad nor angry. Her equanimity was magnificent.

The cardinal leaned forward in his chair. "You are fearless, as they said."

The Dame smiled and Hugh had to resist a sigh. Her smiles affected him. "Eminence, why should I fear?"

"You could be—likely will be—turned over to the Inquisition."

"Fear is meaningless." The way she said it she clearly meant, *The Inquisition is meaningless.*

Diableteur stepped forward, towering over the silver Dame. This confrontation would be too interesting. The black-robed Diableteur bent over her, his melted flesh revealed to her in all its horror. Calm, she looked up into his face. Black giant hovered over diminutive lady in silver.

She smiled.

"You *are* fearless," Fiesco said.

She continued to stare at Diableteur. "Such pain you have, brother." She reached up a hand to touch the scarred flesh.

Hugh sucked air through clenched teeth, astonished.

The Diableteur jerked away.

Hugh couldn't resist a chuckle. He had never seen this before. "It seems Diableteur has finally met his match!"

No one else laughed, but Hugh couldn't stop himself. He even felt a little pride.

"I see nothing amusing in this, my lord," said the cardinal.

"I have not been so entertained in many a year, Eminence" Hugh said, still chuckling.

The Dame stepped closer to Diableteur and reached out again.

Diableteur stepped back.

"You have nothing to fear from me," she said.

Diableteur replied in his tortured, hissing voice. "*But you have everything to fear from me.*"

The cowled head turned and Diableteur faced Hugh. Hugh stopped laughing as the streaming light from the window caught the monster's hideous misshapen features.

Seigneur, stepped between them. He was as tall as Diableteur and equally terrible in his own way. "The Dame remains under my protection," he said, in his own raspy voice. He stood an arm's length from the Diableteur. "I captured the Dame. I shall decide her fate."

Hugh smiled. This was very nearly a speech from the taciturn Seigneur. He rarely spoke. He feared nothing. Hugh knew Seigneur's true name, from the days when they had crusaded to Jerusalem—before Seigneur lost his eye to a Saracen torturer—but after the horrors of Joppa, the great crusader had given up the colors of Castlenau to become the soulless and nameless Seigneur. Hugh doubted he could best Seigneur in fair battle. In one way he was very like the Dame. He seemed empty of emotion and was perhaps the only man alive who could face Diableteur without madness.

"That is presumptuous," Cardinal Fiesco said.

"It is custom," said Hugh, rising to the defense of his old friend.

"The Church's needs outweigh any ancient laws of capture!" shouted Amiel.

"No," Seigneur said. Then he did something extraordinary. He stepped close to the Dame and held out his arm. She folded her arm around his.

"I see," Fiesco said. "How very complicated." He glanced back and forth between Diableteur and Seigneur, as if pondering who would triumph if he set one upon the other, the black or the white. "And would you agree to a ransom, Seigneur?"

Seigneur said nothing.

"I am a poor woman," the Dame said. "We renounce all lands and goods when we take the way of Christ."

"Surely your people can find a ransom?" Hugh said gently.

"My people know that this miserable shell, my body, is nothing. It is meaningless."

"Blasphemy," said Amiel.

Cardinal Fiesco ignored him. "And what of the relics?"

"Relics, eminence?" The Dame stared at Fiesco, revealing nothing.

"I am told certain relics are horded in your mountain."

"Rumors," she said, her voice a bare whisper. "There is nothing that would interest a holy man such as yourself in that impoverished castle."

Cardinal Fiesco stood for the first time. "Men would gladly die for a glimpse of the very cup of Christ."

17

A CROWD HAD GROWN on the *Lices Hautes,* the long stretch between the two city walls. These early arrivals had come to witness the *plaisance,* the practice sessions leading up to the May Tourney. Most of them pressed close to the field, careless of the combatants. Already a mêlée churned up dust as a dozen knights fought on foot with blunted weapons. The clang of weapons and grunts of exertion mixed with the howls of victory and the cheers of the crowd.

They had come here at Adelais' insistence, winding through the rambling alleyways of the *Lices.* The only open areas were the Jewish market, where the Baug had their camp, and the tourney field of the *Lices Hautes,* along the western stretch between the Tour de la Vade and the Tour de la Peyre. It was here that the knights practiced their skills. Away from these two open areas, the narrow *Lices* overflowed with shacks, paddocks, alleyways, wayrooms, and hundreds of exiles living in the filthy trap between the two walls.

Mauri ran off, barking, as if after a bitch in heat, and was now lost in the crowd. Ramon was about to chase after Mauri when he caught a glimpse of the old stooped man with the gray beard.

Guilhem! Guilhem the old Hermit.

Guilhem bent and picked up Mauri. He stroked the little dog's head and nodded at Ramon, but when the troubadour moved to greet him, the old mystic shook his head.

Ramon turned away.

"I hate this sport," Ramon said to Adelais.

"But I *love* these gorgeous knights and their lovely squires! Look at them, Ramon!" She pulled his elbow and they pushed through the crowd. The spectators became more interested in the colorful fool and Lady Adelais than practising knights and squires, and crowded around them. "Make way! May way good folk!" Adelais pushed through the crowds.

"Come, Ramon, we'll take my father's seat. He won't be here for a practice mêlée!" Ramon shouted after Mauri to follow but lost him in the crowd. "He'll be all right, Ramon! Come! Quickly!" She panted with excitement.

They climbed the steps of the *berfrois,* a steep rise of benches built against the west wall in the shadow of the Tower Balthazar, the tallest defensive tower. The *berfrois* was filled with ladies. The audience soon lost interest in the practice mêlée and crowded around Ramon and Adelais in the steep stands.

"Sing a song!" shouted someone.

"Yes, a song!"

Smiling, Ramon bowed.

"We're here for the bohort," cried Adelais. She led Ramon to her father's raised chair and sat there. Ramon sat beside her. The audience continued to stare at them, ignoring the grunting and sweating fighters below.

After a time. the ladies lost interest and went back to watching their husbands practise in the *plaisance*. Three of the knights had been bashed to their knees, and their opponents roared their triumph to the crowd.

"I don't see any of the lords." Ramon said.

"Oh, the high lords don't attend these practice fields. This is just for the young knights. Later there'll be the bohort, for the squires. Then we'll see how Perce does today!"

"Does he do well?"

"Oh, very! He's the best of the squires! Young de Mendes they call him!"

Ramon frowned, wondering if that was true. Adelais didn't care what people thought—wandering with a commoner through the streets of Carcassonne, badgering merchants, intimidating the Inquisition. She was delightful, unusual and an enigma.

"Oh, look!" She pointed at a burly knight who fell with his dented helmet lying in the dirt and his forehead spewing blood.

"I despise these events," Ramon said. "People get hurt."

She giggled. "Of course people get hurt. You can be such an imbecile at times. What's the point of fighting if not to hurt?"

Ramon scowled and watched as the bloody chevalier limped from the field to the cheers of the crowd. One of his fellows kicked his helmet after him like a ball and it tumbled across the dirt. "Has Perce ever been hurt?"

"Of course! It's the game! It toughens them for war."

The horns blew and the bloody knights withdrew from the field, clapping each other on the back.

"See, they enjoy it!"

"I don't."

The sweets hawkers descended on the ladies in the stands. The smells of hot butter and honey wafted through.

"Are all troubadours so squeamish? I thought you sang of the glory of war."

"I'm not squeamish. It just seems stupid."

"Really, dear troubadour, do you think they just suddenly pick up swords and fight heroic battles? They must learn the art of war first!" She shook her head as if talking to a child.

Ramon sighed. "I wonder where Mauri is?"

"Forget him. He's having a hump."

Ramon grinned at Adelais, a little shocked by her crudeness. He waved at a hawker selling buttered nuts. He was in no mood for sweets, but it was something to do. Adelais had helped him, but he had yet to figure out how to use his new friendships and position to rescue the Dame and his rebel allies Doré and Osric.

"Oh, here he comes! Here's our Perce!"

"Who's fighting him?"

"It's Darel. Sir Albaric's squire. That's why we had to be here, to support Perce! Normally the crowd thins after the knights are through, but see—they're all staying!" She glared at him. "Don't look so confused. Seigneur and Messire Albaric are archrivals."

"I can't believe your one-eyed Seigneur cares about these things." Ramon folded his arms. "Didn't he resign as champion?"

"He doesn't care. But Albaric does. Don't you understand?"

"I'm not simple. I understand stupid, one-sided rivalry."

"Well Perce cares! He's going to bash that devil's squire to the grave. You watch!"

"I though they didn't kill each other?" Ramon sat forward.

"Sometimes they do. Especially if they hate each other."

"Then why are Seigneur and Albaric not here?"

She frowned. "You don't understand anything. They couldn't be seen here. It would be unseemly." They watched as Perce walked on to the field. "Isn't he splendid?"

Perce wore his family's blood scarlet and carried the Mendes shield with its gold falcon. He had removed his cloak and Ramon could see the sheen of his light fencing hauberk.

Adelais rested her hand on Ramon's leg. "He's beautiful!"

Ramon nodded, sliding away so that her hand fell. "Very noble." He looked left and right. "I wonder where Mauri is?"

"Oh, forget your dog, damn you! Perce is about to fight for his Seigneur's honor!" She waved. "Perce! Dear Perce!" she shouted and again all eyes were on Ramon and Adelais, including the squire's. Perce grinned and waved back. "You kill him, dear Perce!"

Sir Albaric's squire, Darel, entered the field. He wore the blue and yellow of his family and bore Albaric's shield. He was almost a head taller than Perce.

"He's a giant!" Ramon said.

She nodded. "Isn't it wonderful?"

"Has Perce fought this monster before?"

"No, silly. This is why there's a crowd!"

Ramon stood up and shaded his eyes. Perce looked so tiny next to Darel. "I hope Perce is good."

"He's the best—of the squires, I mean. I've seen them both fight other opponents. Albaric went to great pains to train his squire. Quite dashing isn't he?"

Ramon smiled. Adelais was difficult to understand. One moment all compassion and the next sadistic eagerness. She had rescued him from the Inquisitor, now she hoped for blood. "Who *are* you cheering for?"

"Don't be a dunce. Perce, of course!"

The horns blew again. The two squires turned and bowed to Lady Adelais.

"Now, Ramon, dearheart, you remember every thing that happens! I expect an exciting epic song about this!"

"An epic! It's just a duel!"

"Just! Don't be a fool, my dearest."

The final horn blew. The two squires drew their swords and saluted each other with the blades. They lowered their visors and crouched at the ready.

Ramon shivered as he heard the first clang of their dulled swords. Perce sank to one knee, yielding to the force of Darel's blow, but he turned sideways and slid his blade down to his opponent's cross guard. Lifting from his knee, he pushed all his weight under Darel's guard and pressed his elbow into his chest. Darel bounced back two paces and the crowd went mad.

"Bash him, Perce!" Adelais shouted, on her feet. Her eyes shone.

Ramon stood beside her, his hands clenched in white fists. "Be careful, Perce," he whispered. Even as he made the wish, he wondered at his conflicting emotions. He liked Perce and Adelais, though they were French invaders and enemies. How could that be? These were the people who had burned his mother, hanged his father, scorched the South and held his friends Doré and Osric prisoner. The Dame awaited her own trial. How could Ramon spare a moment of sympathy for the likes of these?

Darel swung overhand but Perce turned the blade easily. He spun to one side and sliced crossways. Darel barely deflected the blow. Darel stepped in and stabbed with his dull point but Perce easily jumped aside.

"Stabbing's not allowed!" shouted Adelais and the crowd hissed their displeasure. "He's a cheater," she said with disgus. "Just like his master."

Ramon tried to look away from the spectacle but found he couldn't. Perce weaved in a delicate dance, his upper body bent in one direction, legs in the other. Perce was a blur, his sword biting and deflecting, swinging and upper-cutting. Ramon found himself cheering with the crowd, his hands waving in the air.

Darel's shield hammered against Perce's, and the smaller man took two skittering steps backwards. As he recovered his stance, he barely had time to deflect another sword thrust. The crowd hissed at the illegal move. Perce retreated across the field, meeting blow with blow but yielding to Darel's bullish strength. That was when Ramon heard Mauri's bark.

Mauri ran between the legs of the crowd on to the field toward Perce, his new friend.

"Mauri, come here!" shouted Ramon.

He watched in horror as the little dog ran to Perce, wagging his tail. Perce nearly tripped on him. Darel, seeing his chance, stabbed at little Mauri.

Ramon closed his eyes, unable to watch.

Adelais grabbed his arm and shook him. "It's all right! Perce saved your little beast!" She pointed. "Though it cost him a cut or two."

Mauri yelped and ran away. Ramon shouted for him. Mauri ran up into the stands, jumped into Ramon's arms and licked his face.

"Your damn dog nearly cost Perce his life! Look!"

Blood ran down Perce's shield arm but he continued dueling. He dropped his family shield and fought two-handed with sword alone.

"I will kill you," Darel shouted as he hammered Perce's dulled sword. "You're a traitor, like your Seigneur!"

Perce fell back against the crowd of freemen who had nowhere to go as he crashed into them.

Perce ducked under Darel's blade and ran back to the center of the field. Darel charged him, howling his rage, but Perce stood his ground. He dove under Darel's swipe and brought his dull sword up and inside. As he snapped his blade up and around, Darel's sword flew through the air.

Perce held the tip of his blade to Darel's throat. "Yield to Mendes!"

The crowd cheered, waving and laughing. Adelais shouted louder than the rest: "Perce! Perce!" She started a chant and soon the crowd was shouting his name with her.

Darel scowled. "Never!" he shouted.

Breathing heavily, Perce dropped his practice sword. "So be it. Until the next time!"

He turned and waved at Adelais. As he did so, Darel struck with his shield, hard on Perce's back between the shoulder blades. Perce sagged to his knees and teetered for a moment, then fell.

The crowd fell silent. Perce did not move.

"Shame!" shouted Adelais, and she ran down onto the field followed by Ramon. "Shame!"

The crowd parted for her.

Darel picked up Perce's sword and its dulled blade clanged as he hammered on Perce's back, his visor thrown back and a look of rage on his reddened face. He was out of control.

"Stop this, now!" Adelais shouted.

"Traitors and dogs deserve no protection from rules," Darel shouted, and he continued to hammer on Perce's armor, grunting from the exertion. Perce rolled over, but he had lost his sword. He raised his gauntlets to protect his face from the blade.

Ramon used his spear as a vaulting stick and levered himself over the heads of the astonished spectators. He landed beside Darel just as the sword went down yet again. The haft of Zaleucus shot out and caught the sword. He turned the haft and snapped it up, knocking the sword out of Darel's hands. He struck Darel's helmet first on one side, then on the other, beating the squire back.

Darel was a giant of a man, Ramon's height but much broader and bristling with muscle. His face was purple in fury, eyes unblinking and hideous.

"The bohort is finished," Ramon said.

Darel took a lumbering step forward. Zaleucus hummed and quivered as it vibrated a bare finger's width from Darel's nose.

"You dare? You dare!" Darel sputtered.

"There is no shame in honorable defeat," Ramon said.

Darel would not listen. He bent to pick up his fallen sword. Ramon flicked it away with the long blade of Zaleucus.

"You dare!" Darel spat at Ramon. Forgetting his sword, he lumbered after Ramon. "You dare!"

Ramon tangled the man's legs with the shaft of his spear and took him down hard. He flipped his spear around in a dainty spin. Darel started to rise. The blade's tip hovered in front of his eye.

"Enough of this game," Ramon said quietly.

The crowd clapped and laughed, jeering at Darel who turned and strode from the field, pushing the spectators aside so roughly men and women cried out as they fell.

Ramon had made an enemy for life.

18

THE AFTERNOON AFTER Perce fought Darel in the *plaisance,* Ramon played "Sticks and Toss" with the bruised squire, Adelais and a gang of children under the Troubadour Tree in the courtyard of the inner chateau. It felt like an old habit, games and songs in the afternoon with his new friends. It was odd, this friendship of theirs. Perce was an enemy. Adelais the daughter of Ramon's greatest enemy. Ramon was using them, wasn't he? There was no time for real friendships. Yet there was something about Perce's naiveté—his idolizing of his landless and colorless Seigneur, his unwavering sense of duty, his belief in chivalry—that attracted Ramon to him. And Adelais was a delightful nymph, oblivious to the sins of her father.

Ramon enjoyed playing with the children of the castle. They loved when Ramon sang and screamed with delight when he told stories. Children of the bloody French or not, Ramon didn't care, he adored the young ones. Perhaps, ten years from now, one of Ramon's songs or his light moral fables would lead one of these noble children to hesitate in butchering Ramon's people. Besides, they loved Mauri so much. His dog chased them all over the keep, barking at them, jumping into their arms, nipping at their boots. Children. Children were always innocents. Always.

Time was a precious thing, with Mayday only days away, and already Ramon was tired. The intrigue, the plotting and the planning were exhausting. He performed three times a day for his new lord, worked on building his "friendships" and allies, but soon he must have a plan. The Dame's trial had been announced for the day after Mayday, just three days away. What could he do? He was handy with a spear. He had Arnot ready to intervene, and the Baug ready to help them escape the outer wall with all their tricks and plays. They would hide the Dame in the wagons, dress her in Baug garb and smear her face with grime, then sing their way out of the city. But how could he engineer an escape from the north tower? She was always guarded by at least two soldiers, the chateau was fully garrisoned, the upper city crowded with an entire army of soldiers. Both the lower and upper cities were crowded with visitors—important people, cardinals and lords and famous knights here for the May Tourney. The Dame's trial would ensure the spectacle continued.

Ramon's head throbbed. Perhaps this was all too much for him: his allies in prison, the Baug under the watchful eyes of the Inquisition, no time to sort out who were his real friends, and the Dame's time only days away. He would have to take more chances.

When finally the children ran off to play a game of "Siege" in the haystack, Ramon decided he needed to probe Perce for more information. The three of them lounged under the Troubadour Tree, the sacred symbol of his own art, an immense elm with ancient branches that swept up to touch the turquoise sky. According to his own songs, Dame Carcas—the city's namesake, a troubadour herself and the South's most treasured heroine—planted this splendid tree in honor of the day she tricked the Franks into abandoning their infamous siege five hundred years earlier. After a one-year siege, with food running low, she had set up catapults and tossed "gift bundles" of food into the ranks of the French. She stuffed pigs with the last of their corn. The last of their livestock and food went sailing over the great walls. The pigs split open, spilling out undigested corn. When the French, starving and weary, saw the food and saw that the city folk were so well off they could feed their corn to the pigs, they were convinced Dame Carcas had food enough to last another year, and abandoned the siege. Were all troubadours tricksters? Ramon hoped he could honor his heroine's memory with as clever a ruse.

Ramon sat silent for a while, watching the children and their siege game. Mauri played, too, the dog of the watch, barking at the attackers of the haystack, sitting up on the top of the stack with the defending children. War games for children. No wonder they grew up to be butchers. They had sticks for swords, and half the boys and girls defended the haystack from the attacks of the other half. Ramon sighed.

A steady line of provisioners came and went at the viscount's formidable chateau—once the blessed castle of Dame Carcas and her descendents. Its impregnable walls were the height of five men, and eight towers rose high above the machicolations, built to defend against the French, not to shelter them. How would he get the Dame out of these guarded walls? He could easily dispatch the two sentries at her apartment, but then what? His plan was good, but—as Nevara was quick to say, "Too tricky. Too many things going wrong and we dead. Dead, dead." They must not just rescue the Dame, they must escape the city walls and make it into the Phantom Wood, where no soldiers were likely to follow. They would not follow because no one ever returned from the Phantom Wood. Nevara's magic notwithstanding, it was the rebels in the wood who posed the great threat, and for them he needed the rebel leaders, Doré and Osric.

"Too much tricky," Nevara had said. "You wanting me to lure them into my spell. I can see doing that, yes. But then? And then? No! No! What if you aren't there as planned? What if you fall? What if they change the patrols? What if—"

"Trust me," Ramon had said. "How many have we rescued over the years?"

"Many, many, all with trickies and good luck. But in villages—not in cities with armies!"

"I'm working on a distraction," Ramon had said. He hoped that Perce might be part of this. Still, his plan was so convoluted that there was very little chance he might succeed. Was it worth all the risk? Even if he didn't love the Dame, he must succeed. Even if he died in the attempt, he must try. Loup de Foix, the Dame's own nephew, was building an army in the Caspin Mountains, ready to march on Carcassonne. Thousands could die in such a futile gesture. Unlike the Dame, her nephew was anything but compassionate and sensible. He only knew his aunt was a prisoner. His Caspin rebels, every one of them Cathar Christians, would march to save their sainted Dame, the inspiration of rebels all over the South. Ramon had heard rumblings about the King of Castille marching on

Carcassonne as well, more likely inspired by the Holy Relics said to be in the Dame's possession. Ramon's own Carcassonnians might die as readily as the French invaders if Castille besieged Carcassonne.

He must succeed. And soon.

Ramon forced a smile at his bruised friend Perce. He needed this squire. "How is it you and Darel hate each other so much?"

"It has always been this way," Perce said, rubbing one of his bruises.

Ramon yawned, pretending he wasn't interested.

"That's no answer!" Adelais snapped, and she punched Perce's bruised shoulder, making him yelp. "What a child!"

"I hate you sometimes." Perce glared at Adelais.

"Well, I love you, dear Perce!" She kissed his cheek. "And you dear Ramon!" and she kissed his cheek as well.

"Tell me of the Dame's capture then," Ramon said.

Perce glanced sharply at Ramon. Had he gone too far? For a moment there were only the sounds of giggling children, snorting horses and birds singing in the Troubadour Tree.

When Perce said nothing, Adelais punched him again. "Let's hear the story!" She always came alive during stories of campaigning and knights. "Tell that story!"

Perce scowled. "I am no story-teller."

Adelais scowled. "He loves to tell stories. You'll be sorry, Ramon!"

Ramon smiled. "I will turn it into a song for you. Brave Perce and the infamous Dame." The smile was forced. He didn't want to hear this story. His own folk had died in the capture, defending their Dame. But there might be important information in the story, information he could use.

"You'll have me slaying entire armies," grumbled Perce, but there was a hint of a smile on his face.

"Tell it!" commanded Adelais.

"Yes, my Lady," said Perce. "I nearly died that day. We had followed the rebels for days, until finally, we cornered the vermin in an old castle in the Pyrenees." He glanced at Ramon. "I'm sorry. I forget you are a Southerner."

Ramon forced a nonchalant shrug. "And we are friends. Say on!"

Perce stared at Ramon for a long moment, as if debating what he should tell. "My Seigneur commanded, but there were many with us, including the Diableteur himself!" Perce shivered.

"How terrible!" Adelais mocked him. She feared nothing, not even the Diableteur.

Perce glared at her. "Do you want to hear this?"

"Please!"

"We were sent on a mission to capture the Dame, but she had a retinue of sixty knights. Even if they hadn't taken refuge in the castle, our three hundred men would have been hard pressed to win a battle. On the third day, probably because they had little food for a siege, the enemy began a series of sorties. I was caught under the south wall by one large force, unhorsed and fighting on foot. I was in a bad way, separated from my Seigneur."

"Oh!" Adelais gasped.

A small crowd of off-duty soldiers and stable hands had gathered under the tree to listen to the story. Ramon pretended to be interested, tried not to squirm in horror as Perce shared bloody details of the butchery of his people.

"It was dusky, nearly night, and I had fallen from my beloved charger. A big man with a spear had me cornered against the north wall. My sword parried his spear, over and over, until I could barely lift my arm. Finally I saw my chance. I used the old stonewall for leverage, kicked off and leaped over his spear. My sword went deep into his neck, in and out. A gout of red shot from the man's neck, and I heard a gurgled scream.

"I pulled back and ducked the dying man's flailing spear, but the shaft struck me as he twisted and lunged forward. I sagged against the poor fellow as he died. It was the only thing that kept me on my feet as two of his companions charged me. I could never defend against two spears with one sword, not exhausted as I was.

"I sagged to one knee, knowing I was done. The two enemies grinned. I could see their teeth in the dark smoke. Everything was darkness and smoke and all I could hope for was that the sortie would be withdrawn. A third man appeared in the smoke, a hulking shadow to one side. Another feinted at me from the opposite side. I swung around, shouting. "To hellfire with you." I stumbled back, clenching the hilt of my sword. I swung up and the sword clanged against a spear blade. Sparks flew. I was too slow. My sword quivered, partially deflecting the blade of the lance, but not enough.

"I knew I would die.

"The wind was knocked from me and I fell back, crumpling to the ground. I landed on something soft and wet. I heard a shrill scream, but I didn't see what happened. Then as I recovered, I looked up and saw a gigantic black horse over top of me and my attackers. The great hooves came down again and again on the back of one of my attackers. The man screamed and died. The hooves missed me by a hand's breadth. A second attacker fell to the knight's sword.

I fought for consciousness. I remember spitting blood, but it was not my own, and I smelled feces, and thank the saints, not my own either. I'd rather die than shit myself. I wiped my eyes and blinked, trying to understand what was happening. I lay on two corpses, one the man I had just slain.

"Stand, you fool!" shouted the voice of my rescuer—of course a familiar voice.

I fought the dizziness and looked up at Boone, Seigneur's black charger. Great, black Boone pawed the earth, his eyes wild with battle rage.

A hand plunged out of the shadows, a white, blood-stained gauntlet with horned knuckle plates. I stifled a cry as my Seigneur yanked me, armor and all, to my feet.

"Now mount, fool!" Seigneur wheeled his charger, his sword flashing down in an arc. Seigneur's blade smashed aside a mounted attacker's shield and sliced deep into his shoulder. His white crusader's tunic was painted scarlet with the blood of the fallen.

"I stumbled, clinging to my sword, trying to see in the smoke and darkness. Where was my horse?

"Then I saw my bay stallion, dying nearby, twitching, a spear broken off between two ribs.

"I had no time for grief, but now, weeks later, I still shed tears when I think of him. Damn Southerners—I'm sorry, Ramon. But he was a good friend.

I stumbled on into the smoldering gloom, following my master. The blood-stained Seigneur had been swallowed by darkness. In the smoke, the hell of glowing torches and screaming men, I could hardly be sure. I tripped on a fallen soldier. As I looked down, I froze, horrified.

"Poor Francois. He was a good soldier, a farmer who loved to speak of his wife and children back home in Toulouse and how he enlisted to obtain his freedom from serfdom. I whispered the Paternoster as I ran.

"An axe arced toward me out of the gloom. I parried, then hesitated, almost killing one of my own!

"'Damnation, Perce, have a care!' A fellow squire pulled back his axe and his young face, blood red and twitching with the ecstasy of battle, smiled at me.

"'Franc's down,' I yelled

"'I know.' Then my friend was gone, vanished into the dark hell like a specter.

"I heard the cries of the fallen and the furious. More by instinct than skill my sword met blades with clangs and sparks, until my arms felt leaden again. How many had I wounded? I lost count.

"Arrows whistled overhead. Screams attested to their random effectiveness. As I neared the wall, the bodies grew deeper and the smells more pungent. The stench of rancid oils mingled with the urine of fear and the blood of the dying—the hot oils from earlier in the night, when the attack began, when the vile Southern pigs—I mean the defenders—had poured boiling fat on my friends.

"Outnumbered four to one and still the rebels fought. And why not? They knew they would burn at the stake or face the executioner's axe. There was nothing to gain by surrendering, except, perhaps, the tortures of the Inquisition.

"Damned heretics. Why didn't they see the light? Who cares what they believed? Just go to the Goddamned cathedral like everyone else, confess, take communion, pretend to be a good Christian, and live in peace. Instead they chose to fight against the pope's own army.

"I realized it was growing light. The first horns signaling the withdrawal blew. I stumbled with the rest, but did not retreat. I needed to be sure of my Seigneur, though not because I believed any arrow or sword could hurt my master. In my entire life I had never seen any who could threaten my lord. One look from the Cyclops knight was enough to wilt the bravest. Seigneur was the devil on horseback.

"Then I saw Seigneur, upright and rigid, his white enameled armor splattered with blood, on big black Boone, the devil's own steed. The Friesian stallion emerged from the clouds of dust, smoke, and early morning mist, his legs lifting proudly as he crushed the dead under massive hooves. Hell's horse with the blood rider. That's what the enemy must have felt when they saw that monster charging them. *Christ love us, I feel that way.*

"'Well fought, Perce,' Seigneur said. Boone halted over me.

"'We have yet to take the keep,' I said.

"'They'll surrender when they count their dead.' Seigneur's voice sounded muffled and eerie behind his closed visor.

"The sunrise spread blood-red over the Pyrenees in the west, bathing the valley in the glow of death. Dozens lay on the ground, many dead, some ignored even as they shouted or moaned.

"Tend the wounded," said Seigneur. He threw back his visor, glaring at me. I flinched, but not because of the scars or the missing eye. It was the pure, black joy on my master's face. It never failed to shock me. He grinned, his eye alive with joy. The delight of battle was more intense with Seigneur. As a battle begins, the joy of it takes any soldier, the fear evaporates and the lust of the fight possesses us. But with Seigneur it was pure delight. The Cyclops scanned the battlefield, taking in the fallen and the wounded, enemy and ally alike, the face full of a cold energy and ferocity.

"Tend the wounded," and he meant our own companions. Already our men were putting merciful swords through the hearts of wounded rebels. Better that than face the Inquisition as heretics.

"As I knelt at the side of a fellow squire, binding a deep wound to his thigh, I found myself looking up at the stone keep we had fought for. The old stone keep was a tiny fortress, with crumbling walls and inadequate defenses. I saw the helmeted soldiers on the walls, looking down on us. Too few, now, and judging by the corpses and wounded, half of the enemy must have fallen in this night's battle.

"The scarlet of the rising sun touched the old stone with exploring fingers, creeping down from the ramparts like blood. To me, the keep appeared to be dying. It was dead already, like those within.

"I have to admit I felt sympathy. They had fought bravely, for a cause they believed in. Me, I was just following orders. I hoped the defenders would die by the sword. It was preferable to the inquiries of the Dominicans, or the hard justice of the viscount, the king's seneschal. But mostly I felt anger. I could not comprehend their will to fight against God and God's army, against overwhelming odds. Forty years and still they battled on. Thousands died on swords and hundreds in the flames. Fools. What drove these poor devils to suffer so? Where was the sense in it?

"Their stubbornness had brought me years of battle and hardship, following the Seigneur de Castlenau. I shouldn't have felt anything for them. But I did.

"The crows arrived with the sunrise, picking on the dead and the wounded alike.

"As I worked to help the fallen, I glanced up again at the walls of the crumbling castle.

"Through the haze, I saw her there. The Lady in Silver. Weeping for the dead. Holding out her hands in some unholy blessing, her long shining silver hair blowing in the morning breeze.

"This was the Jewel of the South. The object of Seigneur's latest quest.

"I winced. The Devil's Wench. The Damnable Dame. She looked down on us. Her words cursed us all.

"I whispered the Paternoster and prayed for the souls of my fallen brothers.

"It was for her they had come. For her that so many had died.

"And she cried out with a voice that silenced all the moaning.

"'*No more pain,*' she said, loud enough for all to hear. The moaning of the wounded ceased.

"I stumbled back, afraid of her curse.

"Magic! Witch's words!

"A hand touched my shoulder, and I admit, in that terrible moment, I jumped.

"'Be still,' said Seigneur.

"I studied my master, imposing and tall on foot, no longer in plate armor, but wearing a skirt of shining mail. He was as invulnerable to her curses as he was to the swords.

"Seigneur looked up at the evil Dame on her walls and shouted, 'Surrender and live.'

"She looked down at him. Even at that distance, her face seemed eerily serene. At peace. 'Seigneur, my life means naught. I told you that we would surrender on the yestereve.'

"'Without conditions, my Lady.' Seigneur's voice rose up, gravelly and harsh.

"'My only condition remains that my escort might leave unharmed. I go with you willingly if they can but leave to rejoin their families without harm.'

"And I knew she must have some power, because even I, still covered in the blood of my enemies, still hurting from battle, surrounded by my dying friends, even I believed her. Her evil magic wove a charm, making her seem wondrous and kind.

"'The seneschal's orders are strict,' Seigneur said. 'We bring all heretics in.'

"'I implore you, Seigneur.' The rising sun illuminated her on the wall now, and she seemed to glow. Even as I watched, a great white snowy bird landed on the parapet beside her. She reached out her hand, and stroked its head.

"'The Devil's bird,' shouted a foot soldier, pointing at the Dame.

"The bird flew off, wheeling south and disappearing into low scudding clouds. All eyes watched.

"Satan's own messenger.

"'I beg you, Seigneur,' the Dame said again.

"May as well beg Satan himself, I thought. My master is without pity.

"Seigneur stepped forward and held up a fist.

"After a long silence, he said. 'Your men may leave unharmed. They leave their weapons. Walk away without horses.'

"I stared at my master, stunned. I had never witnessed any mercy from my Seigneur de Castlenau. Not ever.

"'No! I'll not have it!' A knight rode forward on his grey charger. Albaric de Laon, the Lion, Seigneur's rival, vivid in red and gold. He glared down at Seigneur. 'My men have died with yours, Seigneur. I'll not allow these vermin to escape.'

"Seigneur ignored Albaric and shouted to the glowing Lady in Silver. 'Your men may leave. We will capture them another day.'

"'No!' Albaric's sword traveled half out of its scabbard, wet with the blood of the fallen. 'You've fallen under the witch's spell!'

"'Unsheath, and you challenge me, Sir Lion,' Seigneur said, turning to face the mounted knight.

"The sword remained half in, half out.

"'I command here,' Seigneur said.

"'The seneschal will have your head for this Seigneur!'

"No one spoke amongst the soldiers. Everyone watched Seigneur. What would my unpredictable White Lord do now? Even the wounded seemed to be listening.

"'That is between the seneschal and me.' Seigneur's gauntleted hand traveled to the hilt of his broadsword. 'I lead this troop. I ask again. Do you challenge me?'

"Albaric's gray charger stomped. Without a word, the scarlet knight thrust his sword home in the scabbard and wheeled his mount with a cruel tug on the reins.

"I could breathe again. The confrontation between my lord and Sir Albaric was long overdue, and I felt certain that was the night we would see the epic battle. The only sounds were the sizzle of dying embers, the whimpering of the wounded and the cawing of crows. No men spoke.

"I knew that like as not, Albaric would drive a spear through Seigneur's back when there were no witnesses, rather than face Seigneur in the battle of justice.

" 'Your men may go,' Seigneur said again, raising his voice to the Dame. 'They may take no horses.'

" 'They take the wounded with them?' The Dame's voice had changed, and she sounded sad and empty.

" 'They take no weapons or horses. If they can carry the wounded, they may do so. You have my word, no more will be harmed this day.' His voice was suddenly louder, so all could hear. 'If any touch the evacuees, they face my sword!'

"I'll never forget those words. I'd never heard Seigneur threaten his own men with his old Loial. Would Seigneur really kill one of his own to keep his word? I knew the answer. Seigneur did not speak lightly.

"Seigneur is not religious. We have never attended Mass together. Seigneur curses and kills with the worst of them. He once told me he believed there was a Devil, 'The world is evidence of that,' he said, but he has trouble believing in a God 'who could bring such suffering.'

"But I knew his word was everything. Seigneur would die before breaking his bond.

" 'Thank you, noble Seigneur,' said the Dame. 'Then, I come with you most willingly, to the hospitality of the seneschal.'

"I heard a scattering of laughter from the men. The seneschal's hospitality. They knew it too well. Most likely she'd know rats, dark pits and the master torturer's glowing instruments.

"I almost pitied the Dame her fate. Then I remembered what she was. The Devil's own daughter."

Ramon tried not to reveal his distaste and hatred for this beast who butchered his own people. The story had reminded him of what vile creatures these northerners were. How could he have contemplated friendship with Perce?

Stiff, Ramon stood up, and without a word he crossed the courtyard to the stables. A small paddock of horses held a herd of ready mounts. In the midst of them was a great black charger.

Perce and Adelais had followed him, but he kept his back to them, hiding eyes that threatened tears. He had fallen into a friendship with the very brute who helped capture his precious Dame. A murderer.

Numb, Ramon slipped through the rails.

"Ramon, have a care!" Perce snapped. "These are chargers! They are not friendly."

The giant horses crowded around Ramon. Ramon stroked them with his long fingers.

The big black stallion pranced to him, pawing the dirt. This was the warrior horse who killed Southerners.

Ramon held out his hand.

"Ramon! It is trained to kill!"

The black horse's eyes were wide and the teeth clenched. He did not look friendly.

"It's all right—Boone," said Ramon.

Ramon astonished even himself by wrapping his arm loosely around Boone's giant head. Instead of bucking or snorting, Boone pressed his head into Ramon's chest.

"By God, I've never seen this," said Perce.

Ramon stroked the shining neck. Boone nickered.

"You have a way with horses. Boone doesn't like people much."

Ramon kissed Boone on his fleshy muzzle. Boone nickered again.

"I've never seen the like! Boone's more used to killing and maiming than hugging."

"It is not in anyone's nature to kill and maim," Ramon said, his face still pressed to Boone's.

"What's that supposed to mean?"

"Nothing. Nothing." He forced a smile. "I have a way with animals."

"And people it seems. You have us all in your spell when you sing."

Ramon rubbed his neck. "Even warriors must know love." And Ramon hoped it was true. He knew the Dame's power. She offered uninhibited love and compassion. Perce's story, as horrible as it was, suggested the Dame had reached into the Seigneur's black heart.

The lofty roof of Viscount Hugh d'Arcis's great hall, where Ramon sang. Author photo.

Song of the Lovers

19

THE SEIGNEUR DE CASTLENAU rode through the city streets in a rage, a frosty storm moving quickly through the city, his white cloak flowing behind him in the stiff night wind.

He could not shake his fury at the cardinal, his archbishop and their rabid dog the Diableteur, who had announced the Dame's trial, against his objections. Soon she would endure the same torture he had seen applied to Doré the rebel.

Seigneur had threatened retaliation in public, before all the knights of the viscount's court. "She's my prisoner."

"Then you may attend," said the viscount.

"I will not permit this Inquisition."

"You cannot stop it," said Archbishop Amiel. "This is Church business."

Seigneur glared at the gloating archbishop. "I will take the case to my king."

Cardinal Fiesco had intervened with ominous logic. "Why do you protect this heretic?"

"She is mine to protect."

"She is not some plaything," the viscount argued. "She is the most dangerous person in all my lands."

"She is mine," replied Seigneur, implacable and calm.

Fiesco, for the first time, showed anger. "Then your fate can be decided with hers. No one is saying she is not your prisoner, and you are entitled to rewards and ransoms. But that does not prevent an Inquisition from convening to decide her fate before God. And if you disagree with the judgment, and protect her, you might suffer with her!"

Seigneur had managed to rein in his anger and left the room without another word, not even allowing his loyal squire Perce to follow. Fiesco's meaning had been clear. They had the right to try her; he had the right to defend her.

Why did he care? The intensity of his emotions for The Dame, the Jewel of the South, surprised even him. She was a handsome woman, no doubt about that. But his interest was not sexual—she was sworn never to know a man, and Seigneur was no rapist. He knew only that she brought him peace. From the moment she had appeared on the battlements, begging mercy for her defenders, she had Seigneur in her power. Her voice, her peaceful face, her touch—brought peace. Was it magic, an evil spell? Seigneur didn't care. Ever since the jailer at Eregli took his eye in an orgy or torture, he had known no peace. He had tried to find it in the ways of honor and the sword, but the pain and the fury were always with him. Then the Dame—her voice was a healing jewel.

Last night, he had watched the torturer of the Inquisition play with Doré with barely contained rage. He did not know this rebel Doré except by reputation and he was as surprised as everyone else at the revelation that the famous revolutionary was a woman. As the half naked woman was dragged out, scarred, bruised and whimpering, she shook her fist at Seigneur. Woman or not, she reminded Seigneur of himself all those many years before—a lifetime ago: defiant in agony, stripped of humanity by the torturer.

Torture. No matter by whose hands—the Saracen, the French, the Church—it was a degrading spectacle, not worthy of any person, however low. How could any man take pleasure in such sufferings? He had seen it in the black eyes of his jailer in Eregli. The torturer had laughed as Seigneur lost consciousness with the smell of his own cooking meat in his nostrils. His dignity stripped with each layer of burned flesh, he became less than a man that night.

Seigneur's palfrey, his little Odo, pranced through the streets, lifting his knees in a high dance. Curfew was in effect, but Seigneur made no attempt to obtain the donjon.

The few people still on the street ran into doorways as he passed.

Did he frighten them so? Yes, he knew that he did. Friend and foe found him terrifying.

He rubbed his scarred face, feeling old pains throb. At times he could feel the heat of the glowing metal and the searing of his own flesh. He often woke up shivering, drenched in sweat and clutching at his face. He had been handsome once: an idealistic golden-haired squire off to prove himself in the Holy Crusades to his betrothed, Celene, the most beautiful girl in the Isle de Paris and daughter of his father's old friend the Duc de Tulle. Back then he had no scars, two eyes, shining hair tied back in a pony tail. He had been the most eligible young man of the court: Squire Gerard de Castlenau, first son of the most powerful Lord in the Isle de Paris.

All of that had changed in one night of torture. Now he was simply Seigneur, the Cyclops hero of the crusades. He gave up the green colors of Castlenau and the golden stag and took the white. He became the Nameless. He was as ostracized as the Diableteur, another freak who had been changed by his ordeals.

When he was dubbed a knight by his mentor Sir Harbin, he wore only white. His deeds became famous, but his name remained unspoken. Those who knew him, even the great lords and the king himself, respected his wish not to be called Sir Gerard de Castlenau. When his younger brother sent word that Gerard was now the lord, Seigneur de Castlenau, he simply changed his name to Seigneur. Lord. He left his father's estates in his brother's stewardship, never to return, ignoring the pleading of his widowed mother. When his mother wasted away, there was nothing to tempt him back to Castlenau.

Seigneur rode towards the Baron de Montolieu's city house. They would drink late into the evening. He was about to turn his horse for Montolieu's house when he saw Ramon.

The troubadour was speaking with an old grey-whiskered man in grey robes who leaned hard on a staff. Both the troubadour and the old man were sneaking about city streets after curfew.

Seigneur watched silently. Ramon leaned forward and kissed the old man on both cheeks. The old man turned into an alley and Ramon marched the other direction, towards the chateau gates. Seigneur noted the troubadour's furtive manner. The mysterious old man in gray had the look of a troublemaker or a rebel, in spite of his age. Or perhaps he was one of the old heretic Perfects. But there was something about

Ramon's purposeful stride as he marched toward the castle that changed Seigneur's mind. He spurred his horse into an abrupt canter across the bridge, ignoring the sentries. He kept the troubadour in sight and was surprised to see Ramon enter the low door that led to the dungeon in the bastion.

He dismounted and followed Ramon. He jogged without a sound across the yard and followed the bobbing torch in the passageway. He slowed as he heard voices ahead, and paused, listening.

"I am instructed to sing for the prisoners." Ramon's voice, clear but soft.

"Sing?" The sentry laughed. "Who commanded you?"

"The Seigneur de Castlenau!"

Seigneur froze as the guards laughed. "Well, what a waste! All right, go in."

The Seigneur felt no emotion at the lie involving his *name*, but he was intrigued. He waited until Ramon had entered before approaching the guard. The soldier snapped to attention, clearly confused by all the happenings, but he did not dare question the Seigneur.

Seigneur slipped through the arch. Ramon had taken the only torch and Seigneur watched from the shadows as the troubadour crossed the deep pit, gingerly stepping over the dead and the dying. Doré and Osric no longer hung from the wall in chains but were anchored to the floor. Prisoners stirred as Ramon passed, calling out for water. Seigneur stayed in the shadows, conscious of his white cloak, wrapped in the reek of the pit. Dozens of Inquisition prisoners lay in chains, most half-naked and scarred, unconscious or moaning their despair.

Again, Seigneur's mind journeyed back to Eregli, to the jailer who had played with him for weeks, until, at last, Seigneur had strangled him with his own chains and made his escape to the desert. Wounded, naked, he had almost died in the days that followed, pursued by infidel soldiers. Only hate had kept him alive.

"Ramon?" Doré—the woman—said. "What are you doing here?"

Seigneur settled against the sloping wall, his eye watchful.

"I brought food." Ramon knelt in front of them and unwrapped a bundle. They stared at the treasures in disbelief: hard cheese, a loaf of bread and two apples.

The two rebels wolfed down the humble leavings from the kitchen as Ramon squatted on his heels, watching.

Guilt, Seigneur thought. Ramon had been captured with the two renegades, but while they languished in the pit, he was free. Or perhaps he needed to meet the infamous rebels again, now that he knew of Doré's humiliation and that she was a woman. The entire city was buzzing with the news. Knights who had pursued the Grand Duo fruitlessly for all those years became the lead characters in Ramon's jokes over the great feast.

No. It had nothing to do with professional curiosity. Ramon's furtive behavior made it clear he felt guilty. Guilt was something Seigneur understood well.

"Ramon, your charity is appreciated. But foolish," said Doré. Her breasts were covered by the tunic, and she looked manly again.

Ramon sounded uncertain. "You need to keep your strength."

"Why? What use is strength here?"

"I cannot very well rescue the Dame by myself."

Seigneur held his breath and leaned forward, pressing on the wet stone. A centipede crawled up his gauntleted hand and wriggled up his arm but he ignored it.

Doré and Osric stopped chewing. They stared at Ramon for a long time then Doré smiled and rattled her chains, pulling them taut. "Ramon, you overreach yourself. You are a troubadour. Are you going to take your staff and bash more heads?"

Ramon laughed. "That is why you must keep up your strength."

"Ramon, come closer."

Seigneur watched as the troubadour came within reach of the rebels. Doré leaned forward and kissed Ramon's forehead. "You should leave this alone. You're no warrior."

"And you're no man. Unless you have both testicles and breasts."

"You think strength lies in your sex?" Doré sounded disappointed.

Ramon smiled, his teeth glittering even in the torchlight. "I jest. The two strongest people I know are women." He leaned closer. "But you should not assume a fool cannot fight."

Osric, the big brutish mason, rattled his chains. Seigneur stared at the big man. Even Seigneur might fear to face such a giant, and he remembered it took an entire troop to subdue the man in the Auberge de Terre. "But we cannot help you, good jester," Osric said.

Doré stared at the troubadour. "I know you love the Dame. We all do. But have a care."

Osric reached out and patted the boy's shoulder. "Your sentiment is appreciated, but—Did you hear something?" They all looked in Seigneur's direction. A rat squeaked. "A rat."

"The Dame's trial is certain to go ahead," Ramon said. "I overheard the archbishop. We must do something." Ramon froze abruptly, like a nervous hare then his head swung back and forth. "What was that?"

Doré listened. "A dying prisoner," she whispered. "What is your plan?"

Ramon leaned closer, his voice dropping. Seigneur heard only snatches. "I have ... confidence of ... they trust me ... the seneschal ...the Baug Balar ..." Seigneur heard little, but it was clear that Ramon's appearance in Carcassonne had been no accident. Seigneur found himself liking the boy all the more, in spite of his urge to arrest him and throw him in chains. A brave boy, with a clear sense of purpose, a plan, and talent.

"As I gain the confidence of the court," Ramon said, his voice slightly louder, "I will find a way to free you."

"And then?"

"And then I need your help to free the Dame. Once we are out of the castle, I have my friends ready to help." Ramon pulled a skin of wine off his belt and handed it to the rebels.

"There's more."

Seigneur leaned forward.

"Yes. Even with the Baug's help, our only hope of escape is the Phantom Wood."

"The haunted wood!"

A rat chattered at Seigneur's boot, the only sound.

"They won't follow us in there."

"With good reason," Osric rumbled.

Ramon's teeth flashed white. "I'm told your men live in that wood."

"Is this so?" Doré said, sounding suddenly suspicious. "An unreliable rumor."

"I know you have little reason to believe me," Ramon said, his voice rising.

"You do seem friendly with the French."

"How else to rescue the Dame?"

"Ramon. Everyone's friend."

"You don't trust me."

"We trust no one."

Ramon nodded. "There are more complications. I know not, yet, whether this is ill or good."

"A hopeless cause cannot be worsened," Doré said with a light laugh.

"A cardinal from Rome has claimed the Dame. Seigneur, the viscount and this cardinal fight for the right to the Dame."

"A cardinal? This is bad news."

"And Diableteur has returned."

The silence was broken by Mauri's growls in the darkness. Seigneur glared at the little dog, standing a few feet from him, squatting on his forelegs and yipping.

"Mauri! Leave the prisoners!"

Seigneur stooped and picked up a bone. He stared at it—a human bone. Christ Lord Jesus! He tossed the bone. Mauri's tail wagged furiously and he chased it.

Doré said, "You are just a jester, Ramon. What can you do against such as these? And that damned Seigneur!"

"Be careful of that *devil*!" Osric said.

Seigneur's fingers drummed the goatskin hilt of his old sword. It pleased him to be feared.

Doré's voice hardened. "The Seigneur is a creature of darkness! He's not fit to wipe the shit off the Dame's shoe."

Seigneur slid closer along the wall in the shadows. This comparison pleased him less. The dog was back, barking again, wagging his tail playfully. Seigneur tossed the rib bone once more, and off Mauri ran.

"That unholy bastard watched as they poked me with the hot iron!" shouted Doré. She lifted her arms and revealed the welts.

"Doré, I'm sorry," Ramon said.

Doré made small fists. "This is what Seigneur enjoys!" she snarled. Seigneur froze as Ramon crossed in front of him with the torch and retrieved a bucket of water. Ramon washed Doré's wounds with the water.

"This is monstrous," Ramon said. "You should say whatever they want to hear."

The rebel woman looked at him with suddenly fierce eyes. "I'll never recant. These eaters-of-shit don't deserve it!" Doré shook her head. "It matters not. We are irrelevant. Only the Dame is important. If you can help us, we must rescue the Dame."

Ramon squatted in front of them. "Oc, I know. But—" The boy's voice dropped to a whisper. "I have something of yours."

"Of mine?"

Ramon held out something in his hands and Doré fell silent for a long time. Seigneur's breathing seemed suddenly loud. The dog came back and sat in the shadows in front of him, wagging his tail.

"It was the Dame's, Ramon." Doré held out her hands and clasped them over Ramon's. "This jewel is the nine-pointed star of our Lady. It symbolizes her spirit, our light—and the disciples of Jesus."

"There were twelve apostles," Ramon said, his voice carrying some awe.

If Ramon held a magic amulet, such a thing could have him in chains before the Inquisition.

Osric snorted. "Twelve, less the traitor and the two doubters. The nine faithful of Christ."

Ramon held it out again, as if it were on fire. "I do not want it."

"It will protect you."

"It helped you not."

Doré laughed again. "It took an entire troop of the seneschal's men to capture us. I feel plenty protected." She held up her hand. "Nay, Ramon. Take it. It is blessed by the Dame herself!"

"I found it in the chateau market. One of the guards must have sold it to a merchant. I wanted to—"

"Don't worry about that, Ramon. You really believe you can help us? You really believe there's justice in the world?" She pointed at the star jewel in Ramon's hands. "Look at it! No one can lie in its presence."

"Is it true?" Ramon brought the jewel closer, staring at it.

"That is the Jewel's legend. No one can lie to the Dame. No one can lie in the presence of this nine-pointed star." Doré laughed. "Keep it."

"I'll keep it for *you*."

"It's yours, now. Wear it with pride. If you ask someone a direct question, as long as you wear the jewel, they must tell the truth."

"I will rescue you. I will rescue you, and we will together save the Dame."

Seigneur had heard enough. He stepped out of the shadows into the ring of torch light, with Mauri at his side.

20

THE DAME'S SENTRY looked startled, and took a half-step back. The Seigneur de Castlenau was used to the reaction. Everyone feared him, even his friends. The raised scars that erupted from the uncovered socket of his missing eye always served him well.

"Jaspre," Seigneur said. "Is all well? How is your wife?"

"Fat, my lord."

Seigneur laughed. He liked Jaspre. "You were on duty the other night?"

"Not guarding the Dame, my Lord. I was on the south gate."

"The night the troubadour came to the city?"

Jaspre's eyes revealed confusion, perhaps a little fear. "Seigneur? How could you know?"

Seigneur's eye rolled down in a wink. "I know all, good Jaspre. Tell me your impressions."

"I don't understand, my lord?" Japre did look confused.

"When you saw him what did you think he was?" He wanted Jaspre to understand, but not to lead him.

"A fool."

"When you heard him speak?"

"He made me laugh, Seigneur."

"Did you trust him?"

Jaspre's forehead furrowed, concentrating. "My Lord, no. I wouldn't trust him."

"Good." Seigneur nodded. Jaspre was smarter than he looked. "And what else?"

"He was fearless, lord."

"Explain."

"Faced by armed guards at curfew, he joked with us, not intimidated by anything I said or threatened. Fearless."

Seigneur nodded. Fearless. That was just how Ramon seemed to Seigneur as well. It was why he liked him. "Anything else?"

"No, Seigneur. He wasn't the oddest one that night."

Seigneur stepped closer. This is what he wanted. "Is that so? Who could be odder?"

Jaspre blinked rapidly, worried he'd done something wrong.

"Jaspre, you did well. I am proud of you."

Jaspre's smile was nervous. "Seigneur, it was the witch. And that Templar."

Seigneur stepped even closer. "Templar? The same night?"

"Moments later."

"What of him, then?"

"Arrogant, my lord."

Seigneur laughed. "Is that all? He is a Templar after all."

"I don't know, lord. I felt as if he'd as soon kill me as talk to me."

"And this witch? The white-haired sorceress, no?"

"You know?"

"I know all, Jaspre. What bothered you about her?"

"Nothing at first, lord. She was—delicious." Seigneur laughed, encouraging him. "But the hair. And the eyes."

"Is that all?"

"No. The bird!"

"Bird?"

"This demon-bird landed on her shoulder, a great white owl."

"And she arrived right after the troubadour, no?"

"Oui, lord, she did! A strange night, fog'n all! I still get nightmares, lord."

Seigneur reached out suddenly and clasped the man's shoulder. "You're a good man, Jaspre. I could use men like you."

"I would be honored to take the white, lord!"

"Speak to no one of these things!" He stepped past the flustered sentry and entered the Dame's apartment.

The Dame smiled at Seigneur. She rose and curtsied.

"Do not bow to me, Dame. I am not your better," he said.

She sat on the straw bed, facing him, her placid face studying him as she waited for him to speak.

"Are you comfortable, ma Dame?" He glanced around the drafty stone room. It was better than the pit, but hardly comfortable for a lady of standing. A straw bed, two narrow slits as windows, a chair and a small hearth.

"May we talk as we did on the trail?"

"You need not ask, Seigneur. I enjoyed our conversations."

He held up a jug. "I brought you a jug of spring water."

As she swept past him and retrieved two wooden bowls from the mantel, he breathed in her wildflower scent, still sweet after a week in the tower. Hyacinth, he was certain. What must he smell of? Dust and dried blood? Musty old man. Perhaps the reek of the prison.

"Are you comfortable, Lady?"

She held out the bowls and he poured water. "Oh very, Seigneur. Your viscount has been kind."

"So far," he said.

"Though I think tis the doing of the delightful young Adelais. She was most eloquent, insisting I be treated as a countess."

"You are a countess."

She shrugged. "By birth. It's of no merit."

"Adelais disagrees."

"She is kind to me. She visits every day."

"She has some influence with her father." He set down the jug, wondering at the power of this woman. This Dame, this countess of Foix, inspired men and women both, people such as the rebels Ramon, Doré and Osric to risk their lives for her. And the soldiers who died defending her in the Pyrenees. She wanted none of it, wanted no one to come to her rescue, but it seemed that men and women would die for her. Even the viscount's daughter was her champion.

"I must thank the dear child," the Dame said.

"She'd just laugh at you."

The Dame smiled and drank lightly from the bowl. "Yes, I suppose she would. She's delightful for all of that."

"Troublesome, more like." He frowned. "I pity Lantar."

"Her future husband? He is fortunate."

"I doubt he'll be able to handle her. She's a wild thing."

The Dame's smile lit the room. "Well, Seigneur. What shall we talk about?"

His face must have betrayed his confusion. She set down her bowl and looped her slight arm through his.

He felt the heat rise to his face. "What is it about you that compels me, my Lady?"

"I know not, Seigneur. I feel equally compelled by you."

He pulled away his arm. "I need no dishonest flattery."

She laughed as she often had on the long journey to Carcassonne. "No dishonesty, lord. I am known for my tedious honesty."

He glared at her, his eye squinting. Her smile refused to fall before his scowl. "It has been suggested that I ravage you."

Her sudden peel of sharp laughter surprised him. "I am sure there are younger women you can have your way with, Seigneur."

He slapped his hand loudly on his sword scabbard. "But you are the Holy Dame, sworn to chastity since childhood! I'd be famous if I took your flower."

Again the delightful laugh warmed him. "That is a foolish notion. I am a widow with six children."

Seigneur frowned and looked down at his boots, suddenly conscious of the fresh mud.

"You thought me a virgin?"

"You are of the Perfecti."

"I was a wife and mother first. I vowed chastity *after* my husband died and my sons grew up. I dedicated my life to God only then, to my shame."

"There's no shame in motherhood."

"No, never. My children are a great joy to me. I thank God every day for them."

Seigneur remained silent.

"Are you disappointed in me?" she asked. "Was I so perfect in your dreams?"

"You still are, my Lady."

Again she placed her hand over his arm, her hand so frail and tiny against the gnarly trunk of his sword arm. "Knock me down from your altar, Seigneur. I am no angel."

"But you are the Holy Dame."

She sighed. "I try to teach and guide my people. I strive to control my own cravings—yes, Seigneur, I have cravings. We all have them. You struggle with yours every day."

He pulled away his arm. "What do you mean?"

"You struggle with your lust. I see it in your eyes—no, my Seigneur, don't be embarrassed—"

"You misjudge me, ma Dame!"

"I doubt that, Seigneur. And for me, if I had not foresworn, I would be tempted." She leaned closer. "Your scar doesn't terrify me. You wear it like a badge of terror, but I don't fear you."

"You should fear me. I've killed many."

"I have no doubt."

"Lady, you vex me!"

"I am sorry." She leaned closer and he could taste her breath, sweet like ripe fruit. "I *am* tempted. But I cannot. My life is God's now."

"Then I must hate God."

"God knows your heart, Seigneur. I know your heart. You were a good man. You can be a good man again."

"Do not preach to me, Lady."

She kissed his scarred cheek. As always when she touched him, he felt a peculiar, unnatural warmth. "Seigneur—may I know your name?"

He looked away. "I have no name, no colors, no past." He rubbed his mangled cheek.

"I must know your name," she said gently.

"I have none!" He said it too sharply. Regretted his outburst. Could he even remember his name? No.

Not since that day.

Not since his shame.

Tortured by a man who enjoyed his work too much. He had been captured as a young knight in the Holy Land, stripped of his rank and his armor, humiliated. There had been no talk of ransom or prisoner exchange. His jailer wanted only one kind of satisfaction.

The jailer took a special interest in him, caressed Seigneur's body with blades, glowing implements, whips, stripping away manhood, pride, ideals.

He left a hollow shell, a scarred thing with no hope of returning home to his betrothed.

Seigneur should have died that last night. He had become his tormentor's plaything, a challenge in a dark game he could never win. Seigneur lost himself in God, found strength there, and resisted all the pain with inhuman grace.

The night the torturer took his eye with a white-hot poker, Seigneur bucked in his chains, dangling from the rafters of the dim chamber. The torturer tried three times for the eye and each time the agony was searing, but each time his eyes survived the attack. The reek of burning flesh made him nauseous, but he swallowed it, refusing to give the beast satisfaction. He convinced himself this man was Satan's own creature. He called out to God, to his own personal saint, and to the Virgin. For all his years as a crusader, God sent no angel to take away his pain, no miracle to save him.

Then, like a knife, the hot metal plunged into his eye. His flesh, bubbled and dissolved before the heat, molten flesh pouring down his cheek. And the sizzling ...

Again, he did not scream. He would not beg mercy. He trembled, pulled on his cuffs until they tore flesh, bit into the tip of his tongue to prevent the scream, spat at the torturer. Then, mercifully he passed out. He erupted to consciousness later, driven there by waves of agony that made him wish for death.

The torturer's face greeted him when he woke, and through a cloud of anguish, he realized something. He had seen the man torture others in the dank underground pit, and had seen the man grin with satisfaction. With Seigneur, who offered no screams or pleas for mercy, the torturer grew angry. He never asked questions, never asked, "What is the strength of your troop?" or "Where will your forces attack next?" He just played.

Seigneur fought to stay conscious and a plan began to form.

It was two nights later that he had the strength to attempt it. The man had tended his eye, bandaging the wound, obviously wanting to keep him alive. And what next? Would he slice Seigneur's manhood? He shivered at the thought, though it hardly mattered since he no longer felt a man.

That night the torturer sculpted lightly on Seigneur's chest, peeling back skin. As usual, he worked late, long after his assistants left. He had made Seigneur his special project. He would elicit a scream and hear Seigneur beg for mercy before he would allow him to die. He was intent on perfecting his work as an art.

Seigneur worked his plan and waited for his moment.

The torturer came too close with his glowing stick, his face inches from Seigneur's, glowing like a demon's in the red light.

As the poker caressed his chest, Seigneur screamed for the first time.

"No! No more!"

The man smiled.

Seigneur feigned unconsciousness and the Saracen went for his bucket of cold water. He sluiced water over Seigneur's head, but Seigneur didn't twitch or move, pretending death.

The torturer stepped closer, touched the glowing poker to Seigneur's abdomen.

By now Seigneur was numb to the pain, and his eye socket still agonized him. The new pain was nothing. He didn't twitch. Didn't breathe. He hung limp in the chains.

He peered through the slit of his one good eye.

The torturer leaned closer, reaching out with one hand for a pulse, the other still holding the glowing poker.

It was his fatal mistake.

Seigneur's chained legs swept up and wrapped around the man. The man shrieked, but in a chamber of horrors and screams, no one would come running to aid him. Seigneur wrapped the chains binding his hands around the man's neck. The man swiped at him with the red-hot rod. He tightened the chains, not wishing to kill the man right away. He needed the man to hold on to his heated iron.

The man was strong and struggled in Seigneur's grip. Seigneur choked him and, with his legs, pushed against the man's back, pressing up until his hands reached the poker. Once he had it in his hand, he finished strangling the torturer. He let the poker slide between his hands until the glowing tip touched the restraining bolt on his cuffs.

He fought a scream as the heat seared his hands along with the bolt. After long moments the bolt slowly loosened. He alternated fingers, keeping them far enough from the glowing tip to avoid damage, but close enough to cause pain. Then, surprisingly, he was free.

He became less than a man that day. He felt delight in slowly killing the torturer's assistants when they came to the chamber three hours later, then the guards. None of them were a match for his fury.

It would be the last joy he felt in life. It was also the last day he used his name. He no longer lived among the human. He stole enemy garb and weapons and fled to the desert.

The desert nearly claimed him as it did claim three of his stolen horses. He survived by eating their flesh and drinking their blood. The pain never left him. Weeks later, he made it to the crusader camp, nearly dead, more animal than human. No one in the camp recognized his face, at first assuming him to be an enemy. Later, it became clear he was one of them, even though he refused to give his name. He was close to death by then. Some of his wounds festered, he was delirious from days in the desert. The priests said last rites. No one allowed he might live.

His ferocity shocked everyone in the camp. Finally someone recognized him, and his men claimed him back—the same knights who rode with him to this very day—and took him to their tents. But he wouldn't speak to them, wrapped in such dark rage that he drove away his comrades, filled with such sizzling hate, hotter than the red hot implements of torture, that all he wanted was a chance to kill more Saracens.

His mission became death. He knew now that he could never return home. His fiancée would scream when she saw him. His father would never accept the monster into his chateau. His only purpose in life was to kill as many Saracens as he could.

After his recovery and weeks of clumsy retraining with weapons, learning to coordinate with one eye, struggling to wield a sword without depth perception—he found he could use his phantom eye, his memory of depth, to compensate for the loss, even in lance work—after all of that, he was reborn the nameless Seigneur.

A decade later when his father died, he refused to return home. His fiancée had long since given up hope that he would return. His mother died of the wasting. He sent a letter to his younger brother to steward Castlenau. And still he fought on in crusade after crusade, as the nameless Seigneur. He cultivated the nameless persona. He would be feared by enemy and friend alike. The dull ache of his eye never left him and on rainy or cold days he felt other twinges and pains. They strengthened him, reminding him of his rebirth as the nameless Seigneur, feared and respected by all.

Within a year of his escape he had become the most feared apparition on the battlefield. Saracens fled when they saw the white knight. He never lost another battle, refusing to ever be captured again and face the humiliation of torture. He would die rather than be taken prisoner. It was the secret to his strength. He was no longer hampered by fear or compassion. Though none loved him, his prestige grew. He was famous for never taking prisoners. He would inflict no horrors on even his enemies. Where the Seigneur campaigned, the defeated enemies who were wounded were put to the sword. Even fellow knights and lords were not taken prisoner.

Yet all that had changed not so many days ago when the Dame stood on the battlements and pleaded for mercy. He had felt nothing as he slaughtered her men, but when she pleaded for their lives in exchange for her own, something stirred in him. She did not fear him, but her fearlessness was of a different quality than his own. She met her fate with joy.

After her men departed safely—an act of compassion the soldiers still talked about in the barracks—she walked across the bridge over the dry moat and smiled at her captors. She approached Seigneur and curtsied. Before climbing into the wagon, her prison on the trail, she insisted on kneeling to bless the dead.

He watched, impassive but curious.

Finally, at sunset she agreed to climb into the wagon that would be her cage for many days.

He had held out his arm to help her climb.

He felt heat where she touched him.

He pulled away, shocked. His arm and his scarred face tingled. Warmth spread through him. His empty eye socket itched.

"What just happened?" He stepped back and felt afraid for the first time in years.

She looked at his face, not shying away as most women did. She looked up into his terrible flesh and smiled. "Seigneur?"

"What did you do?"

"I did nothing."

But she had. The endless pain he had endured since Eregli had drained away. The itch and tingling gave way to warmth. The pain was gone, the phantom pain that had driven him mad in battle, that kept him awake at night. Suddenly, he felt no ache, no ghost eye in his empty socket. Even the twitch was gone from his cheek.

"I want none of your witchery!"

She leaned forward to touch his face. He pulled back, afraid for the first time since the Saracen torturer. "I offer no magic."

"Do not touch me!"

His men cowered from the Dame and he saw that they were terrified. What had she done to their Lord? Only Satan's own daughter could make Seigneur pull away in terror.

"Your pain is so deep, Seigneur," she said. "There is no need for it." She smiled at him.

"Undo your magic," he said, touching his face. Not only was the pain gone, he had sensation in his cheek. He could feel the touch of his fingers. "This is devilry. I'll have none of it!"

She pursed her lips. "Perhaps you just forgot the pain." Then another smile.

"I want none of this. Pain is my strength." He leaned close, dropping his voice so that his soldiers could not hear.

"It eats at you."

"Give me my torment."

"No."

He had half drawn his sword. "Give it back to me else I kill you now."

She reached out one of her long fingers. "Then kill me. I have no powers to restore your agony."

"Give it back!" Seigneur was overwhelmed with sensations, his face was alive with them. He felt the cold of the night on his skin. With the pulsing pain gone, he could concentrate on sensations he had long forgotten.

"I cannot give anything back. I took nothing from you." Her voice was surreal. Peaceful. Hypnotic. "The pain was an illusion."

"Sorceress!"

Seigneur touched his face again. He felt the lines of the scar. He ran his finger along his lips, inside his mouth. He could taste his own salt.

The journey back to Carcassonne had been a difficult one for Seigneur. No one wished to ride in the wagon with the woman he called a sorceress. His own squire, Perce de Mendes, took the reins for the first two days. As they rode the high mountain trails, he found himself regaining more and more sensations in his face. He tasted food and wine for the first time in years.

What had she done, this witch? She had cursed him. Taken away his strength.

Curiosity, horror, or gratitude—or all three—drove him to her wagon each night to shout at her some more. "Lift your curses!" He continued to threaten her over the next few days, but as he became accustomed to his new feelings, his threats became conversation. She was the first woman who could stare at his disfigured face without wincing. She didn't seem to notice, though he wore no cover on his empty eye socket. She always smiled.

"How is this possible?" he asked her each time he came for a visit.

She always answered, "Sometimes the peace I have found for myself is felt by others? I don't know, Seigneur."

His deeper feelings returned with the sensations in his face. He could be more than a killing machine. Yes. He could be a man again.

Now this. Now she would know his name. This woman was to be tortured—even as he had been by the Saracens—then she would be tried and burned at the stake as a witch and heretic. And she cared only for his name.

She leaned forward and touched his face. He no longer resisted her touch; he craved it. He felt her warmth, her magic. "The Seigneur de Castlenau must have a name. I would know it."

"You would know too much!"

"Dear Seigneur."

"You took my pain. Now you wish to give me a name."

"I wish to know your name. Not give you one."

"I have no name!"

She sighed.

He leaned over the small fire, staring at the flames. He hated fire. "Ma Dame. I beg pardon."

"I've heard the Seigneur does not beg pardon from any man."

"You are not a man."

In the long silence, there was only the sound of the wind whistling through stone, and the snap of the fire.

"Do you regret sparing my escort?"

"No."

"But I heard your troops mocking you."

He shrugged. "I care not for them."

"What do you care for?"

"Honor."

"And what else, Seigneur?"

He closed his eye. "Nothing else. Honor."

"And there's no honor in slaughtering my guard, is that it?"

"Yes."

"Yet you've killed many."

"Too many to count."

Her eyes glistened with unshed tears. "I am very sorry for you, Seigneur."

He struggled with the anger for a moment, closed his eye again, opened it to see her smile. "I spared your men because only you mattered. My orders were to return you to Carcassonne. Why sacrifice more of my men?"

"So, you bring me back to face the fires."

He turned, began pacing the room, his hand clenching the hilt of his sword. "I told you. Honor."

"That's all that matters?"

"Yes."

She laughed, a light bird-like twitter.

He spun, eye blazing, but the smile on her face melted him. "Lady, you vex me. You vex me so."

"I surely see that, Seigneur."

"You tempt me. You smile at me as no other has."

"It is love."

"But I want a different kind of love."

"Then I cannot offer."

He stepped forward until his face was a hand's breadth from hers. "You wish it, perhaps? After all those years without a man—"

Her smile did not fade. "I am sworn to God. Only *He* may take me. You would have only an empty body."

He turned, angry, surprised to find he was breathing heavily. "I can help you."

"Seigneur, you've been kind. It is enough. Others in your place would have abused me."

"The cardinal has already convened the Inquisition."

"I know."

"Are you so fearless?"

"My heart beats like yours, Seigneur. I can be afraid. I am a weak old woman."

"I have never met anyone so strong."

"Seigneur, my strength is God."

"What God?"

"God."

"They say you worship the Devil himself."

Again, the bird-like twitter.

"I don't believe in a Devil, Seigneur."

The world was full of disease, death and evil. Seigneur himself had slaughtered hundreds, had endured torture, the mocking laughter. There had to be a Satan, an Evil One. It was God he was uncertain of.

"Suffering is of our own making," she said. "Our journey is to find God within ourselves."

"You follow Christ?"

"Of course. I love Christ the enlightened."

"Then why not renounce heresy? Save yourself? Make confession, take the sacraments. I can guarantee your safety." His voice rose in spite of himself. Did he care so much for this woman? This heretic?

"I cannot be so shallow, Seigneur." She took a deep breath. "Mine is the way of the spirit. I have preached it for many years. How could I renounce it now, just to save myself?"

"But you will be tortured!"

"I would lie if I told you I am not afraid. Yet, I have found my peace. I am ready."

She had found peace, even in the face of her impending torture and burning. How could that be? She did not lie. He saw it in her smiling face. Perhaps she would feel no pain, just as she took away his pain.

"Let me help you," he said finally.

"It would ruin you. I want no others to suffer."

"It is not your choice."

She sighed and came closer. Her small hand caressed the fold of the scar on his face. "Dear Seigneur. I'm ready for my end. I've done all I can in this evil world. I can know peace."

"I cannot."

"I know." She pressed her face into his chest. "I'm sorry for you, dear Seigneur."

He pushed her away. "Don't be sorry for me."

"I am."

"I want no pity."

"No pity. Unconditional love."

"I will help you."

"You will not."

"I have no choice."

"There are always choices."

She looked so strong, meeting his gaze, her hands defiantly pressed to her hips—and yet so frail.

"Seigneur. Seigneur, I know you are powerful and influential. But the Inquisition is above even your influence. You would only condemn yourself."

"You are still officially my prisoner."

"You are a stubborn man."

"I am an old man. I tire of crusade."

"I know."

He had set events in motion that could not be stopped. He had become a rebel. His love for this woman had changed him. Others knew of his plans. Tonight he had stepped out of the shadows in the pit to confront Ramon and the rebels, and, to his own shock and theirs, he had made them an offer. They had not believed him. Ramon had even tried to kill him with his puny spear. Seigneur easily restrained the boy, and by sparing his life had proven his sincerity.

But why had he taken the path of rebellion? He was the vaunted Seigneur. But with no hope in Church or king, why should he not fight for this precious Jewel of the South? Did it matter who he fought for? Who he died for? Either way he would die, and for his crimes he must burn in hellfire for eternity. Better to die in hope of rescuing this angel, this Dame.

Only a few hours ago he had seen the disbelief in Ramon's eyes and the intense hatred in Doré and Osric. They believed his words to be a trap, even after he reassured them, "Why must I trap you? You have condemned yourselves already with your words. I do not need to trap you to have you all executed."

Ramon had stared at him long and hard before saying, "I believe him."

"Believe this monster!" shouted Osric. "He has killed hundreds of our people!"

"I know."

"Then why?" Osric shouted.

"I have a friend," Ramon said, his voice low, as if he talking to himself. "She can see the future."

"Watch your words!" said Doré. "We are in the Inquisitor's pit."

"Nevara predicted a man, a man who seems to be an enemy, would help us."

"Not this man," Osric said. "He is a butcher!"

"Are you any less a murderer?" Seigneur asked. "How many of my people have you slain?"

"Not enough!" The giant mason spat at Seigneur, making it clear he would never believe. "He killed two of my best friends."

"You murdered dozens of mine," Seigneur grumbled. "I have no time for debate. You are in chains. I am not giving you a choice. Ramon, you could be in chains with one word from me."

"But why would you help the Dame?" asked Osric.

Seigneur had answered, "She took away my pain."

Doré had nodded. Osric smiled. And Seigneur told them his plan, a plan the Dame could not know. She wanted no one to rescue her, no one put at risk for her.

Now, as Seigneur looked into her smiling face, he realized how precious she had become. Her beauty was in her serenity, and it brought him a kind of peace that changed him.

"I wish no daring rescues," she said, her voice breezy and warm.

"I will do as I will!"

"My fate is done."

Seigneur kicked a chair across the room. "I do not believe in fate."

"Fate does not require your belief."

"If only I had never found you."

"Wishing does not change what is. What must be." She reached out, but he stepped back, away from her touch. "You do not have to fear me, Seigneur."

His face heated. "I do not fear you."

"I love you."

"Be quiet, Lady. You perturb me." He was stunned to realize he was shouting—loud enough for the door guard to hear him.

"But it is true. I cannot lie."

"You'd give your body to me?"

"Not willingly."

"Then why do you taunt me with your words of love?" His eyes were drawn to her womanhood. He had not known love. Never. Though he had bedded whores, no willing woman had ever given herself to him in love. But this woman touched him, took away his agony, proclaimed love.

She stepped closer and took his rough hands in hers. "My belief is that this world—this world of suffering—is an illusion. To escape the illusion, we seek peace. Serenity. Release from the carnal."

"Heresy!" He said, but he could feel no real revulsion. Her words made sense to him. He had seen such suffering, much of his own making. The world really was hell. And she promised a release.

She squeezed his hands. He felt her heat, felt his own arousal.

"We believe that Christ taught us a way to escape the hell of this world. We believe in love, peace, harmony, perfecting of the self. By taking away the craving, you take away the pain."

He pushed away her hands. "I know nothing of these things. I fought for Christ in crusade. That is all I can do, even though I be condemned to hell for the many I have killed."

"There is no hell except this world, Seigneur."

"More heresy!" He must turn and walk from this room, never to return. Testify against her vile words. But he would not. His path was had been chosen. It had been chosen for him the day she took away his pain.

"This world is hell." Her eyes glistened, threatening tears. "We seek to escape it, to break the cycle of suffering with love."

He half closed his eyes. Peace. To know peace. It was too late for him.

She stepped closer and took his hands again in her own. "I would know your name."

He snatched his hands away and left the room.

21

THE HALL WAS SO CROWDED that many of the viscount's guests sat in the reeds on the floor. Delighted to show off his famous new entertainer, the viscount had proclaimed an open invitation to all his vassals. They drifted in—squires, off-duty sentries, bored garrison soldiers. Every lady of note in the city sat at the tables, while the lesser ladies crowded Ramon's bench on the floor and sat in the straw. Mauri ran from spectator to spectator to beg morsels. Ramon sang song after song, and always the crowd rose to its feet and shouted for more. Even the cardinal and the archbishop attended every performance.

"Sing of the Grail!" one soldier bellowed.

"No, Guinevere!"

"El Cid! Sing of El Cid and the Moors!"

Perce sat with his master, the Seigneur, somewhat astonished at Ramon's popularity. When Ramon had entered the hall, the women screamed, lifting their arms. They reached out to touch him. It was a bizarre phenomenon, although, as an admirer of Ramon's voice, Perce understood it. When Ramon sang, his voice transported listeners to mysterious worlds, places where their dingy and miserable lives were left behind, a place where flowers were rubies and sapphires, night skies were filled with diamonds, knights shone golden in their perfect armor and carried magic swords. The cheering continued after each song, led by Adelais, who ran from table to table, gesturing with her arms and chanting, "louder, louder." Soon even the men joined the shouting.

Seigneur had given the audiences a new name. "*Ventiladors*," he had called them. Fanatics.

For three nights in a row, Ramon's adoring fanatics came, the crowds growing each night. Two days before Mayday, the viscount announced Ramon would sing in the main square for the entire city, and the men and women in the great hall shouted acclaim.

Perce's peculiar friendship with the young heretic grew, inspired by Adelais' enthusiasm and a genuine fondness for the odd Southerner. His jokes and songs became addictive, and Perce found himself finding excuses to spend time with Ramon, though it conflicted Perce in a profound way. He adored the troubadour, but he knew that Ramon would eventually run afoul of the Inquisition or even the great lord viscount because of his unyielding mouth. He just would not be quiet around his betters. Each day Adelais made Ramon sing more songs under the Troubadour Tree. Afterwards, Perce and Ramon always played a game of tiles, or sparred in the courtyard with the soldiers—also "ventiladors"—cheering Ramon on. They usually played in the old kitchens, surrounded by the savory smells of cabbage and mutton. This afternoon had been a little disturbing for Perce, not just because of Seigneur's shocking revelation that he was leaving Carcassonne. Ramon had been full of surprises as well.

Everything was changing. He felt it. It had changed the night they had captured the Dame. Before that damned witch, everything was pure and simple and he was on his way to his dubbing. His master was an enigma, but a simple one, a feared and terrible killing machine. Perce had thought long on his career. Should he leave his Seigneur, the man seemingly empty of love, yet whom he loved as a father, for it seemed madness had touched his black lord? Their relationship had always been about loyalty, and he had been grateful to be squire to one of the most famous lords in all of Christendom. But now, here was

Perce befriending heretics, and his lord cavorted with the very heretic queen herself. With the coming of the Diableteur, the cardinal and the Templar the situation had become even more ominous Something was about to happen.

"Your spirit's not in the game," Ramon said with a smile, as they played yet another game of tiles. Mauri sat on his shoulder, a squat little ball of fur, balanced like a bird as Nevara had taught him. It always astonished Perce.

"Nor is yours," Perce said.

Ramon threw out a squire tile. "Sorry. I can't help thinking of the trial."

Perce snatched up the squire and laid two more beside it. "Three squires." He threw out a tile. "She is condemned. Forget her. And your rebel friends."

"They are my people. Sometimes I hear their screams."

"Sound travels in Carcassonne. But this is dangerous talk, Ramon. Don't assume your magic songs can save you from the viscount if you sympathize with rebels."

Ramon drank some flat dandelion brew. "But they will burn."

"Or worse. They chose their path." Perce rapped the table with his knuckles. "You play a dangerous game, Ramon."

"I love games." Ramon threw out an archer tile. "Your one-eyed master is remarkable."

"Oui. There's not a man more feared and respected in Christendom." Perce snatched up the archer and tossed a knight.

Ramon played with Perce's thrown-out tile. "I think your Seigneur is looking for something."

Perce looked at him sharply. "What?"

Ramon shrugged. "I have no idea. But he has the look of a man on a quest." He slid the knight tile in front of him on the table and placed two knights beside it on the table. "Three chevaliers."

Perce scowled, annoyed that Ramon could beat him, even distracted. "You believe in your heroic songs too dearly. There are no heroes in the world."

"You're a philosopher." Ramon threw away a builder.

"My philosophies are born of battle and killing." The squire picked up a tile from the unused pile and laid it in front of him with two from his own stack. "Three lords command your three knights." He tossed out a bishop.

"Perhaps you are looking for something too."

"My spurs and knighthood." Perce snorted. "Revenge for my father, perhaps. But you'd do well not to bring that up. I blame *you* heretics for my family's disgrace."

"What makes you think I'm a heretic?"

"Aren't you all? I've hardly met a Southerner who wasn't."

"That means your church will need to burn the entire South!" Ramon's lips tightened with anger, the smile vanishing for perhaps the first time since Perce had known him.

Perce held up his hand. "Leave this alone, Ramon. I like you—don't ask me why—but be careful what you say. I am loyal to king and Church."

Ramon sighed and finished his drink. "Why is it that warriors, as hardened as you and your master, can be so charmed by a song?" Ramon picked up the bishop tile and put down his other two. "Three bishops command your three lords."

Perce saw the stubborn anger in Ramon's bloodshot eyes. They fell silent. He could see Ramon was no longer interested in the game. Perce couldn't win anyway. Only a set of kings, popes or Templars could win the game now and it was apparent he had none in his stack. Perce pushed the tiles into the center of the table, signaling his defeat. "You win again, troubadour." He began to stack the tiles, staring at them as he gathered his thoughts. He loved Ramon's voice, perhaps he had even started to love the man as a friend, and that disturbed him greatly.

"Will you attend the May Tourney?"

Ramon shook his head. "I despise martial games."

"Nonsense. It's the stuff of troubadour romance."

"I don't want to see you hurt."

"How adorable." Perce scowled.

"Will Seigneur fight Sir Albaric, too?"

"Seigneur? What makes you think they would combat?"

"Sir Albaric hates your lord, and—and Albaric, he's younger."

"You notice a lot." He looked away, embarrassed to show his fears. Ramon had highlighted his own fears. Seigneur might be undefeated, but Albaric was much younger and stronger and filled with hate for his rival. Perce fought a feeling of panic. If Albaric challenged, honor demanded Seigneur accept. Perce forced a laugh, but it was a hollow sound.

"Tomorrow you sing on the great stage in the square," he said, trying to keep his mind off his Seigneur.

"I am ordered to sing."

"You do not sound happy."

Ramon grinned. "I am always happy."

That night, Ramon sang again in the great hall and again the ladies crowded around his bench, eyes fixed with wonder on his pretty face.

Even Perce's stony-faced Seigneur listened, his eye closed and his face expressionless—as serene as Perce could remember. Perce felt it too. There was something truly magical in the youth's voice. You could feel yourself transported by the lyrics. As soon as Ramon fell silent, they shouted for more. Only the cardinal from Rome, guest of the viscount, regal as an ancient Roman emperor in his throne, seemed unaffected by Ramon's songs.

"This boy is wondrous," said Seigneur in his gruff voice. Perce felt pride in his new friend Ramon.

Ramon stopped singing. He set aside the lute and picked up his little dog. They looked ludicrous together, the lanky troubadour and the rat-like mongrel. Of what use was such a dog? Not enough meat to eat, not big enough to be useful in war and not aggressive enough to be a dog of the watch. About as much use as a singer in a land of war.

Perce tensed. "Do you mean to announce, lord?" Now that the singing was finished, he knew his strong-minded lord would announce.

Seigneur gazed at Perce for a long moment. "Oui," he said, a typical one-word answer. Then, as if thinking better of it, he said, "You are released from me, Perce."

"Never!" Perce scanned the room. Why tonight? Why when there were so many hundreds to hear the shame? And especially with the powerful Cardinal Fiesco sitting at the viscount's right, a man said to be the next pope. "I will never leave you, Seigneur. You are my sworn lord." The depth of Perce's conviction surprised him. Seigneur never revealed any emotion. He remained as mysterious as the day he had first taken Perce as squire, a bawling eight-year-old boy orphaned by the attack on Chateau Mendes. The Southerners—Ramon's people—had killed his entire family. Seigneur had taken him in, trained him, raised him, becoming his adoptive father. Whatever Seigneur decided, Perce would follow. Perce felt the change in his master. The constant fury had faded, like a storm blown out and replaced by a placid sunny day. What had happened to his stormy lord?

Seigneur stood. "I would speak." He said in his gruff voice.

Seigneur never spoke in the great hall, and his announcement caused an immediate stir, then a deep silence. Everyone stared at him.

"Yes—Seigneur de Castlenau?" prompted the viscount, sounding astonished.

"I have made a decision." He stared intently at the dais.

Beside Perce, Sir Albaric, Seigneur's rival, and his squire, Darel, stopped their drunken laughter to listen to the Seigneur.

"I have decided to return to Jerusalem."

The astonished silence continued.

The viscount stood up, staring at the former city champion, the Seigneur.

"The Khwarizmenians?"

Seigneur nodded. "Jerusalem may fall again."

"But we need you here, Seigneur." The crowd in the room roared agreement.

Seigneur held up his gauntleted hand, silencing the room. "Knights and lords are meant for crusades, for noble deeds!"

"I will not have this, Seigneur!" The viscount's face flushed angry. Perce understood the anger. A reasonable man would have told the viscount in privacy, not in front of hundreds. Of course, Seigneur was not a reasonable man.

"I do as I please, my lord viscount. I owe you no service. I swore no oath of fealty."

The viscount, lord of all the South, glared at the colorless Seigneur. "We have fought side by side—"

"And may have that honor again. But the crusade in France is finished. My work is done. I will take what is mine and leave. I have no taste for this Inquisition." He spat into the rushes and glared fixedly at the cardinal.

"The Church appreciates your loyalty," Cardinal Fiesco said, his voice carrying sarcasm. "You have brought us this heretic Dame."

Seigneur moved around the table and stood in front of the cardinal and the archbishop. "You misunderstand me, Eminence."

Perce couldn't predict the reaction, but he knew the room might soon erupt in violence. Reluctant, Perce moved to join his lord, stopping only to give his rival squire Darel a kick on the way by. Seigneur's eight knights, who had fought with him on many campaigns, left their various tables and stood with Seigneur, a row of white crusaders.

"I sense a rebellion," the Archbishop Amiel said unhelpfully.

"What means this, Seigneur?" said the viscount, his voice rising.

"I will take my leave after Mayday," Seigneur said, his hand resting naturally on the worn hilt of his sword.

The silence was thunderous.

Then the room filled with shouts of excitement. Most in the room had counted on the Seigneur and his men to lead any force against the heretic stronghold at Montségur, the castle of the Dame. It could hardly be a *holy* crusade without Seigneur.

Shouts filled the hall

"Castlenau leaves us!"

"Seigneur, goes to Jerusalem."

The viscount held up his arms. "Silence!" He shouted his command three times before he restored order.

Perce glanced around at his many friends, at the many knights who had fought at his side. They were all on their feet.

"My friends, we have fought together in honor," Seigneur said. "You will always have my gratitude. You have but to ask and Seigneur will be your ally again. But I cannot support this vile Inquisition."

"That is impertinent," said Archbishop Amiel

"You overstep yourself," said Cardinal Fiesco, although his voice was calm.

When the viscount spoke, he too was calm. "Seigneur, I know not what has brought on this rash announcement. But I must respect your wishes. You have fought long and well for the king and we owe you only honor. We certainly will not forestall you."

Seigneur turned slowly. "That is wise, lord. For none could stop me."

The viscount nodded his assent.

Archbishop Amiel, however, was beside himself. "Does your glib comment mean that you believe the Church's Holy Inquisition is unjust?"

Seigneur turned his back on him. "I made no glib comment. I have stated my beliefs. I am a chevalier and crusader. I am no butcher."

"Heresy!" Amiel's face puffed up red in rage.

A new voice spoke up, an unfamiliar voice but a very familiar frowning face, the Templar Arnot. "It is *no* heresy. The Brothers Templar have as much authority before God as you do Lord Archbishop. I see no heresy here. Only a noble knight whose fight is finished." He glared at the archbishop's livid face. "And Seigneur enjoys the protection of our Order. You'd do well to remember it. We certainly will."

The Cardinal Fiesco stared for a long moment at the Templar. He seemed to be smiling, but he said nothing.

The viscount nodded. "So be it, then. We wish you well. Go in peace, Seigneur. You have our gratitude and our hospitality for as long as you need it."

"Thank you, Lord Viscount."

The Seigneur left the main floor, his knights and Perce following him.

"*He* must be happy, Seigneur," Perce said.

"Who?"

"Him. The *cockroach*." He pointed at Sir Albaric.

"Don't let anyone hear you. Sir Albaric is still your better."

"Seigneur, I—"

"Settle yourself, Perce." He placed his hand on Perce's shoulder, an unusual expression of bonding. "This is the business of lords."

They returned to the table of champions. Sir Albaric stood up, smiling. "Congratulations, Seigneur."

"On what, messire?"

"On alienating the church and viscount in one rash moment." Sir Albaric laughed.

They stood a sword's length apart. Although their words were civil, their hatred was apparent. "Perhaps as city champion I shall challenge you for the Dame?"

Seigneur stepped closer. "You must do as you must. I would regret killing you."

"Bold words, old man," said Sir Albaric.

Seigneur smiled, but it was an ugly expression, alien to his scarred features. "I never turn from a challenge." He bent and picked up his ale bowl. "Come, we drink to chivalry!"

Perce raised his bowl. "Esprit de chevalerie!" Their bowls came together. All the knights at the champions' table shouted the toast. Even Sir Albaric drank.

Ramon's sweet luting and voice defused the tension in the vaulted hall, calming the rumble of rough voices. Perce lost himself in a song of Gilgamesh, trying to forget the confrontation of moments ago. Such a splendid voice. Such a shame that it may end in the fires or on a gibbet.

"What do you think of the castle's new troubadour?" Seigneur asked Perce, his voice a whisper.

Perce hesitated and set his bowl down. "Seigneur?"

"Ramon. You seem to be friends."

Perce shifted. "I suppose so."

Seigneur's face was suddenly fierce and his big-gloved hand closed over Perce's hand. "Tell me, quickly, *écuyer*, where are your loyalties!"

The demand was so sudden and the grip so fierce, that Perce blurted out, "My Lord Seigneur de Castlenau!"

"Even if it means a delay in your dubbing?"

What did that mean? Was this a test? Did Seigneur not wish his only squire to advance to knighthood? But to Perce it didn't matter.

Knighthood was all he ever dreamed of, it was what he lived for, but Seigneur had raised him as his own. Seigneur, for all his faults, was the only family Perce knew. Finally, carefully, he answered, "Even then, my Seigneur."

Seigneur's lip trembled. Was that a smile? "Be ready for *anything!* Obey me *without* question!"

"Is something wrong, Seigneur?" Perce began scanning the great hall, suddenly alert. "I am ready, Seigneur. Can you tell me more?"

Seigneur shook his head once. "Remember your oath. Without question."

Song of the Chariot

22

MAYDAY DAWNED CLEAR and sunny, yet full of dread. Tomorrow, the Dame's trial would begin in a rare public spectacle. Ramon woke from a troubled sleep filled with dreams. He had not dreamed of his mother's burning since Nevara gave him a sleeping charm, but last night it came to him in vivid and horrible detail. Except, in that terrible moment, when the flames wrapped around his beloved mother, and the flesh began to melt, she transformed. Suddenly, it was the Dame tied to the post, flailing in agony atop the piles of snapping hot faggots. The fear still clung to him.

Ramon plunged into the early morning revelers outside the castle, with Mauri at his heels. He hoped the festivities, and his friends at the Baug Balar, might give him some focus. He didn't trust the Seigneur, though he had no choice but to follow the white lord's instructions: "Be ready, the day after the trial begins." Ramon's plan stood a much greater chance of success with Seigneur's planned distraction, though Ramon assumed a trap. Could Seigneur truly be infatuated with the Dame? Osric hadn't believed. Ramon wanted to believe. For some reason, Doré did. But why would Seigneur risk all, his status and his wealth, for a heretic Dame?

"The Dame's power should not be underestimated," Doré had said after the Seigneur left them alone. Ramon knew this, of course. As a child, he had seen the miracle of the Dame. But still, could even one so pure as the Dame heal a monster as corrupt and black as the Seigneur, a man credited with butchering hundreds of Ramon's own?

The streets were dusty with revelers, most costumed and celebrating, crowding every space from the inner bailey of the castle across the stone bridge to the inner market, then through the barbican to the city's main market square.

Ramon pushed his way through the steady stream of celebrants, Mauri hard on his heels and yipping if he got separated by the crowd. He found his friend Perce in the main square, haggling with the baker over buns. "Fair day, troubadour!" Perce said. The squire held out a seed cake. Ramon took the cake in one mouthful.

It seemed to Ramon that Perce knew nothing of Seigneur's plans, judging by the oblivious smile on his face. Ramon was determined to enjoy his friend's company. In a day or two, they might be enemies again. "Ummm. I smell nutmeg tarts!" Ramon pushed into the crowd and bumped into a burly tradesman.

"Watch your purse today!" Perce said as he caught up. They wandered the city, stopping occasionally to watch the mummers, acrobats and minstrels. Ramon's favorite treat was St. John's bread, sticky locust seedpod cake that stuck to the roof of his mouth, as sweet as honey.

Hours later, bloated but satisfied, Perce and Ramon sat on the stone bridge spanning the castle's dry moat. At Ramon's side was Mauri, whining for crumbs.

The sun was hot on their faces but the breeze cooled them.

"A pleasant day," Ramon said.

Perce nodded.

"I'll miss you."

Perce glanced at him. "How did you know we're leaving?"

Ramon shrugged. "I just assumed after Seigneur's announcement you'd soon depart."

"Probably true."

"*You* don't know?"

Perce shook his head. "I don't." His face showed his tension

"Oh." Ramon tossed Mauri the last of his bread. "Well, I'll miss you."

"So you said."

Ramon smiled. He knew Perce was not about to admit a Southerner could be his friend. *We're enemies,* he thought. North and South. Catholic and Cathar. The *oïl* and the *oc*. How could they ever be friends?

"Come. Let's have a diviner egg."

"*Heresy.*"

Ramon sighed. "It's just an old pagan tradition. For fun."

"Well, I don't want to know what is to come. I'm satisfied with not knowing the future."

"After your Seigneur's great announcement don't you want to know as much as possible about your future?"

"Ramon, you are an annoying acquaintance. Mind your business!"

"Diviner's eggs are just for fun!"

"I want no part of your pagan ways!"

Ramon shook his head. "I'm not a pagan, Perce."

"You're still a heretic."

"Truth told, I'm not much of a believer either way."

Perce frowned. "I am. And I don't believe there's room in this world for heresy. God's will must be done."

"Too many things have happened to me to make me religious. I have a hard time believing God could permit all these atrocities."

"A dangerous admission to a holy crusader."

"But not to a friend? All right, then, an acquaintance?"

Perce puckered his lips in thought. "Let's go see our fortune," he said at last.

Ramon laughed and they joined the crowd in the outer market.

They didn't get very far before a piercing voice stopped them both. "Perce! Ramon!"

Perce struggled to hide a frown. "Adelais."

The yard was full of hawkers and merchants. The threesome bought another cuckoo-foot ale and pushed through the crowd in search of diviner eggs. Mauri did his best to keep on Ramon's heel though his occasional yelp indicated his displeasure as the crowd kicked or shoved him. The smells were wondrous—fresh loaves, seed cakes, spiced wine, lamb roasting on the spit—disguising the spring stench of cesspits thawing after a long winter and dumping into the River Aude.

"This is my favorite day!" Adelais practically danced between them, pulling them along. Perce's not so subtle attempts to pull away were unsuccessful.

"Does the viscount know you dance in the streets?"

She laughed. "Of course not!"

"You'll get *us* in trouble."

"Oh, from what I hear you're already in trouble. My father's furious with your Seigneur."

Perce looked away. "My Seigneur is within his rights to withdraw."

They made their way to the Baug Balar in the lower city, arm in arm, laughing and eating as they walked. The Baug square was already crowded. It seemed the entire city had migrated to the colorful tents of the Baug and Ramon was glad. The Baug, at least, would make money today. The crowd jostled them, oblivious of Perce and Adelais' nobility. Everyone was equal on Mayday. The temporary pavilions were up, all blazing color and flags and everywhere the musicians played and the jugglers juggled and the performers danced. The crowd roared on the far side of the market square where Nevara's horses were performing. Ramon desperately wanted to see Izzy and the other horses, and led his friends slowly through the crowd.

Halfway through the throng, they came upon the knife-throwing twins, his childhood friends Atta and Hatta. The threesome watched for a while, as awed as the rest of the crowd by their skills. Of course the mischievous twins saw Ramon and ran to him immediately.

"A new volunteering!" one of them shouted, in thickly accented French.

Ramon tried to hide in the crowd but Perce shoved him from behind. Atta—or Hatta; Ramon could never tell them apart—grabbed him by the arm, and shouted, "Cheering for our new victim!"

Hatta—or Atta—winked at him, and Ramon knew he had a message. He gave Perce his precious lute and his spear Zaleucus, and allowed himself, reluctantly, to be led to the boards where they tied their victims.

"You must see Magba," Hatta or Atta said, as he tied Ramon loosely to the throwing boards. "She's doing the diviner's eggs."

Ramon nodded.

"Don't cut our troubadour!" shouted a delighted Adelais, clapping her hands. "He is to sing tonight!"

A roar of acclaim from the crowd made it clear that they knew Ramon was to sing as well. The Viscount had announced a great festival of song, led by Ramon, on a makeshift stage in the upper market square around the castle

"Worrying not," Atta or Hatta shouted over the crowd. "I not hurting your singing birdie." He leaned in quickly and whispered in Novgorod. "At least I hope not!" He kissed Ramon's cheek. "We miss you, boy."

Ramon couldn't watch. He trusted them, had stood for them a hundred times over the years, but he could never stand on the boards without wincing. He peered through slitted eyes. Adelais covered her mouth, hiding either a smile or her fear. Perce grinned and pointed, and the crowd cheered. Mauri barked, looking up at him with a quizzical look on his little face.

Then the knives flew. Atta and Hatta threw knife after knife, sometimes three in one throw, sometimes with their back turned. Ramon felt the wind of the knives, heard them thunk into the thick wood beside his face. He hoped he didn't wet himself. More knives flew. The audience roared and threw coins. Ramon opened his eyes and breathed again. Dozens of knives traced his outline on the wood behind him, some just a finger's breadth from his flesh, one planted firmly near his groin.

Hatta or Atta untied him, fingers brushing Ramon's skin fondly.

"Day after tomorrow," whispered Ramon, as Atta or Hatta worked the last rope. "Be ready."

"As we planning," whispered Hatta or Atta.

Then, released, Ramon delighted the crowd with a dancing acrobatic tumble. Three handsprings and he landed beside a giggling Adelais to the applause of the crowd.

"That was wonderful!" said Adelais, grabbing his arm.

"You are braver than you look," allowed Perce with a smile.

Arm in arm they pushed through the crowd toward the grand pavilion. Outside the great tent, another massive crowd had grown around the bear stage, built on a raised platform. Umar, the giant husband of Magba and father of the children of the Baug, wrestled his beloved bear, Yiffi.

"Must be a tame bear," said Perce.

"If you are so sure, why don't you wrestle him?" said Ramon.

Perce laughed. "Let's see those famous horses!"

"First the diviner's eggs," Ramon said, pointing at the sign on the great pavilion.

Perce groaned. "The lineup is too long!"

Adelais pulled his arm. "I want my fortune told!" She forced them to join the long line, and they watched Umar wrestle Yiffi as the lineup slowly wound inside the tent. Yiffi growled and raked at his master with a full rack of claws extended, delighting the audience.

Inside the pavilion were many more delights. The Baug dancers performed their miraculous tumbles and throws for the hundreds in line. The audience screamed appreciation as the girls—all Magba's daughters—flew threw the air on their long ropes, dancing magically in the air. Ramon, who had watched them practise all his life, knew just how dangerous their graceful acrobatics were. All of them had broken bones more than once. But the performance this Mayday was perfect as they swung in unison by ropes tied to the huge support poles.

They were surprised to see Adelais' father in the audience, surrounded by bodyguards, clapping along with the rest. The archbishop was there as well, with his new companion the Templar Arnot. All of them were uncharacteristically smiling, pointing up at the acrobats as they performed.

Finally, the lineup wound down to the small platform where Magba sat in all her glory. She had taken on the guise of the old wise woman, her loose robes nestled about her to hide her latest pregnancy, white hair wound up into a great bun. She looked like the most ancient of the ancients, the wisest of the wise, but her grin was wide and welcoming as Ramon sat opposite her. He pulled an egg from the barrel and handed it to his adoptive mother. Magba clenched his hand, and her fingers caressed him for just a moment. Their eyes met, hers crackling with energy, but he dared not demonstrate his true feelings. She tapped on his wrist in the old Baug performers' code. It was their secret way of communicating, useful for the "reading of the minds" act. Magba tapped out, "Diableteur arrest us in two days."

Ramon tapped back, "Pack. Be ready."

"We ready."

"The wagon trap?"

"Yes."

"The forest?"

"Yes."

Ramon tapped, "Two days, I rescue the Dame."

Magba blinked her eyes once. Yes.

Then, Magba rolled her eyes and became the witchly old fortune-teller. She cracked open his egg and stared at its contents. Then loud enough for the audience to hear, she shouted, "Ah, love, love, and *love*. I see love in your future, young Master. What's this? Blindness. No, a blind girl? You will love a blind girl. No, you are the blind one. You don't see her. She's a deaf mute." Magba smiled, thinly and winked. "It is true. I speak truth!"

Ramon feigned disgust and threw a *denier* in the coin pot, wondering if Magba was teasing him. A deaf mute woman? That had to be a joke. He smiled at Perce as he stepped off the platform. "Oh wonders. I'm to love a blind deaf-mute." Adelais roared with her piercing laughter.

"She'll have to be. That way she won't see you," Perce grumbled.

"But she also won't hear my songs," Ramon said.

"Then how can she love you?" Adelais said. They all laughed.

"At least there's love in your future," Perce said.

"Don't despair, dear Perce. I love you! Now go!" Adelais pushed him up onto the platform. Scowling, Perce picked out an egg for himself and handed it to Magba.

"Oh...hoo...oh," hissed old Magba, frowning. "Now, this is not a good fortune."

"What a surprise. Tell, then, old hag."

"Ahhh—" She swirled the double-yoked egg. "Bloody yolks. Not good at all! Betrayal! War. More war. Death. Confusion. The carrion of battle. A siege, with all lost!"

Perce scowled. "All this from an egg?" He stood up to leave.

Magba reached out her hand to stop him. "Beware, young man! Beware the scarred monster!"

Perce wrenched his arm away. "Silence, witch!" and he jumped off the platform.

"Nonsense!" Perce snapped. "It's all *nonsense*."

"Of course it is," said Adelais. "It's meant to be. She knows you. Everyone sees you with the Seigneur—*the* scarred monster. That's no miracle."

Ramon smiled at bright-faced Adelais. "What of you? Do you not wish to know your future?"

She gripped Perce's elbow tighter. "Oh, I already know!"

Perce snatched his arm away.

They wandered the Baug most of the day, and Ramon was full of joy at being amongst his dear family once more. Days of sleeping on the dunged floor of the viscount's great hall or in his stables, alone, with only enemies for companions—he only realized now how much he missed these people, his family.

Ramon forced Perce and Adelais to play another fortune-telling game, the St. John's Wort. He drew a yarrow sprig from a wooden bowl, eyes closed. It was a healthy upright sprig. "True love, love eternal," barked Elas, one of Magba's daughters, who held the bowl.

Perce drew a wilted sprig.

"What does this mean?" Perce asked.

Ramon laughed. "Nothing. Tis a game."

"But in the game what's the meaning?"

Elas frowned at Perce. "It means you'll never find your true love."

Perce laughed. "Wonders. All your pagan fortune telling brings me misery. Endless war. No love."

Ramon rapped his shoulder. "It does not mean 'no love.' Just not your 'true love.' It's the way of the chevalier, is it not? War and romance? Many women, mayhap?"

Perce nodded and finally smiled. "True 'nough."

"So it just means you'll have many loves."

"That's a consolation."

Adelais pulled out a sprig, then pouted. "It's wilted." She hit Ramon.

"You make me play silly games!"

Ramon pushed Perce and Adelais together. "Then you two belong together."

Perce glowered. "Beware, troubadour. I tolerate your nonsense only so far!" He rapped the hilt of his sword.

"I'm an entertainer! Be entertained! Come, the horses!"

The big crowd-pleaser was always the horses. Even with aggressive pushing, they couldn't get anywhere near the front of the audience.

"Lift me up, squire," snapped Adelais.

Grumbling, Perce lifted Adelais up on his shoulders.

"Oh, they're magnificent!"

Ramon knew they would be. He caught only glimpses between the heads of the crowd, but he had seen them perform a thousand times. He saw his own horse, Izzy, up on his hind legs, forelegs slashing the air in perfect unison with twenty other horses. Then they wheeled on their hind legs, pirouetting around each other in perfect time to the music in a graceful horse ballet.

"I needing volunteers!" came Nevara's voice at one of the breaks.

Adelais held up her hand and shouted, "Here! Here are three!"

"Please," Nevara called back. "Letting them through, please!"

Ramon was delighted to be close to his beloved Izzy and the others, but Perce grumbled as Adelais dragged them on to the small field. Only when they were among the horses did Ramon realize how large the crowd was. It seemed thousands. Coins littered the ground, some gold.

Izzy nickered when he saw Ramon but didn't break formation. The twenty main performers were lined up in a perfect row, with Nevara, shining white, standing bridged and perfectly balanced on the shoulders of two horses.

"Lying down for me, please!'

Ramon was glad for the dry spell. The mud had hardened into ruts, so they would not be lying in muck.

"I'm not lying in the dirt," snapped Perce.

"Oh tish! What a baby!" Adelais lay down on the earth right away. "Here? Is here fine?"

"Now the others. Laying down beside brave girl." Nevara pointed.

The "brave" remark was too much for Perce, who lay down immediately. Ramon lay beside them. "No! No! A little further apart!"

"What happens now?" Perce said, sounding uncharacteristically nervous.

Before Ramon could answer, came the thud of hooves, the herd at full gallop. He grinned. He had done this many times, but he knew Adelais, Perce and the crowd were in for a stomping delight. Before Perce could react, the horses were galloping over them, first thundering past their heads, hooves lifting lightly and splattering them with dust, then prancing and wheeling over them in a delicate ballet.

No hooves touched the three prone volunteers. Ramon smiled up at Nevara on the shoulders of Izzy and Wizi. "Don't move," Ramon said, but he didn't need to tell them. The hooves landed as close to their heads as Hatta and Atta's knives had earlier. Adelais squealed in delight. Perce seemed petrified, but neither moved. Izzy's long tail swished across Ramon's face.

Trying to sound brave, Perce said, "They best not defecate!"

Next, one by one, the herd jumped over the three in a long line of graceful horses leaping. The audience hollered and clapped.

"Thanking you!" shouted Nevara. "Going now, please!"

Ramon, Adelais and Perce stood up, dazed and thrilled, and joined the audience, now having earned the right to stand at the front. Perfect strangers clapped them on their shoulders.

"I'll never forgive you for this, Adelais," hissed Perce, but he was grinning with the rest.

The stairs and the beam astonished the crowd more than anything else. One horse at a time, the horses stepped daintily up the wooden stairs built into the back of a Baug wagon. Then, to the adoring shouts of the crowd, they walked across a beam of heavy wood, the height of a child above the ground, paused in the middle, reared and stood on hind legs.

It had taken Nevara months to train them to do this stunt.

As dusk fell, the celebrations continued, noisy and cheerful. For this one night, the curfew was lifted and the townsfolk were ready to make full use of a rare starry evening. The dancing began early and

Perce was very popular with the young ladies. Breathless and laughing, they danced most of the evening to the sweet tinkle of clochetes and the strumming of the rebec.

They danced the Maypoles in the middle of the Baug Balar square with the rest. Ramon sang to his largest crowd ever. It seemed no one wanted the day to end, for tomorrow the Carcassonnians would return to the misery of their lives. And the Dame's trial would begin.

It was a moonless night, full of stars. Torches blazed. Carcassonne resembled the city of old, before the days of the butchering conqueror de Montfort. The happy days of the Vicomte Trenceval de Carcassonne, the last *true* lord of the city. Ramon wasn't alive back then, but he remembered happier times, walking hand in hand with his mother Musette. Strangers and friends alike greeted them with a hug or a wave. Burc, his father, arm-wrestled his friends in the street and warned Ramon to behave. Ramon ran off and played with Jaspre and little Linette, his childhood friends.

Now an adult, Ramon drank chilled spice wine, played games and ate slices of stewed apples and honeyed cakes.

"Won't your father be worried?" Perce asked, late into the night.

"I don't know," Adelais said

"He might have me flogged!"

"He might."

"You're not very reassuring."

"Oh, for a crusader you're such a coward!"

Ramon smiled. "He's not a ladies' man, remember?"

"Ramon!" Perce glared at his friend. "If I paid attention to your romantic nonsense, I'd spend *all* my time with the ladies."

Adelais giggled. "What's wrong with that?"

Ramon patted Perce's shoulder. "My songs also sing of the esprit de chevalerie."

Adelais' eyes shone with excitement. "Ah, Perce, would you tourney for your lady?"

"I don't have a lady."

"But if you did!"

Perce shrugged. "If she was my one and only."

"What about to protect the honor of any lady?"

"You listen to Ramon's songs too much, Dame Adelais."

"Don't call me that!"

"Desist! Adelais, I'm not a chevalier. I can't be anyone's champion."

"But soon!'

"But not!"

Ramon held up his hand to both. "It's Mayfest. No fighting!"

They seemed close to a face-slapping. Finally, Adelais smiled. "Perce, I'm sorry."

For a while they walked in silence, used to pushing through the crowds by now, watching the noisy revels. Ramon knew they weren't admitting their true feelings. Adelais' longing was obvious and he felt sure Perce protested too much. Of course Magba had predicted neither would find their true love, and that seemed likely.

Later, the anger forgotten, the three of them locked arms, Adelais in the middle, and laughed at games of blind man's buff, bowling and dice. The dice games were the most exciting as freemen and nobles alike gambled on the rolls.

They made their way outside the city walls, following the crowd to the river for the wishboats.

On the River Aude, hundreds of candles floated like stars in the sky. "Wish boats," said Ramon. "Come, I have enough coin left for three boats."

They knelt by the shore and watched the little wooden boats, crudely carved, floating on the murky water.

"Another pagan tradition," Perce said.

Ramon ignored him. "You write your wish on a parchment, place it in the boat and light the candle. If the boat reaches the other side of the river without the candle expiring, your wish will come true. If not—" He shook his head.

"I don't think my luck is up to this, friend Ramon," said Perce

Ramon looked at Perce. "That's the first time you called me *friend*."

"Well, don't get all teary-eyed. If you weren't a Southerner I might have called you friend days ago."

"Oh." Ramon's hand instinctively touched Doré's truth gemstone, the nine-pointed star of the Dame. Doré had said no one could lie in its presence. How close did some one have to stand? Was it even true? He hoped so. For it meant he had made a friend among enemies, a friend he would certainly need.

"Well, luck or not, I'll try it."

"Me as well!" said Adelais, dancing lightly from foot to foot.

They paid a *denier* each for the boats and wrote their wishes. Perce gave a tremendous shove to his boat and nearly swamped it. "You'll sink my boat," Adelais said as their two boats collided. The boats pressed together as if to kiss, lifted on a wave, then parted. They watched, anxious, as the tiny boats drifted, flames flickering. Perce's almost sputtered out.

"See, Perce, it heads for the shore."

Perce nodded and Ramon realized that his friend was taking this seriously. Ramon patted his shoulder. "What did you wish for?"

"That you'd leave me be for a while!"

Ramon chuckled.

"No, I wished—*Can* I tell you my wish?"

Ramon shook his head. "I don't know. Perhaps not."

"Then I'll not ask yours."

It became difficult to watch the course of the little boats, mingled in with hundreds of others. Perce pointed. "I think that's mine!"

"I think so."

"I'll get my wish."

"And there's mine!" Most of the boats were reaching the shore of the batter berm, driven by the rippling breeze.

"So what did you wish for?"

"Can't say."

"Won't say."

"I wished for a summer lover," whispered Adelais. Her boat had ground ashore.

"You would," Perce snapped.

"What of you, Perce?"

"I wished to become a chevalier."

"Oh grand. Then you can be my champion!"

"Not likely."

They both looked at Ramon. "I wished for peace." He frowned. "Mine sank." He touched the Dame's nine-pointed star. It seemed they all spoke the truth.

Adelais laughed. "Well, what did you expect? Such a waste of a wish. There'll never be peace in our lifetimes." She winked at him.

Ramon frowned.

Adelais seized his arm. "No frowning! No scowling! Stop that, this instant!"

Ramon bowed his head. "Yes, my Dame."

She punched his arm. "Come on. No droopy faces. Look, the baal fires. Let's dance!"

The baal fires lit the village at the foot of the hill below the city and the festivities continued. The younger girls danced around the bonfires. The single girls had to dance around seven different bonfires if they wanted to be married in the next year. Many of the girls got lost and danced around the same fire twice meaning they'd have to wait until next year. Adelais ran off to join them.

"Now's our chance to escape!"

Adelais skipped around the fire, laughing. "She's beautiful, Perce," Ramon said. "A spirited and intelligent gem. Are you sure you want to run off so quickly?"

Perce watched her mischievous play. She had made it around four bonfires. "She's dangerous, Ramon. And she's already engaged to a royal nephew. Sir Lantar."

"Is it too late? Surely you can only benefit from being a suitor of the seneschal's daughter. You're from a noble family after all."

"So many have thought. The viscount is somewhat protective."

"Hmm."

"The Chevalier de Castelnaudary proclaimed his desires publicly. He was never seen again."

"Hmm."

"Is that all you can say?"

"I still think you're a fool. She's certainly worth your attentions. Just be careful. Take it slow. Seek the viscount's approval."

Perce sighed. "I'll not have time. I believe we'll be leaving soon."

"You don't have to go with your Seigneur. You're old enough to be a chevalier surely?"

Perce scowled at him. "I'll not hear such disloyal talk. My loyalty to Seigneur is absolute!"

Ramon kept his hand on the Dame's truth gem. "I'm sorry. I meant nothing by it. But even if Seigneur asked you to do something you don't agree with?"

Perce looked dangerous for a moment, his eyes hard and angry. "What do you mean by that?"

"Nothing."

"I would die for my Seigneur."

Ramon reached out his hand. "I'm sorry. I know you would."

Perce glared for a moment, then blinked and finally reached out his hand. "Friend Ramon, let's hurry. Before she makes it around the seventh baal fire!"

They ran off laughing, pushing through the crowd.

It pleased Ramon that he managed to lift the spirits of his friend. And if he believed Doré on this truth gem, it seemed that Perce was loyal to Seigneur.

Ramon sang for a great crowd, the beer flowed faster and happy songs and laughter filled the night. Ramon saw many knights and their ladies in the yard, dancing alongside the farmers, traders and serfs. On Mayday, everyone was equal. He saw no churchmen.

Twice they nearly ran into Adelais, but she managed both times to slip out of sight. The dancing continued to the music of *clochettes* and *fipples*, drowning out the song of minstrels on their *mandores*.

They ended the night dancing the *Threading the Needle*, an immense line dance that seemed to have no end. Great *nakers* beat out the pace and a lively group of *chalumeles* made the song. Then, with loud shouts, all the townsfolk seized burning logs from the baal fires and threw them into the river. Acrid smoke and the hiss of dying coals filled the night. The crowd roared when a log cracked, an auspicious sign.

Ramon and Perce lay winded on the grass, leaning against the buttress of the south wall in the deep shadows of the city. They listened for a while to the night creatures. Finally, Perce broke the silence.

"I'll miss you, Ramon," he whispered. "Tell me one more of your jokes. A raunchy one."

Ramon smiled. "Wouldn't you rather have a song?"

"Your songs make me cry. A joke!"

Ramon sighed. "There was a knight and his horse, stationed far out in the desert near Joppa."

Perce smiled. "I like it already."

"The knight had been alone for two years and no one ever came by. He hadn't had sexual relations in years, and he was desperate."

Perce laughed.

"That wasn't the joke!"

"I know. It just felt familiar."

Ramon smiled. "So the knight decided he would try to have sex with his horse. Still sound familiar?" Perce shook his head, smiling. "But he tried and he tried and every time he came close, his horse ran away. Soon the knight was chasing his horse all over the desert. Finally, days later, he came upon a beautiful damsel, alone in the desert. 'Fair damsel, how did you come to be here alone?' he asked, all out of breath. 'My caravan was attacked,' she answered. 'Rescue me, Sir Knight, and I promise you anything you desire.' So he rescued her and carried her on his reluctant horse to the nearest castle. When they arrived, the grateful damsel, looking ever more beautiful after her bath and a change of clothes, said again, 'Anything you wish, Sir Knight, this was our bargain.' And the knight thought and thought, and remembered how he hadn't had sex for many a year. Finally, he said, 'Lady, would you be so kind as to hold my horse for me?'"

Perce roared with laughter until passersby stopped to see what was so funny. No more jokes were forthcoming, and they sat in silence for a long while, listening to the song of cicadas and wolves.

Ramon said, "So you leave soon."

"Seigneur seems all a ready."

"What of the Dame's trial?"

Perce shrugged. "That I don't know. I do know Seigneur has grown unfortunately attached to that heretic. She's of noble birth, the sister of the Count of Foix. I fear another confrontation with the viscount over it. Either way, I'll be glad to quit this place! I suppose we could go off to Castille and fight the Moors."

"What of Adelais?"

Perce bowed his head. "I'll admit I'll miss her. But she's risky. And mayhap I'll be back."

"A chevalier by then, no doubt."

Perce frowned. "No doubt."

Ramon nodded. Mauri barked at him.

"I will not likely eat tomorrow at all!" Ramon patted his stomach. His pockets were full of sweet leftovers.

"Sleep well, friend troubadour." Perce lurched to his feet and staggered toward the arcade of the barbican.

Ramon, too tired, didn't follow. "Fare well, friend Perce." He watched him go, and for some reason it felt like a final goodbye. He enjoyed Perce's friendship, northerner or not, and it was certain that Ramon's path would make them enemies. He waved one last time and fell asleep in the wet grass.

23

THE SEIGNEUR DE CASTLENAU stood as the Dame entered. She wore a simple silver gown, her hair clean and combed. She looked exactly as she had on the day he captured her. Perfection.

Her entry hushed the throng who had gathered in the viscount's great hall, the only room large enough to accommodate the hearing with so many witnesses. The Dame slowly scanned the room, revealing no obvious emotion at the overwhelming assembly who had come to see her condemned, and she took in all the colors of France: the red and silver of Montileau, the green and yellow of Fanjeaux, the white and red of Arnot the Templar, the scarlet of Cardinal Fiesco. *She's wondering what all the fuss is about,* he thought. Seigneur's heart raced as if he had just fought a great battle.

Dame Esclarmonde, Countess of Foix, The Lady of Montségur, the Silver Dame, the Jewel of the South, stood before the tribunal which sat at the viscount's feasting table. She stood, calm and regal, her back tall and straight, less a woman facing certain burning than an empress from an ancient tale. Even with hundreds of spectators, the only sound was the snap of the fire and the clink of armor.

Seigneur sat with Perce at the front of the court, a place of honor for the famous lord who had captured the heretic queen. Ramon sat beside Perce. Flanking the tribunal's temporary table sat the viscount and his vassal lords to the one side, including a smug Albaric de Laon, now sitting in the chair of the champion, and on the other side, God's representatives, the cardinal from Rome, Archbishop Amiel and the Diableteur himself. Beside them sat the lone Templar representative, Brother Arnot, companion of the Master Marshall himself.

Presiding over the court were two Cistercian monks Seigneur knew well from past campaigns and the Master Inquisitor Brother Duranti, a Dominican. The court chairman was Frère Ferrier, a fanatic Cistercian who had taken up the heretic crusade with a passion. The Seigneur had known him for thirty-three years. As a young knight in Sir Harbin's retinue, Seigneur had shared in the victorious siege at Béziers. Simon de Montfort's enthusiastic first crusade against the South had been an exciting time for Seigneur, and the short siege was full of adventure and tall tales, watching the high walls of the city by day and sitting around a friendly fire at night, listening to stern knights tell their tales of fearsome Ottoman horsemen and dark-skinned Saracens. Seigneur's own capture as a squire in the battle for Ascalon had been a popular fireside tale, although Sir Harbin told it at the expense of Seigneur's dignity. The other knights slapped his back in praise of his bravery but he hung his head in shame.

The siege of Béziers was short and when the overly confident enemy, sure of their superior numbers, sent out a sortie of fresh knights, his master Sir Harbin had led an inspirational charge through the city gates before they could close them and captured the east gatehouse.

Béziers surrendered on that dark day, and Seigneur watched from the ramparts as Simon de Montfort marched into town with Frère Ferrier, his spiritual advisor, at his side. The grim army filled the streets, their bloodlust unfulfilled. Seigneur had expected raping, pillaging, a few revenge killings, but nothing could prepare him for Frère Ferrier's proclamation. The excited young monk, himself only twenty at the time, stood up on the Cathedral steps and loudly proclaimed: "Kill the heretics! God will bless you!"

"But which of these townspeople are heretics?" Simon de Montfort asked. "We stand on the cathedral steps. Surely there are good Christians here?"

Ferrier smiled, waved his arm grandly and shouted, so all the soldiers could hear: "Kill them all! God will know his own!"

With a roar the soldiers poured out of the big cathedral square, bloody swords cleaving, hacking and hewing the screaming citizens of Béziers. Seigneur had watched in numb disbelief from the tower, and his master Sir Harbin had shaken his head and said, "A siege always makes soldiers lust for massacre and booty." None of Sir Harbin's men, nor the Templar Knights, participated in the massacre that followed, but they watched, stunned, as forty thousand townsfolk were slaughtered. Even the Catholic priests were slaughtered like sheep, hiding behind their altars. The days that followed were enlightening for the young knight who was ten years later to become France's greatest Seigneur. As he helped to clear the streets of bodies before plague could set in, his youthful heart had begun to harden.

Now this same bloody Frère Ferrier sat in judgment of the Dame. Would he make the same proclamation? "Send her to the flames and let God judge." Ferrier stood up abruptly, his cold eyes studying the court. "In the name of Christ Almighty, and the Mother Church, and his Holiness Pope Gregory, I convene this Court this third day of May, in the year of our Lord Twelve Hundred and Forty-two!"

Seigneur glared at the Cistercian. This ferocious monk—this terrible man who had ordered forty thousand Southerners put to the sword in Béziers—was now a venerable, respected judge and the Dame's Inquisitor.

Frère Ferrier sat in the middle of the tribunal. With him sat Frère Balfour and the Dominican Frère Duranti. To one side was the clerk, Frère Jaie, who stood to read the charges.

Jaie scanned the audience—a cardinal, two viscounts, a Templar, an archbishop, two bishops, three dukes, a score of lords, more than a hundred knights, many ladies. His voice was high and trembly and echoed off the vaulted ceiling.

"Dame Esclarmonde de Foix, Chatelaine de Montségur, Countess of Foix, you are herewith charged with heresy and witchcraft. Hear now what is charged. You are charged with perverting the sacraments of the Church. You are charged with separating yourself from the unity of the Church. You are charged with erring in the exposition of Sacred Scripture. You are charged with following a false sect. You are charged with following articles of faith different from the Roman Church. How say you?"

The Dame stood in the middle of the hall and smiled.

"How *say* you, Dame?" Jaie shouted.

When the Dame remained silent, an angry murmur of voices filled the room.

"Dame you must speak in your defense."

The Dame remained silent, but the smile did not fade. Jaie sat down and lifted his quill to make a note.

Frère Duranti, the chief Inquisitor of Carcassonne, stood on the raised platform. He smiled and extended an arm. His voice was warm. "Dame, you do not understand the seriousness of these charges. We wish your redemption. Please."

When she said nothing, he came down from the raised platform. "Dame, please. Dame Esclarmonde, we love you. We wish only to save you."

Still nothing. His smile finally faded.

"Dame de Foix! If you are found guilty of heresy, you shall be handed over for *debita animadversio*. In Carcassonne, death by burning."

The Dame, serene and smiling, said nothing.

"Let the clerk record that the Dame, accorded the opportunity to plea, refused to answer the charge!" Frère Duranti sat down, his eyes squinting, his mouth quivering.

Seigneur shifted in his seat, his hands sweaty inside his gloves.

Frère Balfour spoke next. "In the name of the Father, and of the Son, and of the Holy Ghost."

The Court responded as one voice. "Amen."

Balfour rose. "We, Frère Balfour, by Divine authority of the bishop of Carcassonne, having special licence from the Reverend Father in God, Peter, by the grace of God archbishop of Carcassonne and Narbonne, and being in this place, day and hour his diocesan deputy; and we Frère Duranti of the Order of Dominicans, Inquisitor appointed to investigate all heresies in the Kingdom of France, being the representative of Apostolic Authority resident in Carcassonne for the purpose of hunting out all those tainted with the poison of heresy or suspect thereof; and we Frère Ferrier, by Divine authority of the archbishop of Narbonne, having special licence from the Reverend Father in God, Sinibaldo Fiesco, by the grace of God cardinal in Rome, Vice-chancellor of His Holiness Gregory, charge that Esclarmonde de Foix is before God Almighty a defiler of Holy Scripture, a practitioner of witchcraft and an enemy of the only Church of Christ, by the grace of God Almighty and the authority of Holy Father Gregory. How say you Dame Esclarmonde de Foix? How do you say to the charges?"

The only sound was the patter of rain on the slate roof. The Dame did not speak.

Frère Ferrier stood up. "If you do *not* answer the charge, this court must pass you over to secular authority, who will seek your confession with diligence! In the absence of the full proofs of two eyewitnesses, or a confession, they will—on the strength of the partial proofs presented in the writ—seek the full evidence of your confession by any means. Do you know what this means, Dame?"

The Dame did not acknowledge. Seigneur watched her completely impassive face with a peculiar pride. She knew. She knew Ferrier meant torture. She behaved exactly as he would in her place—as he had when the Saracens captured him twenty years ago and threatened him with torture. And they *had* tortured him, for days on end, without any regard for humanity—just as the Inquisitional court intended to do to the Dame. He had endured and never spoken, just as he knew she would not. But he couldn't bear to think of it. Would the torturer take her eye? Would he strip her skin with her pride? He had a vivid picture of her in chains, a red-hot poker in the hand of master torturer Francis. He smiled at her as he brought the glowing point closer and closer to her eye. And she did not scream as the smoke of burning flesh filled the room and the her eyeball exploded.

Seigneur's anger grew as he remembered the torture room and the pain of his own ordeal.

Frère Ferrier gestured for the Bailiff. "Let the clerk record that given the opportunity to speak in her defense the Dame has refused. Let the *inquisitio specialis* begin! Take her to the master torturer and obtain her confession!"

The Dame did not move, apparently without fear as the Bailiff's guards stepped forward to seize her.

"I will speak for the Dame!" a voice roared out. Some of the ladies gasped and all eyes turned on Seigneur. He had expected to shock them, and he stood for a long, dreadful moment, first in the awful silence, then assaulted by the roar of friends and enemies alike. He waited, watching Jaie's quill flying across the page.

Red-faced, Frère Ferrier stood up. "You, the Seigneur de Castlenau? Defend a *Southerner* and a *heretic?*"

Perce stood up beside Seigneur, showing his support, although Seigneur saw the terror on his young squire's face. He hadn't expected this, and he regretted not telling him, but Perce would have spent the last week pleading with him to change his mind, distracting Seigneur from his mission. Next Ramon stood beside Perce. Three against so many.

Seigneur put his arm around Perce's shoulders. "Sit, my friend."

Perce stared at him, his mouth agape. Seigneur had never expressed affection, not verbally, certainly not in public. The blood drained from his face. Seigneur shook his shoulders one more time. "Sit." Finally, Perce sat, and beside him Ramon. Adelais, the daughter of the viscount, sat between them.

"What is your interest in this matter?" Ferrier asked. "You are not an advocate, surely?"

Seigneur glared at the mad monk, the butcher of Béziers. "I have an interest in justice," he said, his voice flat and without passion. "I have been taught the king's justice and have administered justice on behalf of my lands. I have fought for God and justice all of my life."

"But what business is this of yours?" demanded Ferrier again.

"I claim interest by right of capture. The Dame is *my* prisoner!"

Again the roar echoed in the rafters, and many chevaliers and seigneurs rose to their feet, cheering.

An exciting trial after all, was what the crowd was thinking. You could always count on Seigneur for a thrill.

"Why should I grant this right? Accused heretics are not provided a defense advocate unless handed over to the secular court for sentencing."

"I demand it!" Seigneur shouted, his pride and smouldering anger bursting into flames. No one in the great hall had ever heard him yell, not even Perce. Not like this. "I have administered the justice of God throughout the lands of the Saracens and Moslems, in the Holy Land, in Spain and here in France. I will not be denied!"

"It will not be permitted, Seigneur."

"The Dame is a chatelaine. A noble. That entitles her to special consideration."

"She is a *Southerner,*" he spoke the word as if it denoted a form of animal. "A *Southern* noble has *no* status among us. Please sit."

A new voice joined the fray. "It will be permitted, Brother."

The Templar Arnot got to his feet and walked slowly to Seigneur's side. He was dressed splendidly in his white tunic, his mail gleaming and freshly oiled, and conspicuously, on the greaves of his shoulder armor, was a new symbol. He pointed at the symbol now. "As charioteer and armor-bearer of the Master Marshall of the Poor Brothers of Jesus, under authority of the Grand Master of the Temple of Jerusalem, I stand with Seigneur."

Curious eyes stared at the embossed symbol, a chariot drawn by two rearing horses. The sacred symbol of power in the Templar order revealed his rank as only one level below the Master Marshall himself.

This time there were no shouts.

"This is a court authorized by *Cupientes*," said Ferrier. "You have no authority here, Brother."

The Templar stepped forward. "Templars have authority directly from the Holy Father."

An awkward silence fell between them. Finally the Inquisitor shook his head. "I know the Templars answer to none but our Holy Father. But your autonomy does not give you authority over this court."

"The Knights of the Temple recognize Seigneur's prior claim of capture. We enforce that right and protect his prisoner." He drew his sword. The doors of the hall swept open, and eight knights marched into the room, their booted feet beating a perfect rhythm on the stone flags. Seigneur's eight white knights bore a new symbol on their freshly painted white shields—the charioteer of the Master Marshall, and, in the left corner the cross of the Templars.

Templar Arnot glared at Inquisitor Ferrier. "I have deputized these good knights as charioteers in the name of the Temple. They have my authority."

"But this is an appalling breach of protocol!" shouted Ferrier.

All of the knights drew their swords with an ominous scrape of steel on leather scabbards. Seigneur drew Loial, his famous blade. Perce and Ramon stood again and joined them, standing to the right of the Dame. When the viscount's own daughter stood with them, a look of naked horror and dismay came into the viscount's face.

"This will not be permitted," shouted a new voice, and the archbishop practically vaulted from the platform to the right of the Inquisitors, brandishing his crozier like a weapon.

"As charioteer of the Master Marshall, I have the authority, Your Grace, in matters where we have been asked for help before God. We have been asked. We will reinforce the Seigneur's prior claim."

"Master Brother Arnot," the archbishop leaned forward, spittle flying as he shouted, "this affront will be drawn to the attention of His Holiness. Yet again you have shown the arrogance of the Templars."

Brother Arnot smiled, serene in the face of the archbishop's fury. "If that is your wish, Your Grace, I have no objection. But today, it changes nothing."

Arguing was pointless. The Templars had the right to defend lawful claims. They didn't answer to archbishop or cardinal. "Very well. Be it on your own risk, Seigneur. This Holy Court will record and consider all words you speak here. Remember that defense of a heretic can be considered a crime!" Archbishop Amiel rapped the floor with his crozier and returned to his seat. He whispered in the cardinal's ear, but the pope's chancellor shook his head and scowled.

The silence was excruciating. Finally, Seigneur spoke. "The court knows my reputation."

"The court concedes your illustrious history, Seigneur," said Ferrier through clenched teeth.

"I wish it on the record," Seigneur repeated.

"There is no need."

"I would like to hear it!" said Adelais, the viscount's daughter. "Seigneur fought alongside my father in many campaigns. We all owe him dearly!"

Frère Ferrier nodded at the clerk, Brother Jaie, who recorded the request. "Very well. Proceed Seigneur."

Seigneur looked at the Dame and she smiled at him. "You should not do this," Dame Esclarmonde whispered. "I am going to die either way. Nothing you can do will change that."

Again he felt the strange pride in her courage. He turned away without answering and stepped closer to the tribunal's raised table. The "deputized" Templars, his own knights, surrounded the Dame. "I am the Seigneur de Castlenau, count of the realm of France." The crowd rumbled in surprise.

"Seigneur is a count!" someone exclaimed.

The Viscount Hugh d'Arcis stood up slowly. "I can confirm this. Seigneur is Count de Castlenau." He glared hard at the Seigneur then turned his angry eyes on his daughter.

Tumult broke out, everyone shouting at once. The *milites* who had fought with Seigneur cheered—"The Count! Count de Castlenau!"—until Frère Ferrier sternly warned them to silence.

"I was, until my resignation, champion of the city, champion of Seigneur the Viscount Hugh d'Arcis!" He nodded his head at his old friend. The soldiers cheered again, louder and longer in spite of the Inquisitor's warning. Hugh nodded but continued to stare at his daughter.

"I have fought in four major crusades, three under Holy Father Innocent and one under his Holiness Gregory. Together with the Poor Brothers of the Temple we recaptured Jerusalem!" He glared at Ferrier. "I have fought with honor against the Albi heretics in Béziers, Toulouse, Carcassonne. I have taken up the cross and fought in the Holy Lands. I fought against the Moors in Spain. And it is becasue of my skill that the Dame Esclarmonde de Foix stands in this court!"

The cheers were piercing. Frère Ferrier pounded his staff to bring silence. "The Court is suitably grateful to you, Seigneur. You are surely one of France's greatest crusaders." He ignored a few derisive calls from other knights. "But why do you wish to speak for the heretic?"

"I fought at the fall of Minerve, thirty-two years ago." He nodded at Frère Ferrier. "I believe you were there also, Frère. I remember your court gave them a choice of abjuring their faith or death by fire. As I recall, only three recanted, and one hundred and forty burned. Do you remember, Frère?"

Frère Ferrier did not answer and folded his arms over his chest.

"I recall especially well that the heretics threw *themselves* into the fire—*singing*. Do you remember their song?" He stepped back beside the Dame and held out his gloved hand to rest on her shoulder. "I will remind you, Frère. They sang of *this* Dame. She was just twenty then, and I had never met her of course. I was barely twenty myself. And I listened to them sing of the Dame as they burned. And what I remember most is that they did not cry out in pain. I hated their heresy, but I admired their bravery."

Frère Ferrier stood slowly, his face calm. "What is the point of this, Seigneur? The heretics used their sorcery to dampen the pain. You are only proving this witch's power."

Seigneur released the Dame's shoulder. "Oh, her power is far greater than you give her credit for. I do not argue here that this woman is innocent. This only she may speak to and, bravely, she declines." He looked at each Inquisitor in turn. "But as a captain of many campaigns, I know from experience that a martyr is more inspiration than an old woman."

"What mean you, Seigneur?"

"This is no simple heretic. Before you stands the spiritual leader of the Cathars. Burn her and you start a new war. Are we ready for a new crusade?" The audience murmured.

The Seigneur strode forward and stood directly in front of the three monks. "I am not qualified to argue religion. I know only that if you hand this woman over to the Shérif for torture and burning, then thousands, tens of thousands, hundreds of thousands will rise up to follow her that did not before. *Remember* the silent passion of the one hundred and forty nameless heretics burned at Minerve? The heretics now call them martyrs, and they are inspired by their example. The martyrs are honored in songs of heroism. They inspire the bravery of the Albigensian rebels—even to this day!" Seigneur lifted his arms for emphasis.

He stabbed his finger at the Dame. "Imagine it! The word spreads throughout the Occitan that the Dame has been tortured and killed. And *she* did not speak one word in fear or defense. Look at her!" All eyes looked at the Dame, driven by the thunder in Seigneur's voice. He was feeling it now, a passion he had never before felt.

"Look at her! She smiles at you in spite of her predicament. Imagine the songs Ramon Troubadour will sing of how she smiled bravely at her torturers!" He pointed at Ramon, standing with the Templars, and the troubadour nodded. "It will inspire the heretics. It will double their numbers. They too will smile and die bravely, and thousands will replace them!"

The room was silent. No one argued. Even the Viscount d'Arcis stared at his ex-champion in silence. Brother Jaie's quill scribbled.

The three monks leaned into a huddle and argued among themselves quietly. Finally, Frère Ferrier spoke.

"The court appreciates your wise words, Seigneur." He smiled coldly. "However, this is not a political forum. Your words may be true but *our* business is before God. Heretics must be saved from their errors. God will give our cause strength to fight the thousands you claim will rise up to follow their wicked queen."

Seigneur looked at the knights and lords in the hall. "I have fought for almost forty years among heretics! I have killed many Saracens, Infidels, Ottomans, Moors, Jews, Albigensians and Cathars! Many of you have fought with me! Duc de Tulle you fought with me in Joppa!" The old noble nodded. "Baron le Puy, we fought the moors with Alfonso at Toledo!"

The old baron winked at his friend and called out: "That was many years ago, but I remember well, Seigneur. You saved my balls!"

Seigneur smiled. "Many bastards for the old baron." The audience laughed. "I have fought with most of you in this room! You know my deeds and you know I speak only the truth!"

"No! I argue that!" an angry voice yelled out. Sir Albaric rose, face excited with opportunity, and stepped before the court. He bowed to the Inquisitors and faced his rival, Seigneur. "I am not afraid to fight the heretics! Our cause is just! God fights with us! If thousands rise up to fight us because of *this* witch, then I say so be it! This is God's will then. He wishes the heretics exposed so that we can send them to hell!"

The room was silent as Seigneur and Sir Albaric glared at each other—the colorless and nameless lord and the golden knight of the Lion. The two crusaders were a stride apart, hands on the hilts of their broadswords.

Seigneur controlled his expression. If he smiled, his plan would be revealed. Sir Albaric must be allowed to continue. To challenge him.

"Seigneur is a traitor to Church and king!" shouted Albaric.

Soldiers loyal to both stood up, howling encouragement or protest. They called for an honorable *outrance*—to the death. All three Inquisitors hammered their staffs for order, unheard. Archbishop Amiel shouted at his guards to restore order. And the Viscount Hugh d'Arcis sat on his dais, watching, not revealing his feelings.

But it was the Dame who restored order to the court. Her voice was calm when she spoke out for the first time, but loud enough, and everyone fell instantly silent: "I will have no blood spilled on my behalf!" She stepped between the two knights. "You may kill me or not as you please. I have reconciled my life. It matters not. But none of you have yet found peace. Do not shed more blood. It will condemn you."

She turned from one to the other of the two warriors who towered over her, silver hair tossing like a proud horse's mane.

Frère Ferrier broke the silence that followed her words. "Cast no spells in my court, Enchantress!" he roared.

She stood motionless, her arms held up and her blue eyes full of sympathy. She turned to gaze on the stern monk. "I know no magic, Frère, other than love. My power is Christ's love."

"Blasphemy! You will not use the Lord's name in vain in this court!"

"I do not, my son."

"Father!" Frère Duranti snapped. "You will address me as *Father*!"

Her smile seemed less sad, perhaps a little good-humored, and she curtsied. "Yes, Father."

"How dare you speak in the name of Christ!"

She stepped forward and spoke quietly, as if she didn't want to embarrass them. "I love Jesus most Holy. He is my Lord and ideal."

"Satan's cheating words. You lie, Sorceress!"

She shrugged. "God bless you, Father."

"I do not want your curses!" Frère Balfour shrank back in fear.

"You need not fear me."

"Take this witch away!" Frère Balfour yelled.

The bishop's guards rushed forward with spears lowered. The Templars drew their swords again and circled the Dame.

Esclarmonde de Foix smiled. "God will forgive you, my children!"

Frère Balfour's voice was shrill. "Remove the heretic!"

One of the bishop's guards stepped forward. The clang of Arnot's sword reverberated throughout the court. The bishop's soldier stepped back.

The Viscount Hugh D'Arcis rose. "My dear Count de Castlenau. We have always been allies. Let us not fight now."

Seigneur looked at the viscount, then back at the Dame.

"Do I have your promise that no harm will befall the Dame while in your custody? On your honor, my Lord!"

Adelais stood up, hands on her hips and stared at her father. He scowled back at her and nodded once. Archbishop Amiel stood in protest, but the viscount's gloved hand rose in stern warning.

"Seigneur, I promise the Dame will be safe in my keeping. There will be no torture. No Inquiry. Not until the outcome of your claim on the Dame. Until then, I will protect her."

Seigneur bowed his head. "That is sufficient." He waved back the deputized Templars who sheathed their swords.

Finally, the guard led the Dame from the stunned court. As the great doors closed, the uproar was so loud that Frère Ferrier's staff could not even be heard as he pounded the floor for order.

Ferrier shouted. "Seigneur, we are moved by your eloquence, but cannot allow your advocacy."

"I am not an advocate, Brother. I argue by right of possession. The Dame is mine by right of capture. I have officially surrendered her to neither the Church nor the king. As I am not a vassal of either, she is mine by right."

Again the roar of excitement filled the room and Ferrier was red-faced in his efforts to silence the court.

"Seigneur. I understand your arguments. I certainly agree not. But possessing—and worse, *protecting*—a heretic makes *you* guilty with her."

Seigneur stepped forward. "Only if her guilt is proven. My guilt could not be established otherwise."

Ferrier looked at the archbishop, helpless. "Lord Archbishop?"

Reluctantly, the archbishop nodded. "Seigneur is correct."

"I challenge that!" snarled Sir Albaric.

"On what grounds?" the viscount demanded. Seigneur knew he had no wish to lose his rights to the Dame, but in front of witnesses, especially the Templars, he had little alternative.

"I subscribe my right of property over the prisoner," said Albaric. "I also fought to capture the Dame. I was there. She is mine."

The viscount asked, "Sir Albaric, how will you prove your claim?"

"By judicial combat."

A distant rumble of thunder and the beating of the rain on the roof were the only sounds.

Seigneur turned to face his old adversary. "Messire Albaric. You would joust with *me* in the mêlée? I have no wish to kill you."

"I have challenged! Say on!"

The viscount held up his hands again. "This is not seemly. A count should not joust with a knight."

Sir Albaric turned to face his lord and held his two fists together. He fell to one knee. "Lord! I am your Champion. The *Champion* of a viscount can surely joust a count in honorable combat."

The viscount sounded sad. "So be it."

Sir Albaric whirled, his face red in triumph. "Then, as Champion, I challenge you, Count de Castlenau!"

Seigneur shrugged. "I can but accept, but I joust only to the death. Be warned."

The archbishop of Narbonne smiled. "And if our noble Messire Albaric wins by right of arms, what then?"

Albaric bowed. "The Dame will be given to the Church for judgment."

"Let it be so, then."

24

THEY CAME TO SEE A MAN DIE.

It seemed to a weary and worried Perce that every chevalier within a day's ride had come for the tourney, to see Seigneur's "long overdue disgrace," and already the field was crowded with every freeholder, serf and tradeperson from Montilieu to Montréal. All the hangers-on from the Dame's trial, the barons and dukes and counts, all of Seigneur's old comrades in arms, nearly every Dominican and Cistercian monk, and—of course—every lady of birth and woman of no consequence—all had come to see the old Seigneur die. The prevailing gossip was harsh—Seigneur was quite mad. Perce tired of the pitying looks, the withering stares and the sympathetic words. "At least Seigneur will go with a sword in hand," was repeated so often that Perce learned to nod and walk on in his busy preparations. Everyone wanted to know, "Is Seigneur ready? Will he put up a good fight? It's as if the Devil himself took him."

Perce hadn't slept. He had refused to dwell on the insanity of the last two days. He was in his prime. Within weeks he would have been knighted, Sir Perceval de Mendes. If he renounced his lord it might still happen. Renounce and join Albaric's crew, or the viscount's guard. But Perce wanted none of it. He had sworn his loyalty to Seigneur, and he would follow him wherever he led.

He oiled his master's saddle, sanded his mail, sharpened his sword and tested the balance of his lances. Seigneur's knights, aging *milites* who had fought at Seigneur's side for more than a decade, would hear nothing of leaving him and seemed inordinately proud of their new shields emblazoned with the sacred symbol of the Templar charioteer. They had ridden so long with no insignia and no colors, it was a relief to the old knights to finally ride under emblem. The knights' squires helped with the preparations, grooming Boone for combat, offering their best weapons, guarding Seigneur's pavilion from supporter and foe alike.

No, Perce did not understand his master's madness. Oh, he knew the cause—the damnable Dame and her magic. His master had not been the same since that night when she had stood on the castle walls in the Pyrenees and cast her spell. She had convinced his Seigneur to spare her knights, something that had never happened before. She had snared his old black heart. He had gone to her every night for weeks, and her magic and womanly charms preyed on the old man's loneliness. Yet loyalty was loyalty. He despised the Dame. He despised Ramon, the trickster, if only because he also seemed to be in the Dame's spell.

He would not even speak with laughing Adelais, so deep was his shame. He owed Seigneur everything: his life, his upbringing, his skill at arms, his love, his loyalty. He hadn't realized it before the trial, before his Seigneur's stunning renunciation, but now he knew that Seigneur was his life, his family. Even his quest for his golden spurs could not take priority over his love of his old Cyclops master, though in all likelihood, Seigneur would die on the field today, and Perce would be sent to oblivion with him. Seigneur, though unbeatable with the sword, was no master of the lance. Because of his lost eye, the judging of distance was difficult. No knight in all the lands could best Seigneur with a sword, but with a lance, half of France could probably obliterate him. His reactions were also slower than the younger Albaric's.

The fields outside the south wall of the city blossomed with pavilions, merchant stands and temporary paddocks. The hammers of the city carpenters rang sharply as they erected a temporary *berfrois* in the flat field where Seigneur would meet his enemy. Merchants set up temporary markets and the carnival atmosphere drew ever larger crowds from the city. The whiff of sweet pastries and candied pears drifted up and over the walls. The freemen who rented their land for the tourney would become wealthy with their short leases, charging at least a *sou* for every pavilion and ten *deniers* for a merchant's cart. They no longer cared that their freshly cultivated fields were destroyed.

The carnival atmosphere sickened Perce. He tried not to listen, and he ignored the sympathetic nods of Southerners, the children playing their jousting games, and the laughter that pervaded the muddy field. It hardly seemed proper.

Impromptu market squares grew up on both ends of the battlefield, jammed with hawkers and merchants and their carts full of game, fish, wax, spices and peppers. Soon after, the mountebanks arrived, and the moneychangers with their wares of cloth and silk. The minstrels and jongleurs came from every village within a day's ride, hoping to witness an event that would make a great song, a breakthrough song that might elevate them to the status of trouvères.

Perce watched the turmoil with a scowl. He wanted to take his Seigneur's jousting lance, crash into the crowd, overturn the carts and shout his contempt like His Lord Jesus in the Temple of Jerusalem. Didn't these fools know how important this judicial joust was? This was no gay tournament. God's justice would be decided!

He ignored it all as best he could.

The tent village grew around the tourney field. He knew many of the visitors and couldn't ignore them. As he wandered through the tent village he forced smiles and held up his hand to greet them: "My Lord Duc de Gies ... Messire Pepevel ... Lord Iven ..." He bowed to each.

The ordeal was endless. He closed his ears to the conversations and wagers around him. He did not wish to know whom the Duc de Gies favored in the joust.

Friends arrived as well, old friends from the crusades: "Well met Duc de Tulle ... Welcome Baron Le Puy ... Are you well, Count Henry of Bar...?"

It was all without meaning. The visitors clustered their courts on either the north or south of the jousting field. Seigneur's old friends—Chevalier Geoffroi, Lord de Castres, Sir Buiron—camped around the Seigneur's plain white pavilion.

On the opposite end of the field was the gold lion of Sir Albaric de Laon.

Conspicuous by his absence was the Templar Arnot. He had left his shield for Seigneur's joust, emblazoned with the rearing horses and the chariot, but he disappeared in the morning, not to return.

The tension was palpable.

Freemen did a brisk trade servicing the needs of the many visiting lords. Feeding and watering the hundreds of horses was a massive undertaking, and a lucrative one. The viscount's stable master exploited his opportunity, organizing stabling for a fee. The viscount taxed the profits.

The greater lords—the viscount of Montauban, Cardinal Fiesco and King John of Aragon, who had been visiting his nearby fief of Montréal—were guests of Viscount Hugh d'Arcis in the castle. King John of Aragon's arrival created the biggest stir. He had arrived on lathered horses, having ridden hard to attend the joust.

Perce scowled. His preparations were endless. While Sir Albaric had a retinue of squires to attend him, Perce was alone—*écuyer*, groom, armorer. Seigneur's knights helped, sparing their squires wherever Perce needed help, but it was important to Perce that he test each weapon himself. He sharpened the swords with his worn whetstone, including Seigneur's old Loial. The other squires scrubbed Seigneur's mail shirt with coarse sand and oiled the links. Perce hardly saw Seigneur. He had no opportunity to confront him over his madness. His work was endless.

Boone and Odo ate well on hot grains. Only Boone would fight the joust, for Odo was too small and not made for war. Unlike Sir Albaric, with his string of Andalusian chargers, Seigneur could rely only on his single charger and one palfrey. Seigneur must count on Boone's training or he would be unhorsed by Albaric's youthful strength.

Perce did not eat, and he hadn't slept the night before. And as he toiled in preparation for the contest amid the mounting excitement around him, he fought tears—to his shame.

They had faced many terrible battlefields. Joppa, where every one of Perce's friends had perished. Malagón, where the Moors ambushed them. Battle after battle. And always the old warrior Seigneur had survived, with Perce at his side.

But this—this battle could not be won. And even if, by Holy Mary's grace, Seigneur's superior experience in battle won out—and that would be a miracle worthy of the Mother of God—his lord would be ostracized, hated, shamed, then tried by the Inquisition for defending heresy.

Perce put down the Seigneur's dented helm. He remembered the blow that had put the dent there. The Caliph Mohamed an-Nasir had unhorsed his lord then struck him with a mace. Perce had cried out and galloped forward, his bloody sword in hand, but he was too far away to help. The caliph lifted his arm for the deathblow. He swung. Perce cried out. All around him the crusaders died, their gore staining the sands, but Perce saw only his Seigneur, lying in his own blood, the infidel over him crying out to Allah.

Seigneur rolled away from the hooves of his enemy, tearing off his freshly dented helm. With a roar he drew his broad sword, slick and red with the blood of the infidel and drove it into the Caliph's splendid horse—a desperate tactic for Seigneur. Perce had never seen him kill a horse before or since.

They won that dark day, or rather, did not lose it, but at great cost. Many of Europe's mightiest knights fell. But the Seigneur struck their only great triumph; he killed the Caliph.

After their victory, on that night of mourning, they sat together and recalled old friends with tales of their battles. They buried hundreds. A sorrowful Seigneur buried the Caliph *and* his beautiful horse in the same grave, the Caliph mounted in the saddle. It took seven exhausted men to dig the grave, but Seigneur insisted. Abbé Yves, their crusading spiritual advisor, had been appalled at the respect paid to an infidel, but Seigneur had won the battle for them and was entitled to any whim.

Some survivors of the Moorish crusade were here now, in the fields of Carcassonne, to see their old hero battle Sir Albaric. They would be remembering as well.

A voice interrupted his grim remembrances. "You seem preoccupied," Ramon said.

"Go away."

Ramon sat on a log. "I know how you feel."

Perce looked away. "You have no idea." How he hated this troubadour. The betrayer. The plotter. The heretic. Seigneur had told him everything, in case he didn't survive the joust, and Perce had felt betrayed by all he loved, both his master and his friend.

"Ramon, leave *now*. I feel in a mood to kill. Mayhap your little dog. Mayhap you."

Ramon didn't move. They sat in silence.

The rumbling of preparations around them continued. Across the field Albaric's squires sharpened swords on a stone wheel, the sparks flying. Merchants called their wares. Children ran everywhere, giggling and shouting.

"I'm your friend. Talk to me," said Ramon.

"Talk to you!" He glared at the troubadour. "Talk to you about what? About secrets? About plots?" He looked away.

Ramon's eyes widened. "You know?"

Perce nodded.

"Then you know it means a lot to your lord."

"Just leave me, Ramon. *You* have work to do it seems. As do *I*."

Ramon extended his hand. "You won't betray us? Your Seigneur?"

"I would die before that." He snatched his arm away. "But I'll chop off that hand if you touch me again!"

Ramon remained standing, arms hanging limp at his side.

"No I won't betray you." He stabbed his finger at Ramon. "And I won't forgive you. Either of you!" He turned his back and continued oiling Seigneur's saddle.

"Perce, we may not see each other after today. I want to—"

"Go, before I kill you."

Ramon sighed and rose to his feet. He started to say something then shrugged and left with Mauri, who wagged his tail oblivious to the controversy.

Perce regretted his outburst. Today, he might lose Seigneur. Today, he might become a fugitive. Today might be the last day to say goodbyes. He watched Ramon walk across the muddy field, his head hung low, but he didn't call out for Ramon to come back.

"That wasn't very nice," said a high lilting voice as he worked the Seigneur's tack.

He sighed. "How long have you been listening?"

Adelais giggled and sat beside him on the log. "I heard everything."

"Everything?"

"Everything." She touched his arm, and he flinched. "Dearest Perce, we love you. Don't you know that? It doesn't matter what you do or say. That can never change."

"I'm leaving, Addy."

"I know."

"I'm leaving in disgrace."

"Never that!" She rested her boylike head on his shoulder. "You have more supporters than you know. Both you and your master."

"Your father?"

She clucked and wagged her finger at him. "Oh, Perce, Perce. There's a difference between friendship and duty, between love and necessity. My father loves Seigneur. But he is a creature of duty."

"As am I."

She sighed. "I know. Your duty to your poor condemned Seigneur."

Perce pushed her away. "What do you want, Adelais?"

"To ask two things." Her smile was that of the nymphet. She was irresistible in her cheekiness. "I would come with you."

"You're assuming Seigneur survives."

"Either way. I come with you." Her intense eyes locked on his.

"No."

"Why?"

"You are to wed into the royal family."

She laughed. "That will never happen. Trust me."

He couldn't help but smile. "Even so."

"Even so? That's what you have to say?" She punched his arm. "Damn you, Perce, I'm not marrying that foppish nephew of the prince."

"Even so."

She punched him again. "You don't want me?"

"I didn't say that."

"No, you said, 'Even so.' Twice!"

"Just so."

"Then I ask my second question."

He shrugged, picked up the saddle and continued cleaning. "I can't stop you."

"No, you can't. I ask you to return after you become Sir Perceval de Mendes. Return and ask for my hand."

"I can't."

"Why?" she shouted.

"You'll be married."

"No. I won't!"

He handed her the bridle. "Here, make yourself useful." And he marched off to find Seigneur.

Seigneur was alone in his pavilion, eye closed in meditation. Perce sat beside him on the threadbare Arabian rug that served as Seigneur's bed.

"Are you hungry, Seigneur?"

Seigneur offered no answer. They sat for a long time in silence. Perce knew this was the Seigneur's habit, to sit on the old carpet—once owned by the brave Caliph who dented Seigneur's helmet. His breathing was calm and shallow.

Together they waited. Perce wanted to say so much. He wanted to tell Seigneur how foolish he was. He wanted to scream, "How could you do this? You are Christendom's greatest crusader. She is a heretic!" But the words didn't come.

It was Seigneur who finally spoke. "Perce."

"Seigneur."

Seigneur placed his hand on Perce's shoulder. Perce trembled at the show of emotion. "You will be Messire Perce after this day. I have arranged it."

"I want no honors but to serve you, Seigneur."

"That is no longer possible."

Perce closed his eyes, unable to restrain the tears.

"Today, I die in combat with a great chevalier. This is as it should be. I have lived for honor. I must die this way."

"Seigneur—"

"Be silent." The hand squeezed his shoulder. "You will be dubbed by my friend Count Henry de Bar. He knows my wishes. You are to be Messire Perce. Perhaps, for a time, you'll be *faidit*—a knight without lands. Always remember, lands are less important than honor to a knight. You may fight in many more holy crusades. You are welcome to join the Brothers of the Temple of Jerusalem if that is your wish. And some day you'll claim back your fief and be Seigneur de Mendes. That is what you've always wanted."

"My only wish has been to serve you." He fought the tears.

"All of this is yours. Boone—you must be patient with him. You cannot master such a beast. You can only be his friend. Odo, of course, is yours, as is my armor—"

"Seigneur!"

"My pavilion, and my precious Loial." He drew his sword from its worn sheath. "Loial has been with me longer than you. It was given me by my mentor, Sir Harbin." His fingers rubbed the worn leather, where it had melded into the ash handle. Perce had offered many times to retool the leather but Seigneur always refused.

"I know. Seigneur, I—"

"I commanded your silence. You owe me this. You are not Seigneur de Mendes yet."

Perce closed his tear-filled eyes. His lips trembled.

"These are my wishes. I've made them known to my allies, including the viscount. Oh, he may disapprove of me, but he's still honorbound by my deeds. He will ensure no one usurps your rights. None in Carcassonne would dare defy him." He ran his fingers along the old double-edged blade, admiring its fine edge. "You've sharpened Loial." He touched the dent that Perce had never been able to remove, from the blow that had killed the Caliph. Two dents from the Caliph. "A fine job, Perce."

"I cannot listen to this."

"You will." Seigneur spat into his palms and rubbed the saliva into the worn leather of his sword's hilt. "I am *old*, Perce. I don't even remember how old. I was twelve when I left for the crusades and I've only returned once to Castlenau."

His fingers caressed the scars on his face. Was he remembering his return to Castlenau at sixteen, scarred and one-eyed? Perce had heard the story only once, from Sir Harbin, Seigneur's old master and it had almost made him cry.

Seigneur had failed in his first crusade in the Holy Land, captured and tortured by the Saracens. After the recapture of Ascalon, he had returned home, head hung in shame, with only a borrowed horse for company.

His father greeted him coldly. According to Sir Harbin he said only, "What triumphs can you speak of?"

His mother screamed and did not look upon his scarred face for several days.

And Celene, the girl he thought loved him, had waited for his return, but when she saw his monstrous scar, she spurned him.

Sir Harbin had perhaps embellished the story, but Perce always felt weepy when he thought of the idealistic young squire returning, only to be snubbed by those he loved because of his appearance. In sympathy, Sir Harbin had made him his *écuyer*. Seigneur had ridden off to the crusades once more—this time, never to return to Castlenau.

Seigneur sheathed his sword and picked at the mud on his boots with his *pavade*. In a calm voice, he continued: "I've always felt I served God this way. I have been a crusader for almost my entire life. We no longer fight in the Holy Land, protecting the pilgrims. Now we call it a crusade in our own lands. We kill our own. I'm not reconciled to that." He sighed. "I've lived by honor, and I will die that way. I have made my peace."

"But why now? Why allow your name to be tarnished by heresy?"

Seigneur's voice was suddenly curt: "That is not your business. I admire the Dame. That is all you need know. She is a heretic, I know. But I didn't fight in the Holy Lands against heresy. None of us did. We fought to free Jerusalem and keep it safe for pilgrims." He caressed the embroidery of the old silk carpet, a trophy from the caliph, the one man Seigneur admired above all others because he was the one man who almost killed Seigneur. "It does the soul no good to have the nobility of crusade corrupted this way. The Inquisition is a perversion." He sighed.

Perce scowled. "Seigneur, this Dame will be your downfall."

"So be it then."

"She is a—"

"Don't say it! I will not hear *that* from your lips!" Seigneur's voice had risen. "I do not ask you to help her. I only ask you not to hurt her. Promise me."

Perce glared at Loial. Soon it would be bloodied again.

"Swear it."

"I swear it, Seigneur."

Seigneur stood up. "You have been a good and loyal squire. If I have not shown my friendship, I am sorry. You will make a great chevalier. I'm proud of you, as a father might be of his son."

Perce fought tears again. He stood up to face his Seigneur—but his lord was gone.

Song of Justice

25

A CLOUD OF DUST shrouded the frenetic activity of the Baug camp. They were nearly ready. All but the grand pavilion was down, and the majority of the wagons, loaded with the children, had left the city by the main gate, unnoticed in the excitement of the joust. Only four wagons remained, and they had a part to play in Ramon's plan.

Ramon found Nevara with her remaining horses, readying them for the flight. Izzy nickered as he approached and ran to him, prancing and nuzzling, pushing playfully, curling back his lip to smell him, little front legs pawing impatiently. Ramon hugged and kissed him until Mauri became jealous and barked, running in circles around them both. He left his arm slung around his beloved Izzy and approached Nevara.

Bubo flew around her in circles, serenely bombing camp stragglers with white droppings. Bubo dropped down and landed on Ramon's shoulder, perching precariously. Bubo tolerated him, but Ramon never stroked the big bird, afraid he would lose one of his luting fingers. The talons pressed painfully through his tunic.

"You look upset, beloved," Nevara said in Novgorod, the smile of welcome fading. She waved off Bubo and hugged Ramon, pulling his face close to her mountainous bosom. She stroked his hair.

"Your lion-wrestler," Ramon said in langue d'oc, in a low voice. "The man you sent to help me."

She tilted his head up.

"Today, he will die."

She laughed at him then. "We all must dying, beloved. And he may surprising you, yet, no?"

Ramon felt her strength, basked in it for a moment. "Is everyone safe?"

She wagged her finger at him. "We not being helpless here, Ramon the fool. Only eleven remain here to helping you."

"That's too many."

"Our fastest riders! No knight can match our Baug men and my horses!"

"And Magba?"

"She leads the Baug."

"She's gone?"

Nevara nodded. "She wanted to stay here with her brave sons. Ha. But not letting her, no."

Ramon sighed, relieved. His plan was too intricate, too dependent on each element to be considered anything but a dangerous tile game, with many lives at stake. Ramon couldn't suppress a tremble.

"Not worrying, my love. You plan is good one."

But too much could go wrong. Diableteur was no fool. Would he stop his men from entering the pavilion? Would the soldiers be fooled by the archers? Would Seigneur survive long enough to give them time to escape? Could they even escape the castle with the Dame? It all seemed improbable now in the cold reality of the empty Baug camp.

"The traps?" he asked.

"All ready. The soldiers, they in for surprising! Many surprisings! My special wagon."

"And the forest?"

"Umar's axe has been busy."

Umar, Magba's strong-man husband, could fell a small tree with one blow from his massive axe.

"And my other snares?"

Nevara laughed. "Always worrying. Worrying, worrying, worrying."

Ramon drew a long breath, held it, and stared hard at Nevara. He had never doubted the Baug's skills before, she was saying. He had always had faith in Nevara and Magba and Umar and Atta and Hatta and Eline and Magba's sons and daughters—his adopted brothers and sisters—and the acrobats and her splendid tarpans. Why did he feel such terror and doubt?

"Carcassonne is a city with an army of thousands, not some village full of superstitious folk."

"Worrying, worrying." She shook her head, still smiling.

"The Baug are in the forest?"

"Yes, yes."

"Good." Magba and the Baug could stand against a few ghosts and rebels in the Phantom Wood. They were as safe as they could be. If the soldiers challenged the rescuers or searched their wagons, all would be lost, but at least the children of the Baug would be safe. The soldiers might hesitate to follow them into the Phantom Wood. People never returned from that dark place.

"This is for you, dearest," said Nevara. She rummaged in the back of her covered wagon and pulled out a gray cloak. Ramon had never seen anything quite like it, the way it seemed to absorb light. It was as dull as a drizzly overcast day. "A concealing cloak," Nevara said. "Made on my own loom, charged with a concealing enchantment."

Ramon didn't have to ask what it was for. His bright colorful clothing might be his way into the dungeon, but the way out would be treacherous and desperate, and camouflage would be valuable. Or not. Nevara's magic was always unpredictable.

"And the other trickies." She held out a bag.

Ramon rummaged through the contents of the shoulder sack. He found a pouch of Nevara's fire-powder and one of Ena's famous ropes. Ena, head trainer of their acrobats, made all the ropes herself, long silky ropes of the strongest natural fibers, her own secret weave, and nearly invisible to the eye. The ropes of the Baug were highly elastic and nearly unbreakable, and in the torch light of the great pavilion, almost invisible. "Thank Ena for me."

"Hoping it is long enough," Nevara said gently. "A rope and my magic powder. A concealing cloak and the wagon. The Seeing Smoke and Umar's axe. And your dummies. Risky, risky, risky."

"It will work," Ramon said, partly to convince himself. A dozen things could go wrong, and he didn't have to tell her that the Dame was worthy of the risk.

"Coming back to me, beloved." She kissed him then, shocking him with her ferocity. A hard kiss on the lips. Her lips parted and he found himself responding, felt his own heat, his own desperation. They stopped kissing when Mauri barked at them.

"What is it, Mauri?" Ramon patted his head, and Mauri jumped from the ground on to his shoulder. Even then he kept barking then growling, his little eyes glaring up the long tract of the *Lices Hautes*.

Nevara closed her eyes for a moment. She scowled. "Diableteur. He comes."

Ramon scanned the wide marketplace, bright in the sunshine, dusty with life. "I see nothing."

"He comes," she said in her own language. "He comes."

Then Ramon caught sight of the black shape slowly descending the winding roadway between the two walls. Diableteur was not alone. A long row of black-robed enforcers marched behind him. At least they weren't mounted on their white horses.

Mauri jumped off Ramon's shoulder and ran in circles around him, snapping and growling. The horses grew restless and whinnied, a nervous high-pitched sound.

"You must go!" Nevara said, pushing him. "Go now."

Ramon watched Diableteur's slow march, a black cloud sweeping in to obscure the Baug brilliance.

"I handle this thing," Nevara said. "Following your own plan, fool!"

Diableteur was closer now, frightening even in the bright spring afternoon, his scythe gleaming in the sunshine. "I cannot leave."

"Having faith, beloved."

Ramon tapped his spear, his Zaleucus. "I have."

"Having faith in me."

"But there are forty-four of them!" Ramon felt the rise of panic, a feeling he hadn't experienced in years, not since the night the Diableteur had come to their shack by the south wall to arrest his mother.

Ramon's life must be a fulfillment of his mother's dying curse.

He must kill this thing.

"The Dame first!" said Nevara, reading his mind. "The Dame, then returning to us. I can handling this."

Diableteur seemed to grow in stature as he marched towards the Baug. Ramon's people noticed the creature now. Magba, Atta, Hatta, Eline, Umar, and Magba's eleven sons, all gathered in front of Nevara and Ramon, facing the heretic-hunters. Eline's bow was drawn, an arrow notched.

Nevara pushed Ramon again. "You knowing us! You knowing me! Go!"

Ramon didn't move. Fourteen Baug men and three women stood with swords and spears now, facing the threat. Ramon had grown up with these men, sons of Magba, his own brothers. How could he leave them now?

Ramon stepped up beside Atta and Hatta, pushing between the twins. They had three knives in each hand. On either side of them were Magba's sons, varying in age from fourteen summers to twenty-four, all seven of them with drawn bows.

The horses became restless, stomping and neighing, stirring up the dust. The smell of horse dung became pungent as the herd pawed the ground.

Eline's first three bow releases came in quick succession and barbed arrows appeared inches before Diableteur's boots. At the same time Atta and Hatta threw knives. They landed so close to the three arrows that the shafts vibrated.

"That being close enough," shouted Nevara, stepping forward in front of the Baug. She was splendid in the afternoon sun, her white gown lifting in the breeze. "Not welcoming here."

Ramon felt the fury in Diableteur's hidden eyes. This was a creature used to darkness and the night, a thing of fear. It didn't know how to react when someone stood against it in the sunshine.

The black soldier to the side of the Diableteur shouted at them. "By order of the Inquisition, we detain you."

The Magba's sons erupted in laughter, and that seemed to confuse the black hunters. Ramon laughed with them, swept up in the energy of his people.

"See, Ramon, all in control," whispered Nevara. "Now go or all is lost!"

Ramon found he couldn't move. He saw his enemy, the black thing that had killed his mother, within spear-throwing distance. Just one throw.

"Never throw Zaleucus," Guilhem d'Alions, his old hermit mentor, had warned him. But his arm seemed to move of its own accord, drawing back Zaleucus.

It was Mauri who saved him. He circled Ramon's boots, barking up at him and reminding him of his obligations.

"Another time, creature from Hell," said Ramon.

And he ran for a side alley and did not look back, the tears already flowing. Everyone was dying today. Seigneur for the love of his Dame. And, perhaps, his own beloved Baug.

26

BOONE PAWED THE GROUND. He knew war was upon them and it excited him. He reared, nearly knocking Perce to the ground.

"Easy, Boone. It is almost time."

Across the makeshift jousting field, Sir Albaric's splendid retinue were ready. A dozen of his red and gold banners, emblazoned with fire-breathing dragons, flew around the perimeter of their camp. Three of Albaric's squires had a string of big Andalusians fully tacked for war. Oddly, Albaric's senior *écuyer* Darel was not on the field.

Albaric's snorting chargers were much bigger than Boone, taller and heavier. Unlike Boone, they wore a full *barde* across their chests and a complete *bacul*. Over their heavy armor were splendid red coats, embroidered with four gold dragons.

Poor Boone. A lighter horse than Albaric's destriers, yet a princely horse, he wore only a leather *bufle* over his breast and hindquarters and a *crinet* to protect his neck. He needed no splendid embroidery. Perce had groomed his coal-black coat to a high sheen.

The crowd excited the horses. The entire city turned out, lining the east side of the field right back to the river, thousands of people chattering. To them this was a rare spectacle, an entertainment. They had come early, after the curfew horn had sounded, jostling to get the best positions—perhaps not realizing those on the front ran the risk of injury or death if the combatants tumbled off the field. Perce had seen it happen. In Paris he had been honored to see his Majesty King Louis in the joust. Even with blunted weapons, two in the audience had died and dozens had been badly injured.

In the judicial joust, the combatants didn't use blunted weapons.

On the west side of the field stood a hastily built stadium for the lords and ladies. In the center sat the viscount, the cardinal and the archbishop. With them were the king of Aragon and several honored guests.

The pennants of all the great families of the South were planted along the west perimeter: the griffins of Perpignan, the rearing stags of Agen, the unicorn of Valence. The viscount's own yellow eagle banners dominated the west field, guarded by soldiers with spears. The royal crown of Aragon was represented by a row of gonfalons.

Perce placed his own family banner near Seigneur's pavilion. Seigneur never wore the crest of Castlenau or carried its banner. Beside Perce's lonely red flag was the Templar's piebald banner, white above and black below, unfurled by Arnot, and the charioteer flag, symbol of the Marshall's lieutenant.

The first fanfare blew and the crowd became more agitated. The battle master cleared the field and inspected it one more time. Then the horns blew the summons.

Seigneur emerged from his pavilion, followed closely by his friend, Arnot the Templar, both in full mail shirts and white mantles. Seigneur wore a light coat of chain down to his knees, rusty in spite of Perce's sanding. He did not wear the traditional greaves on his shins or the armor breastplate common in the joust. He wore only the mail and a *gorget* to protect his neck. His sword, Loial, his old mentor's plain broadsword, was at his side. His gauntlets were of simple leather, without studs or armor. His dagged tunic and knee-high boots were white, decades out of style and on anyone else would have been absurd.

Perce frowned. Seigneur's success in the crusades had relied on bursts of unexpected speed—what he called the 'berserker tactic.' Boone would weave and dance and rear, then lunge, then wheel again while Seigneur feinted, ducked, blocked and stabbed. Bewildered enemies fell in their full plate armor. "Chaos fighting" was what the viscount called it: Seigneur's light charger, his beloved Boone, and his featherweight mail made him the fastest warrior on the battlefield, and he used it to full advantage, appearing where he was least expected.

But today Seigneur faced a fully armored chevalier, covered head to toe in plate. Could savvy battle experience and speed win out against raw strength and armor? Perhaps when Seigneur was *younger*.

Perce held the reins out to his lord. He felt a hot pride. No fancy banners or insignia could make him feel any more admiration. He wished only that his lord wore a full suit of armor. Seigneur smiled at him and took the reins. Perce bowed from the waist.

"Don't bow to me, dear friend."

Friend. Again, that unfamiliar word.

Arnot presented a shield decorated with the Templar charioteer and the discreet red cross. "Seigneur, I would consider it an honor if you would carry my shield. It does not carry your colors, but it is light and strong."

Seigneur cocked his head. "I cannot bear the symbol of the Templars."

Arnot smiled. "You have fought the Holy Wars. You have shed blood for Christ. You, before all others, have the right to wear the cross of the Temple."

Seigneur nodded. "I will bear it with pride."

The two men had nothing more to say. Seigneur took the shield and Arnot stepped back with a wave.

Seigneur stood beside Boone, calming him, a single arm casually looped over his charger's neck. Perce and his Seigneur looked at each other but said nothing. What else could be said? Seigneur nodded.

The final call sounded.

Sir Albaric emerged from his pavilion, surrounded by his squires and sergeants, splendid in full armor: full breastplate and back plate, armored vambraces and greaves, shining bright gold in the sun. Under the plate he wore a suit of mail. A shining gold lion.

Perce scowled. It was correct and right to wear full armor, but it seemed somehow cowardly next to Seigneur's simple shirt of mail. In place of the traditional *pavade*, Albaric wore a *patula*, a short sword, to add to his arsenal. On the opposite belt was his broadsword. A fourth squire carried his helm and a massive jousting shield. But where was Squire Darel? It should have been Darel, Perce's rival, who bore his shield. He was still absent from the field. Was he being punished for losing against Perce in the bohort?

The viscount's voice roared, silencing the din of the crowd. Perce could not catch every word the seneschal of Carcassonne spoke: "Your Majesty, Eminence, my Lords and Ladies, Lord Archbishop ... welcome ... two knights wish to engage in ... judicial ... before God's law ... let none interfere ... the law of combat ..."

Perce stopped trying to make out the words, mere formalities. He watched Adelais, sitting straight-backed and smiling next to her father. What did she have to smile about? Either Seigneur would die and Perce would be disgraced, or Seigneur would live and Perce would be disgraced.

Seigneur needed no assistance to mount his Boone in his light armor. Perce handed him his helm. Oddly, the dented helm was proof of his Seigneur's hardiness. The Templar shield seemed out of place, yet it comforted Perce. The bloody cross of God, the sacred symbol given the Templars by the Holy Father under writ. Surely it had power to protect his lord.

Seigneur spoke softly to Boone, who pawed the ground with excitement.

Two old warriors going to battle, the white Cyclops on his black horse.

The archbishop rose to bless the warriors, his arms held out, though Perce could hear no words. He bowed his head anyway and crossed himself, mouthing his own silent prayer for his Seigneur. Perce's tunic clung to his damp skin, and he shivered. Why was he so afraid? Before battle there was always the rush, the thrill, but never this cold fear. Did he fear Albaric so much? Albaric might have the advantage of youth and strength and armor, but Seigneur had never been defeated. Or was it because this joust was so valueless.

Four heralds in the princely yellow of the seneschal rode out, one to each quarter of the field. They blew their horns and the chief herald announced, "My Lord Seneschal Viscount Hugh D'Arcis. Your Majesty, Lord King of Aragon. Your Eminence. Your Grace. Gentle ladies. Noble men. People of Carcassonne! The seneschal of his Majesty King Louis, most glorious high king of all these lands, commands you to bear witness to this judicial joust. May God guide the hand of the just!" Again, the horns blew and the heralds rode back to the center of the field, their capes fluttering.

The crowd leaned forward over the ropes, their sudden silence as ferocious as their earlier chatter. The only sounds were the snorting horses, excited and ready, pawing the still muddy earth. Parents held up their children and pointed at the two knights. Gangs of older children, hid under the wagons, closer to the field than their parents, lying on their chests in the dust.

The honor of signaling the beginning of the joust went to the most noble witness, His Majesty King John of Aragon. The tall king stood as straight and tall as a young oak tree and drew his sword.

Only last night King John had shown Perce that sword. The king had come to Seigneur's pavilion. Perce had been so surprised he fell on his face before the king, splendid in his purple robes trimmed in fox. Seigneur had merely smiled and said, "Welcome, Majesty."

Perce served them wine, his hands shaking.

"I was in my fief in Montréal when I heard of your joust," King John said, stroking his black beard. "I had to come, of course."

Seigneur shrugged, sipping his mulled wine. "I am gratified, Lord King."

"Do you remember when we played with our wooden swords?" the young king asked.

Seigneur's forehead creased. "I remember a stubborn brat who wouldn't follow instructions."

The king laughed loudly and held out his bowl. Perce's hands were still shaking as he poured wine. "Your squire seems all in terror of me, Seigneur."

"Put down the jug, Perce. Sit with us." Seigneur gestured at him. "Bring that bowl of dates."

Perce had sat on the threadbare rug, the sultan's rug. He felt ridiculous sitting on the ground with his Seigneur and a king, all of them cross-legged like boys on a hunt.

"I don't snarl," said King John, his teeth shining even in the dim torchlight.

"No, Your Majesty!"

"Relax, Perce! I trained John as a boy, just as I'm training you. He became a king. Who knows what you'll be."

Perce dropped his head.

King John shrugged. "Oh, well. A good boy he seems."

"He's adequate." Seigneur smiled. "More than adequate. I jest, Perce." He looked at the King. "How is your mother?"

His dark face flushed. "She's in heaven, Seigneur."

Seigneur reached out and Perce was astonished as they clasped hands. "Your mother was a dear woman."

"She asked about you often."

Seigneur nodded. "The curse of the crusader, never to return to visit friends and family."

The king chewed a date and spat out a pit. "I know. Almost as devastating as the curse of kingship."

Seigneur lifted his bowl. "I drink to your kingship. I was sorry to miss your coronation."

They clashed bowls. "Now what, pray tell, is this all about? Hugh fumes about you defending a heretic. God's curse, Seigneur! You fought in holy crusade at my father's side!"

Seigneur drank the hot clove-laced wine. "John, I don't talk of religious matters. You should know that."

"*John* is it? You're as bold as ever, Seigneur."

"I whipped your naked bottom when you were a naughty bratling. Don't hold me to formalities."

King John laughed heartily and reached forward to clasp Seigneur's shoulder. "Of course I won't. Dear Seigneur, my love for you is born out of many such whippings!"

Perce drank his wine, his trembling hands causing little waves on the surface of the bowl.

"Seigneur, my dear Seigneur, you must have a care. You have many friends. I count you among mine. I see our old friend Templar Arnot is here! But the Church has grown. These are dangerous times."

Seigneur nodded.

"You know what you are doing?"

Seigneur shrugged. "I haven't any idea what I'm doing. For once, I'm following my heart."

King John put down his bowl. "I'm astonished Seigneur. Truly astonished."

"As is my squire, it seems!"

They both laughed at Perce's hanging mouth and pale face.

"Well Seigneur. There's nothing much I can do for you. Other than to tell you what you already know."

"What's that, Majesty?"

"I liked it better when you called me John." He smiled. "Only that you are always welcome in Aragon."

Seigneur nodded. "I know. But I'd never risk Aragon. I have no intention of making *you* the target of the next crusade."

The King scowled. "I lost half of my kingdom to Louis in this last crusade. I'd welcome a chance to strike back."

"I know."

"My father died defending these heretics of langue d'oc."

"I know."

Perce had refilled their bowls and they had talked through half the night of the battles Seigneur fought with King Peter, John's father. Finally, reluctantly, they had embraced, and the king had left Seigneur to get some sleep before the joust.

Perce looked up now at King John, standing between the viscount and Cardinal Fiesco. All three of them were splendid in their brilliant colors, the purple of the king, the yellow of the viscount and the scarlet of the Church. The king regarded Seigneur, his dark face showing no emotion. He nodded at Seigneur, who nodded back.

"Lords and Ladies, noble combatants," King John shouted. He held up his sword, glittering with gems. All faces turned and watched the sword as it swept through the air. "I commence the joust. May God's justice prevail."

A cheer overwhelmed the rest of his words.

Perce watched, helpless, as his Seigneur rode to the starting flag.

27

ARCHBISHOP PETER AMIEL of Narbonne shifted his ample posterior and reached out for another spiced apple. They smelled delightful with a hint of cinnamon and cloves.

"You seem to enjoy the spectacle, Your Grace?" Cardinal Sinibaldo Fiesco, the pope's right hand, frowned, his fierce black eyes like daggers impaling Amiel.

Archbishop Amiel dropped the apple slice, his thick fingers clumsy. "No, Eminence. I am most distressed by such secular acts."

The cardinal sat in the place of honor, beside His Majesty King John of Aragon. The archbishop looked at his empty hand, fragrant with cinnamon. His page, Boden, brought mead. Again, he noticed the cardinal's puckered brow. He looked at the boy—the face of an Adonis, sculpted from young flesh as firm as white marble—then at the aging cardinal. It had been so long since he had enjoyed the pleasure of Boden.

"Your Grace, his Holiness is displeased."

What a surprise, thought Amiel. But he said, "We make progress, Eminence."

They turned on cushioned seats as the two chevaliers took the field to the roar of the crowd. Seigneur's shining black charger lifted his knees high with pride. Opposite was the gold glory of Sir Albaric the Lion.

"This is all unexpected," Fiesco continued. "I was dispatched by His

Holiness on news of the capture of the Anti-Popess, the Dame. Now I must witness this degrading sport."

Amiel fixed his gaze on Seigneur. Seigneur had been the Church's hero for decades. Seigneur had captured the Dame, the Anti-Popess. And in the moment of Amiel's greatest triumph, the fall of Montségur imminent, it was Seigneur who mocked the Church. "Eminence, this is but a small inconvenience. Even should Seigneur win this battle—and that's fairly unlikely, God willing—he gains only possession of the prisoner."

"And why should one of our most noble crusaders wish to possess this creature. She is a heretic and a Southerner!"

Amiel shrugged. "That I don't understand myself. Lord knows Seigneur has killed hundreds of *her* kind. But she will not leave Carcassonne, I assure you."

"I am not assured. But I'll hold you to this."

The clang of lances on plate interrupted their debate.

"A good blow!" King John of Aragon leaned forward, almost off his seat with excitement.

Seigneur's lance scored a direct hit against Albaric's shield. Seigneur's horse wheeled sharply, stepping nimbly out of range of Albaric's counterstrike.

Adelais rose to her feet, cheering wildly.

"Have you ever seen so splendid a stallion!" King John shouted.

"No, Majesty," replied Viscount d'Arcis. "Boone is a Friesian, born of princely heritage."

"Splendid!" replied the king.

Amiel sneered at their excitement. Martial games for petty martial lords. But it wasn't just the lords. The ladies were on their feet, cheering. Lady Adelais, the viscount's daughter, led the excited chorus, ignoring her mother's disapproving glare.

"Seigneur is wonderful!" she shouted, her small bosoms rising and falling like a blacksmith's bellows. "Look!"

"Adelais, sweet, sit down." Viscount Hugh put his gloved hand on her forearm and pulled her so hard he left his handprint in her flesh.

A moment later she was on her feet again, screaming her delight.

Boone charged at full gallop. Seigneur's lance dipped at the last moment and Sir Albaric leaned back in his wooden saddle, shield taking the blow.

"What speed!" King John nearly fell from the stands in his excitement, his ivory white teeth flashing against his olive skin.

"Seigneur is famous for it, Majesty," replied his old comrade the viscount.

Amiel could see their excitement: their bodies straining forward as if their seats could not contain them, the slightly parted lips, the animated gestures. Such children.

"Disgusting," hissed the archbishop.

"It should not be permitted," agreed the cardinal.

"Fiercely done!" shouted the king, his legs coiled under him as if to pounce.

"A magnificent strike, Majesty," agreed the viscount.

Cardinal Fiesco plucked at his ermine trimmed sleeve. "You know, I was a part of the Lateran Council that abolished this nonsense."

King John frowned at him. "No power in the universe will stop an honorable challenge, Eminence. It is the way of Chevalerie. It is the *esprit* of the chevalier."

"Si, Majesty." The cardinal's lips curled into a disgusted smile as another roar escaped the crowd.

Archbishop Amiel enjoyed the cardinal's discomfort. His gloat was short-lived as the audience roared once more. Everyone came to their feet, and even Amiel found himself gripped by the spectacle.

Seigneur swayed in his saddle. Shards of Albaric's lance protruded from Seigneur's shield. Amiel rose with the rest, holding his breath. Would Seigneur fall, to be trampled under the hooves of Albaric's Andalusian? Amiel fervently prayed it would be so. He whispered the Paternoster.

Then Boone, as if sensing his master's need, stepped sideways and Seigneur righted himself in his saddle.

"Ah. It is as I said, Eminence," said Amiel. "Seigneur de Castlenau will fail. He is too *old*."

King John snorted a laugh. "How little you know of such things,

Your Grace. Experience is a greater weapon than youth and endurance." He pointed.

Seigneur drew his sword, swung it quickly behind Albaric and knocked him forward with an echoing blow that dented Albaric's back plate.

The audience cheered.

"It seems these heretics of Carcassonne favor the Seigneur," said Fiesco.

"Oui, Eminence. He is a hero to many, even before his support of the Dame," answered Amiel, pursing his lips in displeasure. *These damnable heretics!* They had no sense of duty or holy obligation. They cared only for their Lady, their cursed Dame Esclarmonde de Foix and their pagan festivals and their crops. And they dared to show their support in front of the archbishop and the pope's own cardinal vice-chancellor.

"Heroes are dangerous to the spirit."

"Oui, Eminence."

King John grew excited again. "See Seigneur's strategy! He wears out Sir Albaric!"

Seigneur and Boone circled Sir Albaric, thrusting and feinting, turning and sidestepping, both of them swinging their swords. Albaric's swings seemed stronger, yet even to Amiel's untrained eyes, Seigneur was more controlled, feinting rather than committing, blocking more than striking, and his devilish black horse seemed to read his mind, for the Seigneur used no reins at all. How could this graying old man stand against so magnificent a chevalier?

"What a splendid horse!" King John shouted. "If I could have but forty of those my enemies would flee my caballeros!"

Viscount d'Arcis nodded. "Oui, Majesty! Boone is a fine stallion. I have bred him with some of my Trakehners."

Archbishop Amiel saw the cardinal's shrug. Mundane matters. Why was the cardinal still here? Why had he come at all? Of course the Church wanted the relics reputed to be held by the Dame, and the Dame herself must be neutralized as a threat to God's peace, but the pope's own vice-chancellor? Amiel assumed they did not trust him. Either Fiesco, or His Holiness himself doubted Amiel would return the relics to Rome.

He leaned close and whispered, "Idiotic games."

For the first time the cardinal smiled, revealing that he was still quite a dashing, handsome man in spite of graying temples. "So, Your Grace, what news can I give His Holiness?"

"The Dame will be tried and found guilty, no matter who wins this battle, Eminence. Then Montségur will fall, the relics will be restored, and my mission will be complete."

"Your mission is never complete for Mother Church."

"I erred, Eminence. I meant my current quest."

"One would hope so. The battle against heresy should never relax. They are everywhere, these heretics, as dangerous as the plague and nearly as virulent. We banned the Jews from France but they are still everywhere, openly defying us! We required all our bishops to seek out heretics in their sees, but no matter how many we find, there are more. We can only succeed if we are vigilant!"

"Oui, Eminence! Only last week we sent three to the fires! They seem endless!"

"I have ordered the Diableteur to move against this pagan rabble. The Baug are they called?"

Amiel stiffened in his chair, shocked at the cardinal's boldness. "Eminence, they are very popular. Very popular."

"This is why I ordered their arrest."

Amiel didn't like the way the cardinal had usurped his God-given authority, nor the smug look on his too-handsome face, but he said nothing.

The crowd rose again, shouting, some cheering, most hissing displeasure. Amiel forgot the cardinal for a moment, assuming the worst for the Seigneur. The Seigneur hung from the near side of his saddle, dangling so low his sword dragged on the earth as Boone swung around at full canter.

"First blood!" roared Viscount d'Arcis.

Blood flowed down Seigneur's leg.

"Ah. Sir Albaric's strength is turning the battle," said Amiel, nodding as if he knew it was inevitable.

Seigneur galloped across the field and the Combat Master blew the horn. Sir Albaric trotted back to his pavilion to change horses while the Seigneur remained mounted. His squire tended his wound, binding his leg.

"I am leaving the Diableteur in your county, Your Grace."

Amiel half closed his eyes. The occasional visit by the Diableteur was barely tolerable, but the idea of a broader mission, a permanent presence … Amiel shivered.

"I have engaged the Diableteur to more aggressively seek out the heretics in Carcassonne."

"The *Diableteur*! But Eminence! That is not needed!"

"We disagree."

Amiel looked away, certain the "we" meant him and the pope. Diableteur at large in his county! That devil! The shame was too much to bear. "Eminence, *we* are mastering the problem."

"Are you?" The cardinal gestured at the excited crowd, cheering for Seigneur. "I see thousands here who do not seem to have Mother Church at heart."

Archbishop Amiel nodded. "It is truly a staggering task, Eminence. But we are winning. Now, with the Dame in our possession they will lose heart."

"For fifty years they have not lost heart! Since they were conquered they have not lost heart!"

"But the Dame—"

"Yes, but *who* possesses the Dame?"

"This will be settled today."

"And what of this Templar?" Fiesco pointed. "See, the Seigneur carries the emblem of the Chariot." He smiled, staring at the Templar. "I have sent for the Master Marshall of the Temple. He is three days' ride away."

Amiel stared at the cardinal, wondering if he was mad. "You asked the Master Marshal here?" His tone conveyed what he really meant: why would you wish to complicate matters?

"I have." He smiled again.

"But why?"

"Simply put, I do not believe this Templar. This Arnot. It all seems too convenient."

Amiel shrugged. "Seigneur campaigned with the Templars for decades."

Fiesco shook his head. "I know a farce when I see one."

Amiel blushed. How many roles had he played for the vice-chancellor of the Church since he arrived? Too many. Could Fiesco see through them all? As if in answer, the cardinal said, "We're not speaking of you." Amiel felt his own heat and knew he was blushing. "Amiel, this Templar isn't right."

"They care for the relics. Surely, there is logic to the Templar's arrival."

"They never travel alone. Never. If this Arnot is the Charioteer of the Master Marshall, the very brother knight of the great master, then he might never leave his side."

"Except on a mission of grave secrecy."

"The Templars always deal in secrecy, Amiel."

"But even the viscount knows Arnot. From the crusades."

"So? What does that mean? It means he is an opportunist, nothing more. Most crusaders join not for God but for the opportunity to loot." His tone conveyed another message. It seemed to say: *You are a fool, Amiel.* "I know a fraud when I see one."

Amiel shrugged. "Eminence, she'll never leave this county. The Dame's dead already, regardless of the outcome today."

"I trust it is so. For your sake."

Amiel looked away. He cared little about the Templars and their incessant plotting. But—the Diableteur permanently in Carcassonne! It was an affront! He shivered. He had been in Avignon when the Diableteur had caused mass hysteria. His own deacon had refused to attend the trials that followed. Amiel had stood in a tower of the pope's French palace and watched the long line of tradesmen, huddled with their families in carts that overflowed with their possessions, fleeing the city in a long line. Houses had emptied.

No one was safe from the Diableteur's accusations of sorcery. In Bordeaux the witch-hunter had accused and arrested a holy bishop of the Church on charges of devil-worship. A holy bishop! Cardinal Fiesco and His Holiness did not trust Amiel. It did not bode well for Amiel's future.

Amiel tried to return his attention to the tourney field. Seigneur remained at his pavilion, mounted but bleeding. Amiel squinted into the afternoon sun. He saw the flash of gray, the stooped figure with the staff, and his gut tightened.

"Lord Viscount!" he snapped. He pointed at the stooped figure by the Seigneur's horse.

Viscount Hugh D'Arcis followed the gesture. Instantly, the county lord sat straighter. He clapped his hands. "Sir Lantar!"

"What is it? What is going on?" Cardinal Fiesco also squinted at the Seigneur.

Amiel ignored Fiesco. He was right! What a catch! If only they could move quickly enough! "The old man, there, by Seigneur's horse."

"So? An old man."

"The heretic of heretics, Eminence!" Amiel's voice carried his excitement. "That is the Perfect Guilhem d'Alions!"

"In God's name!" The marshals were about to blow the horns.

But Amiel remained focused on the old hermit, the Perfect from Alions. Perhaps more than the Dame herself, the old hermit Guilhem d'Alions was the most dangerous Cathar in the South! He was the teacher, the true leader of the rebel movement in Occitania.

Amiel watched as the Viscount's yellow soldiers, led by the splendid purple unicorn of Sir Lantar, moved through the crowd, their spears opening a path, toward the Seigneur's pavilion.

But not quickly enough! He must not escape! The old hermit had a knack for disappearing. He'd appear at burnings, give the *consolamentum* to the dying, then vanish before the soldiers could arrest him. Now, here he was! And with the Seigneur.

He glared at the Seigneur, once his ally, the man he had championed, the knight who brought him the Dame. It was *his* fault. Under his breath, he cursed him. "Death to you, Seigneur!"

Song of the Hermit

28

"STOP FUSSING, PERCE."

Perce shook his head, holding the makeshift bandage. The smell of blood, sweet like rotting fruit, choked him. "It still bleeds."

"This is not the first time you've seen me bleed! Attend to Boone."

Perce ran his hands over Boone's flanks and his quivering legs, lathered from exertion. "Seigneur, Boone seems fine, for now. He has heart."

Seigneur nodded, reached forward and stroked his stallion's neck.

"I notice that Sir Albaric is head shy."

Seigneur nodded. "He tosses his head to shield his eyes."

Perce blinked sweat from his eyes and tightened the girth on his Seigneur's saddle, bent low. He dropped the girth strap, straightened and turned when he heard Seigneur's puzzled voice. "Who are you, grandfather?"

Perce stared at the old man with the staff. Was he a supporter of Seigneur or a troublemaker? Perce had no time for him either way. "Move on, father, we're busy here!"

"I bring a blessing," said the old man, his voice crumbly and dry, as if he rarely spoke. Yet for all of that, there was power in the voice, a mastery that commanded attention. Perce studied him more intensely. He was stooped, yes, but still taller than Perce. In his youth he must have been taller even than Seigneur himself! But the man seemed frail, leaning heavily on a crude staff that was worn about the tip, cracked and dry from age. His beard was as white as Nevara's hair, but crinkly and dry, as if it might disintegrate at any moment, and his face held no definition, merely folds of tired flesh creased into deep wrinkles and lines. But those eyes! Piercing gray eyes that remained defiant of age, timeless and full of blazing energy.

"Move on, old man," Perce said, again.

The trumpets blew.

"Do not be rude, Perce." Seigneur stared at the old man, leaning on the pommel of his saddle. "Your name, sire?"

The old man nodded, then smiled. "Guilhem. Guilhem D'Alions."

"My God!" Perce dove for his hilt. The legendary old heretic hermit! If he could arrest him, his spurs were assured.

"Stay your sword, Perce!" Seigneur, his strength returned, no longer winded from the first round, glared at the old man. "What do you wish of us, hermit?"

"I liked grandfather better," said the old man. "You fight for my daughter. I came to bless you."

"Your daughter?"

"Spiritual daughter, my son." The young gray eyes twinkled incongruously in the stern ancient face.

"I want no blessings. I fight for my heart."

"Yet you have them. I bless you in God's name."

Seigneur crossed himself. Perce half drew his sword. "We want no curses here, heretic!"

"Perce!" Seigneur snapped. He scanned the crowd. "The viscount's soldiers come, old man. I suggest you vanish. I hear you are good at this."

The old man nodded then reached up and touched Seigneur's wounded thigh with long bony fingers. "Be strong for the Dame."

Perce shoved the old man roughly. "Do not curse us, old man!"

Seigneur said, "The bleeding has stopped." There was a little awe in his voice.

"Seigneur?" Perce forgot the old man and turned. Seigneur seemed to sit straighter in the high saddle, his face alive with new energy. The bleeding had indeed stopped.

Then the soldiers arrived, shouting and pushing through the crowd. "Where is the old man?" snapped Sir Lantar, his mustache twitching.

Perce wheeled around again, dizzy with all the happenings, but he was too late. The old man was gone!

"Search for him! Fan out!" Sir Lantar and his men plunged into the crowd and Perce watched as they converged on another troop of soldiers coming from the other direction. His opportunity for triumph was gone, and Lantar, the vile royal nephew who promised to marry Adelais, might succeed where Perce had failed. Envious, he watched Lantar round a pavilion. Lantar was a knight. Lantar would marry Adelais. Lantar was allied to the king and Church.

What was Perce? He had no chance of his spurs, aligned as he was to a lord who proclaimed support for heresies and gave up his prestigious role as champion. He would be lucky if he didn't end up on a stake himself. What happened to the glory? It would all be gone: Adelais, his spurs of knighthood, his future, the opportunity to reclaim his father's fief.

If only he had arrested the old hermit. Was his vow to Seigneur so deep he gave up what he believed in? He believed in the crusades, in God, in abolishing heresies, in knightly chivalry, in justice. How could loyalty to one man be more important?

But Seigneur was that important. He was his adopted father, lord, friend. Seigneur was all that mattered. He turned to his lord, who sat straight and youthful in his saddle. Their eyes met. Perce held up his hand, red with Seigneur's blood, and his lord clasped it. He watched his master take the field once more. A rebellious tear ran down Perce's cheek to mingle with Seigneur's blood. Yet Perce felt pride.

The two combatants charged each other on the third blast of the horns. Clumps of mud flew into the air, tufts of grass were tossed like stones flung from a *trebuchet*.

Albaric swung his sword but Seigneur turned the blow with the Templar shield and struck with Loial as he passed, hitting Albaric's shoulder vambrace with a twang. The crowd cheered as Albaric lurched forward, almost unhorsed.

Boone reared and spun on hind legs. Seigneur charged from behind as Albaric remained facing away from him, swaying in his saddle. Loial flashed, striking plate armor with a loud clang.

Blood!" shouted someone in the crowd.

Seigneur had finally drawn blood. His ancient sword had found the gap between plates, and penetrated Albaric's mail shirt.

Sir Albaric howled, his spurs digging deep into the flanks of his charger. Seigneur, who needed no spurs on Boone, pursued him and hacked one more time before Albaric managed to turn and face him.

Perce ran forward a few steps as Seigneur took a slicing blow. Again the Templar shield saved him and Boone took off at full gallop down the east side of the field. Albaric did not pursue, knowing the limitations of his big charger against Boone's speed. He drew up his big horse.

Seigneur slowed to a canter and turned in front of his pavilion. Boone pawed the earth and his ears came forward. Perce noted with satisfaction that Boone was eager for the charge. He never tired of the battle.

The two knights charged again, meeting nearer to Albaric's pavilion because of Boone's burst of speed. A cry went up from the crowd as Albaric leaned forward and stabbed at Seigneur's horse.

Perce took a step forward, worried for both Boone and Seigneur, but Boone was ready for treachery. He half-pirouetted, launching into the air and swiveling out of the way, then reared, his hooves striking hard on his enemy's flank. The flying capriole! Perce had seen Seigneur training Boone on the high art of Castillian horsemanship, but had never seen Boone use it in battle. Now with Boone airborne, his hooves flashing, Perce understood its power. Albaric's horse stumbled, squealing in pain, but Albaric was already swinging his sword back, stabbing once more at Boone.

"Foul!" shouted Perce. The crowd took up the cry, chanting, "Foul! Foul!" It was one thing to kill a warrior's horse in battle. It was not done in the joust.

Perce sighed, relieved, as he realized Boone was unhurt. He had taken a glancing blow off his leather bacul. Boone's sudden surge of speed was awesome. Seigneur circled the field and charged Albaric's trotting mount. With a clang their swords met and Albaric pitched backwards, nearly unhorsed.

Perce lifted his fist in triumph and cheered with the rest.

Thank God for Boone. Seigneur's precious stallion had been a gift from Frieslander Prince Hodr, a fellow crusader. He had been a colt when Seigneur took him, gentling the beast with a patience that Perce did not possess. Boone and Seigneur were inseparable.

He had heart, that horse.

Boone charged again, nostrils flaring, ears forward in excitement.

At the last moment, Albaric hauled harshly on his reins and the larger Andalusian swung broadside in front of Boone's charge. Boone veered but too late and the two horses collided. Boone's lighter weight and greater speed handicapped him this time. He tumbled to the ground with a shriek and threw his Seigneur from the saddle.

The crowd roared as Seigneur and Boone went down. Albaric remained mounted, his bigger horse trotting back around.

"Seigneur!" shouted Perce, his voice lost in the din. He watched, helpless, as his Seigneur lay in the mud. Boone rolled completely over and flipped to his feet. He stood over his Seigneur and pawed the ground, glaring at the approaching Albaric.

But Seigneur did not move.

29

THE SENTRY'S LEG SLIPPED as he started awake, saved from falling by leaning on his spear. "Qui va là?" He looked at the troubadour and his little dog. "Oh, you two. This day I did not expect you."

Ramon smiled. He knew what the man meant. The entire city except for a skeletal garrison were at the Seigneur's judicial joust, the most exciting event in living memory.

"A shame you must miss the joust," Ramon said.

"You, too, friend jester." He had come each day and they knew him well: Marcel and his mate Normande on this shift; Bevis and Cordel on the next.

"Oh—I hate these things." He clucked, and Mauri jumped onto his shoulder in the way that always delighted Marcel.

"But the Seigneur and the Lion! What a battle! If only I could sneak off!"

"Why don't you? I can stay here."

Marcel seemed to think about it, but he shook his head finally. "Non. It'd be my head if I was caught!"

Ramon nodded. "I understand." He looked around. "Where is everyone?"

"Oh that lucky dog," He bent and ruffled Mauri's head. "Sorry, Mauri! That bastard Normande switched with Jaspre. He be at the tourney, damn his hide. Jaspre is making the rounds. The rest are at the tourney." He spat on the ground, disgusted. "You are a fool to miss the joust, jester!"

"A fool am I!" Ramon danced a little jig. "I have no appetite for war games." He held out the tray. "Speaking of appetites."

"You brought food again." Marcel licked his cracked lips. "Bless you, Ramon, tis no wonder we all love you."

"Pier's hotchpotch. And dandelion ale!"

Marcel sniffed the steaming mutton stew and his stomach rumbled. Ramon handed him a small bowl and a flask of ale. Marcel set aside his spear and wetted his cracked lips with ale. "Ah. God's own angels will fly you to heaven, Ramon. Will you sing for us today?" He bent to scratch Mauri's ear, right where he liked it, and the dog squatted, wagging his tail.

"Not today. Tomorrow perhaps." Ramon forced a smile.

Marcel began to wolf down the food. "Merci, little jester."

"Well, I'd best go in. Farewell, Marcel."

Marcel didn't acknowledge him, probably busy with dreams of jousts and festivities.

Ramon pulled a torch from the wall and bent his head into the low tunnel. He loathed the pit. Every night he had nightmares of it and in the dreams he saw himself hanging naked from the wall shackles, whipped and starving. For the hundredth time, he thought of how fortunate he was that he had never been imprisoned here. But for his voice, he might languish in the pit alongside his friends.

The second sentry station called the challenge.

"Tis I, Ramon."

A face appeared in the dim torchlight, very young and grimly unsmiling, but familiar for all that. "The troubadour?" He seemed shocked by Ramon's colorful clothing and the dog perched lightly on his shoulder.

"Well met, Jaspre. You remember me from the gate?"

"I do. And now you visit the pit. More jokes for us?"

Ramon shook his head. "I'm here On the business of Seigneur de Castlenau."

"And your dog, too."

"Mauri. Hush!"

"Mauri, come here!" Mauri jumped from Ramon's shoulder and Jaspre bent to stroke his head.

"I didn't mention it afore, but I knew a Jaspre once," Ramon said with a sigh. "In this very city. Jaspre, the son of—" he scratched his head. "Son of Chacier Blacksmith."

The guard straightened, his face showing his astonishment. "Well, that's *me*!"

Ramon tried not to reveal his own surprise. Jaspre had been a childhood friend though he had looked nothing like this burly man before him. They had played games of *Sticks and Toss* and *King of the Castle* and even banded together to defend themselves from the larger children. It seemed so long ago. He shivered. Tonight of all nights! Why must he meet Jaspre now, on the night when the guards might lose their lives? Of course he hoped no one would die this day, but it was a jester's hope. In truth, many would likely die.

Jaspre studied Ramon with new interest. "Of course. Ramon Burcson is it?"

"You remember?"

"I never would have guessed from our first meeting. But you always had those long horse-legs. Cheval they called you."

Ramon laughed with him. "I remember. And they called you *Freki*."

"*You* called me Freki!" He held out his hand and Ramon seized it in his own. "*They* called me something cruder." He laughed. "I never knew what Freki meant."

Ramon smiled. "Freki was Odin's wolf. A fierce creature."

"You named me for a Northman's wolf?"

"A god's wolf."

Jaspre's face, childlike, smiled. "I like that. Odin's wolf!"

Ramon leaned against the damp wall. He had little time, he needed to get on, but how could he rush past Jaspre without raising his suspicions? And didn't he owe him more? It was over twelve years ago, the last time he had seen Japsre. Why couldn't he have met him earlier? Why tonight of all nights? It seemed an ominous portent.

"Have a care. That slime doesn't wash out."

Ramon brushed off his shoulder. "You became a soldier after all. I remember we played many soldier games."

Jaspre laughed. "With little Linette as our enemy."

Ramon nodded. "And how is Linette?" He was remembering castle and siege games, with Jaspre as the castle lord and Linette, Jaspre's sister, as the invading army.

Jaspre's smile faded. "She is in heaven. The pleurisy."

Ramon squeezed Jaspre's hand. "I'm sorry. She was an angel."

"And now she's with the angels."

Ramon felt his sadness, as dark and dank as the pit. This only made Ramon feel worse. He hoped he could find a way to spare Jaspre from either injury or death, or retribution from his liege lord if he failed his duty.

"You always wanted to be a soldier." Ramon said.

"A knight, actually. But that is for my betters. I'm not born to it."

"I'm sure you serve well. Mayhap, we could meet after your shift?" Of course, he hoped never to see his childhood friend again. If he did, it would mean Ramon had failed, and he would likely be hanging in chains along side the Grand Duo.

Jaspre nodded eagerly. "I'd enjoy that, Ramon. You can tell me what brings you home to Carcassonne."

Ramon nodded. "And I can sing you some of my silly songs."

"I had heard of Ramon Troubadour. Now I realize it's you. You're famous now, especially with the ladies. Including my sweet Avice."

"Not Avice the spinner?"

He squinted in the gloom. "You know my Avice?"

"She spins the countess's wool. She often comes to hear me sing."

"Funny, isn't it?"

They laughed together.

"We're expecting our first child."

"Oh, my congratulations, good Jaspre! Another little soldier."

Jaspre kicked at a rat. "Damn things! Can't abide this pit! I'm usually on the wall garrison. With everyone at the joust I was reassigned."

"Oh, that's why I've not seen you."

Jaspre nodded. "Well, I'm off after curfew. Perhaps we could meet on the morrow?"

"Let's do that."

Ramon took his leave and made his way into the darkest depths of the pit. He felt profound melancholy. He'd never meet with Jaspre. In fact, with luck, he'd never see him again. He remembered how Jaspre was always eager for play battle and Linette was his reluctant playmate. Jaspre led many mock charges with Ramon at his side. He hadn't thought to ask of Jaspre's mother or father.

Jaspre would fall asleep like the other guard, taken to a dreamless place with Nevara's drugs. At least he need not die.

Jaspre was the enemy now, and Linette was—dead. His eyes sparkled with tears and he tasted salt. Life could be so cruel. It was no wonder the Perfecti preached that hell was on this earth, that heaven was escape from this existence.

Several voices lifted in a symphony of moans. Many of the prisoners looked forward to his visits. He knelt and gave morsels of food to many as he passed on his way to visit Doré the Costonot and Osric the Hammer.

"Ah, there you are, Ramon. You are late today." Doré smiled. They were chained tightly to the floor—after Osric nearly strangled one of the sentries, the soldiers had shortened the chains—and normally Ramon had to feed them himself by dropping morsels into their hungry mouths.

But this time, he knelt and put the food on the floor. Several rats descended on the bundle, squeaking, but Mauri charged at them and they scampered away. Now Mauri did his rounds, going from prisoner to prisoner, licking their faces.

Doré frowned. "No food today, friend troubadour?" His stomach rumbled.

Ramon leaned closer. "Today is the day," he whispered.

Doré smiled, nodding, and the smile transformed her from man to attractive woman.

Ramon held up a smithy's bar he'd hidden in his cloak.

Doré was startled. "Did Seigneur's ruse work?"

"Actually, no. Not a ruse. Seigneur is likely to die." Ramon fell silent, sadder than he might have believed possible. Seigneur was a famous enemy of his people, known for his brutal enforcement of the viscount's laws.

"That's for the best!" snapped Osric his broad face grinning. "He killed many of my friends! Hundreds of our people were captured or killed by that monster!"

Doré cocked her head to one side. "But the Dame's love has transformed him."

"He's a creature of hell!"

"We all are," Ramon said, working on the hand cuffs with the smithy's bar.

"Then I hope he dies! He'll be released. And we'll be rid of him!"

Doré sounded sad. "I think—I know—he loves her."

"Have a care, Ramon," snapped Osric. "My hand!"

He paused as the smithy's bar scraped the rock. "Sorry. Stop moving."

"Be careful!"

"Sorry."

Osric held up one hand, clenching and unclenching his freed hand.

"You risk much, Ramon," said Doré when he began working on her cuffs.

"I know. But I'm counting on you. You aren't famous for nothing, I trust? I've seen you fight." Ramon inserted the claws of the crowbar into the second cuff. "Perhaps we can talk about this another time. Unless you want to keep hanging about?"

Doré smiled.

The crowbar drew blood. "Have a care, friend troubadour."

Ramon snapped the second cuff open. "Sorry."

Doré rubbed her raw wrists. "And now what? Assuming we obtain freedom."

"I rescue you because I need your help rescuing the Dame."

"And then?"

"I have arranged delays and tricks. I will take care of the garrison."

"You?"

"Me." Ramon grinned. "I need you to protect the Dame. To get her safely to the Phantom Wood."

Osric glared at him. "That's a plan?"

"It is all I have time to tell you. Just take the Dame in the Baug wagons. Protect the Dame and my people."

"The Baug?"

"The Baug. They are my family."

Doré touched Ramon's shoulder. "We'll do our part."

Osric rubbed his raw wrists. "I will delight in ringing a few soldier's necks."

Ramon's eyes widened, alarmed. "No! I beg you not! Tonight, with all the guards at the joust, my old childhood friend Jaspre has been assigned duty. I couldn't bear his death." He thought of Linette. Poor Linette.

Doré swayed as if she were drunk. "That is if I can stand. I've been shackled for what seems like many moons."

"Just a few days." Ramon's smile faded. "We must hurry. We have little time."

"What about us?" cried a feeble voice in the darkness.

Ramon knew he should leave them. If any of the other prisoners were found wandering about, the remaining soldiers would know there was an escape. He studied the haggard faces in the torchlight. No. He couldn't just leave them. He handed a man the bar. "Free yourselves."

Then Ramon led the way out of the safety of the pit into the dangers of the Viscount's castle.

30

NEVARA CONCENTRATED on her work. She chanted the stormbringer. She had worked on the storm since the previous night, working with her elementals, and now, as the dark clouds loomed abruptly south of the city, she knew her spirit servitors had felt her need. It made for a terrible image. The market square was bright with late afternoon sunshine, the tall pavilion of the Baug colorful and glowing from the merry fire within, but high black clouds boiled over the castle on the hill above Diableteur, a terrible image that intensified the creature's darkness. Perhaps this was his storm. The dark creature brought a storm to wash them away.

No one had moved since Eline had sent her arrows flying to mark a boundary for Diableteur. He studied them now, a statue, unmoving. The wind of the coming storm lifted his long trailing sleeves and cloak but never enough to blow back his cowl and reveal the horrors within. His forty-four soldiers—like Templars, half-knight and half-monk, dressed in black mail over black leather, faces obscured under cowls—also did not move, as if Nevara had cast a freezing spell on them. They were armed with crossbows, bolts drawn. Long broadswords hung on their belts. Thank the Goddess the Diableteur's deathriders were afoot. Against their white horses, even Nevara's magic would not be enough.

In the standoff, the only sounds were the distant clanging of swords as Seigneur and Sir Albaric continued their combat, the rumble of approaching thunder, and the nervous snort of Nevara's horses.

Diableteur moved, bending stiffly from the waist. His sleeve trailed over one of Eline's arrows. He pulled it from the dusty earth and snapped the shaft with a sharp and jarring sound. Over the Diableteur's shoulder, forked lightning lanced across a black sky.

He stepped over the remaining two arrows and the knives.

Eline drew rapidly and fired another volley of arrows. With perfect precision they pierced the earth just in front of Diableteur's boots.

He stepped over them again.

Thor's own thunder rumbled. The sun finally disappeared behind the leading edge of wind-blown clouds.

"You will coming no closer," shouted Nevara, and she raised her arms to the sky. Obligingly, more lightning flashed, silhouetting the crenellations of the castle walls.

"Cease this magic, witch!" The Diableteur's voice was windy, loud but low and raspy. He planted his scythe in front of him, blade up, haft down. *"You condemn yourself!"*

Nevara pointed a long finger at the castle behind the Diableteur. The unholy creature turned his head. Forks of lightning split the sky. A bolt struck the Tour des Casernes, streaking across the slate roof tiles.

Diableteur's cowl again faced Nevara.

"Bubo!" shouted Nevara. Her ghost owl guardian swooped from his perch on the peak of the tower of Saint Martin, screeching, his wide wings catching a glide. The Diableteur didn't see him coming. Bubo struck the *Diableteur,* raking talons snatching at the cowl.

The *Diableteur*'s hands reached up, but too late.

The cowl fell back.

Diableteur's hollow eyes stared at Nevara. *"You wish to see me, witch?"*

Nevara tembled. She thought her attack would distract the creature, but instead it was she who remained frozen in terror. How could any man survive such injuries? It was clear this was no man but a creature of the underworld itself.

A molten ripple of flesh clung to its hairless skull. The eyes were sunken, and it had no nose, only two gaping holes. The skin had healed over the boney shape, but the flesh beneath had never reformed, melted away by the blast of heat that sculpted this creature of hell.

"Well? Are you satisfied?" It yelled now, the voice a raspy hiss that echoed from the walls that rose around them. *"It will be the last thing you see, before you die."*

The hollow eyes stared and she found she couldn't move. Even in her darkest nightmares she hadn't expected this. This could be no living human. There was nothing left of a man about that head, just bone and skin fragments molded into a terrible new shape by fire.

Nevara pointed at him. "Kill that devil!" she commanded.

The Baug archers notched arrows, one after the other, and they flew true and straight, but Diableteur's forty-four deathwalkers did not return fire. Diableteur spun like a dervish, cloak flying in the wind. Eline let fly again, and Atta and Hatta threw knives. The Diableteur did not duck or step back or dodge.

And he remained untouched.

Even Nevara did not command this sort of magic.

His words were as chilling as the north wind that swept over the embrasures of the hilltop castle: "*Kill them all!*"

Crossbows lifted. They fired one volley, forty-four quarrels, then swords left their black scabbards. The forty-four deathriders howled with one voice and surged past their master. The first drops of rain fell as the forty-four charged.

The acrobats of the Baug leaped and vaulted, diving behind a wagon as the bolts hissed around them. Then they returned and formed a new line with arrows drawn.

Eline's bow hummed, six arrows in the air before the first struck.

Nevara chanted a charm on the arrows and they flew true, straight at the Diableteur and his deathwalkers. Some of the deathwalkers fell, but Diableteur weaved and spun around, his cloak flowing around him majestically. Every arrow missed him. He held one aloft in his hand. He snapped it.

Dark magic! Could her own elemental magic stand against such darkness? The white against the black?

The rain came hard now, icy cold and slicing in from the north.

Eline fired again, this time aiming at the deathwalkers. Arrows flew from a dozen Baug bows. Some glanced off hidden mail, but other barbs dug deep into thigh, calf and neck muscle. Men fell, but the rest charged faster. Yet always, through the flurry of arrows, Diableteur marched on, spinning and whirling with blinding speed, untouched by arrows and knives alike.

Atta and Hatta threw knives in handfuls. The blades plunged to the hilt into eye sockets as men screamed and fell in pools of their own blood. Black walkers fell, but most continued the march.

On the ground lay seven men, some dead, some bleeding and screaming for mercy. Only one of the Baug was wounded, a wicked crossbow bolt through his forearm, but young Saurimond, Magba's son of seventeen summers, ignored the pain and managed to draw his bow. Soon other soldiers would arrive, even with the city walls depleted by the tourney. A handful of skilled young boys and Nevara's magic against the black arts of the Diableteur and an entire army!

"Now!" Nevara shouted.

Magba's sons fell back into the great pavilion, followed by Atta and Hatta, and lastly Eline. Nevara stood at the doorway, arms raised, her face as stormy as the sky.

"Enter if you dare!"

The charge of Diableteur's men faltered. They had thrown their empty crossbows aside, but now dozens of men in black stood with raised swords, just a few strides away.

Nevara prayed to the Goddess that Ramon's plan would work. She had faith, but Diableteur was no fool. She ducked into the pavilion and ran to the great fire. Her hand plunged into the bag at her shoulder and pulled out the secret herbs. It had taken her months to distill her precious formula, the *Seeing Smoke,* months of mixing mushroom essences with dried herbs, poison yew, and the secretions of the horned toads found in the Phantom Wood.

She cast the mix on the tall fire in the center of the pavilion. Magba's sons and the remaining Baug formed a small circle around the fire, backs to the fire. Atta and Hatta passed the flask and each drank—the pure essence of distilled horse milk fermented to a fine wine and laced with the extract of Muscimole. At any other time, such a blend would induce a deep, dreamless sleep, but with the zest of battle on them, and the Seeing Smoke churning around them in clouds, it would keep them from dying.

Of course, the Diableteur could set fire to the pavilion and be done with the Baug. That had been Nevara's argument with Ramon. "Not Diableteur," he had said. "He will want the trial." But would he?

Nevara waited. Would they fire the tent? Or fire crossbow bolts in at the helpless Baug?

The flap drew back and Diableteur's men entered the smoky pavilion, fanning out along the perimeter, encircling the Baug with swords held ready. A ring of dozens surrounded the seven sons of Magba, Atta, Hatta, Eline and Nevara. Some coughed, especially the Baug who stood closest to the fire, but no one thought much of the sweet smoke, as pleasant an incense in the Basilica. Nevara's own eyes burned and she felt tears on her cheek.

Diableteur seemed to materialize in the smoke. As if from nowhere, he appeared, wrapped in coils of Nevara's own poisons, barely three strides from her.

Nevara stepped back. Diableteur stepped closer.

Then the rapture took his men. One fell, twitching and choking. A second pointed at the smoke hole and shouted. Others looked up. One screamed. Long sinuous coils of smoke wrapped the center pole and climbed up to the smoke hole like a giant snake. The Seeing Smoke brought terrible visions to some, while others saw wonderful sights. Others saw nothing, but collapsed into convulsions. Swords dropped. Abruptly, Diableteur's men seemed to be under attack.

The sweetness of herbs filled the tent. She called her blend the Seeing Smoke because she used it in small quantities to "see" her spirits. Only the liquid extract of Muscimole could counteract its effect. A whiff of the Seeing Smoke opened the mind. A deep breathing brought terrors that might frighten even a creature such as the Diableteur. Many men might die faced with horrible mind-demons that seemed to rend the flesh and speak in vile tongues. Too much smoke induced a strange paralysis, and, if untreated, death.

More of Diableteur's men were down, screaming and thrashing at invisible creatures as if to fend off the Devil himself.

Nevara felt a little giddy at first. She sensed the fear in the Baug pavilion. On the edge of her hidden eye, she glimpsed dark creatures in the smoke, fiends with red eyes and drooling fangs and gaping mouths that could swallow a man whole, looming over them all, gibbering and moaning. But the Muscimole kept her grounded. She yawned. She found herself fighting a sudden urge to sleep.

"You shall all perish!" she shouted and threw a black powder on the fire. Flames roared up, yellow and white, and choking black smoke filled the tent. "You shall be torn apart by demons and dragged to the lowest level of hell itself!" Her voice thundered. Diableteur's men moaned, some screamed and more fell to the ground in shivering heaps.

Only Diableteur stood, seemingly unaffected. He threw back his hood again, revealing the horror within.

Tendrils of the Seeing Smoke coiled around Nevara's head. She felt dizzy as she stared at the creature. Even with the Muscimole, her vision wavered as she stared at the apparition of Death. Walking Death. The grinning skeleton of the reaper. She nearly screamed. Then, she remembered the Seeing Smoke. She concentrated on Diableteur's face. The fangs shrank to human teeth. The skull melted into tortured flesh.

She shivered. What must Diableteur's deathwalkers be seeing, without her antidote?

"The Goddess protects us!" She threw the last of her black powder on the fire. It roared upwards, the flames surging up to lick at the lower poles of the tent. Black, vile smoke, reeking of sulphur, churned from the fire and filled the closed space, until even Nevara could not see.

When Diableteur recovered, he would find the pavilion empty of all but Nevara's demons, and some of his dead men.

Song of Fortune

31

IT RAINED, at first only scattered drops, but soon a gusty wind blew in a rampart of black clouds, and the sky opened. The rain bounced off the muddy ground, forming instant puddles.

Doré the bastard let the rain wash over her pale skin, skin that had not felt the sun or sky in too many days. The rain was cold on her tender skin but she enjoyed the pain as it washed over her scabbing wounds. It helped wash away the memories of violation. They had taunted her, tortured her, played with her, and soon, she had no doubt, they would have raped her. Her rage boiled blood red and she wanted to kill the first French dog she came across. *Ah.* Never had anything felt so good as that rain. It was fortunate the bailey was empty, because she stood still, face turned to the angry sky, ignoring the urgent pleas of Ramon and Osric.

The air was so clean, so perfectly sweet, it intoxicated. She had learned, in the pit, to breath lightly, to filter out the stench and the filthy taste. Her chest heaved as she took ragged draws of the damp, clean air, musty with mud but perfumed with the distant scents of pine and grass and the nearer smells of the kitchens.

Ahhh.

If she died in that moment … to breathe clean air … it was almost enough.

The rain was a bit of bad luck. It meant that when the judicial combat finished, the cityfolk, lords and ladies would hurry back to the shelter of their hovels, homes and castle.

But so far it had been all good fortune; it had been too easy. There had been only two guards, already unconscious and tied up in their cellar. She had wanted to kill them, but Ramon had refused her.

"Who are you?" she shouted back, not caring if the whole garrison came down on them. "Who are you to say who I can kill?" She stabbed the air with one of the captured swords. "Do you know what they did to me?"

But he didn't, and he stood there like a blubbering fool, even when she pressed the point into his ridiculous green tunic. "Kill me then. If that's all you care for!"

Osric had taken her in his arms, hugged her and kissed her on her lips, draining away the leading edge of her fury. But it had been difficult to walk out of that pit without killing at least one of the guards.

With a bit of searching they had found their own weapons—Osric his hammer, and Doré her twin patulas, wickedly sharp short swords that were a gift from her first lover and teacher, the young prince of Castille. They also found their clothes, which was a blessing; Osric didn't fit into a normal man's clothing any more than slight Doré did. It felt good to be clothed again. She wrapped her long travel cloak around slender shoulders and enjoyed the warmth after a month of chills and shivering in the pit.

She had come to love Ramon for his daily visits with warm morsels from the kitchen and his delightful songs, and she was beyond grateful to the troubadour for the rescue, but she doubted Ramon's elaborate plan. Potions and spells? Distractions and traps? And now this yapping dog, threatening to bring down the garrison on them. Why did he have to take that creature everywhere, even into the pit? He kept yipping.

"Keep him quiet, for the love of God and all," said Doré.

Ramon tried soothing words and finally resorted to clamping his hand over Mauri's jaw. Mauri whined and wriggled. The dark clouds and rain helped camouflage their slow approach along the east wall, towards the Tour du Degré, the north tower where they held the Dame. The few soldiers on the wall were facing outward, alert to outside threats, and most were on the south wall, peering at the distant field and shouting jeers or cheers as they watched the joust.

She turned to face Ramon and—he was gone! For a moment, in the dark, against the haze of pouring rain, Ramon had vanished. Then abruptly his smiling face appeared again. He wore some sort of camouflaging cloak with a hood, and when he wrapped his face, he merged with the gray stone next to him.

"I go to the stables to saddle horses," Ramon said. "You rescue the Dame."

Doré leaned over and kissed him. Ramon might be a fool, but he was very brave. She'd be under the torturer's brand again tomorrow, or worse, if not for him. He'd risked all for them. They would likely all be captured again, but he had given them a chance.

"The Dame can ride?" Ramon asked.

"She can ride with the best of us."

Ramon nodded. "Remember my plan."

Doré shook her head. "What plan? We're to ride to the postern gate. You say it will be open. Then on to the west gate we're to join your friends. That's a plan?" She stared hard at Ramon. "How does the gate magically open?"

"I'll open it."

"You. You'll open it?" She laughed.

"I'll open it."

"Even assuming you can, how do you escape?"

Ramon winked. "Magic."

She grabbed his arm. "What about pursuit?"

He tossed a leather pouch in the air and winked again. "The horses will be asleep."

Without another word he crossed the bailey unchallenged, his concealing cloak tossed back. When a guard on the wall noticed him, Ramon waved at him. The guard waved back.

Doré watched the enigmatic man. Quietly he said, "Osric—are you strong?"

"For the Dame I am the strongest."

Doré smiled. How she loved big, brave Osric, always ready, always dependable, a bull of a man, her lover and mate for life.

They passed the kitchens on the way to the north tower. Delightful aromas assailed them, tempting them to kick in the door and raid the pots. Osric's empty stomach growled and for a moment—just a moment—they stood, inhaling and forgetting their mission. Just one hot meal. Even if it meant they were caught. Loud voices from inside the kitchens startled them out of their stupor.

"It's unfair, Piers! Why should we miss the joust?"

"Shut yer big mouth, stinkpot. That's the fifth bloody time you've complained."

"Don't you think it's unfair?"

"Of course! But your damnable whining won't change anything!"

Doré crept around the perimeter of the bailey and slipped unseen up behind the single guard on the tower door. With Ramon gone, she didn't hesitate, slipping the short sword from its scabbard. She leapt from the shadows, flying waist high in the air, the blade plunging down and into the man's neck. He was dead before he could scream and the limp body landed in a puddle of rainwater. For all her days in the pit, she hadn't lost her famous ability to leap high and strike.

"Should we leave him?" Osric asked. He spat on the corpse.

Doré shrugged. "We must be fast. We'll be discovered soon 'nough. Leave him!"

Ramon had told them the Dame was in the highest room in the tower. Doré and Osric leapt up the stairs, taking two at a time. The guard at the top of the stairs saw them coming, but Doré yanked a knife from her belt with her left hand and threw it. It tumbled once, flew true, and buried itself in the man's throat. He twitched and groaned for a moment, but he couldn't manage a dying scream. Doré felt icecold satisfaction, not because of the kill, which was strangely unsatisfying, but because she had not lost her ambidextrous skills. Broken fingers made her right hand unusable.

They pushed open the door and entered, bloody and reeking. The Dame stood at one of the arrow slits, looking down. She turned and frowned at them.

"Osric and Doré. Always killing." She sighed.

"We're here to rescue you," Doré said.

The Dame crossed the floor gracefully, her dress sweeping the stone floor. "Dearest Doré, I'm reconciled to my death. I need no rescuing."

"Ma Dame, we have no time. If we don't go now, we'll all perish."

"Well, dear ones. I must reject your help. You still have time for escape."

Osric bounded to her side in two strides and knelt to her. "Ma Dame. I must beg you." He kissed the hem of her dress. "We are not alone. Others will die. Seigneur has jousted on your behalf to distract the court—"

"I have seen. Terrible. Terrible."

Doré ran to the arrow slit and glanced out the arrow slit. The crowd to the south of the city vast. The two knights hacked at each other with swords, and the crowd cheered in spite of the storm.

"Ramon the troubadour has rescued us, so that we may help you. No one will leave without you, ma Dame."

The Dame Esclarmonde de Foix lost her normal composure. Her smile faded. She bowed her head as if in prayer. "Well, friends, we must go then. But I ask you—especially you big Osric, for I know your rashness—not to kill on my behalf. I could not bear it."

"I have killed, ma Dame, but only in need. But I kill, if I must, for the cause, not for the Dame."

"God will forgive you, my son." She placed her hand briefly on his head.

"We must go, ma Dame. Anything you need? Please be fast."

"Just my cloak."

She paused at the door, looking down at the guard with his gashed throat, and the tears came. She knelt, ignoring Doré's pleas, and said a blessing. When she stood, her eyes were full of fury. "You did this in my name," she said. "I cannot forgive this."

"Do not forgive us, ma Dame. Just come with us!"

The bailey was still quiet. The downpour had sent most of the wall sentries to their towers for shelter. The rest had sought shelter in the great hall.

The sky was dark and heavy with clouds, black and angry over the city. Lightning strafed the sky and thunder rumbled, roared and clapped. Anyone sensible was indoors, especially if they wore armor, and no armed man could be on the open ramparts.

The Dame glared at Osric when she saw the second guard lying in a puddle of water, his face in mud colored black by his blood. She knelt in the mud, cupping his head in her hands and spoke a blessing.

"Ma Dame, no time!"

She frowned at him, standing with great dignity. "I'll not have more of this on my behalf."

"No promises—"

She put her hands on her hips. "I mean this, Osric. You too, Doré." Her white hair clung to her face, plastered back by the rain, and Doré saw her nipples pressing through her dress. She looked away, embarrassed. "As you say, ma Dame, but—"

A roar of drunken voices interrupted her. Realizing the laughter came from the great room, Doré scanned the bailey then moved along the stone walls, staying in the deep shadows. It wouldn't be empty for long. The change of shift could happen at any moment, a troop of satiated sergeants would burst from the big double doors and spy them. The only traffic in the courtyard were the stewards, kept busy running back and forth with casks of beer from the undercroft to the great hall. The odd trio—giant, dandy and lady—managed to reach the stable without the alarm being raised.

Ramon greeted them with a grin. A string of horses stood wtih him. One of the stable mates lay unconscious in the straw.

"I gave him an early night's sleep," Ramon explained.

The Dame smiled at Ramon, and he bowed awkwardly. "My precious troubadour."

He blushed. As instructed, he had saddled several sturdy horses. A smaller horse was clearly for the Dame and a big charger for Osric. The rest were Spanish barbs, known for their endurance and speed.

"Well, mount up," Ramon said, suddenly in charge. "With any luck, the Baug has made the west gate."

They watched with admiration as the Dame swung up into a man's saddle without effort.

32

BROTHER JAIE wasn't sure where it all went wrong. At first, he felt glorified by the high calling of the Inquisition, honored that Brother Duranti would invite him to clerk, in awe of the archbishop and trembling when he met Cardinal Fiesco. He had achieved something, he did the work of God, he sat in the shadow of great men, and he helped heretics find themselves. So why did he feel so empty?

The doubts began at the very first trial he clerked. The feeling of wonderment left him the first time the seculars were invited to extract confession. He endured it because he did see dozens renounce their heresies and rejoin the Church. Wasn't that worth a little pain? But no matter how many prayers he said, his life began to feel empty. He thought he saw lust in the archbishop's eyes. He almost certainly saw cruelty.

He made his way from the Tour de Justice, along the inner wall that connected the city wall to the castle, his cowl drawn up on his bald pate against the pouring rain. He looked down off the high wall. From here the steep hills rose up to meet the seneschal's newly fortified outer curtain.

He leaned out between the merlons, further and further, slick with the hard rain. Lightning flashed, illuminating the dark tapestry of the Phantom Wood, all the more frightening in this sudden spring storm. The green forest swept up and over hills to the west, untamed, haunted by the ghosts of the thousands who died in the crusade, it was said. He shivered. Oddly there were no guards on the wall. Just lean a little further. A little more.

His fingers gripped the slick stone. No one could see him. It would be deemed an accident. An accident, not suicide. Not a mortal sin. No one would care about the clerk of the Inquisition, a young monk from nowhere with no name that no one on earth cared about. Not even God.

Tonight he had witnessed the torture of the wishboat maker. The poor fellow seemed oblivious that his trade superstitious and a sin. He blubbered his confession the moment he smelled his own flesh burn. The stench was still in Jaie's nostrils. He turned his head up, allowing the heavy rain to sluice across his face, washing away the vileness. At least the wishboat maker, Ren was his name, had confessed. He would not burn. Three years in the pit would cleanse him.

Jaie shivered. How could this be God's will?

His world collapsed the day master torturer Frances peeled back Doré the Costonot's clothing to reveal that she was a woman.

Nothing was as it seemed! Nothing! He could no longer sleep. He rarely ate. His brethren noticed his wild mood shifts, and even the archbishop commented on it. Duranti threatened to remove him, and he would have been grateful for it. The self-flagellation in his cell only helped him understand the pain of the heretics under the torturer's art. It did not move him to purity, or to ecstacy. It brought only pain.

End it.

He served a church that would tolerate only one doctrine, that preached love and practised the Devil's ways. How could he not have seen it?

End it.

He nearly slid from the sloped scarp. Instinctively, his hands flailed for the wet stone. He was not just a hypocrite, he was a coward. He could not even end it.

He crawled back to the wall, soaked through, trembling, horrified at his own weakness, angry at everyone. Everyone. Even the archbishop. Even God.

He looked both ways along the curtain. No guards. Where were all the guards. Of course they were in the Pinte et Posterne tower and the Tour de Justice, sheltering from the storm. He was alone on the walls.

No. Not alone. The troubadour strode across the Cour du Midi in the chateau. He blinked rain from his eyes. The troubadour was unmistakable with his colorful vest and green hat, and that little rat-dog running at his heels. Jaie shrugged. He had, like everyone else, taken a liking to the troubadour. The day Ramon had confronted him with his raw jokes in the marketplace, Jaie had felt a change in his life, his despair suddenly running deeper. He didn't blame the troubadour.

Jaie blinked again. The troubadour had vanished before his eyes! One minute he was there, the next he was gone in a wink. Magic! Jaie found himself drawn back to the castle battlements, where they connected with the outer city wall. He peered down into the courtyard, holding his cowl with one hand to shield the rain. Others were gathered below, but not the troubadour.

Who—? The Dame! Unmistakable in her silver gown. And the rebels, Doré the Costonot and Osric the Hammer. Jaie felt a blush of heat. Doré the woman! Why had her sex changed him so? He ran along the wall, heedless of the puddles and the slick stone.

The troubadour was back now, he saw his face against the stone.

Then this was—an escape!

Jaie ran for the postern gate.

33

SEIGNEUR DE CASTLENAU was grateful for the rain. It washed the sweat and the blood from a dozen cuts, stinging him awake. The judicial had called a remount.

Boone was tireless, as always, but Seigneur felt the exhaustion heavy on his old muscles. How long could his arms hold Loial, his former master's sword, in numb fingers long past cramping and wet with rain? Albaric must have been feeling it as well, carrying the weight of his heavy armor, but after six breaks to change horses, he seemed as fresh as ever. Boone, in those short rest periods, recovered, snorting and pawing the muddy earth, glaring at yet another fresh Andalusian stallion. Boone against six! Seigneur was so proud of his beloved princely horse.

Light mail or not, Seigneur was done. He could barely lift his sword arm. He had given the renegades as much time as he could, and he could only pray to a God who no longer answered that the Dame had been rescued. The audience, in spite of the rain, stayed with the tourney.

This was his moment. Today, he must die in front of friends and enemies alike. So far, it had been a battle Ramon could weave into a great epic song—if the heretic troubadour survived the night. But Seigneur must not die by exhaustion, fading away like an old man falling into a sleep from which he never woke. He must die with Loial in his hand and Boone between his legs, fighting.

His strength came from the small piece of torn cloth tied to his helmet. The shred from the Dame's dress fluttered as he rode, reminding him of Her. The Holy Dame. His Precious Lady.

Perce, loyal Perceval de Mendes, waited at the end of the field with a flask of wine, and water for Boone. Boone trotted up, legs lifting high in the deep muck.

"Call a draw!" Perce said for the tenth time. "Before God, call a draw!"

Seigneur turned his face up to catch the rain, allowing it to run into the empty socket of his missing eye. The water pooled there, cool and stinging.

"No, good Perce. I'm enjoying this."

The Templar Arnot handed him the wine flask while Perce gave Boone water. "By the Holy Mother, I've never seen such a battle!" Arnot said, his voice both excited and sad. "I would have fallen an hour ago!"

Seigneur drank deep of the wine, allowing it to run out of his mouth and down his cheeks.

"A fresh sword, Seigneur?"

Seigneur handed him back the flask. He balanced Loial across the pommel of his saddle. Dozens of dings and dents marred the edge. Sir Albaric would have a fresh sword on each new horsing, but Seigneur had stubbornly refused. "There's magic in this old blade."

"I believe so," said Arnot, grinning up at him. "At least my old shield has not cracked."

Seigneur nodded. "A good shield, brother."

"Blessed by the Marshall himself."

The shield had taken a hundred blows, dimpling and creasing, but it had never cracked or shattered in spite of its light weight.

"Now, in the hour of my death, will you tell me true?" Seigneur's eye glared at Arnot. "When did you leave the order?"

Arnot seemed speechless.

"I've known since the beginning." It delighted Seigneur to play these games. "The Master Marshall and I meet from time to time. I spoke with him only three months ago, and I asked about you." Seigneur should have been catching his breath, but this was too much fun, the look on Arnot's face, and it might be their last conversation. "So I'm guessing you came with our friend the troubadour, but that part is a great mystery."

Now Arnot smiled. "You kept my secret."

"Why not? We fought together in Joppa, no?"

"And it was useful to keep the information?"

"Oui. Useful. Besides, who ever heard of a beardless Templar."

"I couldn't grow a beard fast enough for Mayday." Arnot laughed.

"If I know, others must guess." Seigneur found it difficult to speak. Exhaustion took him hard, and he swayed in the saddle.

"Thank you for keeping my secret." Arnot reached up his arm.

Seigneur clenched it down to the elbow. "Why not, friend Arnot? At least I know you are Arnot, unless you lied all those years ago."

Arnot continued holding Seigneur's gauntleted hand. "I grew tired of crusades sooner than you."

"Not too tired for games."

"Never that!"

A horn blew. The rain intensified, but Seigneur remained mounted, afraid he might not have the strength to remount otherwise. "We have a little time before the last horn. Tell me how you came to leave the order. How you met Ramon."

"That's a story for another time."

"There will not be another time, friend Arnot. I am reconciled to this."

"Will you call a draw?" Arnot said, gently.

"Never."

The next horn blew.

"Where do you draw this strength, old man?" Arnot grinned at him.

"All my friends are here. I must put on a good combat, no?"

They laughed. Even Perce smiled a little. Seigneur's eight knights gathered around, their heads bowed in respect.

"I should have perished long ago," said Arnot.

"We all should have."

"So the story is for all of us here," Seigneur said, between long draws of breath. "You gave us your coat of arms in some great fraud. A worthy fraud I hope. Tell the story."

"You want me to stand here in the storm, telling this long tale, while you sway in the saddle?"

Seigneur finally released Arnot's arm, realizing he had been using the ex-Templar as a support. "I am about to die, old friend. Give me the rabbit's version of the tale."

"I owe you that."

"You do. And quickly. Two more horns!"

Arnot nodded, but he glanced about them to make sure none but Seigneur's loyal knights and Perceval were within earshot. "I lost my faith in Joppa."

"We all did, Arnot."

"But in the Templar order you are sworn to God. Faith is not something you fight without. I became a killing machine, volunteering for every suicide mission. I had seen too much death, too much brutality to believe any God could sanction such things.

"I could take it no longer, and one night I quarreled with one of the younger brothers, son of a baron. Fighting among brothers is forbidden, but it didn't stop me. I had seen him too many times on the field of battle, sadistic and too pleased to kill. It's a long story, Seigneur, but just to say, he was a killing bastard and that night I killed him. He would torture no more Muslims.

"For that I would die, lieutenant of the Master notwithstanding. So I left with nothing but my armor, my horses and my sword, little enough, but all property of the Temple, I suppose. The Master Marshall—we were brothers, friends—for the sake of this friendship, did not pursue right away."

Seigneur nodded. "He said as much, Arnot. You were his greatest crushing defeat."

"I'm sorry for that." Arnot closed his eyes and continued his story. "The first galley out went to Venice, and there I stayed. The Doge took me in as a mercenary, and for years I fought and killed for Venetian glory. There were many opportunities to earn gold coin. I fought at the whim of the Doge, and I grew rich. But when you lose your faith, you become bitter. I continued killing, for money rather than God, and it made me nasty. I became a drunkard. Not just an occasional falling-down-drunk session, but night after night, waking up in a brothel with a hangover."

"Nothing wrong with that, brother," Seigneur said, with a rough laugh.

Arnot didn't laugh with him. A horn sounded. "Only one more horn!"

"Say on! I would know this before I die."

"I spent years as a mercenary, but I shaved my beard and dressed opulently, and those were difficult years. The Temple Grand Master himself sent assassins to find me. No, not the Master Marshall, for love and brotherhood I suppose. But Templars came for me, dressed in black, hired assassins for a bag of gold. Between my faithless profession, the drink and the constant fear, I decided to end it."

Seigneur snorted. "Suicide for you? I doubt that, Arnot."

"Not that way. I decided to end it in a haze of alcohol, lust and debauch. Or, like you now, with a sword in my hand. You haven't much time, Seigneur! Let's just say, a certain troubadour came to the golden halls of the Doge. He sang for the Doge one night when I was there at the back of the grand hall, passing out from too much in the cups. Well, I guess you all know the power of Ramon's voice. He brought me out of the gray void, and soon I was laughing along with the rest and listening to this girlish boy, as taken with him as the entire city of Venice. He stayed ten days, developing such a following with the ladies of Venice that the Doge commanded him to stay. And we became friends. I don't know if this Ramon always deliberately seeks out the most in need, but he found me, or I found him. I couldn't get enough of that voice. Would I be exaggerating to say it saved me, that voice? And his stories. My haunted old soul came alive."

Seigneur stared at him. He understood Ramon's power. It had stirred him, too, although it had been the Dame's power that stimulated his own dark self, bringing light and hope.

"But Ramon is more than he looks."

Seigneur laughed at that.

"I followed him on his seventh day in Venice. The golden-haired entertainer became a dark creature at night, and I was intrigued. He crept under the old bridge by the prison and I saw him hand a bag of coin to the Doge's prison-keeper. Three condemned prisoners were in the shadows and Ramon put them in a gondola. He was nearly away with them. I had no boat. I had no choice but to confront him then, or lose him entirely in the night. I jumped out of the shadows, expecting them all to fall down in fright."

"He didn't, did he?" Seigneur smiled. He knew Ramon that well.

"No, he jumped in front of his prisoners with that ridiculous little spear and challenged me then and there. It's a longer story than I have time for, Seigneur. Suffice to say, he gave my life the purpose it lacked since the Templars. Rescuing people. This boy, he goes around rescuing heretics from the Inquisitors by whatever means he can. Bribes in bigger cities. In small towns he sometimes breaks them out of their cells. The three he rescued that night were sentenced to hang as Bogomils."

"Bogomils! We fought alongside the Bogomils in Joppa!"

"Yes. Christians, but heretics, so we are now told. This Ramon, he makes friends wherever he goes. The Bogomils are sworn to help Ramon whenever he needs them, as am I. My hazy world had no purpose, but he seemed to have enough for both of us. There's something infectious about the boy. I couldn't help but take up with him. I had enough money, anyway. I just needed purpose, or it was time for me to leave this world. I've been with him since. We go from village to village rescuing heretics and witches."

"And what drives this Ramon, then? You I understand, old friend."

"For that you'd have to ask Ramon."

"I have."

Arnot laughed. "I'll warrant he gave you a long speech about compassion."

"Something like that." The last horn blew. Seigneur nodded at his friend. He lifted his voice louder so that the Seigneur's eight knights could hear him. "This story stays with us, my friends."

The knights nodded. They, like Perce, had served most of their lives with Seigneur.

"And you are free from my service," Seigneur said. He hadn't fully recovered, but his breath was fully returned. He could, at least, fight to the death without fear of embarrassment.

Arnot placed a hand on Seigneur's wounded thigh. "Farewell, my brother."

Seigneur turned Boone toward the field, then halted his mount and leaned down to tussle Perce's red hair. "You'll be Sir Perceval tomorrow. Make me proud." Seigneur was already proud. He had taken this scrawny runt, a bawling boy, from the dead arms of his mother! He had slugged the boy and told him he was a man, demanded he stop his crying, and then he had taken him in for love of his father. Now, as he realized he would never see Perce's grinning, freckled face again, he realized how deeply he loved him.

Had the Dame changed him so much? It seemed so. From her he had learned true fearlessness, the one trait he admired above all others. A man could die happy if he had courage. In fear was only misery and disgrace.

Today he would die happy.

He kissed the white cloth that hung from his cheek plate. Her scent was on it. She probably didn't even know he had torn it from her gown, and it had become his charm this day. It had protected him so far.

Seigneur bent forward and stroked Boone's slick black neck. He hoped Boone survived the battle. He knew Perce would take him in and care for him. How strange that Seigneur, known for his lack of emotion, should find so many loves at the end of his miserable life: the Dame, who could love him, but not physically; Perce, who loved him unconditionally; Arnot, an old comrade in arms; his eight loyal knights who had never left him from crusade to crusade; Boone, his beloved horse. And watching him now were so many old comrades, from King John of Aragon to old Baron le Guy. He had more supporters than he ever knew.

Boone snorted, glaring at Albaric on his new horse. Albaric looked as fresh as when they commenced the combat. Seigneur was done.

He took the field. A roar rose from the crowd. They loved him too. How could that be? Their cheers gave him new life. Boone felt it too, his legs lifting high. The roaring continued, unstoppable now, even as the lightning flashed and the rain pelted.

Albaric, splendid in his red and gold, bore a fresh sword and shield. He tossed his head, a gesture of pride and triumph. He repeated the gesture, then again. This was not pride. The man's helmet, a full helm, had only slits for his eyes. It was a handicap! The rain ran down the eye slits, distracting him, maybe even blurring his vision.

Seigneur smiled. His own helmet, an open chapeaux de fer, flanged outwards, channelled the hard rain away from his face. At least he had one small advantage.

Song of
Strength

34

RAMON WRAPPED HIMSELF in Nevara's cloak of concealment. It worked wondrously well in the gloom of the storm. Dark clouds boiled overhead, completely hiding a sun which must be low in the sky by now, and thunder rumbled. Occasional flashes of lightning illuminated him on the wall, but he was gray cloak against gray stone and hardly visible.

He made his way to the Postern Tower, the highest in the castle, alone and hopeful he would not see any sentries until he reached the postern gate. He carried only his spear. He had left even Mauri behind with the Grand Duo.

The new mud from the sudden spring storm stirred up the old smells of moat sewage, raw in his nostrils. Nevara's Storm. Thinking of her brought a stab of anxiety. Had she used the Seeing Smoke? Was she even alive?

His companions, Doré and Osric, were too weakened from their tortures to creep the wall and incapacitate the guards. One fool against how many guards? With Seigneur's diversion, the rescue of the Dame had been easy—at least so far. The Dame sat on a horse with the others, in the stable, Mauri squirming in her lap, waiting for Ramon's plan to unfold. They would wait until he gave the signal, then charge the postern gate, ride out into the narrow strip between the two walls and, hopefully, into the waiting wagons of the Baug Balar at the west gate—if all went well with Nevara's snare. Even with diversions and Ramon's traps and tricks, they would need much luck and magic to succeed.

The postern gate could only be opened by a hidden latch in the Tour Pinte et Poterne, the Tower of the Small Postern. If he succeeded in opening the gate, they had every chance of success, with most of the garrison outside the walls, though it was doubtful Ramon himself would escape. A small sacrifice for the Dame.

Ramon did have Ena's miraculous elastic rope, Nevara's magic powders and concealing cloak, and the Baug's old flying tricks, but could he create enough spectacle to allow the Dame her escape? He was a passable acrobat, but he didn't have the skills of Ena's troop.

A flash of lightning illuminated the tower, blinding him for a moment. He could open the gate only from the upper level of the tower.

The door was ajar. He skulked along the outer curtain, pressed against the crenellations. He had almost reached the door when it flung open and a guard stepped out. He flattened himself against the stone.

It was Norvice, one of the older guards, but he was not on patrol. He turned inwards, facing into the long Cour du Midi, and unhitched his breeches. He arced a long stream of urine into the gardens below.

"Don't be pissing on anyone below, Norvie," shouted a voice from within.

Ramon took this moment as his own. While Norvice was distracted, he slipped to the door, his little spear held tight in both hands. He peered inside, uncomfortably aware of Norvice only strides away.

Only Norvice's partner was in the tiny square room. Ramon didn't hesitate. He made a long-legged leap through the doorway, and struck the guard on the back of his head with the shaft of his spear. The man grunted and fell against the table in a clatter of cups.

"Wait for me, Pierre!" shouted Norvice. Ramon slipped behind the door and waited. Norvice stepped back inside, still tying his breeches. "The sergeant'll have you in the stocks for drinking," the old guard said, nudging his friend. Ramon caught him lightly behind the ear, and Norvice fell on top of his fellow guard.

Ramon went quickly up to the hidden latch. He pulled hard on the stone lever and felt it give. The gate was open.

He stepped out onto the inner wall and simulated the whistle of a night bird.

"What are you doing here, jester?"

He spun on his heels at the sudden voice in the dark and dropped into a martial crouch, his spear held ready.

The clerk of the Inquisition! Brother Jaie.

He stared at the monk, for a moment so startled he couldn't think.

"Brother, what brings you to the wall?"

Jaie's youthful face scowled, clearly suspicious. "I came across the curtain from the Tour de Justice. I saw you and your friends skulking about. And the Dame."

Ramon didn't ask the obvious question. It was clear Jaie hadn't raised the alarm. He stared at him hard, not bothering to play the jester or the troubadour. Jaie had seen his crime. For a long time they stared at each other. The clop of horses below made them look down at the same moment. Doré led the Dame's horse, followed by Osric.

Ramon must act quickly. He must hope that Jaie, facing him as he was, would not cry out and alert the chateau as Ramon's spear haft knocked him to oblivion.

Before either could speak, a flutter of wings made them cry out in surprise. Ramon cursed Nevara's bird as it landed on the rampart between them. The monk stared with wide eyes at the white bird.

Bubo flapped his wings warningly then settled. On Bubo's leg was a note. "Good boy, Bubo."

Bubo huffed a little "wuh-wuh-wuh" sound.

"Hold steady, Bubo," Ramon said, forgetting the monk for a moment. As he untied the note, Bubo's beak swept down and tore at Ramon's skin then he flew off and disappeared into the stormy black sky.

Ramon rolled open the note, desperately hoping at least that part of his insane plan had worked out. Nevara's runic script was urgent and curt.

My magic working.
Diableteur pursuing us.
Meet us West Postern.
N.

He shivered at the thought of the Diableteur and his forty-four hard after the Nevara and Magba's sons. Death hunting the children.

"I can help," the monk said.

Ramon stared at him. He had half-forgotten the young Inquisitor. He couldn't have heard correctly.

"I promise you, before God, this is no ruse."

Ramon spun his spear in an elegant twirl. "Why would you help us then, brother?"

"Perhaps I was snared by the magic of your songs." Jaie's scowl had faded and he looked so earnest that it could only be an act. "Perhaps because I can't stomach the Inquisition. Perhaps because I care. Perhaps because I have nothing to live for."

"Perhaps. Or perhaps, you hope a clever delay will save you?" He crumpled Nevara's note. "I have no time for this."

Yet the monk could be useful.

He had opened the gate. Now he must draw off the wall sentries.

In that moment, the horns of hell sounded.

Guards emerged from the Orientale Towers, the twin towers over the main gate. They spread out along the wall in both directions. More guards emerged from the Casernes Tower. Then the Tour du Major. Soon the would spot the Dame and the Grand Duo.

Ramon threw back his camouflaged cloak.

He thrust his spear so the tip touched the monk's chin. "Yell. Scream for help."

"What? I want to help."

Ramon flicked his wrist. A prickle of blood appeared under the young man's cleft chin. "Scream!"

The monk screamed like a pig at slaughter.

The soldiers hesitated, turned then pointed at Ramon. From two directions, the guards ran along the curtain with crossbows and spears. Two more guards appeared at the Tour de Saint Paul.

Ramon prodded the monk. "Run. Up the stairs in the Postern Tower!" The monk wasn't part of the plan, but soldiers were more likely to chase if they thought a hostage was involved.

The monk scrambled into the tower. He shouted in alarm when he saw the unconscious soldiers within. "Up the stairs!" Ramon shouted. He poked the monk harder with the sharp blade of Zaleucus.

"I'm your friend!" the monk screamed.

"Then run!" Jaie scrambled up the narrow stairs, pressing his hands against the wet stone for balance. The stairs were barely the width of a man, with no rail, a design meant to slow attackers. This was the tallest of the castle keeps, its open roof surrounded by merlons. It was Ramon's only hope. He paused to snatch a loaded crossbow from the rack and chased after the terrified Inquisitor.

The horn blew again. Angry shouts came from behind him. He clung to Nevara's bag, slung the crossbow, snatched a torch from the wall, and ran up the treacherous stairs, wet from the rain that poured in through the defense slits.

Alarms continued to sound. He peered out an arrow slit. Soldiers milled on the wall below the tower. At least he had drawn them all to the curtain. At any moment they would see the Dame and her guardians.

"Keep running," Ramon shouted, pointing the loaded crossbow at Jaie. The monk's hands went up defensively. He turned, slipped, nearly fell, clutching at slick stone, then scurried on up the stairs.

Ramon turned and carefully balanced the crossbow on the ledge. He aimed carefully, not wishing to kill. Crossbows were easier to aim than the short bows of the Baug, but from so high up, with the storm raging and the darkness and wind, it would be easy to miss entirely or to kill a soldier.

He squeezed.

The bolt shot right through a soldier's calf. The man screamed and pointed up at Ramon.

The soldiers were on the stone steps now. Ramon threw down the useless crossbow. Should he throw the monk off the stairs? He was clumsy and slow and would likely betray Ramon. But no, it was not in him to kill a monk for no reason, and it would be useful to have a hostage and a further diversion. The soldiers might dally with him longer if they thought they were on a rescue mission. His sweaty fingers fumbled for Nevara's powders. He opened the smaller sack and emptied the powders as he ran. The stench of sulphur made him gag.

He paused. Dozens of torches appeared below. Almost certainly the entire wall battalion was after him, as he had hoped.

There was no way off the tower. Ramon was trapped, and the soldiers knew it. Ramon's diversion would leave only a couple of gate guards for Osric and Doré to deal with.

The soldiers were gaining on him. Ramon pressed against the wall, running with rain. The wind howled through the stairway like the screaming of the damned. He hoped the wind would fan the flames.

He waited. They were just below him now, angry faces turned up, illuminated by their torches.

"Halt! Halt in the name of the seneschal!"

The last soldier passed the powder.

Ramon tossed his torch. It tumbled in a clumsy arc, bounced off the stone wall and landed on the step where he had poured the powder.

Nothing happened.

The last soldier turned back.

"Have a care!" Ramon shouted

Ramon shielded his eyes as Nevara's powder exploded in searing flames and churning smoke.

The soldier screamed then he fell, arms flailing, eyes staring up at Ramon as he plunged to his certain death.

Ramon ran on up the stairs. The way behind was closed by flame, and the soldiers were trapped with him. He had lured them to the highest tower, hopefully long enough to let the Dame escape. The gate stood open. The soldiers pursued him. But there was no escape for him and his hostage.

35

ARCHBISHOP AMIEL WAS BORED. How many hours could these two knights dent each other's helms? The crowd was not tired of the spectacle, nor King John nor the viscount—and certainly not his delightfully exuberant daughter Adelais—but Amiel just wanted the warmth of his palace, the comfort of his page boy and a cup of mulled wine.

Even after the storm raced in, chased by a north wind, the crowd didn't disperse. Lightning terrified Amiel, and he cowered under one of the berfrois' support beams, glaring surreptitiously at the cardinal vice-chancellor. Fiesco had not lost interest either, watching intently as the two knights circled each other. Amiel had to admit the swordplay had been the best he had ever witnessed, but they were too evenly matched, too tireless.

"Eminence, perhaps we should retire to the palace?"

"But this is just so interesting," Fiesco replied, holding his hat on his head against the wind. "What is it?" he asked Archdeacon Verdun, Amiel's own clerk, who had appeared abruptly before them. Verdun leaned close, speaking in rapid whispers directly to the cardinal. Then Verdun knelt.

Amiel assumed the news was dire. His own clerk would always come to him first. "What is it, Eminence?"

Fiesco paled, suddenly slouched in his chair. Terrible news. Had Emperor Frederick besieged the Vatican again? Fiesco said nothing, staring at the field. He trembled.

"Eminence, what news?"

Tears ran down the cheeks of the pope's vice-chancellor. He bowed his head and said a silent prayer.

"Is it His Holiness?" Amiel asked and whacked Verdun's shoulder. "Tell me!"

Fiesco's lips trembled. "His Holiness, our father Gregory, has fallen into the sleep without waking." He crossed himself and closed his eyes, his lips moving in prayer.

The Pope comatose. But it was too soon! Too soon for Amiel to campaign for the office. He didn't have the relics, only the Dame, and possession was yet not certain.

Amiel knelt beside Verdun. "I pray for our Holy Father Gregory," he said.

King John of Aragon and the viscount fell to their knees beside the archbishop.

Fiesco heedless of the combat on the field, clutched a rosary in his trembling hand. "We must say a Mass for His Holiness."

"Yes," Amiel said. "A Mass." He kept his head down. Fiesco would rule the church as long as Pope Gregory remained comatose. If the pope died, he would call a convocation and eventually a new pope would be elected—by all accounts almost certainly Fiesco himself. But until the new pope took office—or Pope Gregory recovered—Fiesco ruled the Church.

What appalling news! A change of leadership always brought sweeping changes, uncertainty, political unrest, rebellion. There would be campaigning in Rome, the cardinals would assemble and the in-fighting would begin. There was, perhaps, still time. Perhaps this would draw Fiesco back to Rome where he belonged, leaving Amiel with a free hand to deal with the Dame and to collect the Holy Relics that would ensure he became a living saint.

The king and the viscount rose to their feet, looking as pale and shocked as Fiesco. Amiel wondered how he looked. Suitably shocked? Horrified? He hoped so.

"I must return to Rome!" Fiesco said, eyes still wet.

"Of course, Eminence," Amiel said. "I'll arrange everything."

Fiesco remained standing. "We must go."

Amiel nodded. Of course, it was the right thing to do. But Seigneur. The Dame. So much depended on this joust.

"Can I offer you an escort, Eminence?" asked King John of Aragon.

The cardinal stared at the king. No doubt King John worried for his unstable crown. Aragon's borders moved with the wind, and heresy swept his lands like the plague. A new pope might be bad for Aragon, might even call a crusade against King John as Pope Gregory had for the Occitan. King Louis of France, the viscount's overlord, would worry about weakness in Rome, and later he might become concerned about too strong a pope being elected. Amiel would have to bide his time for the next election, and hope he could capture the relics. Had he suitably ingratiated himself to Fiesco? He thought back on the last few days with Fiesco staying in his palace. Did Fiesco know about his little vices? If he rescued the relics, would the likely future pope reward him suitably? As his new vice-chancellor, for instance?

Fiesco as leader of the Church! It could take months or years before an election was called, but until then, Fiesco was the de facto ruler in Rome, and with all the uncertainties in Europe and the Holy Land, there could be territorial disputes, a stalled Inquisition, new wars or crusades. His Holiness Gregory had been in a pitched battle for his entire papacy with the emperor Frederick II, now under excommunication. Would Frederick move on the Church? Already his armies surrounded the Vatican. There could be no worse time for this.

"Eminence, His Holiness will be a saint," said Amiel. It was a shallow statement, but he was too flustered to think of much else to say. Gregory had, on the whole, been a great pope, systematizing the Inquisition and the rules that defined heresy, canonizing Saints Dominic and Francis of Assisi, and he stood against Emperor Frederick for breaking his vow to commence a new crusade to the Holy Land. A great pope. A saint. This little man beside him, this Fiesco, how could he measure up to Gregory? He was nothing.

"You assume the worst," Fiesco said.

"I pray for the best," Amiel said properly, but he sighed. Now the relics in Montségur, and the Dame herself, were vital. Vital! They could create a pope who could make a difference. They could inspire a new crusade. They could solidify the infant monastic Inquisition. All that was required to make it happen was for this damnable Seigneur to fall from his horse.

He felt a moment of hope as Seigneur swayed in his saddle. A fall would constitute a clear win. Then Seigneur leaned forward across the lathered neck of his black horse, regaining his balance, and he brought his sword up in a clumsy block. The horse stepped sideways. Damn that horse. He was the devil's own mount, that beast, with dancing feet and moves that Amiel had never seen. How could a horse move sideways like that?

Seigneur counter-attacked as his horse wheeled hard against the flanks of the bigger Andalusian. Instead of a swing or a feint, Seigneur's sword stabbed tight and true.

Amiel shuddered. The sword plunged deep under Albaric's armpit as the knight raised his sword for a killing blow. Seigneur's blade thrust in, then out, and in the moment before the rain washed it away, bright red appeared.

"A killing blow!" shouted King John, the Pope's coma forgotten. He rose to his feet, and with him the viscount.

Adelais jumped onto her chair and shouted, "Seigneur! Seigneur! Seigneur!" Many of the spectators took up the chant. Soon everyone was chanting, "*Seigneur! Seigneur!*"

"God's mercy," said Amiel, standing with the rest. It couldn't be! It couldn't! But Albaric slumped forward on his horse. The panicked stallion suddenly cantered. The knight bounced from his saddle and landed in a sad, metal heap in the deep mud, face down.

The pope and Sir Albaric lost to them in one terrible stormy day! The Devil was in the world this day!

Seigneur vaulted from his horse, sword in hand, for the killing blow.

But the damnable Seigneur didn't whack off his head or plunge in his sword for the kill. Instead, he rolled his rival over and opened his visor.

Albaric was indeed alive. Seigneur pressed his sword tip to the space between helm and plate. The crowd hushed as Seigneur's voice rose. "Yield your claim."

"Never!" Albaric shoved away the sword with his gauntlet. "Kill me if you like. I do not yield!"

Seigneur shrugged, sheathed his sword, and turned to face the viscount. "My lord viscount? Your judgment?"

Viscount Hugh d'Arcis played with his mustache and smiled. "I find in favor of Seigneur de Castlenau."

"Never!" shouted Albaric again. Blood ran down his arm, washing across his plates.

"I have made my decision. See to your wounds."

Seigneur bowed. "Then I take the Dame."

"We shall talk later, Seigneur," said the viscount, with a light wave of his hand.

Seigneur turned to leave the field, his boots ankle deep in the mud.

Albaric struggled to his feet and lifted his sword.

"Seigneur!" shouted King John of Aragon.

Albaric's sword swung around, carried two-handed, and struck off Seigneur's helmet with its fluttering white cloth.

At the same moment the alarm horns sounded from the chateau.

The viscount turned, shielding his eyes from the rain.

"To the city!" he shouted. His knights and soldiers broke for their horses.

The horns blared again. Everything became chaotic as the viscount ran for his horse.

At the edge of the field, Seigneur and his knights were mounting with that traitorous Templar. They headed west, parallel to the city, while everyone else headed for the main gate. Adelais had disappeared. She didn't follow her father. Amiel scanned the crowd for her and saw the little boy-like sprout jumping down off the berfois. She vaulted on to her horse.

And rode west!

Amiel shouted for his captain of the guard.

"Your Grace?"

"Assemble the men. We head for the west gate of the city!"

Cardinal Fiesco looked at him as if he were mad. "What are you doing?"

Amiel pointed.

Seigneur's white cape trailed him as he rode at full gallop to the west, with his white-robed knights and the Templar close by him. A lone rider, Adelais, rode hard to catch up.

"God's curse on that man," said Fiesco.

36

DAREL WAS NOT HAPPY. Sir Albaric de Laon, his master, had left him in the donjon. Perhaps, even now, Albaric was delivering the crippling blow, splitting open Seigneur's head so his brains spilled out. He knew his master. He would play with Seigneur, wound him, kill him little by little, make him beg for mercy.

And Darel was missing it all.

He waved away the servitor. He was not drinking. Rubi stroked his brown hair. *I'm sitting here listening to stories instead of supporting my master's triumph*, he thought. Out loud, he whispered, "Damn you, Perce."

"Master?" Rubi looked at him, her eyes red with ale.

"I said naught!" Darel snapped.

Rubi leaned forward, her breath harsh, and caressed his pouting lip with her own. He ignored the bitter taste of pickled olives as her tongue slipped between his and ran along his teeth. When his mouth refused to open she withdrew. Her hand reached down to his crotch, and she massaged his bulge.

He felt it stir, swell slightly, then he pushed her to the floor with an angry buck of his knee.

She looked up at him, her eyes flashing.

"I want you, master," she said, her voice slurred with drink.

"Go away, damn you." He sat straighter and fixed his eyes on the viscount's juggler, tossing apples and dropping as many as he kept aloft.

She slid along the floor and slipped her hand between his muscular thighs. "I *want* it master." She stroked. "It's *so* big."

She smelled sour, like fermenting apples. He let her caress his manhood for a moment, let it swell again against his leather leggings, thought for a moment about having her, quick and hard, but finally he kicked her away again.

She stood, hands on her hips, but when he refused to look at her she laughed and slid instead on to Gerome's lap. She nuzzled his ear.

Gerome looked at Darel.

"*Merde*! You can have her, Gerome. I don't want her."

Gerome shrugged as she nibbled his neck. "You're sure, Darel?"

Darel didn't even look at them as Rubi's mouth traced up Gerome's chin. "I said so, didn't I?"

It wasn't Rubi who infuriated him. He could think only of Perce. Because of *him* Albaric refused to allow Darel to attend the joust. "If *you* can't even beat Seigneur's squire in the bohort, you're not ready to bear my shield." It was a slap in the face. "I thought better of you." *The other cheek.* Darel had nearly fallen on his knees. That night he had bashed the heads of two of Albaric's grooms, ignoring their pleas for mercy.

What had happened? He was bigger and better than Perce. He worked hard at growing muscles and training with the sword. None of Albaric's squires could equal him.

Rubi tunneled her tongue into Gerome's mouth and he moaned. His hand pinched her upright nipples. She stopped her wet exploration and smiled at Darel.

Darel looked away. His fingers drummed on the table top, glaring about the hall. The few remaining soldiers were drunk, some already passed out, their heads resting on the table or sprawled without dignity on the stale floor reeds. Not a single knight was left in the castle.

"Just us lowly butt-lickers," he growled.

Rubi smiled at him. "Umm. There's an idea."

He yanked his knife from his belt. "Be still or I'll cut out that vile tongue of yours!"

She smiled then shrugged and she went back to kissing Gerome.

Leveret shouted, "Stop that minstrel's damnable wailing! Where is that rapscallion Ramon?" He guzzled more beer. "I want real music! Find that damnable troubadour!" He slammed his bowl to the thick oak table, spilling brew, and the minstrel scampered from the hall.

Other soldiers took up the call for Ramon's ballads.

"Perhaps he is at the joust!" Gerome wiped his mouth.

"Go back to your lip sucking, Ger!" shouted Leveret.

"Nay, I saw him earlier this day," said Normand.

Darel frowned. Where was the troubadour? The troubadour had not missed singing at a main meal in a week. Darel stood up slowly, eyes penetrating every corner of the room. Something felt wrong.

"Gerome, come with me," Darel snapped at his junior. "Bring the guard!"

The young *écuyer* looked up, wiping away the froth of his ale. He had the sour look of 'leave me alone I'm off-duty'. He said, "What is it?"

"Gerome. Get your tongue out of there! You don't know where it's been. Bring Normand!"

"What is it, Darel?" Gerome threw Rubi off his lap, retying his breeches.

"Quickly, oaf! Do not waste time!" Darel strode to the big doors.

"Is he drunk?" Rousset growled.

"Insolent!" Darel snapped. He led them into the bailey and the pouring rain.

The tower sentry lay face down in the puddle at the foot of the tower.

"The Dame!" Darel shouted, shielding his eyes from the pelting drops. "Quickly! Rousset and Jaie check upstairs!" Wiping the cold rain from his face with an angry brush of the back of his hand, he scanned the courtyard. "Gerome! Normand! With me!" He ran towards the stable. "Sound the alarm!"

Song of the Hanged Man

37

HENRI WATCHED THE RIDERS walk slowly toward the open gate. For some reason, Norvice had opened it. Then the alarms had sounded. He held up his hand, squinting into the rain.

In the dark of the archway, his first impression was of a mountain of a man on a big charger, a woman in gray, and a smaller man. Their faces were wrapped in their hoods to ward off the slanting rain.

He snapped his spear forward. "Halt!"

The big destrier pranced forward, nearly trampling him, but the rider—*Dear God, a giant of a man*—hauled back the reins roughly and the charger stepped backwards, splashing Henri with muddy water. "Aside, soldier. Aside and we will not kill you."

Henri shouted the alarm. Two more guards came running from the shelter alcove. The giant turned in the saddle, a sledgehammer in his huge hands.

"The Hammer!"

Henri stumbled back. An escape!

The Grand Duo were famous killers. This giant was a monster. His spear felt suddenly tiny and useless. He wished his normal sentry companion was with him. Jaspre always knew what to do.

"Pierre! Jean!" he shouted. "The Hammer and the Dandy!"

Jean's mouth hung open like an idiot but Pierre already had his spear couched.

A shout came from the stable. "Traitors!"

Henri looked as Darel de Lâon, Albaric's squire, followed by four of his men, came running across the yard. Thank God! Reinforcements.

"Stop them!" Darel roared.

Stop them? Who could stop this monster of a man? But Henri shouted, "Stand!"

The giant rammed Pierre with his warhorse. The stallion snorted, striking the falling man with his big hooves. Darel was too far away to help. Henri thrust his spear at the big charger but the horse reared, his eyes flashing. Jean shrieked as the hooves struck his shoulders.

"Stand, traitors!" Darel's voice was a roar as he entered the arcade, his sword in hand. Henri staggered and fell to one knee. *Thank God for Darel!*

"Go! Flee!" the giant on the horse shouted. "Take the Dame!"

The Dame! So that was it! Henri grabbed at the reins of the Dame's horse but she was past him. The giant on his horse turned to face the Darel's soldiers. He spurred his big mount into the four men, and his mason's sledgehammer arced through the air. Darel stepped back and deflected the blow with his shield, then staggered to one knee. His shield split into two halves, wood splinters flying.

Normand thrust with his spear but missed the monster, then the horse wheeled on him, knocking him like a limp doll against the wall. More soldiers ran from the great hall. It was too late for the giant to escape. Soon he'd be overwhelmed. Darel sliced his broadsword with the force of two arms, but the giant's war-trained horse reared. It was then that Henri realized the horse was Darel's own stallion!

Shouts rang out in the castle, echoing despite the din of heavy rain. Dozens of men at arms ran toward the small gate, swords drawn, but the Dame and the Dandy were out and across the archway.

The giant's horse reared and trampled two foot soldiers. The hammer slammed down on another, and he shrieked as his shoulder popped from its socket. Henri threw his spear, and the tip flew true at the giant. The man was fast for his size and threw himself aside in the saddle.

Henri glanced up on to the allures, and saw the first crossbows appear. It was finished. If this giant didn't throw down his weapons, he would die with shafts buried in his heart.

But the giant's horse flew across the arch, hooves slipping on the slick stones. The first bolts flew. One buried deep in the haunch of Darel's stallion, but this just drove him to run faster. They were outside the castle with the Dame!

"Pursue!" shouted Darel. Some of the men had already run for the stables. They came back a moment later, shaking their heads.

"The horses are all asleep or dead!" shouted Gerome.

"Then run! It'll be our heads if they escape!" Darel ran, sword in hand, and the soldiers after them. Henri didn't dare follow. Darel might be right. It likely would be their heads. But if Henri left his post now, there was no hope for him.

38

RAMON DROPPED the heavy oak trapdoor and threw the bolt. They were trapped on the flat stone roof, lashed by rain and wind, but for the moment, the soldiers were below them on the stairs, under the locked door.

From this tower, he could see the entire castle and city below. Soldiers pounded on the oaken door, but Ramon ignored them. He pushed the inquisitor in front of him, careful to keep him nearby in case the monk tried to open the bolt.

Holding on to the monk's arm, Ramon looked down between the two walls. His entire design lay before him. The great field lay to the south, the pavilions in tatters from the wind, and the city folk streaming back through the main gates at the Narbonnaise entry. Doré the Dandy and Osric the Hammer rode at full gallop between the city walls toward the west Postern. No horses pursued, thanks to Nevara's sleeping drug, but rows of foot soldiers pursued at a run, and crossbowmen fanned out along the walls on high alert.

To the north, coming round the long sweep of the narrow roadway, was Nevara, snowy brilliant, arms raised. With her were Eline shooting arrows, Atta and Hatta throwing knives, and Bubo circling above. They stood against a small row of Diableteur's black cohorts on foot. And Diableteur.

"No!" The icy cold wind of childhood terrors nearly blew Ramon from the roof. Diableteur. Death.

The four Baug wagons jammed the west gate as planned. The front wagon would have its front wheels sabotaged so that it could be moved only with difficulty. The guards of the gate struggled to move it even now.

Diableteur faced Nevara. The wall sentries besieged Ramon. The people of the city flowed back through the gates. And Doré, Osric and the Dame galloped to their escape.

There was a chance. A chance of success. A small one.

Lightning raked the tower above them. More crossbowmen assembled on the wall. The ghost owl Bubo beat wings wider than a man's armspan and dove at the archers, claws extended. Startled, the men tumbled back.

Nevara ran for the gate, pursued by the Diableteur and his men. Nevara, Eline and Magba's sons rode their tarpans at full gallop through a barrage of crossbow bolts.

The tarpans, brilliant little horses, weaved as they ran. One Baug man, one of Magba's dear sons, slouched forward. He clung to his horse's neck and rode on.

The rescuers made the west gate, the horses leaping over the stuck wagons. Three guards lay in the mud, their heads caved in.

A line of knights, barely visible in the dusky storm, rode hard at the foot of the hill below the city, angling directly for the Baug.

Night was upon them, perhaps the escapers' only advantage, but they must make it to the Phantom Wood. Even in bright sunshine, the ancient wood loomed terrifying, eerier still in dusk and storm, full of gnarly old wood and a hundred treacherous paths to nowhere. Giant elms, half dead and drooping, hid a shadowland filled with ghosts, phantoms and rebels. It was the forest of Doré and Osric.

Ramon shivered, boyhood fears rising. Like most Carcassonnians, he lived in terror of the wood, said to be haunted, definitely deadly. No one hunted the wood. No one traveled there but the desperate. Some said the living dead walked the wood, and if they touched you, turned you into creatures of the night forever damned. A land of desperadoes, evicted by the viscount, so hungry and poor that they would kill you before you had a chance to speak. Now it was their only chance of escape, yet Ramon would rather face a hundred of the viscount's soldiers than that dying wood.

Yet they were far from that dread sanctuary. Nevara and Magba rode at full gallop down the steep slope, outside the walls. With them rode the Dame, her silver robes unmistakable.

Ramon sighed. At least they had their chance.

The monk, Brother Jaie, cowered against the wall, leaning on a merlon, his eyes wide.

"We are trapped!"

"I am trapped," Ramon said.

He turned north. Izzy and three other horses were passing the Tower de la Poudre. Not much time.

"I would come with you."

Ramon stared at the monk. Ramon faced almost certain death, trapped with dozens of soldiers just below him, separated only by a thick oak door. What did this monk hope to gain by proclaiming friendship, this Inquisitor who witnessed the horrors of torture, who oversaw the trial of so many people?

"We're going to die here, Brother," Ramon said.

Jaie nodded. His youthful face wore fear, white and cold, in the dim stormlight. "I know. It is time for an end to suffering."

Ramon shook his head. "No time for puzzles, Brother. You have one more use to me." He dug into Nevara's pouch and yanked out Ena's fine elastic rope.

"You mean to hang me?"

"You wish death, perhaps?" Ramon said as he uncoiled the rope. It wouldn't do to tangle the precious rope, not with his riders only a minute away.

"Wish it? No. That would be a sin." Jaie crossed himself.

"I see." Ramon smiled. "Can't live with your horrors any longer, Brother?" He tied a loop with quick fingers.

Ramon lunged and grabbed Brother Jaie by his cowl. He flipped him down, hard to the stones, and wrapped the rope around his ankles.

"What are you doing?"

"You wanted to hang, didn't you, Brother?" Ramon couldn't resist a grin.

"Not like this!"

"No. Like this!" And Ramon threw the man from the tower. The monk fell only a few feet. Ramon wrapped the rope around the open square of the merlon.

"Help!" Brother Jaie dangled, head downwards.

Ramon lowered him. The wind caught him and buffeted him against the slick stone. His head hit a ledge. His hands flailed as he tried to grab a crevice. Ramon lowered him faster now, leaning all his weight into the rope. This was no more dangerous than the acrobatics in the Baug. Except that here, the soldiers were likely to rain crossbow bolts and spears on him.

The soldiers in the stairway below pounded on the trapdoor, making it shake and shudder.

Ramon swung out on the other end of the rope, extending his legs until he was walking down the stone wall backwards, facing up the tower at the boiling storm clouds.

He played out the rope and skittered down the wall. Brother Jaie had fallen faster and faster, almost to the ground, when the rope snapped taut and Ramon jerked to a stop. He was still the height of three men above the ground. He swung on the rope, pushing out from the wall in greater and greater swings. Brother Jaie screeched as his head hit the foundation.

Now Ramon's greater weight pulled Jaie back the other way and he began to ascend again as Ramon passed him on the way down.

Amazingly, Jaie shouted, "Take me with you!" as he passed.

The two of them swung back and forth in perfect equilibrium, the monk an arm's length above. Soldiers at the merlons looked down, readying crossbows. They had broken through the door.

"Wait for it!" Ramon said. "Be ready."

"Ready for what?" shouted the monk, his upside-down face just above Ramon.

"This!" Ramon released the rope. It snapped up and Ramon fell.

Jaie screamed, and as the rope uncoiled from the Merlon, he fell too.

Ramon tumbled, letting his fall carry him in a graceful spiral.

He had timed it wrong. Izzy was already past him. Ramon turned into a tuck, then a tumble, and hoped he wouldn't break any bones.

He hit the ground in a spin, deflecting off his shoulder blades. He felt the sharp pain of impact and took a mouthful of dirt, but he concentrated on continuing his tumble until his momentum was spent.

The monk landed in a heap, without benefit of Ramon's training. The mud might have saved him from too many broken bones.

Izzy had cantered back. His muzzle pressed Ramon's face. The other three horses had stopped too, and Ramon saw the twins Atta and Hatta and Magba's favorite son Sarimond.

"Ramon, mount!" Atta or Hatta yelled.

The crossbow bolts flew.

Ramon reached down his arm. "If you really want to come, Brother."

The suicidal monk reached up.

39

ADELAIS RODE HARD into the storm. Full night had fallen and the Seigneur and his knights were visible only because of their white cloaks. She wasn't sure what she was doing, but she was certain that if she let beloved Perce vanish into the night, she'd never see him again.

Alarm horns continued to blow from the walls. What could be so important that the city guard blew the enemy alarm.

What was happening? The last few days had been an exciting time for Adelais. Ramon and the Baug Balar had brought excitement to the dead city, joy to her miserable life. So much had happened, stimulating, exciting events. Her father meant to marry her to that dullard Sir

Lantar, a devastating announcement. Then everything had changed. The Dame's capture! Ramon with his magical voice that took her away to lands of dragons and wizards and knights in shining gold armor. Seigneur's great joust. It was all the stuff of songs!

Adelais lived for adventure, not just in songs. She would have adventures and ride and fight like a man, not do embroidery and sit in her bedchamber preening herself like a useless songbird. Adelais didn't fear swords or lightning storms or the black of night. What she feared was boredom. She feared the manacles of marriage.

She felt that excitement of adventure now! Whatever was happening in the city, it meant excitement for her. Seigneur was a real hero, famous from Jerusalem to London. His epic battle through the afternoon inspired her. Against all hope, he had won. She could win as well.

The Phantom Wood loomed to her left, the one thing in the world that could frighten her. The outskirts of that wood were filled with renegades, starving brigands, her father's escaped prisoners. The depths of the black wood were haunted with hungry ghosts. Though her father's men set at the wood each year with axes, always the forest seemed to encroach on the city, closer and closer each year, as if it would creep right to the city walls. Men might not frighten her, but the Phantom Wood did.

She angled right, away from the wood, but still she followed Perce, her prey.

Suddenly a band of small horses appeared, riding hard across the grassy fields directly toward the dreaded Phantom Wood. The Baug Balar! Seigneur and his knights were riding to intercept the Baug. Were they going to stop them from leaving the city? But why? And there was Ramon at the back of the column, on a spotted black and white horse!

What was happening?

Behind Ramon were her father's men, some twenty men in the viscount's yellow on horseback, and beyond them a larger detachment of foot soldiers. Why were they trying to stop the Baug Balar? Had the Inquisition ordered their arrest?

Adelais felt the beat of her heart, the hot pleasure of her horse at full gallop, the rain hard upon her. Adventure! After the high stone walls of Carcassonne and her father's castle—freedom.

Seigneur's men and the Templar rode around the Baug. They did not stop them, but circled and drew up in a line to face the yellow tunics of the viscount. Ramon turned and rode with the Seigneur.

Seigneur was protecting the Baug! Perce sat on a horse beside his master, and on either side of them four white knights.

Twelve against a hundred.

The Baug horses galloped through the muddy field straight for the Phantom Wood! Didn't they know how dangerous that forest was? No one ever returned from the dark wood, some said because of rebels, others because of ghosts. Even her father's well-armed troops didn't return from the Phantom Wood.

She turned toward the Baug riders. She would intercept them, warn them there was no refuge there. But the clang of swords drew her back to her Perce and the Seigneur. Her father's men had flanked Seigneur's small line and surrounded the twelve horsemen.

Adelais reined in, breathless, terrified. They mustn't kill her Perce! What were they doing? Seigneur was no enemy.

Seigneur's famous black horse reared, knocking a soldier from his saddle to the mud. The man screamed as the horse's hooves came down on him. Seigneur's sword swung, taking the head of another of her father's men. Shouts of the dying and fighting men shrieked above the din of the storm.

The Templar knight's mace swung back and forth, knocking her father's men from their horses like a child's dolls.

"Oh!" She held her breath as a lanceman struck Perce's shield. Her beloved turned the lance and swung in with his sword as the soldier's horse slammed against his own. The man shouted and fell from his horse. "Oh, Perce!"

Even Ramon was fighting, diving in with his little spear. He rode without reins, guiding the horse only with his legs, protecting Perce's exposed right. Perce had power, but Ramon had speed. His spear plunged in and out, a blur, his horse a dwarf amongst the war horses, dancing lightly among them, like a hawk among wolves. The twelve were holding the hundred, while the Baug Balar rode hard for the wood, nearly at the eaves of the haunted forest.

But there could be no doubt that Seigneur and his men must fall.

Terrified, Adelais sat alone in the dark and watched the battle. Swords rang. Men screamed and fell to the bloodied mud. Lightning flashed. Two of Seigneur's knights fell. Then another.

"Stop this!" she shouted, suddenly. "Stop this!" She kicked her horse forward. It shied, dancing in the muck to avoid her reins, but she kicked again. "Stop this! Stop this! I command it!"

No one heard her. The fighting continued.

Song of Death

40

AND THEN DEATH CAME to the field of the dying.

Diableteur and his men arrived, darker shadows in the howling black. Ramon felt a chill, a trembling combination of numb exhaustion and the horror of killing, charged with fear of dying. He was drenched with blood and rain, shivering from cold and fatigue. The Dame, the Grand Duo, Mauri, and even Brother Jaie had already disappeared into the Phantom Wood. Ramon made his stand with Seigneur and his men. The ancient martial skills taught him by Guilhem d'Alions and the Hun twins gave Zaleucus a life of its own, yet he was almost a detached spectator from the horror he wrought. How many had he stabbed with the armor-piercing blade of the lawgiver? He avoided the killing thrust, but many lay in the mud, writhing from his wounds.

He wanted nothing more in life than to face Diableteur, to kill it as it had destroyed his mother and the mothers of a hundred others. Yet only twelve of them stood against dozens of the viscount's horsemen, the Diableteur and his deathriders. Seigneur might be worth a dozen men, but he was exhausted from his epic joust. Templar Arnot had taken down ten of the enemy, but eventually sheer numbers and fatigue would determine the outcome.

The Baug had disappeared into the eaves of the wood.

"Back to the wood!" Ramon shouted. His trap was set. It was their only hope. They fought a pitched battle as they retreated toward the wood. He could barely lift his arms. He was determined not to be taken prisoner by the Diableteur or the viscount. Months in the pit, torture and an end in screaming agony on the flames of the Inquisition would be the best he could expect if captured. If he must die, it would be here on this muddy field, content in the knowledge that he had done what should have been impossible. He had rescued the Holy Dame from the black grip of the Inquisition.

At least Mauri and his precious lute were safe with the Baug.

A knight in full armor crashed into Ramon. His horse shrieked and reared. Ramon could rely only on speed for survival against armored knights, but the muscles in his arms burned. He grabbed a handful of mane, ducked forward and kicked Izzy's left flank. He felt the blade sweep above his head, a stroke that would easily have cleaved him, except for Izzy's quick step to the right.

Whether by the magic of Zaleucus or the automatic reflex of a decade of training, his spear spun out and back and plunged into the eye slit of the knight's helmet. They both shivered, Ramon in horror, the knight in death, as Zaleucus drained the man's miserable life and he collapsed in the mud.

He had killed. He shuddered. He had not meant to kill.

Izzy plunged on through the French line, and Zaleucus sliced and lunged in abandon, sparing only the horses. But men fell from Zaleucus and from the terrible sword of Seigneur, and from the precise blade of Perceval, and from the bloody mace of Arnot, and from the five remaining knights of the white. But always there were more to kill. More to die.

Ramon wanted only one thing: to pit Zaleucus with the Diableteur's scythe of death. Perhaps someday someone would write the song of this day. The song of the rescue of the Dame. The song of death. The Song of Montségur.

Three of Diableteur's guard closed on Ramon, swords swinging together. Ramon whistled sharply, and Izzy reared and spun. The long blade of Zaleucus caught one of the swords. The other two missed cleanly and clashed together. One of the riders fell to the ground. A quick tap of Ramon's heel and Izzy pranced to the right. Ramon swept his spear, longer than even a broadsword. One of the black riders fell under the hooves of his own horse. Two others charged him, stabbing this time. Ramon grabbed a handful of Izzy's mane and swung off his back. His feet touched the ground lightly, and he sprang up and over his horse, his hand balancing on Izzy's withers. He had played this game in the ring, with the other Baug horses, but here, one mistimed move and he would die. Izzy sensed his move and stayed with him as he jumped, spear flashing down. He plunged hard and pierced the man's shoulder plate. The knight screamed.

Ramon barely maintained his seat, but Izzy stayed with him. His long legs wrapped his beloved tarpan and he burst past another swordsman, knocking the blade aside with a quick backswipe of Zaleucus.

He broke through the horsemen and rode straight at the looming shadow of the Diableteur. He left behind Seigneur and his knights, still hacking sword against sword. He lowered his short spear and charged. Alone. A dozen black shadow knights surrounded Diableteur, armed with swords and shields.

Ramon leaned lower in the saddle and kicked, ignoring the pain of a dozen cuts and the sting of rain in his eyes. A sheet of lightning lit the sky, and behind the Diableteur Ramon caught a glimpse of more horrors. Hundreds of mounted soldiers and knights wound down the steep road from the west gate. More rode hard from the north.

It was hopeless.

And all Ramon wanted was to take Death with him—to his own death.

"Mama. Your mouse strikes back." He heard his own voice, a cry in the storm.

Perhaps it was exhaustion. Or the storm. But now he saw Mama, her smiling face looking down on him, a face in the boiling mass of storm clouds. She seemed to loom there, real and magnificent.

"Flee, bébé, flee." The voice was within him, but clearly his mother's voice. *"Run my mouse!"*

The scythe reached out for him. It seemed to grow as if by some dark magic in the stormy night, the blade longer and longer, sweeping.

And Zaleucus seemed to shrink.

A dozen deathriders stood between them, but Izzy didn't shy away. Ramon pressed his left leg hard into his flank, steering Izzy back to his death on the swords of the blacks.

Far away, it seemed, he heard voices. *"Retreat! Retreat!"*

Who spoke? Voices in his numb mind? His mother? Seigneur?

Lightning flashed and the Diableteur loomed, hood thrown back, the remains of its face more skeletal than alive, He laughed at Ramon.

And something magical happened. Standing there, between Ramon and Death, a spectral glowing figure hovered. The Dame. She stood, shimmering silver, an illusion of his tired mind almost surely, but warm and wonderful for all that, her arms lifted, calling out to him. Her voice was large in his mind. *"Retreat, Ramon! Flee!"* Her eyes captured him, drawing him away from Death and suddenly he wheeled his horse, just a moment before he would have crashed into the leading edge of the soldiers.

The Dame shimmered and vanished in a sheet of rain, a dream of his collapsing will, but suddenly he was riding back and back, toward the Seigneur and his few remaining men, away from Death's scythe.

Zaleucus tore into the flank of the viscount's men. He broke through and passed the Seigneur, calling for him to retreat. The Cyclops lord was as surprised as the enemy, but they rode hard after Ramon, the viscount's men right on them. They rode into the uncertain black, guided only by the occasional flash of white above them. Then the forest loomed in the dark and suddenly they were within the eaves.

The viscount's men pursued them into the Phantom Wood.

Dark branches hung over them, spidery leafless branches of ancient elms that raked down like claws.

In the next flash of lightning Ramon glanced over his shoulder. A new rider had joined them, a slight figure on a light horse, galloping alongside Perce.

Adelais! It wasn't a trick of his tired eyes and brain. The viscount's daughter was there, close at Perce's side. Ramon had no time to wonder at her presence.

The trees closed on them, the Phantom Wood drawing in on them like specters. Soon they would have to turn once more to face the viscount's men, or plunge into the thickening wood and risk being knocked from their horses by the lower branches.

A wall of pine stood before them, like the ramparts of the forest. They found themselves turning and turning and riding parallel to the barrier, weaving among the older trunks of barren elms until they could ride no further. The tree line forced them back out onto the open field where Diableteur waited. They must halt and face the viscount's men.

Ramon turned hard and with him were Arnot, Seigneur, Perce, Adelais, and the remaining knights of Castlenau. They would make their stand.

"Stop!" shouted Adelais, holding up her arms to her father's men. "Stop! I am their hostage!"

Perce swept his bloodied sword around and held an inch from her bare throat.

"I command you!" Adelais sounded frightened. "Go back to my father and tell him I am hostage. They will kill me if you pursue!"

Perce would die before he'd even scratch her neck but they put on a good act. The viscount's men probably knew it was an act. They looked at each other in the darkness, controlling their restless horses. Ramon sensed their uncertainty, saw the jerky movement of their heads back and forth.

"Release my lord's daughter!" shouted a purple knight.

"Leave here, or she dies, Sir Lantar!" shouted Perce, his sword pressed closer to her throat.

"I don't believe your ruse," the purple knight said. He was nearly Seigneur's size and grandly feathered in his purple and gold.

"I don't want to die," Adelais pleaded. "Please, my knight. Rescue me another day."

Sir Lantar held up his arm and his men halted. "My fiancée is not to be harmed!" Whether he shouted it at his own men or Seigneur's, Ramon wasn't sure.

Ramon walked his horse up close behind Adelais. This close, even in the darkness, Ramon saw Adelais' elaborate wink. He had no idea where she came from, but she was trying to save them.

"If you harm her, no place in all the land will be safe for you!" shouted Sir Lantar.

"If you go, we will not harm her," Perce shouted back.

The soldiers hesitated, then a burst of lightning revealed they were retreating from the haunted wood to report the capture of the viscount's daughter and the betrayal of Seigneur and the Templar.

"Quickly! Before they discover our ruse." Perce leaned over in the saddle and gave Adelais a quick kiss. "Thank you, Addy. You saved us. Now go!"

"I'm with you," Adelais said.

"You are not!" Perce slapped her horse's flank and the horse sidled away, but she wheeled it back toward them.

"You need me!"

"We do not. The Phantom Wood is not safe!"

Ramon could only stare with the others. Where had she come from? What was she doing? Of course it was obvious. Adelais loved Perce, and, his protestations to the contrary notwithstanding, Perce loved her in return.

"More soldiers come!" shouted one of Seigneur's knights.

"We can argue this later," said Ramon. "Into the wood."

Ramon didn't wait for an answer. He rode poor Izzy back the way they had come. They rode slowly along the tree line until they found the rutted mud trail where the Baug wagons had entered.

They slowed to a walk. The horses snorted nervously, stamping their fear. A blacker shadow marked the way, an arching deep black. Even as lightning flashed, no light penetrated the darker shadows of the forest. The horses smelled death. Even Ramon covered his nose against the pervasive stench.

He looked up.

His last ruse.

They were in the trees. Dozens of them. Shadows.

Sir Lantar rode up hard behind them with a hundred mounted soldiers. "Halt! You will release Adelais or you shall not escape me!"

Ramon turned Izzy, fixed a big smile on his face and pointed up with his spear.

Sir Lantar looked up. He flipped his visor back further from his face. A sheet of rain blew off one of the trees, drenching him.

"A trap!" Lantar shouted.

The first arrows flew, raining around Lantar and his horses.

"Leave now, Sir, or your men will wear new feathers," Ramon said, still smiling. "We have hundreds in the trees."

Lantar's horse pivoted in terror as more arrows flew. He glared up at the ambush.

"Another time, Troubadour. There is nowhere I wouldn't follow you." Lightning lanced across the boiling black sky, illuminating the archers in the tree.

"Don't follow me, Lantar. I am not sweet on you." He wheeled Izzy around, leaned forward in his saddle, and pulled down his leggings. "This is what I think of you."

"I will ram that dainty spear up your hole, fool," shouted Lantar, and he wheeled his horse and rode from the eaves once again.

"I love thee not, Lantar!" Ramon shouted, and the men with him laughed.

It was all he could do. Laugh. Be happy. A few shadows had turned back the viscount's men.

Against all expectation, they had escaped the unholy city. They had rescued the Dame, the Jewel of the South. Their refuge and hope was the great reeking forest of hungry ghosts. The Viscount would send his entire army after them. Lantar would pursue them. Diableteur and his shadows would haunt them.

Death behind them. Ghosts before them.

Epilog

THE VISCOUNT HUGH D'ARCIS rode beneath the branches of the ancient tree. His destrier, Caspin, reared. Hugh easily retained his seat, and stroked the hard muscled neck of his warhorse. "There, Caspin. Not ghosts after all." He stared hard at the rutted track leading into the dark shadows of the Phantom Wood. Even by day, it was frightening, this ancient, rotting wood.

Hugh was not a superstitious man. Unlike his men, he did not believe in ghosts who preyed on any who ventured into the ancient wood. He was no fool either. The displaced of Carcassonne, the thousands he had driven out of their homes after the conquest, lived in there, hungry yes, but not yet ghosts. The starving renegades. The dispossessed. The desperate. Hiding in their trees with their bows.

"Gies!"

His squire rode up, his face revealing his terror. It was not just his squire who wore the fear openly on a pale face. They were afraid of Hugh, yes. This troubadour had mocked him, had abused his hospitality, had killed his men, and had taken the two most important women in his life—the Dame and his daughter. His men should be afraid of him.

Earlier, when he had found the sentries bound in his pit, Jaspre and the others, he had not even questioned them. Hugh's sword still ran red with their blood. Jaspre had begged for his life, screaming that his wife was with child, but his head flew from his shoulders in mid-shout. The head was mounted on a spike by the west gate, the scene of the escape, as a warning to cravens and fools.

Yet it wasn't the viscount's wrath that put fear into his men. It was the forest they truly feared. Of all the sorties and patrols Hugh had sent into that wood, not one had returned.

"A lance!"

The lance swayed in Gies trembling hands. Angry, Hugh snatched it and balanced its great weight. He thrust upwards.

The archer fell to the ground. The man of straw. Hugh stared at the dummy. His laugh was dark and without humor.

"This fool has made of fool of me." His horse pawed the sad sack of straw that had terrified his men in the night. He could well imagine their fear. Shadows in the trees and arrows flying at them. They must have assumed the rebels were in the trees by the hundreds.

"Sir Lantar!"

The purple knight rode up. It had been Sir Lantar who had called off the pursuit, faced with these straw dummies as enemies. "My Lord Seneschal. Forgive me, lord!" He bowed his head.

The knight was to marry Adelais, and he was a distant nephew of the king himself, nor was he a craven—he was a champion in the joust and a veteran of many battles—but he was almost certainly a simpleton.

"You say you turned back to save my daughter?" Hugh kept his voice low, barely heard over the lingering winds of the previous night's storm. The rains had stopped, but the winds blew sheets of water from the leaves of the trees above them.

"Yes, Lord Viscount!"

"Then, you are fool."

"Yes, Lord Viscount!"

"And I am a fool."

"No, Lord Viscount!"

Hugh edged his horse closer to his knight, until their skirted legs touched. "Sir Lantar, we rode together to Toledo. I know you are no craven. I give you this one chance to redeem your life." He half drew his stained sword from the sheath, revealing the fresh blood of Jaspre and the other guards from the pit. "You will return my daughter—your future wife—to me unharmed. You will ride into that wood with these hundreds, and you will return her to me. As long as one of you lives, you will not stop."

Sir Lantar lifted his head. His eyes showed the old fierceness. He would not die today. "I will, my Lord!"

"And Lantar," Hugh said, his voice low. "The Dame as well."

"It will be done!"

"And you will kill this troubadour. Don't bring him to me. Just kill the fool."

"He is dead, my Lord!" Sir Lantar nodded and rode back to his assembled horsemen, hundreds of Hugh's best men, among them seventeen of his best knights, a hundred cross bows, several hundred swords and spears, all of them on horse. A more ruthless man would have fired the forest. The forest was long overdue for a burning.

Yet with his daughter—his sweet Adelais—in that wood, he dared not. *Once she was rescued,* he vowed, *once rescued, I'll burn that hellish wood.*

Hugh watched them assemble into two long rows. They'd be helpless in that wood, unable to ride more than two abreast, no doubt picked off man by man by the rebels. Yet Lantar's honor was impeached by the kidnapping of his future wife. He would get the job done. And if not, losing a few hundred men didn't matter. In the end, even the rebels could not hope to stand against all of these seasoned soldiers.

Hugh stared at the trampled straw dummy. How could it all have gone so wrong? How could a fool, a traitor knight and a troop of entertainers so out-maneuver him? He had led armies in crusade after crusade. He had never been defeated.

He looked back at the city on the hill, now golden and beautiful in the light of the morning. Storm clouds broke apart in tatters, blown by a strong wind, and the sun broke through in full glory.

He saw Diableteur riding south with the survivors of his forty-four. They rode hard, at full gallop, Diableteur's black cloak streaming behind him, his scythe held aloft like a banner. One of his men carried the great black rose on a mast. They made a terrible sight, these black men on white horses following Death itself.

Sir Albaric, the golden lion, headed in the opposite direction. The knight had survived Seigneur's killing blow. The Seigneur had deliberately pulled back, not penetrating the organs with his old Loial, a mistake for a man who normally showed no compassion. An angry Lion now pursued the Cyclops, racing against Death itself, and the wounded lion was deadly. Sir Albaric's men, nearly two hundred of them, rode with the Lion Knight.

Death to the south, the Lion to the north, the royal nephew and his hundreds heading west. Death rode for the Dame and Ramon, and Hugh could pity them.

Tricks would not save the fool and his entertainers. And even if they survived the hungry ghosts, the rebels, Sir Lantar and his troop, the vengeful Sir Albaraic and Death itself, Hugh would be waiting for them at Castle Montségur with an army of thousands. The cursed mountain had waited long enough. It would fall, even if it took every man he owned and a two-year siege.

No one made a fool of Hugh D'Arcis.

Here ends the first book of the ***Song of Montségur*** cycle, ***The Last Troubadour***.
The adventure continues in ***The Last Quest***.

Ramon, the Last Troubadour, and the other children of Magba must escape the Phantom Wood and achieve sanctuary at Chateau Montségur. Against them Death comes with his Scythe and his deathstalkers. Riding to cut them off is a vengeful lion, Sir Albaric de Laon and his hundreds. In the Phantom Wood are the terrible hungry ghosts and desperate renegades. The Dame, Ramon, Seigneur, Perce, Adelais, Nevara, Arnot and the children of the Baug face a pursuing army led by Adelais' fiancé, the ferocious purple knight Sir Lantar. If they escape the ghosts and armies, they must cross the lands of the Mad Duke, into the Weir Mountains, pursued by crusaders charged by the new Pope Innocent to obtain the Holy Relics. And beyond this lies Chateau Montségur, last refuge of the Christian Cathars, with their small village of the faithful to guard the sacred Holy of Holies from the viscount's thousands.

Coming in cloth hardcover, Fall 2008 from Kunati Books (ISBN 9781601640116).

The cycle completes in the stunning finale, ***The Last Stand***, Fall 2009 (ISBN 9781601640123).

The surviving guardians protect the Holy of Holies from thousands of crusading knights who besiege lofty Montségur. The only hope is the complex trickery of a fool, and the heroic bravery of his companions.

About the author

Derek Armstrong

He loves the provocative, controversial and unique.

What the critics say:

"Armstrong's abudant enthusiasm for his material, combined with the semi-satirical plotline, compel us to keep reading, and his prose style keeps us chuckling." David Pitt, *Booklist Magazine*

"Derek Armstrong is good," Michael Korda, *Simon & Schuster*

"Gruesome, suspenseful, and rich with dark humor, Armstrong moves the reader through time and space with a keen sense of momentum and dash. His characters are diverse, bold, unforgettable..." *ForeWord*

Armstrong focuses on "high concept" but with a key difference. Black humor, edgy dialogue and "broad swipes at the zeitgeist" are integral to Armstrong's unique writing. Armstrong is as likely to make fun of his own "thriller" genre as reality television—the target of his attack in ***The Game***. His historical thriller, ***The Last Troubadour,*** makes light of both the Catholic Church and the latest passion for the Holy Grail. He has been called "cheeky" and "daring" and "provocative." Derek Armstrong writes thrillers because, according to him, "they're entertaining and you can be ridiculous and serious at the same time. Thrills and laughs belong together. Really."

Derek Armstrong has won many awards for advertising copywriting Internationally and wrote ***The Persona Principle*** (Simon & Schuster) with co-author Kam Wai Yu, now translated into six languages.

Forthcoming titles include ***MADicine***, the whacky thriller sequel to ***The Game***, this time taking aim at medicine and scientific research.

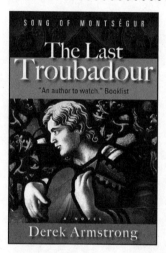

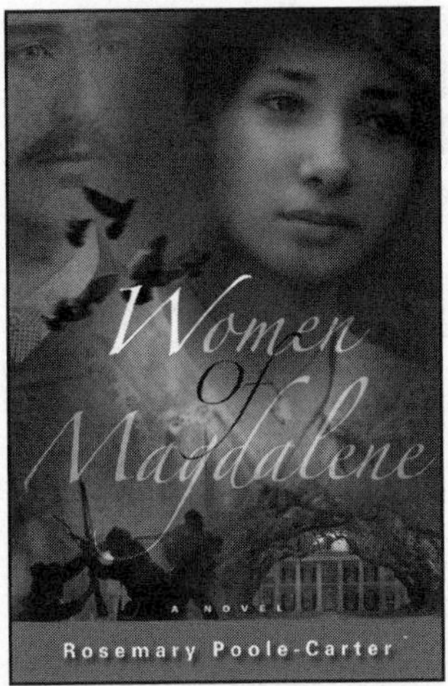

Women Of Magdalene

A hauntingly tragic tale of the old South by Rosemary Poole-Carter

An idealistic young doctor in the post–Civil War South exposes the greed and cruelty at the heart of the Magdalene Ladies' Asylum in this elegant, richly detailed and moving story of love and sacrifice.

US$ 24.95 | Pages 288, cloth hardcover
ISBN-13: 978-1-60164-014-7
ISBN-10: 1-60164-014-5
EAN: 9781601640147

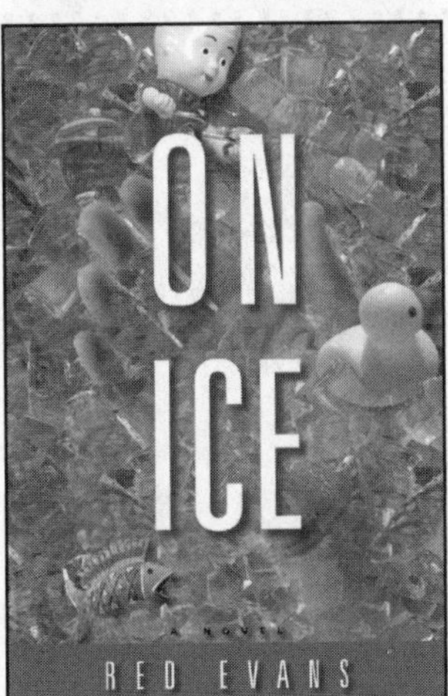

On Ice

A road story like no other, by Red Evans

The sudden death of a sad old fiddle player brings new happiness and hope to those who loved him in this charming, earthy, hilarious coming-of-age tale.

US$ 19.95 | Pages 208, cloth hardcover
ISBN-13: 978-1-60164-015-4
ISBN-10: 1-60164-015-3
EAN: 9781601640154

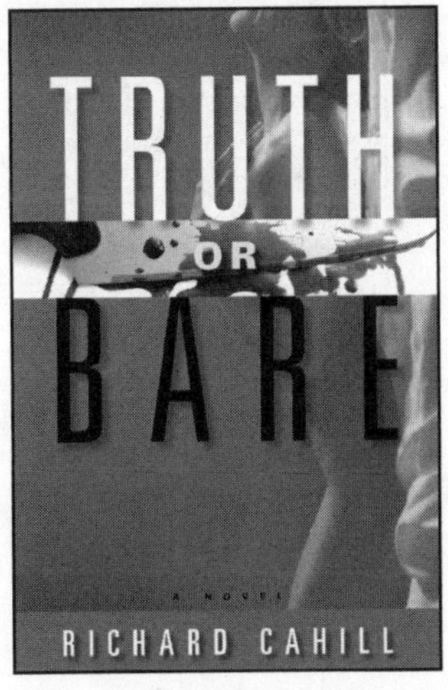

Truth Or Bare

Offbeat, stylish crime novel by Richard Cahill

The characters throb with vitality, the prose sizzles in this darkly comic page-turner set in the sleazy world of murderous sex workers, the justice system, and the rich who will stop at nothing to get what they want.

US$ 24.95 | Pages 304, cloth hardcover
ISBN-13: 978-1-60164-016-1
ISBN-10: 1-60164-016-1
EAN: 9781601640161

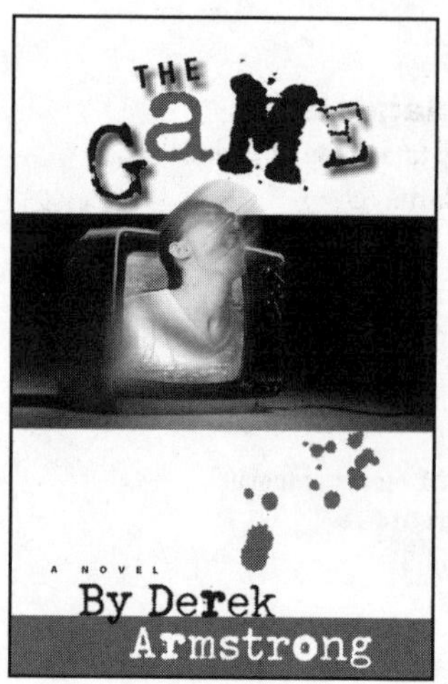

Provocative. Bold. Controversial.

The Game

A thriller by Derek Armstrong

Reality television becomes too real when a killer stalks the cast on America's number one live-broadcast reality show. ■ "A series to watch ... Armstrong injects the trope with new vigor." *Booklist*

US$ 24.95 | Pages 352, cloth hardcover
ISBN 978-1-60164-001-7 | EAN: 9781601640017
LCCN 2006930183

bang BANG

A novel by Lynn Hoffman

In Lynn Hoffman's wickedly funny *bang-BANG*, a waitress crime victim takes on America's obsession with guns and transforms herself in the process. Read along as Paula becomes national hero and villain, enforcer and outlaw, lover and leader. Don't miss Paula Sherman's one-woman quest to change America. ■ "Brilliant" STARRED REVIEW, *Booklist*

US$ 19.95
Pages 176, cloth hardcover
ISBN 978-1-60164-000-0
EAN 9781601640000
LCCN 2006930182

Whale Song

A novel by Cheryl Kaye Tardif

Whale Song is a haunting tale of change and choice. Cheryl Kaye Tardif's beloved novel—a "wonderful novel that will make a wonderful movie" according to *Writer's Digest*—asks the difficult question, which is the higher morality, love or law? ■ "Crowd-pleasing ... a big hit." *Booklist*

US$ 12.95
Pages 208, UNA trade paper
ISBN 978-1-60164-007-9
EAN 9781601640079
LCCN 2006930188

Shadow of Innocence

A mystery by Ric Wasley

The Thin Man meets *Pulp Fiction* in a unique mystery set amid the drugs-and-music scene of the sixties that touches on all our societal taboos. *Shadow of Innocence* has it all: adventure, sleuthing, drugs, sex, music and a perverse shadowy secret that threatens to tear apart a posh New England town.

US$ 24.95
Pages 304, cloth hardcover
ISBN 978-1-60164-006-2
EAN 9781601640062
LCCN 2006930187

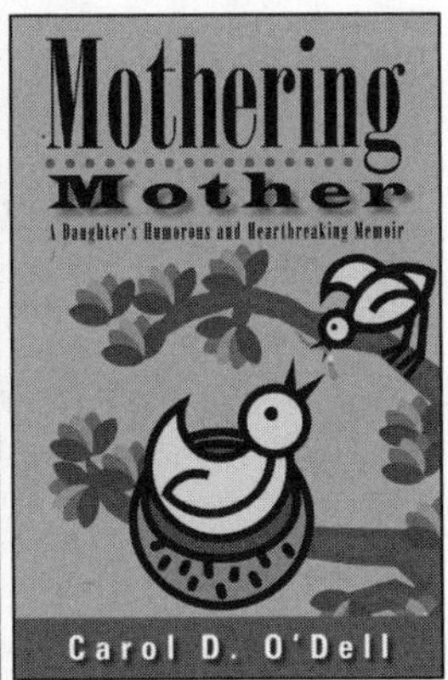

The Secret Ever Keeps

A novel by Art Tirrell

An aging Godfather-like billionaire tycoon regrets a decades-long life of "shady dealings" and seeks reconciliation with a granddaughter who doesn't even know he exists. A sweeping adventure across decades—from Prohibition to today—exploring themes of guilt, greed and forgiveness.

■ "Riveting ... Rhapsodic ... Accomplished." *ForeWord*

US$ 24.95
Pages 352, cloth hardcover
ISBN 978-1-60164-004-8
EAN 9781601640048
LCCN 2006930185

Toonamint of Champions

A wickedly allegorical comedy by Todd Sentell

Todd Sentell pulls out all the stops in his hilarious spoof of the manners and mores of America's most prestigious golf club. A cast of unforgettable characters, speaking a language only a true son of the South could pull off, reveal that behind the gates of fancy private golf clubs lurk some mighty influential freaks.

■ "Bubbly imagination and wacky humor." *ForeWord*

US$ 19.95
Pages 192, cloth hardcover
ISBN 978-1-60164-005-5
EAN 9781601640055
LCCN 2006930186

Mothering Mother

A daughter's humorous and heartbreaking memoir.
Carol D. O'Dell

Mothering Mother is an authentic, "in-the-room" view of a daughter's struggle to care for a dying parent. It will touch you and never leave you.

■ "Beautiful, told with humor... and much love." *Booklist*

■ "I not only loved it, I lived it. I laughed, I smiled and shuddered reading this book." Judith H. Wright, author of over 20 books.

US$ 19.95
Pages 208, cloth hardcover
ISBN 978-1-60164-003-1
EAN 9781601640031
LCCN 2006930184

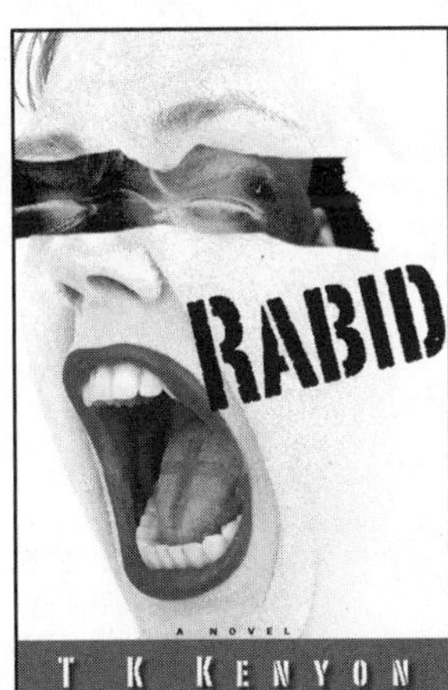

Rabid

A novel by T K Kenyon

A sexy, savvy, darkly funny tale of ambition, scandal, forbidden love and murder. Nothing is sacred. The graduate student, her professor, his wife, her priest: four brilliantly realized characters spin out of control in a world where science and religion are in constant conflict.

■ "Kenyon is definitely a keeper." STARRED REVIEW, *Booklist*

US$ 26.95 | Pages 480, cloth hardcover
ISBN 978-1-60164-002-4 | EAN: 9781601640024
LCCN 2006930189